THE
Diagnosis
of Love

THE

Diagnosis
of Love

MAGGIE LEFFLER

DELTA TRADE PAPERBACKS

THE DIAGNOSIS OF LOVE
A Delta Trade Paperback / March 2007

Published by Bantam Dell
A Division of Random House, Inc.
New York, New York

Book design by Ginger Legato

Grateful acknowledgment is given for permission to reprint from the following:

Excerpts from *Oxford Handbook of Clinical Medicine,* Editors R. A. Hope, J. M. Longmore, T. J. Hodgetts, and P. S. Ramrakha. Copyright © 1993 by Oxford University Press. Reprinted by permission of Oxford University Press.

"Gaudeamus Igitur" by John Stone, M.D., from *JAMA,* 1983 49 (13). Copyright © 1983 by the American Medical Association. Reproduced by permission of the American Medical Association. All rights reserved.

"Backyard, 6 a.m.," from *Grace Notes* by Rita Dove. Copyright © 1989 by Rita Dove. Used by permission of the author and W. W. Norton & Company, Inc.

Excerpt from "You're," from *Ariel* by Sylvia Plath. Copyright © 1961 by Ted Hughes. Reprinted by permission of HarperCollins Publishers.

Excerpts from *The Art and Science of Bedside Diagnosis* by Joseph D. Sapira, M.D., Editor Jane M. Orient. Copyright © 1990 by Lippincott Williams & Wilkins.

Excerpts from *The Library of Health,* Editor B. Frank Scholl, Ph.D., M.D. Copyright 1927 by Historical Publishing Co.

Delta is a registered trademark of Random House, Inc., and the colophon is a trademark of Random House, Inc.

LIBRARY OF CONGRESS CATALOGING-IN-PUBLICATION DATA
Leffler, Maggie.
The diagnosis of love / Maggie Leffler.
p.   cm.
ISBN: 978-0-385-34046-5 (trade pbk.)
1. Mothers—Death—Fiction. 2. Women physicians—Fiction. 3. Americans—England—Fiction. 4. Twins—Fiction. 5. Family secrets—Fiction. I. Title.
PS3612.E3497D53 2007
813'.6—dc22   2006025305

Printed in the United States of America
Published simultaneously in Canada

www.bantamdell.com

BVG   10 9 8 7 6 5 4 3 2 1

To my mother, Martha,
who made every sky seem like something worth fishing

And to Tim,
my double knot,
my one-handed tie with my eyes closed

Dazzled I walk the world my mother gave me,
whose stony streets are paved with emerald.

— "BIRTHSTONES," MONA VAN DUYN

THE
Diagnosis
of Love

CHAPTER I

Signs

> "Sometimes a sign can be equivocal or even contrary to what you'd expect."
>
> —Oxford Handbook of Clinical Medicine

My brother, Ben, says that the story starts here, in the Volvo going 80 mph on our way to Chautauqua, New York. I think it started four months ago when Mama died. Or twenty years ago, when she left for the first time. But Ben says no. He says this is The Beginning, and I defer to him because a) He's six minutes older than me, and b) If it weren't for my ruse, we wouldn't be on our way to Chautauqua in the first place.

I'm becoming more and more nervous as we hurtle down Route 79 in the pouring rain. An ominous oil tanker looms in my rearview mirror, while tandem tractor trailers rumble just ahead. I'm nervous because the last person on earth that I want to be doing me a favor—Dr. Mary Worthington—is doing me a favor: making hospital rounds in the ICU this morning so that I could get an early start on our road trip. No doubt Mary will try to negotiate completely unreasonable paybacks for her trouble. Then there's the real reason my palms are clammy and my heart keeps turning over: I'm afraid that Mama isn't going to show up.

Meet me there, Mama, I pray, gripping the clumsy steering wheel.

"Are you okay?" Ben asks, glancing up from his *Time* magazine. I can't understand how he is able to read in a moving vehicle without vomiting.

"Why?" I ask, downshifting.

"You look funny. And you're driving so...erratically."

"I am not," I say, stamping on the gas as we dodge past the tractor trailer train. I don't remember much from college Physics except that there's something about a pressure drop between two moving objects that will cause one of the trucks to suck the Volvo toward it and subsequently destroy us in a ball of fire.

"Promise you won't get mad?" I ask finally.

"No," Ben says, turning a page of his magazine.

I open my mouth to confess the truth but he realizes it before I can make a sound. "We're not going to hear J. D. Salinger speak, are we?"

I shake my head.

Ben laughs, only he's not happy.

My brother owns about four different laughs. There's his Courtesy Laugh, a lifeless chuckle as if generated from the wind of a sigh. There's his Leader-of-Silliness Laugh, which is startling and infectious and reminds me of a bad guy rubbing his hands together and booming *moo-hoo-ha-ha*. Then there's his Don't-Make-Me-Laugh Laugh, a snicker when he's doing his best to stay in a bad mood but can't. And his Disgusted Laugh, which Ben is doing now, something on the verge between a snort and a scream.

I know his noises well. After all, we shared a womb. Laughing-shakes probably rippled through Mama's belly like electricity.

"Unbelievable, Holly. You made me drive two and a half hours from Pittsburgh—"

"I'm driving," I say.

"All for J. D. Salinger's book tour, which doesn't even exist—"

"He's a recluse!" I say, as if he'd been on the schedule and suddenly remembered he couldn't come out in public. "He hasn't written a book since 1965!"

"Who are we going for?" Ben asks.

"We're going for Mama," I say, even though Mama is dead.

"Come on, Holly. Who are we—" Ben stops and glares at me. "Oh, no. Not What's-his-face."

In fact, we are going to see What's-his-face, also known as Joshua Peter, the star of *Passing On,* a show where the famous psychic talks to people who have already passed on to an alternative universe and now want to communicate to loved ones back on earth.

"Seriously?" Ben's voice reaches a baffled pitch. "You dragged me 150 miles to witness this—this con artist waltzing around pretending to talk to dead people? You're a doctor, Holly!"

"Meaning ... ?"

"You're supposed to be logical—and scientific!"

I inform him that a medical education can only do so much to reshape one's basic psychological makeup. Besides (I think), when it comes to psychics, Ben shouldn't be so narrow-minded, considering he's in seminary and believes that God impregnated a virgin who bore a son who performed miracles. Joshua Peter doesn't even resurrect anybody.

"You need to get out more," Ben says. "You need a boy-friend."

This stings more than I want to admit. As an SUV speeds past, spraying us with water, I steady the wheel and point out in a stiff voice, "I could have a boyfriend if I wanted."

I'm thinking of Matthew Hollembee, a third-year surgery resident who has asked me out on several occasions since we met in July when he rotated through my hospital, St. Catherine's Medical Center. It's funny he should come to mind when I honestly don't know much about him, except that he's tall, thin, and wears thick, black glasses. I also know that before St. Cate's, Matthew's home base was London. And the fact that I've never accepted a date with him doesn't seem to deter him from inviting me out again.

"So why don't you?" Ben asks.

"Why don't I what?"

"Want a boyfriend?"

"It needs to be the right person," I say, feeling unusually prim, feeling like my grandmother Eve, who never stops harassing my brother for "shacking up" with his girlfriend. It still baffles me how my normally gun-shy twin ended up in such a whirlwind affair. They met in New York eight months ago, when Ben still believed he'd make it as a filmmaker and Alecia as a morning news anchorwoman. By June, just eight weeks after Mama died, they'd moved to Pittsburgh together so Ben could start seminary. According to Alecia, my brother's Calling just happened to neatly coincide with her new job as a reporter for Channel Four Action News ("Alecia Axtel, taking Action for You!"). But this still doesn't explain why they bought a dining room set and a couch together. ("Relax. It's just IKEA," Ben told me.) I can't imagine sharing my sacred living space, much less buying furniture with another human being, no matter how inexpensive and convenient.

"How will you ever know who's right if you don't take a risk?" Ben asks.

After a moment, I reply, "What did you think of Matthew?"

"Who?"

"Dr. Hollembee? The guy who saved your life?"

I'm only half exaggerating. In early July, Ben showed up in Saint Catherine's ER with excruciating right lower quadrant abdominal pain. Matthew Hollembee was the surgery resident on-call that night who helped the attending remove Ben's appendix.

"Oh, yeah, him. The guy with the thick glasses. He seemed smart. Competent," Ben says.

"I mean personally," I say, though the circumstances weren't ideal for male bonding: a rectal exam followed by laparoscopic surgery.

"He's nice, Holly. The sort of guy who gets beaten up and stuffed in a trash can in middle school, and now he's got the last laugh because he's a surgeon."

"ENT," I say, and then add when Ben looks puzzled, "He's

required to do a preliminary year of general surgery, but he's going to be an Ear, Nose, and Throat surgeon eventually. Fundamental personality difference." By this, I mean that Matthew is nicer than your average surgeon. Or maybe he's nicer because he's British; I don't know.

"I'm kind of rooting for the guy," Ben says.

"You say it like he's the underdog," I say.

"Every man is the underdog with you, Holly."

WE MAKE A PACT outside the amphitheater not to talk before the show starts. Ben has it all figured out. He's convinced the place is bugged, and that's why the audience has to sit around so long before Joshua Peter appears. Then, he says, the TV crew listens to the conversations, and Joshua Peter uses the information to fool people.

"I'll prove it to you. We'll say we miss someone like..." Ben starts snapping his fingers, "Aunt Velma. And then see if he mentions her name."

"Someone in the audience is bound to have an aunt Velma who died."

"Really? Velma?" Ben is doubtful, but I put my finger to my lips to make him shut up. We're approaching the gate of the outdoor theatre, where an older woman is checking to be sure we have passes. It has stopped raining now and evolved into a humid, sunny August day. There's something about the crowd's nervous energy that reminds me of hope. Just as I'm about to mention this, Ben says there's something about the throngs of people that reminds him of the inscription on the Statue of Liberty: "Give me your tired, your poor, your huddled masses."

Once we're finally in our wooden seats, I start to pray, only I feel sort of funny about it. Ever since Mama died, she's the one I pray to.

Meet me here, Mama. Meet me here. Say something to make me understand.

I am talking about the letter I found when I was going through her things after the funeral, a letter written to my mother in 1983, the year she left home for seven months to go to medical school in Grenada. She had applied to school in the United States and didn't get in. Ben and I were only eight at the time—just six weeks before our ninth birthday. There probably isn't a good age to have your mother leave, even if you know she's coming back, but for me, it wasn't easy. Still, Mama's departure always seemed justified. She had a Calling to fulfill, no matter where it took her. Only it turns out that my mother was pursuing more than medicine that year. She was pursuing another medical student, Simon Berg.

Let the record show Mrs. Bellinger kissed me first, he wrote in his letter, apparently not knowing that her married name was Campbell.

Did you love him, Mama? I wonder now. *If so, why did you come back? Did you always wish, after that, that you were someplace else?* I add that if she's going to answer any of my questions through Joshua Peter, to please do it in code, so the rest of the audience won't find out the truth. I never even showed the letter to Ben. At this very moment it's hidden in a fireproof safe, back at my apartment. I don't want to ruin Mama's memory, but I can't let my questions go.

"Twizzler?" the woman next to me offers. She is sixty-something and has the rotund body habitus of a lady with type 2 diabetes, one who shouldn't be eating candy.

Wiping my wet eyes, I decline. She takes a bite and remarks as she chews, "It could be a while. I hear he meditates before each show."

On the other side of me, Ben snorts.

The woman asks us where we've come from and who we're hoping to get a message from.

"Pittsburgh. And we're not here for anyone in particular," I say, forgetting to mention Aunt Velma. "We were just curious."

The woman doesn't look fazed that we would drive two and a half hours in the rain out of mere curiosity. She just wants an excuse to tell us about her brother Charlie, a star runner who died at a track meet forty years ago when he was struck by lightning. She opens her purse to reveal, among more Twizzlers and a Milky Way, that she's carrying Charlie's medals and a small gold trophy.

Ben emits a sound that reminds me of cattle lowing. I step on his foot.

Over an hour later, Joshua Peter finally comes out, and everyone rises to give him a standing ovation. Everyone except Ben, that is, who grimaces from his seat. Joshua Peter looks pretty ordinary for a psychic—untucked flannel shirt, jeans, and brown hair. As if in church, he gestures with his hands to make us all sit down, then closes his eyes and tells us he's ready to begin.

"I see a woman, a woman who has already passed. She's holding up . . . a Mickey Mouse key chain."

Someone gasps. The camera crew carry their microphones over to a lady whose dead nephew once dressed up as Goofy for Halloween. Thus ensues a complicated story about Disney World and Space Mountain, until someone else pipes up with another dead relation who once carried a key chain shaped like the Eiffel Tower.

I start to notice a pattern. Joshua Peter only needs to say a few key phrases before the audience blurts out their own stories. They go back and forth until finally the same conclusion is reached: "Your loved one is with you." It occurs to me that I've risked death on the highway and a favor from Mary Worthington all for nothing.

This game of free association continues for another hour. Just as I'm getting drowsy Joshua Peter says, "I'm getting something about the eyes. A person who deals a lot with eyes."

"Say something," Ben says, giving me a nudge.

"No," I whisper.

Our mother was an eye doctor. He can't be talking about her, though. There are four thousand people in this amphitheatre, and surely Mama wasn't the only ophthalmologist.

"My aunt has a brain tumor. It's affecting her vision," someone in the front row volunteers.

"My dad had cataracts," someone else says.

"No...I think...It's coming from this section," Joshua Peter says, waving his arm our way. I feel as if we're in the stands about to get hit with a fly ball. *Resist the urge to duck,* I tell myself.

"My brother had a glass eye," the lady next to me pipes up. "He was a track star," she adds, apropos of nothing.

"It's not a glass eye. It's more..." Joshua Peter pauses, shuts his eyes, and puts his hand on his forehead as if concentrating very hard. "I see a hand on the eyes. She's a healer. Like an optometrist."

"Ophthalmologist," Ben blurts, his voice carrying over the crowd. God bless him; he's trying to correct the man. Children of eye doctors always know the difference between optometrists and ophthalmologists.

Microphones come our way.

"Our mother was an ophthalmologist," Ben says. "An eye surgeon."

"Well, why didn't you say so?" Joshua Peter asks, which makes the audience laugh. It's a warm laugh, and I relax despite the attention.

"I'm getting the letter 'V.' She's making a V sign, like for victory. Her name was Vicky? Velma?"

We shake our heads. Clearly, we've been bugged.

Joshua Peter rubs his chin, pretends the spirits are talking to him. "She was sick for a long time?"

"No," I say into the microphone. My mother's name is Sylvia Bellinger Campbell, and she died in a car wreck four months ago. But I refuse to give this away.

"I'm getting jaundice. Weight loss. A liver ailment. Something that made her bedridden," he says.

"Not our mother," I say. "Does this sound familiar?" I offer the woman next to me.

"My neighbor was paralyzed. He was bedridden," she says.

"Who are the twins?" Joshua Peter suddenly asks, which makes both of us sit up straighter.

"We are," I say, glancing at Ben, who is nodding.

Finally, a hit! Only how hard can it be, guessing that we're twins when we both have red hair and matching grins? Though, to be fair, neither one of us has grinned since we got here.

"Okay, I'm with you two," Joshua Peter decides. "The person your mother's telling me about has not passed over, but she's very sick. And she's parallel to your mother, which lets me know they are of the same generation. It's a mother figure to you. Your mother's best friend?" he suggests.

My mother's best friend is Jessica DeMatto, her medical school roommate, who left medicine to become a fashion designer and now makes millions of dollars off of her trademarked, custom-made "Jexy Jeans" line. When we last saw her at Mama's funeral she looked fantastic, not at all like someone dying of liver failure.

I briefly entertain the idea that he's referring to my mother's mother, Eve, who moved in with us when Mama left for Grenada, but it didn't fit then and it doesn't fit now. For one thing, Grandmother is not dying. For another, Mama is our only Mother Figure.

"Our mother's best friend isn't sick," I say into the microphone.

"Though we haven't seen her lately," Ben adds, which makes me glare at him for giving Joshua Peter any room to be right. So what if he guessed that we're twins? For every ninety term-births, one set of twins is born.

"Your father has passed on?" Joshua Peter asks.

"No. He's here," I say, even though he's not really here, he's in Maryland trying to install a central air conditioner himself. Of course, before I can stop myself, a vision of Dad with charred hair, lying unconscious on the floor holding a tangled mess of wires pops into my head.

"Which one of you is moving to England?" Joshua Peter asks.

I shake my head without even looking at Ben this time. This is absurd. Ben will have three full years of seminary, while I have another ten months of residency until I stay on as attending faculty at St. Catherine's Medical Center. It's all been arranged. No one is going anywhere. "Neither one of us."

"Well, your mom says congratulations. Someone is getting

engaged. And someone is moving to England. She's pulling her energy back," Joshua Peter says. "Just know that she's with you and sends her love."

"She's with you and she sends her love," I mutter, kicking a stone, which belatedly I notice is labeled with the word "Hebron." After the show, Ben wanted to wander around the Chautauqua Institution, and so we've ambled down the hill toward the lake, where Ben noticed a topical map of Palestine laid out on a small strip of grass by the water. Scattered around a stream labeled "The Dead Sea," stones lead up to a mound of dirt that has turned to mud with the day's rain. According to the sign, this map was erected in 1874 to teach people about the journey of the Bible. Ben, the seminarian, is intrigued, but I'm so disappointed, I could cry. *This is what you get when you rely on superstition,* I think.

"Sorry I dragged you here. What a waste."

"It wasn't an entire waste. Some of it was right," Ben says thoughtfully. He's ahead of me, slipping through the mud from the rock of Bethlehem to one called Arimathea.

"Like what?"

"The twin thing. And he knew Mama was an ophthalmologist."

"He said optometrist," I say, my foot sliding into a puddle of the Dead Sea.

"Many people don't know the difference. And he mentioned Aunt Velma."

"We don't have an aunt Velma! That just proves we were bugged!"

"But we talked about her before we ever got into the theatre," Ben says, turning away to climb up the small peak labeled Mount Hermon. I don't remember a Mount Hermon in the Bible, and I'm about to ask what happened there, but the wind carries his voice back to me. Ben's saying something about a wedding and a coincidence.

"What wedding?"

"Promise you won't get mad?" he calls.

"No." I stop, feeling the Dead Sea squelch between my toes.

"Mine." He grins. "I'm getting married."

I blink. "To whom?"

"Alecia—who else?" Ben laughs. Only it's not one of his laughs that I'm familiar with. It has a new, full sound, brimming with giddy affection, and it makes me feel sad and alone.

"Really? Alecia?"

"Don't say her name like that," Ben says.

I try to remember something more about the woman my brother has been living with for the summer: a Boston College graduate, a psychology major, a Delta Delta Something who "deactivated." He once mentioned sheepishly that she'd been arrested for having sex on a public beach and was forced to plant palm trees on Key West as community service. Those were her wilder days before she became a TV news reporter. He also said that her mother had been temporarily committed for a psychotic break, and her father is a billionaire.

"Come look at the view of the Mediterranean," Ben adds, gesturing to Lake Chautauqua as if he created it. The sun is reflecting so brightly off the water and silver sailboat masts that it's hard to keep my eyes open.

Nevertheless, I climb over the rocks of Jericho and Pella and Capernaum and Caesarea Philippi to sit next to my brother at the top of Mount Hermon. "I don't know what to say."

"How about 'Congratulations'?" Ben says, giving me a nudge. "Even Mama knew that."

"Congratulations," I manage to sound out. Then, after a pause, I ask, "So, if you're getting married . . . am I going to England?"

"Well, it's possible. Someday you might. I mean, hell, it's not like he said Middle Earth."

Ben laughs again, slings an arm over my shoulder to give me a side hug. I want to run down the other side of the hill, over the stone called "Damascus" and back to the Volvo with its slippery steering, but I can't. My twin is engaged. I have to smile. So I do.

"Thanks for the Courtesy Smile," he says.

I laugh.

"And for the Courtesy Laugh," he adds.

I shrug in protest even though my eyes won't stop giving me away with their leaky tears. "Sorry—my allergies—"

"What are you so sad about?" Ben asks, with such unexpected tenderness that it makes me want to weep out loud. "What were you hoping to discover today?"

"I want to find out if Mama's okay," I snivel.

But even as I say it, I know it's a lie. I want to find out if I'm okay.

CHAPTER 2

Three Sticks

"Do not blame the sick for being sick."

—OXFORD HANDBOOK OF CLINICAL MEDICINE

B ut nearly eight months later—mid-April, on the thirteenth consecutive day of rain—I am no closer to finding out the truth until my patient Clara Storm lets me know it: I am not okay and will probably never be okay unless I get out of Pittsburgh. I'm standing at the nurse's station in the ICU while fielding the unit secretary's questions about how to handle the dead body in Room 305 if we can't get in touch with the family. Just as I am about to tell her to follow the Dead-Body-Without-a-Family Protocol, Shirley, a crabby nurse who takes breaks from caring for people on ventilators by smoking cigarettes, informs me that the ER just called. They are refusing to take the man in 305 back.

"Well, that's not standard procedure, is it? To send a dead body back to the ER?" I ask.

"Well, it's not standard procedure to admit a dead body to the ICU either," Shirley snaps.

"He had a pulse!" I say.

The fact is the man in 305 was barely alive when he was

transferred from the VA Hospital to our ER. His chest was blue, his limbs were set in rigor mortis, and his eyes were fixed and dilated. He'd "been down" for nearly forty-five minutes already, but unfortunately the man's barely beating heart wouldn't stop its obscure electrical activity, and we were compelled to counteract with shocks and drugs and more shocks, all in the hope of obtaining a normal heart rhythm. At last, after one hour of CPR, bagging with 100 percent oxygen, and the rest of the rigmarole of resuscitating an otherwise dead man, his heart quit.

I pronounced him dead at 3:42 P.M. No one objected; in fact, someone muttered that we should've stopped a long time ago, which made me wonder if we could really, truly step away from a man whose heart was still going. I shouldn't have wondered, because then suddenly the man's heart erupted into a flurry of beats like the finale of the 4th of July fireworks. His chest was visibly moving from the contractions of his heart, so I pronounced him alive and made the decision to get him upstairs to Room 305. I figured we'd continue our futile efforts until I could track down a family member to explain the grim truth: that he had no meaningful chance of recovery. Only, somewhere between the ER and the ICU, the fireworks in his heart stopped going off, and now the ICU nurses are mad that he wasn't pronounced dead back in the ER. They've been stuck with the body and all the paperwork.

"Honey, next time you're not sure if someone's dead, call me," another nurse, Wanda, says, patting my shoulder. "I'll pronounce him."

I'm actually grateful. It's lucky that Wanda was there when the ER nurses wheeled him into Room 305. Lucky because by that point I started to lose all sense of what dead really was. The man was cold, cyanotic, and unresponsive when we met, but not completely unlike the lady in Room 311, who is brain dead on a ventilator, and whose family "still wants everything done." Or not unlike the patient in 306, who hasn't responded in the three weeks since he was "found down," hypothermic and hypoglycemic, on a park bench. The man in 305 may have been colder and bluer, but I would have kept going if Wanda hadn't exclaimed—like the child who blurted out that the emperor had no clothes—"This guy is fucking dead!"

I love Wanda because she wears one-inch nails painted like mini American flags. And I love Wanda because she knows when to stop. Or when to start, as in the case of Clara Storm, whose room she's making me walk toward now.

"Forget 305 and walk with me to 302," she says. "Clara needs an art line. But she doesn't want one."

Clara Storm isn't like most of my ICU patients. Meaning she's lucid and, frankly, a little demanding. Despite having a tracheostomy that's hooked up to a ventilator, Clara moves her mouth in constant lip sync to her feelings. Clara says that she's sick of having pneumonia, that she's sick of being on an air mattress that whirs like a car engine, that she's tired of the programs on TV. I'm starting to wonder how I'm going to cope as a regular family doctor—and one of the teaching faculty, no less—when I finish residency in two and a half months. Lately I prefer patients who can't communicate their needs.

Clara requires some convincing that she actually needs the arterial line placed in her wrist. I tell her we want to measure her blood pressure better, that we're not getting a good reading on the cuff, that, no, I'm not just doing this for kicks. I also tell her that it will save her multiple needle sticks, because now when we want a blood gas, we'll just tap into the flow of the art line. Clara looks doubtful. She holds up her index finger and mouths the words: *One stick, one try, no more.*

Wanda also looks doubtful. Clara not only weighs three hundred pounds, but her wrists have become swollen since being on the vent, so I say, "I'll do my best."

Setting up my sterile field on Clara's wrist, a News Break flashes on the TV screen that's bolted to the wall. Apparently there's been a shooting in Oakland at the Exxon on the corner of Forbes Avenue and McKee. I glance up from the circle of iodine that I'm making on Clara's pale, doughy wrist to see one of the Action News reporters standing on the sidewalk in the rain.

"A man authorities have identified as Robert Coleman of Penn Hills entered the Quick Mart this afternoon and shot his ex-girlfriend, identified as Elaine Winter, also of Penn Hills," says the reporter, an attractive, well-built black guy, who I've noticed usually gets sent to the most dangerous areas of town.

"The suspect also killed Dr. Gabriel Linzer of New York before turning the gun on himself," the reporter goes on. "Ms. Winter had apparently broken up with Mr. Coleman earlier today. Dr. Linzer was not connected with the other victims. Authorities say he was a guest lecturer at the University of Pittsburgh School of Medicine and was buying a bottle of water when the gunman entered the store."

"Jesus! Talk about being in the wrong place at the wrong time," Wanda says, using her American flags to tap the keys on the bedside monitor.

I look up at the TV to search for a picture of the murdered doctor, as if I might know him, but they are showing the one witness who was present, an Exxon employee. Apparently he managed to survive by hiding behind the coffee island, which he was cleaning at the time. The story ends with a promise for more details at 6 p.m., then the five o'clock news continues with another major event: Pittsburgh is about to get a new Krispy Kreme Doughnut shop.

"Hey, isn't that your sister-in-law?" Wanda points to Alecia Axtel, who's standing outside a Krispy Kreme in Cranberry Township interviewing customers under her rainbow umbrella— "Live!"—about how they feel about the new store.

"Not yet, she isn't," I say, and then singsong to Clara, just as I poke her with the needle, "Little stick." Clara opens her mouth to scream, but luckily she doesn't have use of her vocal cords right now. Though there's something equally disconcerting about the hiss that seeps out through her trach tube.

"Hang in there, honey. You're doing great," Wanda says, from across the hospital bed, and then asks me, "So when's the wedding?"

"They haven't set a date," I say, fishing in Clara's arm with my needle, trying to tag her radial artery. What happened to her thready pulse? Suddenly it's slipped away. Clara is staring at me, tears squeezing out of her eyes.

"That is some ring," Wanda remarks, staring at the TV, still standing poised, ready to connect my art line to the monitor, if I ever get it in.

She's talking about my mother's emerald, a square stone set in arms of platinum. The sight of Alecia wearing it only flusters me further. The ring should've been given to me, not Ben. True, I was left garnet earrings and a gorgeous sapphire locket, but whenever I remember the emerald—or see it on TV every night between five and eleven—I imagine Mama's eyes, nuggets of green. No matter if Alecia's interviewing an accused pedophile or warning Pittsburgh that a friendly cub named Mr. Snugglesworth has escaped from the zoo, there she stands, gripping the mike with Mama's bright green eye wrapped around her left finger.

At last! A cherry-red flash of blood fills up the tube—I've hit Clara's artery. Oh, how satisfying it is to thread the wire forward and then slide the catheter up into the vessel! "I'm in, Clara. First try. You did beautifully," I say, but really I'm complimenting myself. It's the most satisfying moment of an otherwise lousy day.

Wanda attaches my catheter to the tubing and flushes it with saline. On the monitor, we watch the line that represents Clara's blood pressure arrange itself into a reassuring wave. For a second I grin, until Alecia catches my eye on the TV, still going on about the history of the Krispy Kreme craze.

Reaching for the sterile sewing needle, which I'll need to secure the art line onto Clara's arm, it occurs to me that I forgot to tell her about the second stick. For just a moment, I consider poking her without a warning.

"Clara, I have to stick you one more time, just to tie the line in place," I say.

Noooo! she yells without a sound, which is eerie, like watching a horror movie on mute.

"Clara, I have to," I say.

Tape it, she mouths.

"Tape doesn't work. It needs to be tied on so the line won't fall out. Okay?" I pass the needle through her skin before she can protest.

"There, Clara, there. It's over. That was the last stick," I say hastily, trying to ignore her tears.

Shirley appears in the doorway of the room to announce that there's a problem. Apparently the man in 305's son is on the phone and wants to say good-bye to his father.

"So, what's the problem?" I ask, glancing up from Clara's wrist where I'm still fumbling with the thread, trying to tie a knot. That's the hardest part of all, securing the art line into place. I'm terrible at sewing buttons onto clothes, much less catheters onto wrists.

"The body is already in the morgue," Shirley says.

"So send the son to the morgue," I say.

"What is this, *CSI Pittsburgh*?" Wanda asks, her voice rising to a near shriek. "Now he's gotta go identify the body?"

"We don't send families to the morgue," Shirley says. "There's no one down there after five. We can't have the son just prowling around the bodies in the basement."

"So bring the body back," I say.

"To life?" Wanda asks, and then snorts with laughter.

"To Room 305," I say. "Let his son kiss him good-bye."

"We don't admit patients to the ICU from the morgue," Shirley says snidely.

"That's fine. It's not an admission," I say.

"Yeah, the room is still dirty, right? What's the BFD?" Wanda asks.

Shirley turns and leaves, trailing a loud sigh, and I'm not sure what the outcome of the man in 305 is going to be. But Wanda is my hero, because Wanda made Shirley leave.

"Now we need to talk about access," Wanda says, just as I've thrown out the needle and crumpled up the bloody sterile field. "She's blown every peripheral line. She needs a central."

"Uh-oh," I say, only because I promised Clara one stick, and then it was two sticks, and now . . .

What's happening? Clara mouths, her eyes looking fearful.

I lean in close to explain over the sound of the ventilator and the bed that she doesn't have any access. Clara reminds me that I just put a line into her arm. I reply that it's an arterial catheter to measure blood pressure, not a venous line. "We don't push drugs into arteries," I explain. "And in order to give you medicine by vein, we need to put in a central line."

You promised me, Clara mouths, *only one stick.*

"I meant one stick for the art line. I didn't know you needed a central line, too."

You promised.

"I didn't promise anything!" I say.

Wanda leans in then and rubs Clara's shoulder. The way she makes her voice all creamy, I get the feeling she's trying to soothe me, too. "Clara, honey, you know every time I put a peripheral line into your arm or hand, the vein blows. If you let Dr. Campbell put in a central line, it's going to last much, much longer."

"Clara, we can't give you your antibiotics or your pain medicine without an IV," I add.

You're bribing me, Clara mouths.

"I'm not bribing you, I'm trying to help you!" I shout over the whir of the ventilator and the bed. It sounds like a factory in here.

I watch as Clara's lips slowly form the words: *Don't blame me for being sick.*

"Honey, nobody's blaming you," Wanda says, rubbing her shoulder.

But it's a lie. Clara is right. I am blaming her. For having feelings.

And this is how I know it's time to get out of Pittsburgh.

"Everything all right, Dr. Campbell?" says a familiar voice from the doorway. It's Matthew Hollembee.

I rip off my gloves, tell Clara that I'll be back, that we're not finished discussing this.

"Can I help?" Matthew asks, outside the room, where he's now leaning against the nurses' desk in his scrubs.

"Clara Storm needs access," I say, running my fingers through the wisps of hair that have escaped my ponytail. "She's blown all her lines."

"Not a problem," he says, always the English gentleman. "I'll do it."

"I can do it myself, but she won't let me." My voice cracks with frustration. God, I'm about to cry. Why is it that all emotions—rage, joy, fear, guilt—reduce me to tears?

Matthew straightens and puts a hand on my shoulder. "May I have a bash? Perhaps she'll allow me."

I shrug and tell him to go for it. He's a much better sweet-talker, given the British accent. Nurses, even Shirley, seem to automatically like him because of it. Besides, the body bag containing the man in 305 has just arrived on a gurney from the morgue, and I can only deal with one failure at a time.

"Where yinz want this?" the orderly asks, as if it's Pottery Barn furniture he's delivering.

"In there," I say, pointing down the hall to 305. "In the bed, please. Out of the bag." I turn to Shirley and add, "Can we get him a blanket?" which makes her glare at me. "He's cold," I say.

"Oh, he's cold, all right," she mutters, walking away.

Through the glass window of 302, I watch Matthew leaning over Clara's bed and notice how she's nodding her head instead of moving her lips. He's convincing her just the way he convinced me.

Matthew and I have been "hanging out" for the last month. When Grandmother Eve wanted to know if "hanging out" was the same as "going steady," I said I didn't think so. I said it just meant that we were spending time together, which Grandmother didn't like the sound of.

"But you're a girl, and he's a boy," she said sharply. "What do you do when you spend this time together?"

I said what she wanted to hear: about the dinners and the movies. I didn't mention that usually we were too tired to go out, that usually we were too tired to do anything but sit on the couch and talk or make out.

"So you are going steady," Grandmother Eve decided.

"No," I said. "It's not that formal."

"Well, then you're developing an alliance," Eve said, which sounded about as romantic as forming a committee. But forming a committee did sound better than going steady, so I said yes.

"Righty ho," Matthew says, emerging from Clara's room. "Wanda, get us set up for a quad lumen catheter. Holly, go home."

"Really?" I say, relieved.

"Coming by tonight?" he adds in a low voice, which both pleases and embarrasses me. Matthew would probably be ready for more than just "hanging out," if only I could be convinced. But my work life is frenetic enough without introducing the drama that goes along with a real relationship. I check to be sure no one is listening to Matthew, but Shirley is still tucking the man in 305 into bed, and Wanda is getting ready for Clara's third stick.

"I have to do laundry tonight," I say, which is the truth. Clothes have besieged my apartment; it looks like a Dumpster outside of Goodwill.

"Why not use the machine in my basement? You won't even have to pay," Matthew says. He rents a ramshackle house in Highland Park, while I live in an apartment in Shadyside, which charges me three dollars a load. But the truth is so silly, I can't even admit it to him: I'm scared of his basement. It's wet and dark and there are tangled cobwebs hanging over his dryer.

"If you take my key, you could go there straightaway and get started," he adds.

"I can't do laundry without my clothes," I say, gently nudging his key back to him. Shirley is eyeing us as she emerges from 305, which is all I need: nurses knowing we're an item. I can just imagine the insinuations if we don't answer a page on the first ring. We're hooking up in a call room, they'll suggest. (For the record, I've never had sex in my call room, or any room for that matter. In college I saved myself for marriage, in medical school for the right time, and since residency began, I've saved myself for sleep.)

"We could order pizza ... or Chinese?" he suggests.

Hot food, of any nationality, suddenly sounds comforting. "Okay," I say slowly.

"Brilliant," Matthew says, grinning. His teeth obviously didn't spend years sheathed in metal, being tugged by carefully engineered rubber bands. Instead they're as uneven as piano keys in the middle of a song.

I tell him to give me a call when he gets home, that if I don't answer I'm in the tub.

IT TAKES ME forty minutes to get home from work because Baum Boulevard is as clogged up with cars as my mind is with thoughts. *Don't blame me because I'm sick,* Clara said, or tried to say, which makes me blink tears from my eyes. What kind of a person blames her patients for being sick? Ever since Mama died, if someone complains of chest pain, I wonder why—only I'm not wondering whether it's a myocardial infarction or a pulmonary embolus. I'm wondering, *Why now? Why is he or she doing this to me?*

And then there are the clinic patients, I think, as I make my way across Centre Avenue onto South Aiken. They steal my strength, waving around their problems like sticks of kryptonite. Their desperation makes me weary. I was taught by textbooks and dead people who never made demands. Cadavers don't request permanent disability for a yeast infection or narcotics for pinkeye or pills to make themselves skinny. Cadavers don't expect things of me, get mad at me when I can't fix them, or demand that I touch, look, feel, smell their wounds. Cadavers lay themselves down and say, *Here I am. Tear me apart. Make a mess of me, if you have to.* It occurs to me that I am becoming a cadaver myself, or at least an asexual cynic, starving for a different life, one filled with men and chocolate.

I cut the engine outside my building, rest my head on the steering wheel, and consider curling up for a nap in the backseat. Suddenly the walk from the parking lot to my first-floor apartment seems like hiking into the Grand Canyon and back.

Home is good, I tell myself, finally trudging from the car.

It always surprises me to unlock the door to my apartment and discover how disgustingly messy one's place can become when one is hardly ever there. Dirty clothes are scattered everywhere—on the floor, on the coffee table, on the backs of chairs. Dishes are piled up in the sink, while a lawn of green mold has sprouted over a pan of hard brownies. I drop my doctor's bag on the table and go to put on some music, but all my CD cases are either empty or contain the wrong disc. If you didn't know better, you'd think my place had been ransacked; in fact, the thought itself is enough to make me take pause and glance around. Did somebody else trash my apartment? But no, it looked like this yesterday, and the day before.

Messy or not, this is still my favorite hideout. I dump my white coat on the floor and grab a beer from the fridge. My building doesn't have a scary basement where things are neglected, stored out of guilt, or hidden in some dark corner, like the man in 305. Instead, my apartment is a luxury one-bedroom with high ceilings, wood floors, built-in bookshelves, and a bathtub with old-fashioned feet, which is where I'm headed now. After setting the Yuengling and an *American Academy of Family Physicians* magazine on the toilet seat, I strip off my scrubs, turn the bath water to hot, and splash into the tub. As if on cue, the phone starts to ring, and I groan out loud. It's Matthew, of course. Can't he give me one second of privacy?

I shouldn't be so hard on him. After all, I actually like the guy, like him more than I want to. *It's interesting the way he sort of snuck up on me,* I muse, sinking into the hot water as the phone continues to ring.

The commencement of our "alliance" began one Monday in March, during Journal Club. It was my week to lead the discussion about an article and to decide whether the study in question was Good or Bad (based on its validity). If it was Good, I had to determine if it would change my practice in real life.

Matthew showed up about halfway through my lecture and took a seat at the back. I assumed he was there for the free food, considering that surgery residents don't normally crash the family practice lunchtime lectures, but instead of quickly eating until feigning an emergency page, Matthew raised his hand to disagree.

"Bollocks!" he said, which made everyone turn and look. Of

course, most residents were smiling once they discovered the source of the outburst, none other than "Buddy Holly" (a nickname he'd acquired since coming to St. Cate's, on account of his glasses). "Where is your evidence?" Matthew wanted to know.

"Excuse me?" I said, crossing my arms over my chest. The pens in my breast pocket dug into my ribs.

"If you believe that this is a good study, that this article represents the truth, then you have essentially accepted the null hypothesis," Matthew said.

"Accepted the null hypothesis?" I repeated. He made it sound like I was an atheist, but just because I don't take the Bible to be completely true doesn't mean I don't have some vague sense of God.

"Statistical analysis is a philosophy of chance," Matthew said, getting up and walking over to where I stood next to the marker board. I could feel my eyes growing wider, as if he were about to publicly propose.

"There are never any absolutes. A good statistical analysis doesn't claim to be the actual truth, it says with a certain degree of confidence that the truth lies somewhere between here"— Matthew touched my white-coated shoulder—"and here"—he tapped his own chest.

I stared at the space between us.

"Now, if I may . . ." Matthew picked up a Magic Marker and wrote on the board as he continued. "The null hypothesis states that the experimental findings of an entity X being related to another entity Y are a random pairing, the result of chance— exactly what the experimenter hopes to disprove. He wants better than mere chance, he wants a statistically significant relationship." Matthew underlined the last word. "At the end of it all, the experimenter has the right to either reject or fail to reject the null hypothesis, but no one ever just accepts it."

I suddenly started wondering if he was talking about us.

"Hey, that's permanent marker you used," Mary Worthington piped up from the front row.

Matthew licked his thumb and tried to wipe the indelible ink off the board, but it remains there even now, four weeks later. "Oh, good Lord. I do apologize."

"The surgeons owe us a new board," someone else said.

"Consider it done," Matthew said with a confident nod. Nevertheless, he did look humbled when he took his seat again, and he didn't open his mouth for the rest of the discussion.

Afterward, I stopped him in the hall to ask what the hell he was talking about in there. "It must've been important if it made you ruin our board." I smiled as I said this, hoping to give him an opening to show interest in me again, but Matthew only answered gravely, as if we were discussing reality TV or SARS.

"There is inherent error in the author's methods of math—a critical mistake that people constantly make," he said. "The author has gone and picked one control group and then used the same group again and again to make new comparisons. It sickens me. Studies get published that are meaningless."

"Why meaningless?" I asked.

"Because you can't just select a random group of people and decide that they represent what's normal every single time. There is inherent variability within the control, and if everything else is compared to the one we arbitrarily call 'normal,' all the results become completely skewed."

"I see," I said, even though I didn't quite see anything except that his lashes were thick, his eyes were olive, and his passion was huge.

"The long and short of this is, you must find two independent parameters before you bring them together," Matthew finished.

A strange feeling came over me—hope, desperation, giddy fatigue?—that this was the moment I'd been waiting for, the one that brings two random people together and names it Significant. Here were Matthew and I, just two independent parameters looking for the right conditions.

So, there in the hallway, I asked him to dinner. And we went out that night, and the night after that, and somehow in the last four weeks, we've found the time to hang out quite a bit.

In fact, just thinking about that moment is enough to make

me sit up right now in the tub and consider bolting for the phone before the final ring. Only it's not Matthew on the other end; it's Ben, whose jarring voice fills my apartment and reminds me I'll have to turn the volume down on my answering machine in the future. My neighbors can probably hear his entire, hysterical message through the walls: "Holly—it's me. You won't believe this—have you seen the news? No, of course, not. You don't watch the news. Alecia's uncle was murdered! He was coming into town to give a lecture at Pitt! He was buying a goddamn bottle of water when he got shot—he was supposed to take us out to eat tonight at Laforet!" Ben says, strangely emphasizing the four-star restaurant. "Oh, my God, I can't believe it. I can't believe it!" he shouts. Then more calmly: "Give me a call. As soon as you get this message."

I can't move. I can't pick up the phone. What does Alecia's uncle have to do with me? I don't know him, just like I don't know the man in 305. I wasn't even invited to Laforet. I am the doctor who blames her patients for having feelings. I can only do so much, and right now all I can manage is to shut my eyes and sink lower into the hot water.

Outside, on South Aiken Avenue, ambulance sirens scream *EEEEEEE,* and car radios go *doom-doom-doom,* and cat fights shrill, "Giiiirrrl, you better not be saying what I think you said!" And from the buses, computerized announcements remind me where they are going, night after night: "Downtown!"

The only way to drown out the racket is to try to imagine that I'm someplace else, but the one place I want to be is in my mother's kitchen.

Keeping my eyes closed, I conjure her up. There she is, standing on a step stool and watering the hanging spider plants while I sit at the table, nursing a lemonade and stressing about finals. I am twenty years old, and the pressures of junior year in college are overwhelming.

"What if I don't get into medical school?" I ask.

"Trust me. It's not the end of the world," Mama says, her voice sounding wry, as she moves her stool and steps back onto it to reach her fern plant with the watering can.

"It was for you," I say. "It was the most important thing to you."

"I was narrow-minded," Mama says. "I could only imagine one way to be happy. But there are lots and lots of ways to live your life that you'll find fulfilling, if you open yourself up to it."

"You think I won't get in," I say.

"Holly, I have no idea. I'm telling you there's more to life than medicine. I'm telling you that, believe it or not, I might've been wrong."

I consider this, eyebrows furrowed as I twirl my hair, until finally a smile forms on my face. "No," I say sheepishly. "You, wrong? It can't be."

"I said *might've* been." Mama grins, walking toward me on her way to the sink. "Open up," she orders, holding the watering can by my mouth, as if she's about to feed me.

I swat the spout from my face and, in spite of myself, start snickering. After a moment, we are both laughing.

Oh, how we laughed, I think now. That was the best part about Mama. Because when we cried, we cried, but when we laughed, we did it right—recklessly and hysterically, until we were weak and could barely stand, until one of us, crossed-legged and reeling, beseeched, "Don't make me wet my pants!" Oh, it was funny. It was really, really funny. I start chuckling, except that when I open my eyes, I'm disappointed to find myself back in the tub.

Mama, you said there was more to life than medicine, but you never told me what medicine really was. You never mentioned the constant burdens of decision and negotiation, and that you can never really heal anyone. Of course, that only gets me thinking of other things Mama hid from me, secrets like Simon Berg. *Were you just as disillusioned by marriage and motherhood as I am with medicine? Is that why you left? Then why did you come back? And why do I keep going forward?*

Of course, she doesn't answer. She can't answer. *She's dead, Holly,* I tell myself. *Get used to it. Get over it. Let her go.*

But I can't let her go. As soon as I loosen my grasp she'll disappear, and I'll really have to face a life without her.

Giving up on a sign from my mother, I reach for my *AAFP*

magazine, which has slid off the toilet onto the rug and fallen open to a full-page advertisement featuring a picture of London's Tower Bridge. With wet fingers, I grasp the magazine and bring it to my face to inspect the ad. "Travel Doc!" I read. "Be a Locum Tenens in Europe! Great Way to See New Places!" *"Locum tenens,"* I remember, is Latin for "holding place."

It's funny how quickly decisions are made—or maybe I'm lying to myself. Maybe my mind was made up after Joshua Peter informed me almost eight months ago that I would go to England. Only Mama really knows for sure. But on the evening of April 13, still in the tub, I decide my brother is right, that it's time to take a risk for the first time in my life. I will not be taking the faculty position at St. Cate's or joining the hospital-affiliated family practice clinic. I will move to England and become a Travel Doc. I will hold somebody's place while back home somebody else can try being me.

CHAPTER 3

Family Taboos

> "As late as the 1920s, it was taboo for a doctor to touch the living human heart."
>
> — "Don't Touch the Heart,"
> Lawrence K. Altman, MD

It's been two months since Alecia's uncle got shot, two months since my Clara Storm revelation, and ten months since Joshua Peter predicted that Ben would marry and that I would go to England. The psychic is only half right. So far, Ben hasn't taken a single vow—in fact, there've been rumblings of discontent—but as of tomorrow morning, I will be thirty thousand feet in the air, hurtling across the Atlantic Ocean on a mammoth Airbus bound for the U.K.

Ben drives the U-Haul from Pittsburgh to Maryland, and I follow behind in my Volvo. The U-Haul is filled with all of my furniture and boxes, while the Volvo is stuffed with smaller things: suitcases and clothes. We arrive in front of the family home just before dusk, and our father comes out of the white colonial and down the flagstone walk.

"Isn't there a weight limit on international flights?" Dad asks with a chuckle as he crosses the lawn.

He gives me a hug before my car door is even shut and asks

how I roped my twin into commandeering a truck from Pitts-burgh.

"I told you. She's giving me the Volvo," Ben says.

"Just for the year," I say.

"What happened to the Honda?" Dad asks my brother as we walk back toward the house together.

"Well, Alecia needed a car, so we decided—"

"You gave your *girlfriend* the car that your mother and I bought for you?"

"No, I traded it in to help with the down payment on her new one. We're getting married, Dad," Ben adds. To Dad, "news breaks" require crystals of information to be broken over his head in order for the occasional shard to sink into his brain.

"When?"

"One of these..." Ben starts, and then waves his hand around in lieu of choosing a time frame—it could be days, could be decades. "Maybe I'll start unloading," he says, pointing at the truck.

"What are you planning on doing with all that stuff?" Dad asks me, as if I hadn't called ahead.

"I told you. I'm leaving it here," I say, reaching for the front door that always seemed so enormous when I was small. The brass knocker rattles as I push my weight into the big, red door, and when I step into the hallway, I inhale, searching for the familiar scent of my childhood. Only it smells different now, like sawdust and boiled peas.

"You're leaving it here?" Dad repeats. "Oh, no. No, no, no, no, no."

"Maybe I won't unload the truck," Ben says cheerfully.

My father becomes agitated, insisting that despite the fact that four people once lived in this house, there is simply no room for my stuff. (A retired orthopedist, Dad has been busy replacing everything from the light fixtures to the floors, in lieu of people's hips and knees.) My bedroom is slated to be his new office; the basement, his woodshop for building sailboats; and the attic is already filled with boxes. The contents of the U-Haul will make the house look "cluttered." A strange argument, I think, considering that besides the usual accoutrements of the foyer—a coatrack piled high with jackets that haven't been worn since the 1970's, a decorative box of broken umbrellas, a pair of crutches from my seventh-grade ankle sprain—sitting at the edge of the Persian carpet there is also a toilet.

"So, what's the front hall going to be? A bathroom?" Ben asks, pointing at the toilet wedged next to my mother's grandfather clock.

"Oh, that. I'm replumbing the downstairs bathroom. Had to take the toilet out," Dad says matter-of-factly. "When I shower, I don't want to have to worry about someone flushing the toilet and scalding me to death. With the manifold system I'm installing, the shower and toilet will run independent of each other."

"Isn't that a lot of trouble?" I ask.

"Yeah. I mean, it isn't as if anyone lives here to flush the toilet on you," Ben says.

From his contortions of mild annoyance—angled eyebrows, forehead wrinkles—Dad's face seems to melt into a frown, the expression he developed when we were eight, when Mama left, the same one he's worn most often since she died. "Thanks for reminding me," Dad says now, staring at the toilet on the rug.

Eve, my mother's mother, shows up after that, which disturbs my father even more, because he was supposed to go pick her up. Grandmother still lives alone in an old Victorian out in Howard County, wears her hair in a blond bouffant, and drives herself around in a Saturn sedan, except after dark. Inevitably, she'll have to spend the night, because Dad now has no choice but to invite her. I'm sure this was her plan all along. She probably wants as much time as possible to convince me to change my mind.

"So. London," Eve says to me, as in *Go. Start explaining.* We've just sat down to dinner (thick-as-fog split pea soup and oven rolls, the first meal my father learned to cook after Mama died) and finished a very pious grace. We always say a special grace when Grandmother eats with us. And we try never to laugh, because for the period of time she lived with us when we were children, she instituted a rule that there would be no laughing at the dinner table. If we accidentally chuckled, snorted, snarfed, or guffawed, we would be sent to our rooms for "getting out of hand." Eve often described the dangers of choking on one's food ("You could aspirate-and-die," she said, as if it were one word). For most of my life I've thought laughing and eating didn't go together, like drinking and driving.

"Not London. I'm going to Winchester, actually," I say.

"And where is that?" Grandmother says, raising an eyebrow.

"South of London." For confirmation, I look to my father, who puts down his napkin and pushes back from the table, probably to go grab an encyclopedia.

"Aha!" Grandmother exclaims. "So it is about the psychic! I knew it. I told your father, 'This is about the psychic.' "

"It actually has nothing to do with the psychic," I say.

"I saw it on that episode of *Passing On* last November. He told you that someone was going to England. And I could see it in your face. You thought he meant you. And now you've thrown away a faculty position at a university-affiliated teaching hospital, simply because the star of—"

"He also said Ben was getting married, and God knows when that'll happen," I interrupt, which makes Ben look up from across the table with wide eyes, as if I just fired a shot.

It works. Grandmother stops her tirade and puts down her spoon, heaving a sigh. "Benjamin, when will you stop shacking up with this girl?"

"It's not really a shack," Ben says. "It's actually a very nice apartment."

"Your mother would be appalled to see you living like this."

"Oh, I don't know about that," Ben says, reaching for his glass and downing half of his water at once. "I think Mama is probably delighted when someone loves one of her children."

"Jesus would be appalled, then," Grandmother says, apparently giving up on my mother's sensibility.

"Jesus hung out with the sinners. I don't think anything could appall him," Ben says.

"How do you expect to become a minister when you yourself aren't practicing a holy life?" Grandmother asks.

"In the original intent of the word, 'holy' did not mean being better than someone else. It meant 'set apart by God.' We're all holy here," Ben says, and then hops up from the table, as if he suddenly has to leave. "Ice," he adds when I shoot him a questioning look.

"I'm curious, Ben—is that what they're teaching you in school?" Eve calls after him. "That the church condones premarital sex? Is that what you'll preach someday?"

He halts and lets go of his Disgusted Laugh, which sounds particularly jagged tonight. "I'll be preaching *love* and *forgiveness,*" he says, only the way he spits out the words, they almost sound like "hate" and "revenge."

"But there are very specific laws, Benjamin. Haven't you read the Bible?"

"Dad?" I call, wondering if he's gone off to read the encyclopedia in the bathroom. Only, I can see the toilet in the foyer. Thankfully, it's unoccupied.

"Ice," Ben says again, and then disappears into the kitchen with his half-empty glass of water.

"Have they found out anything more about the suicide-murderer?" Eve asks. There's something about the way she daintily takes another spoonful of soup that makes me feel like we should be discussing wedding gifts for the happy couple instead of a bloody rampage at Exxon.

"They figured out he was depressed." Unfortunately, I'm not joking. Channel 4 actually held interviews with friends and neighbors, who confirmed that the gunman had seemed down, easily tearful, quick to anger, and unable to experience pleasure after his girlfriend dumped him. The medical reporter even used the story as a forum to remind the public to "Talk to Your Doctor About Depression."

"And how is *she* taking it?" Grandmother rarely uses Alecia's name, which is good, since I don't like to hear it from Grandmother's lips. She always sounds mocking, turning "Alecia" into

"A-lee-cee-ah"—four distinct, high-pitched syllables—rather than just "Aleesha," the way Ben says it.

In the kitchen, I hear glass breaking, unless that's just Ben, smashing a block of ice.

"I really wouldn't know how she's doing. I only see her on the news." I reach for another roll. Until this morning, when I had to have every last bit of trash in the Dumpster by 10 A.M., the condolence card that I meant to send was still sitting on my coffee table. I probably should've called, but it was easier to pass on my sympathies through Ben. The truth is, I find it very hard to talk to Alecia. She doesn't have conversations; she conducts interviews. "How are you coping with the loss of your mother? Are you still reeling with shock?" she asked, shaking my hand for the first time. Ben thinks I'm too sensitive, and maybe he's right. But I never expected him to show up with a date to Mama's funeral. Alecia wore a little black dress, which made Ben say, "Wow," and made my grandmother pull me aside to ask, "Who is that tart?" I heard Alecia say, "Good thing I packed this dress after all!" as if we'd thrown them a surprise engagement party. Later I looked out the window and saw her groping my brother against the side of the house. No, we would never be friends.

"Benjamin, I was just asking Holly how your girlfriend is doing," Grandmother says. Like my father, she deliberately avoids the designation "fiancée." I suppose "girlfriend" is nicer than "that tart."

"She's having a difficult time right now, but she's getting through it," Ben says with all the heart of a publicist issuing a statement to the press. I notice that his water has now changed to a Scotch on the rocks. Grandmother probably thinks it's iced tea.

"Winchester, one hour south of London by train," Dad announces, coming back to the table with an England guidebook. I am suddenly thankful that it's my turn to be sacrificed.

Dad proceeds to read aloud, which is how I find out that the market town of Winchester is nestled in the midst of rolling, green downs, that it used to be the capital of England, that knights used to sharpen their swords or swap recipes at the round table inside its castle, and that its "neo-gothic" cathedral was formerly the center of this "once-glorious" city.

"It's career suicide, Holly," Grandmother says, stirring her soup.

"Jane Austen even died there," Dad adds, which makes me uneasy when I think about flying tomorrow with a suitcase the size of a casket.

"Why exactly are you going?" Grandmother asks, holding up her spoon like a judge raising a gavel. "Is this about some need for an adventure?"

I open my mouth, wondering how to explain Clara Storm and the man in 305 and how I've been blaming my patients for the last year, when I realize I'm not exactly sure why I am going. But it has something to do with me, and something to do with Mama, and maybe even something to do with Simon Berg.

"Look, Mama went away for a while, and she came back the better for it," I say.

"*Holly,*" Grandmother says, sitting up straighter and putting down her spoon.

"*Holly,*" Ben echoes, sounding just as disappointed, only he's grinning and sipping his Scotch.

"Not a good analogy," Dad says with gritted teeth.

AFTER DINNER, with both Ben and Dad's help, I unload my boxes and furniture into the basement—"I think I can still fit a boat in here," Dad finally decided—and wait in my bedroom for my last load of laundry to dry. Besides clothes, I've laid out food for the journey: three boxes of Snackwell's cookies, a five pound bag of raisins, fifteen Balance Bars, and fat-free Fig Newtons. I've also set aside my favorite books: Carl Jung's *Synchronicity* (a gift from Ben, who now believes in ESP), *Oxford Handbook of Clinical Medicine* (a gift from my father, who doesn't), and *Ballet Shoes* (a gift from my mother when I was nearly nine and she was leaving for Grenada). Now if I can just make everything fit.

From the back of my closet, I unearth Mama's enormous

tweed suitcase from barnacles of old running shoes, Shaker-knit sweaters, and unused canvas bags. Wedged between cardboard boxes marked "Personal"—filled long ago with my most sentimental T-shirts and stuffed animals—the suitcase requires both muscle and torque to set it free. In the process, I bang my head on a shelf above, causing a track-and-field trophy to topple onto a metal *Return of the Jedi* lunchbox. Stepping back to massage my head, I survey the collection of record albums overhead—no classic rock, just Disney's *Cinderella* and *Snow White* and, curiously, Loretta Lynn's *Country Christmas*. There's also another box, the size of a pair of shoes and covered in paper bearing a tropical print. Reaching up to grab it, I see my mother's writing scrawled on the side: *1983*.

Sitting on my bed, I pore over the contents for a while. Inside are pictures of Mama and her medical school friends: six-foot-six Thor Burnshack manning a grill; Jexy DeMatto feeding a stray cat; Ernie Chang throwing a banana peel off a roof; Jexy and Mama waving from a motorboat—both wearing scuba gear. Then there's the whole gang at the edge of what appears to be a giant crater. My mother's writing on the back reads: *Mt. Soufriere, St. Vincent, October, 1983*. I flip the picture over again to examine the group. Thor looks like Moses with his giant staff, which appears to be a tree trunk. Jexy is a blur dancing dangerously close to the edge. Ernie is sitting Indian style on the ground holding...I squint...a can opener and some tuna fish. And Mama is simply standing there. She looks freezing in her tank top and her red hair is practically covering her face from the wind, but her expression is happy—wildly happy. I can't help wondering if Simon Berg is the one standing behind the camera. I sift through the box until I find one of a young couple on the beach surrounded by open textbooks and stray dogs. She's in a purple one-piece suit and Cat Lady sunglasses. He's smiling and making rabbit ears over her head. On the back someone has written in unfamiliar longhand: *Simon and Sylvia*.

I separate that picture from all the rest and flop backward onto my bed, studying the image. The bearded man looks exotic almost—Italian or Greek—but then it occurs to me that if his last

name is Berg, he's probably Jewish. I wonder what my grandmother would've said about that, considering she forbade my
mother to marry my father because he was Methodist and not
Catholic. Then it occurs to me that maybe Grandmother knew
all about Simon Berg. *My mother knows me better than I know myself,* Mama used to say.

Lying here, staring at the picture of Sylvia and Simon, I think
how happy they look—happy and *alive*—and before I can stop
myself, I think of just the opposite. I think of my mother alone in
her hospital bed, and our last conversation, on the night that Dad
paged me to tell me she and Ben had been broadsided by a truck
running a red light. Ben was intact and Mama "critical but stable." I begged Dad to put her on the phone.

Her voice was raspy but strong—critical but stable. She said
she had a broken pelvis and broken ribs and a collapsed lung but
her pain was well controlled. I said, "If anything ever happened
to you, I would crawl away and die. What would I do without
you to whip my tar?" Mama loved to threaten to whip the tar out
of each of her children, unless she was really angry. Then she'd
become dagger-eyed and quiet.

Early the next morning, I was pronouncing a patient dead
and had the eerie feeling of being watched. When I looked up, a
blue jay fluttered away outside the window, as if it were the spirit
of the patient. But I was wrong: it had to be Mama, because less
than an hour later Dad paged me to say that she didn't make it.

"Didn't make what?" I asked, strangely confused by the
language of death, which—until that moment—I had been flu-
ent in.

"She didn't make it!" Dad repeated, more hysterically this
time. "She died, Holly!"

"I just talked to her last night," I said, woozily making my
way to the sofa in the doctors' lounge. "She was fine."

"She wasn't fine," Dad said. "And this morning she stopped
breathing. They're saying it was a pulmonary embolism, but
they really don't know. And I'm not going to let them do an autopsy."

I remember thinking that he must be wrong, that if I were

there I could show all the doctors that they were mistaken, that she really was alive, and that no one should ever use the word "autopsy" in conjunction with Mama. But then I felt myself being watched again, and I knew that Dad was telling the truth.

The next day I drove from Pittsburgh to Maryland for the funeral, which was the last time I heard my mother's name spoken in the usual way—without pain or longing—and the first time I heard Simon Berg's at all. Mama's friends were gathered in the living room: Ernest Chang, now a pediatrician in San Francisco; Thor, Jexy's ex-husband, a transplant surgeon in Maine; and even Vic Loopinetti—"Ubiquitous Vic," Mama called him—an internist from Key West, whom Jexy reprimanded for showing up graveside in flip-flops.

"She was such a little bookworm until she met you, Jex," Thor said, swirling his white wine. "You were quite the bad influence."

I looked over at Jexy and thought how strange it was to see her dressed in black. "I wasn't the bad influence. It was Simon," she replied.

Why wasn't he there? I think now. *And why didn't I ask?*

"Remember when she started the petition protesting all the petitions?" Vic asked.

"What were you guys protesting?" I asked, trying to pour myself a glass of wine before my grandmother came back into the room. My hands were so shaky that I ended up spilling half of it on the floor.

"Not enough vegetarian options," Vic said. "Not enough electricity."

"Too much information on the exam," Jexy said.

"We kept signing our names over and over, trying to convince ourselves we existed," Ernest said in a quiet voice, hands in his pockets.

"Is it true, Mrs. Bellinger, that you told Sylvia not to wear her stethoscope around her neck, because the patients would have something to strangle her with?" Jexy asked Eve, who had walked in with a pitcher of lemonade. I hastily handed my glass of wine to Vic, who, looking confused, took a sip.

"Well, of course I did," my grandmother said, straightening up as she set down the pitcher. "Grenada was a dangerous place."

"Not exactly," Thor said with a chuckle. "Well, maybe at the end, once the tanks were in the streets."

"Oh, God. Remember the hospital?" Jexy asked, and then turned to me and explained, "There were like a million cots stuffed into a room. Chickens roamed the floors looking for feed, and there was, like, one fan for the whole room. Everyone was sweating to death."

"The autopsies were done in a shack out back by the cemetery," Ernest added. "Sylvia asked if we were supposed to bring shovels."

"What was it that Simon called her?" Vic asked.

"Vee. His silly, silly Vee," Jexy said fondly.

I sit up in bed, suddenly remembering Joshua Peter asking if my mother's name was Vicky or Velma. *I'm getting the letter "V." She's making a V sign, like for victory.*

"How's the packing going?" Grandmother Eve asks from my doorway, making me startle.

"Slowly," I say, and then explain that I was distracted by Mama's old pictures.

Even with her dowager's hump and slow gait, my grandmother always seems so strong that I forget to help her onto my canopy bed, which is high off the floor.

"Where is she? Show me your mother," Eve says, putting on her bifocals with tremulous fingers before reaching for the photo in my hand. If she knows anything about Simon Berg, it doesn't seem to register on her face as she studies the picture of the two of them on the beach towel. With all the textbooks surrounding them, they look as innocent as lab partners. In fact, they were lab partners.

"She certainly was a beauty," Grandmother says with a sigh.

"Yes," I say, only because when I was nearly nine, and Grandmother came to live with us, we were taught that "Yeah" was low-class slang.

Mama is the only reason that I have any faith in my looks, because people always said she was beautiful and that we looked alike. Her skin was delicate. "Fish-belly white," Mama called it. My skin is more tan and tends to freckle. "You got the good nose," Mama would remind me as she pointed to her bulbous one. As far as I know, no one ever paid attention to her big nose, so easily outshone by her welcoming, red smile. But still, when I look in the mirror, I listen for Mama's voice in my head and am glad that I got the good nose.

"You don't remember, do you?" Grandmother asks now, which makes me wonder if she knows the bearded man on the beach towel after all.

"Remember what?"

"You were devastated when Sylvia left. You cried so hard. And when she came home for the summer, you were crushed when you found out she was going away again the next fall."

"She was only gone for a couple of months."

"Seven months, thanks to the invasion. If we hadn't invaded, it would've been two whole years." The way Grandmother Eve has always talked of the invasion, it's as if the United States sent in troops solely to bring Mama home.

"So what are you saying?" I ask.

"I'm saying it wasn't the kindest thing to bring up to your father at dinner."

I hate being reprimanded and hate even more thinking about when Mama went away. The day she left is a memory nearly as painful as her funeral. I recall how quiet the house was that January afternoon, how the grandfather clock's ticking seemed to echo off the front hall ceiling, and how it smelled like burnt meat—an introduction to my grandmother's cooking. When I looked up from taking off my boots, Eve was there, telling us not to track snow in the house. *But it's water,* I thought, and asked instead where Mama was. I wanted to tell her that I'd just been made a safety patrol.

"She's on an important mission," Eve said, as though Mama had become a CIA agent. "And you have to be brave."

Ben seemed to already know what this meant. "Don't you remember, Holly? Mama left for medical school today."

There had been a lot of discussion about her going away,

possibly sparked by an incident in the bathtub the year before. "Look, Mama. What's this?" I had asked, pointing out a speck of green on our map-of-the-world shower curtain. Mama was in the middle of toweling off Ben's hair. She said it was mildew. When the mildew didn't come off with soap, she said it was a country. "Grenada," Mama said. A little while later, she started talking about the medical school down there. *If only I hadn't shown her the shower curtain!*

When I asked if Mama would be home for dinner, Ben said she wouldn't be home for dinner or for my bath or to tuck us in. She was gone. She'd taken a plane to get there.

"Your mother is *helping people*," Eve said. "And she wants you to be brave until she sees you again."

When I asked who was going to tuck us in, Eve didn't even suggest my father, which made me think we wouldn't see him again either. "I am," she said, a declaration, which made me start crying. Grandmother wouldn't know how to make the comforter tight around my legs and arms or how to align the stuffed animals into a halo of protection around my head.

Eve said that my mother wouldn't want me to cry, that Mama wanted us to be strong, which made it sound like she was watching over us right at that second, and that Ben and I were like those poor orphans in *Ballet Shoes* who would probably have to take up dancing to earn money. When I asked if Mama was dead, the question only served to annoy my grandmother more. She snapped that she'd told me where Mama was—on a mission— and that if she'd meant that Mama was dead, she would've said so. "God forbid, Holly!"

After that, Eve was always at our house, packing our lunches, doing our laundry, making our dinner—making our birthday cupcakes for the class and then embarrassing us by bringing them in ("She's not my mother," I remember explaining. *Can't you see that she's old?*). And Dad was always angry. In fact, even after Mama came home again, Dad was angry. But to me, her return was as miraculous as it would be if I went downstairs right now and found her in the kitchen watering the plants. It was as if she'd never left.

"It's not a secret that Mama left the country to become a doctor," I say to Grandmother tonight.

"Yes, but it's not necessary to put Will through that all over again."

"Through what all over again?" I ask. And then, in case she's forgotten, I tap on the picture of my mother's smile and add, "I'm not her."

Eve studies me with narrowed eyes, as if to be sure I know who I really am. Then, apparently satisfied, she kisses my cheek before climbing down off my bed. "Holly," she says, pausing for a moment in the doorway. "It'll happen as soon as you're ready—and sometimes even if you aren't!"

"What will happen?" I ask, imagining the Jaws of Life extracting me from a crumpled car.

"Why, everything," Grandmother says, sounding strangely bright. "Believe me when I say that you have everything in life to look forward to. Trust in God, and don't lose your faith."

What faith? I think, after she's gone. *Faith in the star of* Passing On?

But I can't worry about my lack of conviction right now, when the larger task of packing lies in the way. Only it's far too daunting to sort out what to bring for an entire year. Instead I reach inside my backpack and take out the envelope with the New York return address, the one I've kept hidden—even from myself—for the last year. I'll have to find a place for this, too.

July 10, 1983, I read.

Dear Sylvia,

I have no right to send you a letter like this (and maybe I won't send it, because I don't want to get you in trouble), but you have been home with your family for exactly forty-eight hours now, and I can't stop thinking about you. It seems all wrong that you should be in Maryland right now with your husband and children, and that I am here in New York with Lisette. Of course, before we met, it seemed all wrong that I should be moving to an island to learn medicine away from my family and friends and fiancée, but now I can't imagine it any other way. I know that you don't want to hear this, but for me, Grenada means you, Sylvia Bellinger.

You said that it started for you the night we were practicing the head and neck exam for physical diagnosis, and I removed your ponytail to palpate your skull and lymph nodes. (For future reference, that whole running-my-fingers-through-your-hair is not something you should be doing to your patients.) You said it took my touch to open you up.

For me, it started the moment I saw you. You were standing on the beach with your red hair blowing in the breeze, your arms wrapped around yourself, staring at the ocean, looking statuesque but melancholy. I almost didn't know if you were real until I came toward you shouting, "Pig in the water!" and you turned. I don't even know why the pig freaked me out, except that I didn't know what kind of hellhole I'd arrived at where an evening walk on the beach included packs of wild dogs chasing me for food and a dead pig rolling around on the surf. It was like something out of Lord of the Flies. *But you, of course, were not freaked out. You just looked at where I pointed and your face changed from glum to curious— even fascinated—by the pig. I should have known then that you were a med student, not a tourist. When I said, "Kind of makes you wonder where they get dinner," you smiled and, oh, I was gone. And this was even before anatomy started and you were miraculously fated—or alphabetized—to the same cadaver. Yes, I imagined things, Sylvia, from the night that I met you—things that would horrify you now considering I'd only left Lisette hours before. But I never expected to fall in love with you.*

"Whatcha got there?" Ben asks from my doorway.

"Oh, just..." I stammer, folding up the papers and setting

them aside. "Nothing. A letter. Listen. I'm sorry about dinner tonight. Bringing up Alecia and all."

"I knew it was coming. I mean, Eve just can't help herself," Ben says with a sigh, coming to sit on my bed. "Who's it from?" he asks, tilting his head toward the pages on my night table.

"Oh . . . Matthew," I say.

"Looks like a novella. He must be pretty upset that you're going."

"Um, yeah," I say thoughtfully. Matthew seemed to think the timing was bad, given that our relationship was just starting. I couldn't help thinking the timing was great, considering I couldn't trust myself to make a decision about love right now, anyway. As an afterthought, I wonder, *Is love a decision?*

Ben peers around my room, seems to be taking in the piles of clothes on the floor, the scattered shoes, the random bottle of conditioner on my bookshelf. "You packed Big Bertha yet?" He means my mother's giant tweed suitcase. It's what we always called it.

"Getting there," I say, which makes Ben look at his watch. It's already after ten.

"What's with the food?" he asks, pointing to my raisins and cookies and protein bars. "They do have grocery stores over there."

"I'm sure I can buy all the blood sausage I want," I say.

I can tell by Ben's blank expression that he's already thinking about something else, even before he speaks. "In some ways, Eve's right, you know. I haven't even read the Bible from start to finish—"

"So, you've got two more years to go," I say.

"I think I'm still working out my personal theology," Ben says slowly. Staring across the room, he expels another tight breath of air.

"Everything okay with you and Alecia?" I ask.

"We're going through a difficult time right now, but we'll be all right," Ben says, back in his publicist voice. I wonder if he learned it from her.

"Well, if you ever do pick a wedding date, you're going to give me some advance notice, right?" I give him a nudge.

Ben nods and tells me I'll be the first to know, but I can tell he's not even listening to his own voice. He stands up to leave but turns back at my bedroom door. "You know, Holly, you can eat right, never drink or smoke or have sex, and you can still die in a plane crash tomorrow."

I sit up straighter, feeling betrayed by my brother or my own neuroses, I'm not sure which. "Why would you say such a thing?" I ask, horrified. "You know how I feel about flying."

"Oh, relax. You'll be fine," Ben says. "I only said it because I know you'll be fine."

He sounds so sure that for a moment I believe in him more than I believe in anyone, or at least more than I believe in Joshua Peter.

Ben leaves me alone to finish packing, so I flop back on my bed, prop up my head with pillows, and finish reading Simon's letter.

> *You keep telling me, "I'm not like this." Not like what—happy? Maybe I'm not normally happy either. Lisette has noticed that I'm different. She asked me the other night if I wished I were still there. I told her no. I was thinking about the dust, and the liquid heat—it's like you need gills to breathe—and the sulfur-seaweed rising off the ocean at low tide. You can smell the loneliness, it's so depressing. But maybe I'm just depressed about you. It's hard to believe that after the summer, you will no longer be mine. You are already not mine. You have a family! (Why does that still shock me?) And yet, I have a hard time imagining you belonging to anyone at all.*
>
> *You seemed so self-assured that first lab, when we were nervously choosing our scalpels, telling us all that we couldn't do much damage to the cadaver since she was already dead. It was as if you'd cut up dead people before. You told me later that you were just acting confident, and*

that you knew how to act because you'd been doing it for a long time in your marriage, too. I'd like to believe that the woman who tastes of salt and sweat and sunscreen, who just spent the night on my squeaky twin bed was the real Sylvia. But maybe the real woman is the one who looked terrified when the dean's secretary interrupted our Heart Sounds tutorial to say your mother was coming. I've never seen you look so scared—I thought you'd pass out—which strikes me as odd only now, when I consider the woman who showed up a few days later looking ready for tennis in that pink sundress with her perfectly hairsprayed helmet of blond hair. She didn't look like she could've given birth to someone as carefree as you, Sylvia. And she didn't look like someone to fear either. You said you were terrified because no one knows you better than your mother does, which makes me wonder just what does she know? What else could you possibly be hiding? (Jexy was the one who first told me about your kids. You kept them a careful secret from me at the beginning, Mrs. Bellinger—or what did you say your last name really is? See, I don't even know that about you.)

Every time I read that sentence, it makes me feel like that day in the residents' lounge, when Dad called to say that she was dead and I could barely stand up. *You kept them a careful secret from me.* Weren't we worth talking about? And why did she go by her maiden name and not Sylvia Campbell? Did she really plan to forget about us all along?

You think that it will be an easy transition coming back after the summer, but you're wrong. For one thing, the alphabet hasn't changed. For another, despite what you think, everyone knows. And not because I've told them. They just know. It's a small island, Vee, and you know as well as I that the Rumor Mill thrives on stories like ours. You were already a rumor, even before I got involved. ("*Did you hear she left her husband and children to do this?*" *Jexy asked, and I was floored.*) *The Rumor Mill knows when you study, when you are and aren't awake, when you drink—what you drink—if you screw.*

You're probably right. Ubiquitous Vic is the instigator. He's been telling people that we were together ever since that night in the anatomy lab when he found us dissecting after hours. Remember when he showed up, wanting us to sign one of his stupid petitions? I told him later that nothing was going on—and nothing was, back then— but he said I was smiling too much for him to believe it. I guess there was something about unzipping the black bag after hours, being alone in the lab with the body, which made me feel like we were doing something clandestine. I remember digging through the triceps muscle from opposite sides to follow the path of the radial nerve, and our fingers touched in the middle, and our eyes met, and I forgot everything in that instant that I'd already learned. All I wanted was to learn you, instead.

Oh, Sylvia, if you're wondering why I'm writing this down, it's because I need to. I have to get it out, or I'll never move on. How do you just pick up your regular life as if this didn't happen? How can I stay with Lisette, when she doesn't even know where I've been?

Do you remember the night of our first kiss? You and I walked out to the edge of surf under the moonlight with the pack of dogs barking at our heels. I wondered how long it would be until they keeled over dead, since you told me that my sister, Jude, had been feeding them chocolate bars earlier that evening. We walked right up to the shore where we first spotted the dead pig a few months before and stood staring at the water, listening for signs of swimming or drowning, when the biggest shooting star that I've ever seen came right for our heads. It looked like a basketball of blazing light, like God had tossed over a silent, slow-motion flare. You grabbed my shoulder and gasped. It was the first time you touched me. (Let the record show that Mrs. Bellinger kissed me first.)

Writing this now, I'm realizing that it was almost as if the island, with its shooting stars and phosphorescing algae, was a conspiracy of wonder designed to bring us together. Don't you agree? The first time we made love, the stars were jumping around in silent fireworks so mesmerizing that neither one of us could speak. We lay there on the docks, paralyzed with amazement. Even the dogs stopped barking for once.

Maybe that's why I'm writing this down. New York in the summer is like waking up with a hangover. If I don't write it down, I won't believe it happened. But it was real. The stars moved. And you and I fell in love.

I know that my sister told you that I always get everything I want. Don't listen to Jude. For one thing, Jude has this perception of my life that is radically opposite from the truth. She seemed to think that I was incredibly lucky when I was leaving for school in the Caribbean, apparently forgetting the fifty-seven rejections from U.S. medical schools that sent me there or the fact that it put quite a kink in my marriage plans. Judith loves me but—subconsciously or not—doesn't want to see me happy.

You said on our last night that we couldn't let this happen again and that, for the sake of your children, you had to go home and repair your marriage. It seems to me that your marriage was over a long time ago. It seems to me that to stay together with someone that you no longer love is not helping your children.

The truth is, I never intended to get involved with a future doctor, and certainly not an already married one with two children. That doesn't change the fact that I love you, Sylvia Bellinger.

Do you remember that time in our Heart Sounds tutorial when Dr. Nagarabotha called on you, and you guessed "aortic stenosis," and it turned out we were listening to a tape of the normal heartbeat? He told you to start using the stethoscope on yourself at night. "You can't learn what an abnormal heart sounds like if you don't know what's normal," he said.

Oh, Vee. For once in your life will you pay attention to your normal heartbeat?

> *Yours,*
> *Simon*

"Holly?" Dad asks from the doorway, making me gasp with surprise. In fact, in my haste to get the letter out of sight, I crumple up the last page and toss it onto the floor. Dad, as usual, doesn't seem to notice. "Are you ready?" he asks.

"Ready as I'll ever be!" I say, an expression I used before medical school exams, though I was more prepared to answer those questions than the ones Simon's letter makes me ask. It occurs to me that I have always been better prepared to handle textbook scenarios than real life.

"What time is your flight?" Dad asks. His eyebrows furrow, probably because none of my mess has actually made it into the suitcase.

I tell him four P.M., and that for international flights I have to be three hours early. He says not to pack too much and not to forget my clothes in the dryer.

As soon as he's gone, I pick Simon's letter up off the floor, smooth it out, and replace it in its envelope. Then I put the envelope in my money belt, tucked between my e-tickets and passport. *At least the most important things are ready,* I think, imagining myself in Customs tomorrow. I wonder if when I return in one year, I'll have something to declare.

CHAPTER 4

Welcome to Winchester

> "However lonely you feel, you are usually not alone. Do not pride yourself on not asking for help."
>
> —Oxford Handbook of Clinical Medicine

We just finished dinner an hour or so ago, but the flight attendants are making their way through the cabin, offering bagels, juice, and coffee, as if feeding us again will make us believe we haven't been up all night crossing time zones. Realizing that with breakfast and daylight comes the inevitability of landing, I start to feel slightly shaky and short of breath. It was all well and good when I made plans to leave my life behind, but until this second I never really imagined what it might mean to arrive someplace else.

Stay calm, I coach myself. *Think positive.* But all I can do is worry. First I fret that I may have packed too much, seeing as I couldn't lift the suitcase off the curb at the airport. Then I worry that the skycap never actually put my luggage onto the airplane belt after it was X-rayed for explosive devices because, come to think of it, I never saw him do anything but mark it with a red twist tie before I walked away. Then I dabble in concerns about airport security and the use of twist-ties to stop terrorists, when suddenly the image of my father, waving good-bye, appears in my head. He looks so sad and bewildered that I can't help feeling sad and bewildered myself.

Ever since Mama left for Grenada, my father has oscillated between two states: oblivious or suspicious. Ever since she died, Dad leans more toward assuming the worst about people, especially when it comes to me. Because I "look just like her," I must be leaving because I don't want anything to do with him, because I don't love him, because I'm never coming home. We hit a patch of turbulence and my heart flip-flops with panic as the plane lurches and rights itself. God, I hope to make it home again.

The only way to avoid thinking about the worst is to try to concentrate on the book in my lap, *Synchronicity,* open to Jung's passage about fish. Apparently, when researching the fish symbol throughout history, Jung was bombarded by seven fish coincidences in one day. "It cannot be a question of cause and effect, but of a falling together in time, a kind of simultaneity," he reasoned.

Looking at the rattling ceiling of the airplane where the oxygen masks are tucked away, I suddenly wonder whether anyone will ever "fall together in time" with me. I think of Matthew Hollembee, and how my brother said he must've been upset that I was leaving. Certainly Matthew was not happy to watch me go. Still, he would never have been inspired to sit down and pen a letter like Simon Berg wrote to my mother. Our breakup was as casual as our relationship.

Matthew was sitting in the doctors' lounge, surfing the Internet and eating his lunch. He wore his thick glasses, which—as of the day before—were being held together with adhesive tape after they'd fallen underneath a three-hundred-pound lady during a "suboptimal" post-op transfer from OR table to gurney. As soon as he noticed me, his face broke into a wacky-toothed grin.

"Ah, hello!" Matthew said. "You've got your suitcase with you."

In fact, I was not carrying Big Bertha this time, just my doctor's bag, which Matthew liked to tease me about, always saying I carried far too much around. He's right, of course. I'm still not sure why I burden myself with so many extraneous things when all I really use are my eyes, my ears, my hands, and my stethoscope.

I dropped the bag onto the floor, started massaging my own shoulder, and told Matthew we needed to talk later. I'd just received a large envelope with a London postmark telling me that I'd been accepted for work in the U.K. Matthew said he had to finish tracking down lab results on all the surgery patients before rounds began, if I could just give him a sec.

"Not now. Just call me. I have some news...."

"News? Well, you can't possibly leave, then. Let me have a quick look on the computer, all right?" Matthew asked, and then added as I pointed lamely at the door, "I don't suppose you're toting any rubbers in that big bag?"

"*Rubbers?*" I asked, startled. We hadn't even had sex yet. We hadn't really undressed yet besides our tops.

"I tend to use a lot of them," he said. "Especially where our other intern is concerned. He's absolutely useless."

I frowned, watching Matthew sift through the drawer of the communal desk, apparently in search of an unused condom.

"Ah," he said, producing an eraser.

"*Ah,*" I realized, collapsing onto the blue couch that contained an abandoned pillow from some resident who'd probably curled up there for an hour the night before.

Matthew Hollembee went to work, his face screwing up with focus as he erased lab values from a sheet of paper and scribbled in new ones. Observing him tap on computer keys, twirling a pencil while eating a liverwurst sandwich, I began to wonder if love is when you can watch someone concentrating on something other than yourself, and you're absolutely intrigued. As it was, I felt impatient and couldn't wait a second longer. So I blurted it out: "I'm going to England."

"Sorry? When!" he said, unexpectedly delighted.

"In June."

"Fantastic!" Matthew said. "You can meet my mum!"

"M-maybe." I hesitated, which made him laugh.

"You don't want to meet my mum?"

"I have no problem meeting your ... mum," I said.

Matthew took off his glasses and inspected them, his face turning wry as if recalling the crunch of his frame under the fat lady's thigh. He didn't comment on it, but instead replaced the thick-rimmed lenses, took another bite of sandwich, and asked what was on my mind.

"Nothing, I just ... thought you should know that I'll be going away for a while. I'm going to be doing locum tenens over there."

"I see," Matthew said, chewing slower. I watched him swallow. The liverwurst seemed to stick. "And for how long?"

"I signed up for a year."

"Ah," Matthew said again. "A year. And I am unfortunately rather committed to staying in Pittsburgh for the next four."

"I know," I said with a nod.

Suddenly he seemed to realize he was holding his sandwich. "I feel terrible eating in front of you—do you want ... ?" He held up his sandwich.

"Oh, no—I've got a bagel!" I remembered, reaching into my doctor's bag to grab one of my sandwich Baggies of supplies. "Listen, I know this is inconvenient, since we just started going out, and I know it doesn't make much sense to continue...." I trailed off, debating whether or not to bless Matthew Hollembee, who had erupted into a coughing spell. Why should a blessing only apply to the sneeze?

"I've never really been into transcontinental relationships. Not that I've been in this situation ever before ... Are you—are you okay?" I asked politely.

Matthew rocked back and forth, turning purplish red and crying, but he didn't give the universal sign for choking to death. Just as I wondered if the hands-around-the-throat gesture was strictly an American mime, he pointed down at the coffee table, at whatever I just pulled out of my doctor's bag. Horrified, I saw my sandwich Baggie of fresh underpants lying there.

In the split second it took me to hastily throw them back inside the medical kit, several thoughts occurred to me, such as *This looks odd. He must be wondering—Maybe I should explain—*

Do I reassure him that the panties are fresh? Did I already eat my bagel? An image of myself as a ten-year-old floated to the surface of my swirling brain. I'm crying before a field trip to Gettysburg, because glass bottles are not allowed on the school bus, and Mama, realizing this in the parking lot, has ingeniously poured the fizzing Coke into a freezer bag, telling me to keep it upright. "I just want to be normal!" I say, bawling. Mama doesn't understand. She wonders what other mothers could possibly be using instead of plastic bags. "Cans!" I wail.

This is your fault, Mama, I thought, still furiously trying to come up with actual food from my medical kit. All I could see was my toothbrush, deodorant, a razor, and at last, my bagel. Matthew hadn't stopped laughing, which only made him cough harder.

"I suppose that's for when you find someone by the side of the road in torn knickers?" he finally managed to gasp.

"Right," I said with a sheepish grin, thinking, *At least he knows they're clean.*

"Oh, Holly," he said, getting up to move to the sofa and wrap an arm around me, his stomach heaving with laughter. "This is most unfortunate timing."

"I know," I said, resting my head on his shoulder. "But maybe it's for the best. I can't trust any of my feelings these days. Even the good ones."

Still hugging me, Matthew seemed to consider this. "I suppose you're right," he finally said. "The most consuming feeling your heart knows is fear, and it fires your brain into a circle of worry and worst-case scenarios. Fear doesn't allow for best-case scenarios."

I pulled away from his chest to look at him. "Do you hate me?" I asked.

He swallowed and looked at me so lovingly, it was almost hard to take. "I bear no malice. Truly."

"Well, thank you for . . . bearing me no malice," I said, feeling sheepish again.

We sat smiling at each other until Matthew reached over and

took my pink cotton undies off the top of my medical kit to inspect them. "So this is what you've been hiding all along."

My thoughts are interrupted when a stewardess on the loudspeaker informs us she'll be coming around to collect our trash. The airplane seems to be hunkering lower in the sky, which makes me tighten my seat belt and put Jung's *Synchronicity* in the seat pocket ahead of me. Are we descending into Heathrow or crashing? There has been no announcement about putting up our tray tables.

Mama, just get me there safely. I'll worry about the rest later.

Suddenly, I get the feeling she's heard me. The plane starts to climb, the ceiling stops shaking, and an unfamiliar calm washes over me. For one complete minute I know with certainty that Mama agrees with Grandmother: I have nothing to worry about and everything to look forward to.

Then, instead of popping, my ear suddenly starts to throb with searing pain. It occurs to me that, having given up my job and apartment, I can't go home even if I want to, and that somewhere, many miles away, I left my last load of laundry in the dryer.

FIVE HOURS LATER, after the chaos of claiming my baggage in Heathrow Airport, after a cab has deposited me at Waterloo Station and then a train has taken me an hour into the English countryside, my journey finally comes to an end in Winchester. With my doctor's bag slung over one shoulder, my camera case over the other, I rush to drag Big Bertha off the train. It's only with the help of the conductor that I can wrestle it from the steel compartment. Then, like two Egyptians toiling over a block of pyramid, we manage to heave the Great Slab onto the platform. The sense of accomplishment is so satisfying that I'm almost surprised to hear a whistle, the scrabble of feet, and a slamming of doors. The train disappears, leaving me standing alone on the outdoor platform with my baggage and the rest of my life.

I check the map that was included in my "Travel Doc"

orientation packet to see how far the Royal County Hampshire Hospital is from the train station: just about four inches, which could mean four miles, four kilometers, or literally four inches, since there's no scale. Luckily Big Bertha has built-in wheels. *If only she had a motor.* Just wheeling my suitcase in circles to search for a nonexistent elevator makes me break a sweat; the June heat feels like exhaust from the core of the earth. Finally rolling Bertha to the foot of a flight of stairs leading to the exit, I'm faced with the predicament I've been dreading since yesterday: I can't lift her, not even a single step.

"Never, ever fill up Bertha," Mama warned me once, when I was borrowing the suitcase to take to a friend's wedding. "You won't be able to lift her. And then you'll be stuck."

Oh, good God. Bertha's full, Mama, I think.

"Can I give you a hand?" a voice interrupts my thoughts. I look up from my suitcase to see a guy with a backpack. He has dark hair, blue eyes, and a familiar accent: American.

It takes me a minute to respond. No one has actually spoken to me since my father said good-bye at the Baltimore airport and waved so forlornly. Not even the flight attendants, who simply looked at me and listened to my requests. The stranger is well built and attractive in a J.Crew-catalog-model sort of way, the kind of generic "tall, dark, and handsome" that most girls appreciate but which I find completely uninteresting. Give me crooked teeth and Buddy Holly glasses and deft hands that can slide a line into someone's fat neck. This guy probably knows he's good-looking. Why else would he have the confidence to ask a complete stranger if he can carry her bag?

"What?" I finally say, blinking from the sun in my eyes.

"Can I give you a hand?" He waves his hand as if familiarizing me with the body part. "Can I help?"

Can I help? It's a question that I generally try to say no to, especially when it comes from a stranger; and yet, if he doesn't help, my entire sojourn in England will involve camping out on a train platform.

"I . . . don't want you to hurt your back," I say, hesitating. *I don't want you to touch my stuff.* The last words my grandmother said at breakfast were: "Watch out for the gypsies. They'll steal everything you've got." At least my money belt is securely around my waist.

"I'll be fine," the guy says, reaching for the handle and moving to lift it. Bertha doesn't budge. "Impressive," he says, taking off his backpack and handing it to me. "You take this. I'll meet you at the top."

And with a noisy grunt, he's off, this complete stranger, with my suitcase! Granted, I've got his backpack as collateral, but it feels surprisingly empty, not even the weight of a camera inside to make up for the loss of my entire wardrobe (minus the load in the dryer). I try to run after him as fast as I can, only I've had to pee since Waterloo station, and it's hard to take more than one step at a time, especially the way my doctor's bag keeps bumping into my bladder.

"You sure pack light," he says when I find him at the top, bent over, out of breath, and holding his knees.

"Yes," I say primly, as if talking to Grandmother. I decide it's best not to tell him that I've packed for a year. He doesn't need to know my travel plans. Or, for that matter, where I come from.

"So where're you comin' from?" he asks.

"The United States of America," I say.

He smiles with crooked, full lips and pushes some dark hair out of his eyes. "No kidding. Which state?"

"Um . . . Maryland," I say, too tired and uncomfortable to invent somewhere else.

"Maryland's a nice place. Lived there once when I was little. I'm from all over. Last address: New York."

I nod stupidly, because all I can think about is how bad I have to go. I find myself blurting out would he mind watching my suitcase while I pee?

"Go for it," the guy says, no longer winded. In fact, he sits down on a bench next to my belongings with such familiarity that I wonder if this is all a continuation of the ploy to steal my luggage. But I have to pee too badly to worry about it.

Returning from the ladies' room moments later, I find the American gypsy holding my black doctor's bag on his lap. Has he been rifling through it, searching for Oxycontin? He doesn't look thin enough to be a heroin addict. Maybe he's just a dealer.

"I'll take that," I say, yanking the bag into my arms.

"That's some bag. Are you a doctor?"

"I am," I say, nodding vigorously, deciding he's not a gypsy or a drug dealer at all but a stalker, searching for overpacked women traveling alone. I will definitely not tell him about the Royal County Hampshire Hospital.

"So you practice in Maryland?"

"No. Pittsburgh, Pennsylvania," I say, struggling to get the handle up on my suitcase. Thank goodness Bertha came with wheels.

"No kidding. That's great."

"Not really . . . well, maybe . . . Listen, thanks again."

"No problem, Sylvia."

I turn back to meet his eyes. It's been over a year since anyone outside of my family has said my mother's name like that—with familiar recognition—and I want to hear it again, as if she might actually speak up herself.

"Excuse me?"

"Sylvia Bellinger, MD," the guy says, pointing to the inscription on my black bag.

"It was my mother's bag," I say. "Before it was mine." This is terrific. Now he can access my credit cards with her maiden name.

"So what's your name, then?" he asks easily, apparently unaccustomed to the social convention of apologizing for deaths one has nothing to do with. Then it occurs to me that I never actually said Mama was dead. Maybe he thinks she's retired. *How nice would that be, Mama?*

Well, technically I am retired, I can hear her say wryly.

"Your name?" he asks again.

"Bertha." For a moment I must look startled, as if a chandelier just dropped to the sidewalk. Then, because I can't tell him that I temporarily forgot my own name, I say it again with conviction, "Bertha." It feels like armor.

"Bertha," he repeats. The way he says the name, all slow and thoughtful, as if tasting it, reminds me of Mother Nature and the Big Bang theory and the potential for life forms on other planets. Maybe it's not such a bad name after all. "I've never met a Bertha who wasn't . . . you know, old," he adds.

"It's a family name," I say, which isn't entirely a lie, considering we really did name the suitcase.

"I'm Edwin—Ed," he says, extending his hand for a shake.

"Nice to meet you, Edwin," I say, politely squeezing his hand, wondering if we're both giving fake names. His feels equally old-fashioned. "And thank you for carrying my suitcase."

"No problem. Good luck to you, Bertha."

"Thanks," I mutter, hustling away, remembering how my father wished me luck at the airport, as if it's all I can hope for.

Glancing back at the first corner, I'm relieved to find Ed isn't following me; in fact, he's nowhere to be seen. Finally I can relax. After all, people named Bertha don't get stalked. And certainly not by backpacking models named Edwin.

Just meeting a man pretending to be called Edwin reminds me of the only other Edwin I've personally known: Edwin Clemens, ruler of my third-grade class at Misty Creek Elementary by virtue of his sheer novelty. He came late in the year and left early, when his father got transferred to Ohio. On Balloon Launch Day, people handed him balloons like he was a politician collecting votes. Grandmother thought launches were silly and refused to support the Misty Creek gym class fund-raiser. Mama was in Grenada at the time, and Dad ended up agreeing with Eve, reasoning that balloons never got farther than the power lines, and rubber shards would litter the neighborhood for days after. Ben and I had to beg classmates for balloons and were lucky to gather one or two for the send-off. But not Edwin Clemens. He had so many, they could've carried him away— which is how I always imagine he left, on a tide of balloons bound for Ohio.

What ever happened to Edwin? Where did he end up? I wonder. The image of him as an astronaut competes with one of him hang-gliding behind a motorboat. He was too popular to be up to something ordinary.

The trek toward the hospital becomes a heartening one. Following the map leads me to a bike path by the river, where, on my left, water rushes in a furious stream and, on my right, quaint stone houses show off window boxes filled with marigolds, petunias, and lobelia. Ivy climbs up luxuriant bay windows while honeysuckle and lilac drip over a picket fence.

The English gardens give me a thrill, make me roll Bertha faster and swing my black bag of medical supplies the way Julie Andrews swings her guitar case, belting the song "I Have Confidence" as she nears Captain von Trapp's mansion.

"What will this day be like?" I sing softly. "What will my future be?"

The road to the hospital turns sharply uphill just past a stone church the size of a one-room schoolhouse. Huffing and puffing, I meander behind it among the headstones, which are cracked, sawed-off, and crooked, like Matthew Hollembee's teeth. In fact, for the first time I wonder if breaking up with him was the right thing to do. But if I'd stayed, things only would have gotten complicated. We'd have progressed from "forming an alliance" to full-blown commitment, a gamble of vulnerability too dangerous to allow. And since I left, could we really have sustained a brand-new relationship from two different countries? It made perfect sense to say good-bye.

Though it's a strange feeling, missing someone other than Mama for a change. I feel a little foolish for traipsing through a cemetery with my suitcase, which makes me think of an Emerson quote, "Why drag about this monstrous corpse of your memory?" If only I could convince the dead that I too am here to bury something dear.

Finally, at the top, I reach the Royal County Hampshire Hospital, which looks something like a sprawling church itself, only without the cross. Once inside, I roll Bertha through the refreshingly empty corridors suffused with light from tall windows. We pass hospital wings named Victoria Ward and Nightingale Wing. The names sound like a lark, as if nothing bad happens here, as if dead people aren't admitted for futile resuscitation, as if Clara Storms aren't suffering for months on ventilators, enduring needle sticks and trach suction and bad TV.

"Can I help?" asks a lady who must've spotted me studying one of the posted signs. I turn to see a woman wearing a white dress and a little nurse's hat on top of her head, a combination that reminds me of movies set in the 1950's. I feel like taking a picture for the ICU nurses back home. "Un-fucking-believable," Wanda will say with a snort.

"Yes, please," I say gratefully, feeling less vulnerable about requiring assistance from a stranger whose name tag says "Sister Theresa." No wonder she's so courteous. "I'm looking for the Information Desk."

"Just straightaway. You can't miss it. Go on, now." She smiles and waves me on, as if to let me know I'm already halfway there.

"What about the ER?" I quickly add.

"Oh—the A&E? Just that way, to your left." She smiles and adds, "That's Accidents and Emergency."

"Thank you, Sister," I say, bowing my head slightly. I'm not sure if I'm supposed to genuflect.

Sister Theresa chuckles and gives my shoulder a pat. "I'm a nurse, love. Not a nun. We're called 'ward sisters.' "

"Thanks. I'm new to the area. Just got here from the States."

"Right. So I gathered." Sister is smiling again. "Welcome to Winchester."

"Thank you!" I say.

Walking away, I'm transiently elated, because the Royal County Hampshire Hospital is nothing like St. Catherine's. Already I can feel it: the dead will be allowed to die.

At the Information Desk, I introduce myself as the "new locum tenens from America," and ask the silver-haired candy striper behind the counter if she knows where I can find the key to my flat.

"It's called Parchment House, love," the candy striper says, reaching into a file to whip out a key numbered 3. "Just follow the road 'round the bend. You'll be sharing the dormitory."

I glide Bertha outside and down a handicap ramp to rejoin

the path. Dormitory? It occurs to me as an afterthought. Maybe it'll look like the pictures I've seen of Oxford, where every building on campus looks holy, even the pubs.

I come around a rock wall that borders the road, to find out what "Parchment House" really means. The dorm doesn't have spires, and it's not even stone. Instead it's an ugly shed of cream brick that resembles a bomb shelter.

The inside, I soon find out, isn't much better. Leaving Bertha at the foot of the stairs, I investigate the upstairs hallway. Flickering fluorescent bulbs light the way with an eternal buzz.

Turning the key, I push open "Door Number 3," which reveals one bed, one desk, and one sink, a room more barren than a standard jail cell, which, to my understanding, comes with a toilet. The place also happens to be six feet wide, like the walk-in closet in the colossal apartment I left behind. Even worse, the air smells of mothballs. Disappointed, I leave to prowl around the abandoned hallway.

Signs of life hang nearby—a memo pinned to the door next to mine: "Re: Quiet hours. They now start at 10 P.M. during the week.—Marian."

Marian, I repeat in my head, like it's the coveted lead role in a play.

Maybe Marian will be my new friend, I imagine. *My friend Marian and I went to London. Marian and I saw* Phantom of the Opera. *Marian is setting me up with her brother.*

The sight of the lounge with its blazing orange sofa makes me forget my fantasies of friendship. The plaid-covered chairs and two plastic recliners are mildly depressing, but the orange sofa may be the worst piece of furniture I've ever seen. Its neon color actually hurts my eyes, so I retreat through the swinging doorway on the back wall, which leads to a dank kitchen that smells of ramen. Dishes crust in the dripping sink, while the refrigerator is decorated with pictures—one, a husky blond girl in baggy pants grinning over the caption "Oink, Oink"; the other, a waif in a sundress looking sullen. Hoping that the fun-loving chubby girl might be Marian, I suddenly realize the photos are of the same person.

Walking back downstairs to retrieve my suitcase, I decide the only way to move in will be to unzip the load that is Bertha and carry the contents, armful by armful, upstairs. Just as I'm coming back for my second trip, the waif from the picture—this time wearing a little nurse's hat and uniform—walks through the front door of the flat.

"Don't trip!" I call, since my open suitcase is blocking the foot of the stairs. "Marian?" I add.

She seems startled—both by the monstrosity of Big Bertha and the fact that I've used her name without being introduced. There's something about her pinched mouth and translucent eyebrows that reminds me of Mary Lennox from the book *The Secret Garden,* at least at the beginning, when she was still thin and sour.

"I saw your note upstairs. About quiet hours? Ten o'clock, right?" I say. It must be the jet lag making me try so hard.

"Sorry? Who're you?" Marian asks.

"I'm Holly. I'm new here," I say, dragging Bertha to the side of the landing. "Just moving my things in."

"I see that," she says, folding her arms and looking down. Marian is either trying to avoid eye contact or trying to avoid stepping on my black sandals and brown leather shoes that are scattered over the stairs.

"Where is everyone?" I call after her, before she can disappear behind one of the wooden doors on the second floor.

"It's Sunday," she says, sounding surprised. "They've gone home. Or traveling."

"Oh. Thanks," I say.

"And quiet hours start at nine on Sunday," Marian adds.

Back in my bedroom, I slump onto the rock-hard bed and try to imagine how to make this dreary place my own. If I'd taken the faculty position, I'd still be in my dream apartment right now. I shut my eyes when a bout of nausea overwhelms me. *Oh, God, is this all a terrible mistake? How will I get back home?*

Then I remember Mama's advice about going someplace new. First thing's first: make the bed and get food for the pantry, in that order. And when you walk toward where you'll sleep, call it home, because home is wherever you are at the moment.

Wearily, I move to unfold my yellow bedspread and hang up my fresh towels, because what else can I do? My job has been filled, my apartment rented, my boyfriend rejected, and my life suspended. I can't go back before things have begun, I decide, tacking up two pictures by the sink, the one of Mama grinning, and the four of us at my med school graduation.

Then, to clear out my mind as much as the mothball smell, I pull up the shade. That's when I realize my room has a view of the town and beyond, where acres and acres of green hills spread for miles. The horizon is completely clear except for the occasional wisp of airplane exhaust that hangs in the sky like a faded message. Cathedral bells clang in song, reminding me of peace, as if whatever battle I've been fighting may finally end.

I would take Mama's advice and go in search of food to fill my pantry, but suddenly jet lag overwhelms me. In between the notes of the bells and the trilling of birds and the whisper of trees, sweet silence sings. Home is wherever you are at the moment. *I've come so far just to lay my head down,* I realize, crawling into bed.

You can't put a price on a good night's sleep, Mama says as I drift off.

CHAPTER 5

Ideals

For you will not be Superwoman
For you will not be Solomon
but you will be asked questions nonetheless...

— "GAUDEAMUS IGITUR," JOHN STONE, MD

wake up and have no idea where I am. The birds are too noisy for me to be in Pittsburgh, and the sunlight too bright. My travel alarm suddenly erupts in a barrage of beeps, and I jump to shut it off, as if defusing a bomb. Then, with the clock in hand, awareness returns. I recall the flight to England, the stranger at the train station, my suitcase in the cemetery, and the strange Scottish music that woke me up last night. Did I just imagine the sound of stomping and clapping? If not, what sort of bizarre people have I moved in with?

The Parchment House hallway is empty and silent except for the buzzing fluorescent lights that make me think of killer bees. *Where is everyone?* I wonder, feeling late for something big and important, like a nuclear war. Padding down the barren hall in flip-flops and a towel, I imagine that either everyone's been annihilated or they're meditating. Both images evaporate when I find a memo on the bathroom door: "Re: Orchids in the tub. Kindly remove them, or I won't hesitate to write you up—Marian." I stare at the sign, as if memorizing a clue, and then finally knock on the door. When there's no answer, I tentatively open it, half expecting to encounter Marian herself in karate stance. Instead I find an old-fashioned tub filled with orchids and a rusting shower nozzle hooked where the faucet should be. Removing the plants one by one, I place them on the floor, for lack of a better spot. For some reason the toilet is kept in a separate room called the "WC," which I discovered last night. And there's no shower curtain either, I realize now. At least there's a hook for my towel.

Moments later, squatting on cold porcelain and spraying myself down at arm's length, I wonder if there's a better way to do this. Without the benefit of a curtain, I shower the window, the walls, and the plants, everything but my soapy shoulder.

Walking back to my bedroom in my towel, I'm in the middle of contemplating the fact that I can't plug my blow dryer into the wall socket without a converter, when I notice my next-door flatmate locking the door to his room. He looks intriguing, at least from behind: broad shoulders and an athletic butt, like Michelangelo's statue *David* inside a pair of scrubs. And when he turns, I realize I know him. *I know I know him. But how?*

The guy glances at me, puts his key in his back pocket, and then looks again, longer this time, as I flip and flop toward him. Slowly, his mouth cracks into a grin and my heart unexpectedly lets go like a gaggle of balloons. *I have not lost the faith, Grandmother.* It's Edwin Clemens from Misty Creek Elementary. It has to be. Why else would he be pointing at me and shaking his head, apparently speechless?

"Bertha, right?" he finally asks.

"Oh," I say, halting abruptly, clutching my shower basket a little closer to my chest.

It's not Edwin Clemens at all. It's the backpacker guy from the train station. The other Ed.

"It's you, isn't it?" he asks.

"It's...yeah, ha ha," I say, feeling awkward and naked and dripping wet. Of course, I'm completely covered by my blanket-sized yellow towel, but there's something about not wearing underwear that makes me feel like I'm posing nude.

"I almost didn't recognize you without..." He pauses, seems to take in my neck and bare shoulders. "Your suitcase."

"Well, I almost didn't recognize you without the train station," I say.

"You're not the new locum tenens we've been expecting, are you?"

"I am," I say, nodding. "And I guess I'm also your new next-door neighbor." I point at Door Number 3.

"No kidding? How crazy is that?" He nods, too, nods and grins and then nods some more. I start to feel like he's trying very hard to recognize me, even though he already did. Maybe he's just trying to will my towel to fall off. Finally, Ed looks at his watch. "Well, listen, I've gotta get to the A&E. You working a shift today?"

"Probably. I'm supposed to meet with somebody named Mr. Danvers. I'm sure he'll put me to work."

"He's kind of a hard-ass," Ed says. "But if I needed emergency surgery, I'd want him to do it."

"Good to know," I say, moving to my bedroom door as Ed makes for the stairs.

"See you in the Fish Bowl," he calls.

Inside my room, I lean against the back of the door wondering about the synchronicity of it all: meeting a random guy at the train station, meeting him again in my dorm? What could it mean? And why does Danvers go by "Mister" if he's a doctor? Of course, it's better than calling him "Father," I decide. And what the hell is the Fish Bowl?

After quickly pulling my wet hair into a bun, and my white coat over a skirt and blouse, I check to be sure Mama's medical bag is stocked and loaded with supplies: extra deodorant, clean underwear, a finger puppet (for pediatric patients). Then I sling a stethoscope around my neck and take off for Accidents and Emergencies.

Right away, I discover that "the Fish Bowl" has neither water nor fish. Instead, it consists of a board decorated with names of patients and their chief complaints. Underneath this Great Wall of Problems, nurses in white dresses and doctors in white coats shuffle around, trying to find ways to erase the names.

Walking toward the chaos, I see Ed over by the eraser board. For a second I remember Matthew Hollembee writing in permanent marker on our board at home, trying to convince me we were statistically significant. And then the thought leaves as quickly as Ed turns around. His curtain of dark hair swings over one eye and across the top of his cheek, but he tucks it behind his ear so he can watch me walking around the nurses' station.

Maybe it's his scrubs. Maybe it's the fact that his hands can probably slide an interjugular catheter into a fat lady's neck with as much skill as Matthew Hollembee, but Ed will look better doing it. Maybe it's because if he's a doctor and I'm a doctor, we speak the same language. Whatever it is, the guy from the train station has become completely appealing. *Maybe I was meant to have beautiful children,* it occurs to me. God—or Mama—must have a plan.

"Oh, hey, Bertha. That was fast," Ed says with a smile. There's something about his smile that stops me short. I know that smile. It transports me back to third grade.

"What was fast?" I ask, and then almost simultaneously blurt out, "And I go by Holly, actually. Holly Campbell."

I wait to see if he recognizes my name, if he could in fact be the Real Ed from Misty Creek Elementary. But this Ed only fills up my extended hand with a pager.

"Danvers said to give you this bleep. Had to go deal with an emergency."

"Emergency?" I repeat, examining the pager as if it's flying saucer fuselage. "Bleep?"

"That's what they're called here," Ed says, and then nods. "A neighbor left a message that firemen were shooting his home with water."

"Was it on fire?" I ask, horrified.

"No. They just…felt like practicing," Ed says slowly, and

then smiles again, which startles the breath right out of me. "Yes, it was on fire."

"Oh, I just—" My pager interrupts with two shrill beeps, followed by a prim English accent announcing over static: "Code Red. Victoria Ward. Code Red."

"Code Red," I say. "Do doctors go to Code Reds?"

"Only if you like using a fire extinguisher. That's for fire," Ed says with a laugh. "You worry about the Code Blues, cardiac arrests."

"Okay. Right," I say, nodding and wiping my sweaty brow.

Ed chuckles and wonders aloud, "Is everything on fire today?"

Does he have any idea that we may have met before the train station? Can it really be him? Doesn't he belong in Ohio? The longer I stare at him the more certain I am that this is the aged-composite version of the boy I once knew in the third grade. Of course he would have turned out to be a gorgeous doctor. Edwin was a brainy pipsqueak; teacher's pet...everyone's pet, but a brain.

"Bertha seems kind of...not you," Ed suddenly says. "Is it your middle name or something?"

"No. No, it's not. Did you want to give me the rundown on all these patients?" I ask, pointing to the board looming in front of us.

"Oh, I can't. At least, I shouldn't. You're supposed to get it from a doctor...like Mr. Danvers."

"Why is he called 'Mister' instead of 'Doctor'?" I ask.

"It's a higher title, means Danvers is surgically trained. You'll never hear him go by 'Doctor' unless he's trying to get his car fixed and wants to sound important," Ed says.

"I see," I say, even though I don't. "And why can't you orient me?"

"I'm an orderly."

"Oh," I say.

I'm ashamed to admit that I suddenly don't care about getting oriented, much less hearing about the conflagration of Mr. Danvers' home. I'm let down by Ed's job title: the orderly, which means he's the muscle of this ER. He transports patients, dispenses vomit basins and mops up when they miss. He's the guy to call if a small boy needs to be held down while I stitch up his head. Ed lifts boxes of medical supplies and makes sure they get put on the right shelf. In short, this can't be synchronicity. It's just an interesting side effect of entropy, as random as chance, a simple rule of probability that states, Of the millions of molecules flying around, two that collide and separate will somehow collide again.

"Hell, I can give it a shot," Ed says, pointing to the "Chief Complaints" column scrawled by the names. "Bodley—chest pain. Franklin—bright red blood per rectum—"

"Did you have Mrs. Sandler for third grade at Misty Creek Elementary in Columbia, Maryland?" I blurt out.

When Ed turns to stare at me, I can see flecks of yellow in his deep brown eyes. I feel like I'm being noticed at last.

"Who are you?" he asks.

"Holly Campbell."

"How do you know me?"

"I was in your class."

"I went to Misty Creek for three months before we moved away."

"To Ohio," I say.

"Iowa," he says.

"Really? I could've sworn . . . well, you would know."

"You actually remember me?"

"It's your name. I never met another Edwin Clemens."

"When did I tell you my name?" he asks.

"Just a second ago. I thought you said . . . maybe not . . ." I say, and then trail off, scratching my head. I'm not going to tell him that it's his smile I remember from so long ago. There he stands, four feet tall at the edge of the blacktop, watching his rainbow of balloons spread across the sky—to California, to Nova Scotia, to outer space—as my two tangle and pop in a nearby elm tree. His hands are in the air, his bangs are blowing, and his crooked smile is as mesmerizing as the trail of color growing distant. I can tell by the look on his face, it doesn't matter where the balloons end up. He's flying right alongside them.

"You got that big, laminated card when you left," I say instead. Ed smiles. "You sound a little bitter."

"Mrs. Sandler cried when she found out you were moving. She wasn't supposed to have favorites," I say, smiling, too. *Is this flirting?*

"Did you even sign the card?" Ed asks. He may be joking but it's actually a good question.

"Well, Ed, I see you've found your fellow American," a stiff voice pipes up from behind us, making my face heat up even more than a second ago.

I turn to see Marian—Sister Marian, apparently—standing there with her arms folded across her chest.

"We were actually just discovering that we must've met at, what...age eight? Nine?" Ed says.

The week after my ninth birthday. "Twenty-one years ago," I realize.

"God, I'm old enough for that? To not have seen someone for twenty-one years?"

"Bed one is having chest pain. You might want to get reacquainted later," Marian says, handing me a chart.

"Thank you for seeing me," my first patient gushes, so grateful that it makes me acutely uncomfortable. Angus Bodley is a thin, sixty-something man with a curly mustache and a sweater vest. His blue eyes look hopeful and terrified at once.

"You don't have to thank me," I say, flipping his chart open. "It's my job."

"Ah! You're from America, are you? What brings you to England?"

The trouble with going to someplace new is that everyone always wants an explanation for how you got there. Temporary insanity never seems like the right response. "Just here to learn, sir," I say.

"Well. Isn't that noble? I myself have only been to the States once. It was for a vacation." He sounds apologetic, and then adds, "Oh, dear."

"Oh, dear—what?" I ask, looking up from the chart that Marian has labeled: "Chest Pain."

"There it is again," he says, rubbing his sternum.

I ask him the seven questions of pain and discover his happens to be stabbing in nature, located in the center, radiating left, and is associated with shortness of breath and palpitations. It's lasted as long as an hour and hasn't been made better by Tums or aspirin or nitro. "Each time it happens I feel as if I might be dying," he says, still wincing and rubbing.

"Well, don't do that, sir. Let's get an EKG."

I stick my head out from behind the curtain and wave to Ed, who puts down a bag labeled "Biohazardous Waste" and walks toward me.

"How do I get an EKG?" I whisper.

"Hang on," Ed says, and then jogs over to the machine to wheel it back.

"Oh! You do EKGs," I say.

"No . . . you do."

"R-right." I hesitate.

"Don't you?" Ed sounds curious.

"Of course," I say, directing the EKG machine right up to Mr. Bodley's bedside.

I've never done an EKG. In the States, medicine has become extremely compartmentalized. There is a job description for everything. This means that though I can intubate a patient, I can't program the life support because respiratory therapists— Eric and Ellen—handle that. Though I can slide a central line in the neck or the groin, I can't reliably place an IV because nurses—Wanda and Shirley—handle that. Though I can do a lumbar puncture to rule out meningitis, I can't analyze the spinal fluid because lab support—Sal—handles that. Though I've mastered how to turn on a patient's TV from the hospital bed, I still can't make his IV pump stop obnoxiously beeping, and sometimes no one handles that. I can run a code and read the EKG the paramedic gives me, but I can't actually do one. Until now.

"So this sticky thing will go here . . ." I say to Angus Bodley, who has already unbuttoned his shirt and vest for me. He eyes my hands as I gingerly place one tab to the left of his hairy chest and then connect a wire.

"Haven't you got that backwards? 'R' is for right side, isn't it?"

"Absolutely," I agree, tearing off the sticker unceremoniously, which makes Mr. Bodley flinch. "So you've done these before?" I ask.

"Electrocardiograms? Have had a good few done to me," he says.

"Now I'm just going to attach the rest of these wires to these stickies," I say, more for myself than for him. "Does this look okay? Why is my screen still black?"

"You might want to hit 'Power,' " Mr. Bodley suggests.

"Thank you."

Finally, when the machine prints out a series of waveforms that look familiar, I sigh with relief.

"Everything all right?" Mr. Bodley asks.

I concentrate on reading the EKG for a moment. There aren't any ST wave changes to indicate a heart attack, but the heart rate is rapid, which could mean . . .

"Well?" he asks, growing visibly short of breath.

"When you said you feel as if you might die . . ." I start.

"*Yes?*" he asks.

"Are you referring to a sense of impending doom?"

"Absolutely!" Bodley says. "I feel that way all the time!"

"Okay. I think we need to get a CT scan of your lungs," I say, ripping the stickers off one by one and dismantling the wires. "I just want to make sure you don't have a blood clot lodged in there."

"CT scan! Blood clot!" he repeats, horrified. "Is it fatal?"

"Not if we know about it," I say, which isn't entirely true. Still, it would've been nice if Mama's doctors had even considered the diagnosis before it was too late to save her.

I stick my head out of the curtain and signal to Ed in the Fish Bowl, though it's hard to get his attention since he's flirting with

Marian. From behind, I see the little cap on her blond head shaking back and forth while he smiles and swings his keys. Finally, he notices me.

"We need to get this guy over to CT pronto," I order, too loudly.

People look. From an old lady in a wheelchair who stops gripping her ankle to the pregnant lady who pauses in the middle of describing a rash, everybody turns to witness this event like rubberneckers on a highway. Even Marian turns around to show me her scowling face.

Ed responds quickly, crossing the sea of stares like a lifeguard and shoving back my curtain. "Out of the way, please," he says, and suddenly I wish I were the one being saved.

"But we need another bed. This one won't move," I say.

Ed slams his foot on a pedal near the base to expertly unlock the brakes. Then he winks at me as he rolls Mr. Bodley out of the examining room, making me grin.

"Where, pray tell, are you taking this patient?" a man suddenly demands, standing in the path of the stretcher with folded arms. His white coat billows out behind him like a cape.

"CT scan," I say, as Ed rushes to find the brakes again before I run this guy over. Angus Bodley says "CT scan," too, but his contribution sounds more like a wail.

"And who, pray tell, are you?"

"Dr. Holly Campbell, sir. The new locum tenens," I say, extending my hand.

"Mr. Danvers," the surgeon replies, shaking my hand limply as if to imply I'm not worth the effort of a real squeeze. Danvers has a potbelly, flyaway eyebrows, and a theatrical presence—only maybe it just feels that way, with everyone watching.

"Oh, hi. Nice to meet you," I say, deciding not to ask him about his house and whether it's now a pile of ashes. "I've got to get Mr. Bodley to CT. We're ruling out a pulmonary embolus," I add, accustomed to the American tradition of "we."

"What makes you so sure this man has a pulmonary embolism?" Mr. Danvers asks.

"He has chest pain, sinus tachycardia, sense of impending doom—"

"And have you found S1 Q3 T3 on his EKG, Dr. Campbell?"

"Well, no, but he has sinus tachycardia," I say again, feeling my face heat up with ego and anger and embarrassment. *So he's got a fast heartbeat. So what? Lots of things can cause that,* it occurs to me. But I don't want to pay attention to myself. Everybody's looking, and I'm the physician here. "Unexplained tachycardia in a patient with chest pain—"

Danvers doesn't let me finish, just holds up his hand to make me stop talking. Then he reaches out for Mr. Bodley's hand and says in a soothing voice, "There now, Mr. Bodley, I think we'll not be needing the CT scan."

"No CT scan?" my patient says hopefully. "What about the clot?"

"I don't believe there is a clot," Danvers says with an arrogance that disturbs me.

Who cares what you believe? It's written somewhere: if the diagnosis crosses your mind, then you have to order the test. The moment you ignore your intuition, your patient is bound to drop dead. The only thing sadder is if you never had any intuition in the first place.

"How do you feel at this moment?" Mr. Danvers asks Bodley.

I try mental telepathy: *Please say your chest pain is crushing. Just for me.*

Angus Bodley takes an excruciatingly slow deep breath and then exhales as if demonstrating yoga. "Doing a bit better now," he finally says. "Relieved, I suppose. Got quite a scare when she suggested the clot in the lung."

"I don't think this is anything sinister," Danvers says loudly, so everyone can hear, including the audience in triage. I'm so humiliated that I can't even look at Ed, much less Mr. Bodley, and I find myself meeting eyes with Marian instead. Her expression is the same as yesterday in the hall: flat and sullen.

"Let's put Mr. Bodley back in his room and let him settle down a bit. Bring the man a cold drink, if you will, Ed," Danvers orders, and then turns to stare at me. His hard look is almost scary. "Dr. Campbell, allow me to have a word with you."

Here we go, I think. *Fired on my first day. Now what?*

Staring at the back of Danvers' coat saves me from making eye contact with anyone as we cross the twenty-foot chasm between the examining rooms and Danvers' office. Once inside, he shuts the door behind us and points to a seat. I feel like I'm inside the principal's office.

"Dr. Campbell, I daresay you'll find things here are quite different than in the States," Danvers says, as he folds his arms again and leans back in his leather chair. For some reason, the lean gives me hope, as if there may be more than one right answer.

"We don't just order tests willy-nilly," he goes on. "We actually examine our patients and take a thorough history. Did you even speak to the man before ordering such an expensive test, exposing him to unnecessary radiation?"

"Yes. We...conversed." *But shit, I didn't even examine him.*

"Well, if you had taken a social history, you might have concluded that Angus Bodley is an anxious man. His wife has left him, he's about to be out of a shop unless his 'landmark' grant proposal comes together soon, and everyone knows that this grant will never be approved because his research is a whole lot of bollocks. If you'd have asked the man if he'd ever felt this way before, you'd have found the answer was yes, many times, and that he's never been diagnosed with anything remotely like a heart attack or even heartburn. Mr. Bodley is simply a timid man afraid of dying. You, my dear, gave him the shock of his life." Danvers leans forward. "Congratulations."

At that moment the strangest resolve comes over me. It's as quick as a light switch and just as astonishing. It's a sense that I vaguely knew long ago, before the city kept me awake, before I gave up a social life for a textbook. The resolve is this: I have to help Mr. Bodley.

"I'm sorry," I say. "I didn't know this chest pain was a benign thing."

"You'll never know anything if you don't ask the questions.

And remember, this is not the United States," Danvers says, holding up a finger. "In England, we think more about our patient than the next test. And we do not create terrifying scenarios for them."

"But terrifying scenarios are part of reality," I say.

"Dr. Campbell, presentation is everything in medicine. Which is why we don't say 'cancer' in front of our patients; we talk of *neoplasia* until we're certain. We don't say 'TB'; we say 'acid fast bacilli.' We certainly don't mention *pulmonary emboli*."

"Yes, but—in the States, we like to explain why we'd be ordering—"

"Forget ordering."

"But it's also about preparing the patient," I say.

"Dr. Campbell," Mr. Danvers interrupts in a voice of quiet command. His fingers are poised on top of the desk as if he could start banging out Beethoven's Ninth. Only he's staring at me as if I am the sheet music. "When you can learn to present death as a natural part of life rather than an aberrant evil that calls for war, then you will have prepared the patient. And quite likely, yourself."

EIGHT HOURS LATER, I trudge back up the hill from town. The gnawing feeling of not eating breakfast, lunch, or dinner forced me to forage for food after work instead of sinking into bed. Handles of plastic grocery bags are now cutting into my fingers, but my brain is too numb to care. What exactly happened today? Everything after the meeting with Danvers is a blur. It's hard to remember all the other patients, hard even to remember shopping itself, though somehow my arms are now full.

I squint: home is in sight. On the front step of Parchment House, a girl with short blond hair sits and waits. Marian must've gotten a haircut after her shift. And must've locked herself out. Her feet impatiently tap the ground while her arms are folded across her chest. When she glances up, Marian reminds me of Ben's fiancée, a slender type with the same dark eyes and fighting look, except Alecia Axtel is far from blond. Her hair is so black it shines blue. It's funny, I think, the way you can go to a foreign country and everyone makes you look twice, makes you think that you must've known them in some other setting. Maybe it's just that people look the same no matter where you go.

Marian is still watching me, and I'd jingle my keys if it weren't for the groceries in my hands. She raises her arm with a tentative wave, then covers her mouth with the other hand as if trying to imagine what to do next. That's when I see the flash of emerald and platinum on her finger. It's not her English doppelgänger. It really is Alecia.

My steps slow as I round the corner to the stone path leading up to Parchment House. The bags twist around my fingers and cut off my circulation.

"Holly?" Alecia stands up, looking tentative. "Surprise?"

My brother's fiancée, my sister-in-law-to-be, has bleached her dark hair blond. I can see the almost-black roots in her spiky short cut. Grandmother would say it looks trashy and low class, but I hate to admit that I think it looks glamorous.

"A-Alecia? Is everything okay?" I ask, imagining she's flown three thousand miles to tell me someone else I love has died. Thank goodness the groceries make it impossible to hug. "Where's Ben?"

"Ben's at home. He's fine. But he..." She trails off, runs her fingers through her new hair.

"He...?"

"Doesn't know I left. Oh, hey, let me help you," she offers, rushing toward me to reach out for my bag of milk, which is slipping.

I feel oddly protective of my food and would insist on handling it myself, but one of my fingers is turning blue. "I don't understand," I say. "What are you doing here?"

We near the front step, and I see her two massive suitcases sitting there.

Alecia notices me noticing her luggage. "I'll explain over dinner," she says.

CHAPTER 6

In-Laws

"An attitude of wary open-mindedness may serve us best."

—OXFORD HANDBOOK OF CLINICAL MEDICINE

After pushing Alecia's suitcases into the first-floor hallway and dumping my groceries in the kitchen, we head back down the hill toward the shops and restaurants. I'm starting to feel dizzy with hunger.

"I banged my knee on the plane, in case you were wondering about my limp," Alecia says.

I hadn't noticed a limp, but I don't admit it since I'm expected to pay attention to these subtleties. After today I realize my patients could be headless and I'd ask them: Any problems smelling? Chewing your food? Trouble wearing hats?

"They should really instruct you to uncross your legs when the plane is landing," Alecia says. "You know, 'Seat backs up, tray up, uncross those legs.' It's entirely dangerous, otherwise. That's how I hit my knee on the seat in front of me."

Better yet, they should recommend the crash position, I think, but don't feel like using my voice. It doesn't seem as if any noise could come out of me without a sharp note of sarcasm or a flat tone of hostility.

"I sat next to a dental hygienist on the plane. I mean, what the hell is that all about?" Alecia is looking at me now, forcing me to speak.

I try to sound polite. "Dental hygiene?"

"Hygienists taking vacations. They're a threatening breed, you know? One time, I swear to God, one of them asked me, 'Do you want to have any teeth when you're ninety-nine?' As if that kind of threat is supposed to encourage me. Even the freak on the plane made a show of going off to floss in the little bathroom cubicle. Can you imagine flossing in one of those metal coffins where people pee?"

I don't want to imagine it. We pass a quaint red phone booth, and I resist the urge to run and call my twin. *Ben, your crazy girl-friend is here! Take her home, for God's sake!*

"Alecia, are you going to tell me what the hell is going on?" I ask.

"I'm taking a vacation," she says, blinking innocently. "I have family living abroad that I've been meaning to visit. And you were sort of on the way, or at least...in the same country, so I figured—"

"You're taking a vacation without Ben?"

She sighs. "We needed a time-out. We kept fighting. It started with the wedding plans—the gift registry, the venue, the guest list, everything an opportunity for an argument. I started wondering if this was normal wedding jitters or a sign of something much deeper."

"Like your uncle?" I ask.

"What about my uncle?" Alecia says.

"Well, I just heard you were really depressed after he... died."

"He didn't die; he was murdered. And excuse me for grieving. What, Ben was upset that I wasn't paying enough attention to him?"

"No," I say, wishing I'd never opened my mouth. "He just said you were having a really hard time."

"It had nothing to do with my uncle," Alecia says. "It was Ben. He kept nagging me to talk, kept saying I should see a shrink. He's the one who needs help. One time we were in the car sitting at a stoplight, and it was taking an eternity. I didn't think I'd ever been at a longer red light. By the time it turned green, I'd managed to peel an entire orange. I said to your brother, 'There is no reason a light should be so long that I have enough time to peel an entire orange.' You know what he says? He says, 'That's not an orange. That's a clementine.' Talk about being an instigator! He picks fights just to make conversation!"

"But a clementine is much easier to peel," I say.

"What's that got to do with anything?" Alecia snaps. "God, I should've known. The person who knows him best thinks exactly the same way."

Suddenly I can't remember what stoplights and clementines have in common, but thankfully we've come upon the cemetery, which temporarily distracts her as we wander down the path that cuts through it.

"Hey, what do you think happened here?" she asks, pointing to half a headstone lying on the ground like a tablet smashed by Moses.

I stare at her. "The war?"

"I thought they'd have cleaned it up by now," she says.

I want to call Ben and ask, *This is who you're marrying?* But then I remember, maybe he's not.

"So the wedding is off?"

"Oh, God no. I just need some time to figure out if we're still right for each other." She snorts, adding, "Wedding's off? Are you kidding? I've got my dress."

My curiosity gets the better of me. "What does it look like?"

"Spaghetti straps, silk sheath. Vera Wang."

"Pretty," I say. Weddings generally remind me of the Academy Awards. You may not know how it's going to turn out, but it's fun to see the outfits.

Leaving the cemetery, Alecia leads us straight past the same tiny church I passed yesterday, down another block of the hill, and into an alley. When I suggest we take a left instead, toward the cobblestone High Street, she tells me her way is a shortcut that she stumbled upon on the way to find me. I hope she's not leading us past the Winchester Cathedral. I don't want to see it yet and certainly not with her. Sometime, when I can be there to pray rather than tour, I'd like to go alone.

The thought of the cathedral reminds me of Ben explaining that in biblical times, anything that kept you from the temple made you unclean. I imagine the hospital wards and realize I've been unclean for years now, too busy practicing futility to believe in anything else.

"So, it must've been pretty inconvenient when Ben found his faith," I say as we wander along a ten-foot medieval wall.

"Excuse me?" Her thin, plucked eyebrows go up.

"I mean, you must've been pretty astounded when out of the blue Ben goes from being a respectable filmmaker to suddenly wanting to be a minister."

"*Au contraire,*" Alecia says. "First of all, he never made more than a ten-minute film. Didn't he tell you how we met?"

"Jexy," I say, only because my brother credits my mother's best friend with the luck of their meeting. As a well-known fashion designer, Jexy seems to know important people everywhere. She got Ben a job at the TV station where Alecia was reporting the news. The rest was kismet, as Ben says.

"Jexy never introduced us—I only met her later, once we were dating. She got him the job editing newsreels at my station, and the fact is, he was incredibly miserable. He was The Guy Who Wouldn't Smile in the beginning. But I gave him the benefit of the doubt, just because he was uncharacteristically genuine, at least for the business. Besides, he started to perk up once I agreed to get coffee with him. And he really started smiling once we were going out. Or maybe he was smiling because he got Called. Have you ever seen your brother off-the-wall excited? Just bursting?" Alecia asks. "When Ben had his epiphany, I hadn't seen him that worked up about anything before, except for sex. Jesus and sex. It was contagious. I was reevaluating my previously agnostic roots."

Jesus and sex, I think. *Two things I have yet to figure out.*

"Still, you were mad about leaving New York, just so he could go to seminary," I say.

"Is that what he told you?" Alecia asks.

"That's what you told me. That time when Ben made us go out for sushi? I remember you were really bitter about being in Pittsburgh. You kept talking about the job market for TV, and how this was a setback."

"Well, it was, but . . . I wasn't bitter."

"You said you'd never be Katie Couric now."

"I don't want to be Katie Couric anymore," she mutters.

We reach a stone archway, which Alecia ambles through as if she grew up on the inside of a castle. Of course, according to my guidebook, there's no castle left, only some ruins standing near the cathedral, which was erected in the ninth century, when Winchester was the capital of Anglo-Saxon England. Even the stained glass survived the world wars, but just barely: apparently the English took the broken bits of color and resurrected them into a new picture.

"Isn't it gorgeous?" Alecia says, just as I realize we're looking at the side of the enormous church from across the lawn.

Together we cut across the green and round the front of the cathedral under another arch. For a fleeting moment, I feel aware of my own breath, walking around this place where people have bled and died and worshipped for centuries. I have the strange feeling that, like Mama flying away to Grenada, I too am on the verge of my own history. Finally, we stop and stare at the gray stone Gothic structure in all its glory of spires and stained glass.

"Want to go in?" Alecia asks.

"I really need to get dinner first," I say, apologetically this time.

As we walk across the close toward High Street, I ask, "So when did you give up on being a *Today* show host?"

Alecia heaves another great sigh. "I've been kind of disgusted with the business lately. Last week I was interviewing a man outside an apartment complex where a baby had been shaken to death. We're on live, you understand, and I ask the man how he feels about living so close to a killer. The guy says, 'I'm just shocked. There was a *baby* living here? He never made a sound.

Never even saw him coming or going. This is a heck of a way to find out.' "

Alecia hugs herself in her blue silky sweater as she babbles on. "No one understood how completely bizarre that was. Not my cameraman, not my editor. I just knew, right then, that America is filled with completely screwed-up, backward people, and I had to get out of there, away from all the baby killers and dental hygienists."

"So . . . you quit?" I say, with a small element of panic. It's one thing if she and my brother take a "time-out." But if she quits her job, she may never leave me alone.

"Just a sabbatical," Alecia says. "My boss understood. He said burnout happens to all good reporters."

We've come upon the Firkin, whose chalkboard outside declares that dinner is still being served, and that Monday is karaoke night. I'm grateful for the diversion. Maybe she'll be quiet for at least five minutes while we order.

"American girls in the house!" the bartender celebrates loudly as we enter the pub. The ceiling beams are so low I imagine we've wandered into the living room of a Hobbit.

But the bartender hasn't even heard our accents yet, and I wonder what it is about us that screams American. My Nike running shoes? My tiny, square glasses? Our jeans? Like the rest of her, Alecia's denim is chic—a thought that's confirmed when I notice that the leather label on her waistband reads "Jexy Jeans." Jexy's custom jeans go for over three hundred dollars a pair, but maybe she gave Alecia a discount.

The bartender immediately follows us over to the table we pick, while the few other people at the bar merely stare at us.

Even after reaching our table, he uses the same loud voice. "From New York, are you?"

"I am." Alecia sits up straighter and smiles. "New York City, best city in the world."

What happened to baby killers and dental hygienists? Or is that just the problem with Pittsburgh?

"Welcome to Winchester," the barman says. "Where might you be staying?"

"The Royal Hotel," Alecia replies.

"The Royal County Hampshire Hospital," I say flatly.

"Ah! You're one of the nurses!" he says.

"Holly's a doctor," Alecia says.

"A doctor—brilliant!" The man claps his hands together. "Are you ready to be singing tonight?"

We're both startled. Alecia laughs uncertainly. "I think not."

I join in late: "No-ho-ho," I say, shaking my head.

"Come on!" he says, doing a Chubby Checker twist. "How about 'Girls Just Wanna Have Fun'? Everybody loves Cyndi Lauper!"

"We just"—I pat my stomach—"wanna have food."

"Or how about 'We Are Family'? Heh? A little Sister Sledge rendition tonight?" The man waves his eyebrows around in energetic ripples.

"Look, all we want is menus," Alecia says, suddenly unfriendly. "Can we just have the menus?"

He sobers up and points with his fingers in the shape of a gun, as if about to fire a pistol at one of the lights. In fact, over at the bar, a gangly man with a broken leg propped up on a bar stool actually ducks. Then I realize he's just making sure we have full view of the chalkboard near his head.

"Brilliant," Alecia says, with a sudden British inflection. "Let's order, shall we?"

ONCE WE DECIDE on dinner, Alecia waits a moment until our bartending waiter is out of earshot. "That harassment was just uncalled for." She says the word "harassment" in the fancy way, with the emphasis on the wrong syllable: hair instead of ass.

"Well, he meant no harm."

"What's up with that guy over there?" She means the guy at the bar in the full-leg cast. "What do you think happened to him?"

"I heard him say his legs were crossed when his airplane was landing."

Alecia laughs loudly. The man looks over from his drink, as if he wants to join us. "Hey, should I get us some beers?" she asks.

"Oh—n-no. I don't think so," I say. "I have to work to-morrow."

"I didn't say we'd get trashed. "

"I'm just not thirsty for beer."

Alecia blinks. "You don't want a Bass Ale?"

"Yes. No. Yes, that's correct. No, I don't want one."

"Wow," she says simply, and gets up to go order one.

Suddenly I'm thirsty for a Bass Ale but don't feel like chang-ing my mind after all that. *If she senses I'm getting comfortable with her, she'll stay longer.*

"O-oh, okay!" I call desperately after her. "I'll just have one."

Alecia furrows her eyebrows like she doesn't understand, but when she flips her head to order, I watch as the bartender draws two large pints of amber ale.

Alecia stands over at the bar, one hand on her hip, talking to the broken-legged man who wants to tell her about his last trip to New York. Since it's such a small pub, we're all privy to his sto-ries about the nice people he met, and the misconceptions the world has about mean New Yorkers.

"Well, hey...some of it's true," Alecia says magnanimously, taking a sip of her beer.

Luckily, she doesn't bring her new friend back to the table when she finally delivers our drinks ten minutes later.

"So, I meant to ask," Alecia says, sloshing my beer as she slides into her seat. "What're you doing here?"

For the first time all day, I laugh. It feels good, too, as if the tornado of my life has just dispersed into bubbles. "Funny, I thought I asked you the same thing."

"Did you really quit your attending faculty position?"

"How could I have quit when I never took the position?" I ask.

"Ben said you found the hospital depressing," Alecia says in a newsy voice. I can even imagine the microphone in front of my face when she adds, "Why was that?"

"Everybody's sick and dying. Or trying to die."

"Did you expect something else?"

"I never thought about it," I say. When a ten-year-old makes up her mind to become a doctor, she's not contemplating how it might feel to crush an elderly person's ribs as she's trying to get a heartbeat, or how it feels to secretly hope that the heart won't respond. Because surviving a cardiac arrest in the hospital is rarely a rebirth; instead, it's the beginning of a tug-of-war between pain and death.

"Maybe you just wanted to be like your parents," Alecia suggests.

"So?" I say.

"So, Ben says your father was never around! He was always seeing patients."

"Mama was home," I say.

"Yeah. Okay. Sure," Alecia says.

"What does that mean?" I ask.

"Your mother left!" Alecia says, as if she has the right to make judgments about my family—as if her own mother isn't crazy! "She walked away from her life just to become a doctor."

"It was for less than a year. She came back," I say.

"You just wanted to please her," Alecia says.

"I wanted to be *like* her," I say. A person who loved her job, one who felt "called" to do it.

Besides, my childhood images of medicine were glorified by my respect for Mama and Dad. Wasn't it natural? Between the two of them, they knew almost everything. They even spoke a secret language—hunger was called "hypoglycemia," thirst was "dehydration," and watching TV was "flattening your EEG." The few concepts that neither one of them could explain were very authoritatively classified as "idiopathic." The way I saw it then, Mama and Dad weren't just improving other people's lives; by taking care of strangers, they were protecting us from everything unfortunate, unexpected, and irrevocable.

What would Mama think of me now, if she knew how ambivalent I am about medicine? Although, what do I think of Mama, knowing how ambivalent she must've been about me?

"Hello?" Alecia waves. "I asked you a question."

"Sorry," I say, sipping my ale. *Don't want to keep the TV view-ers waiting.* "What did—?"

"If you're sick of being a doctor, why did you come to England to do the same thing?"

Because this is all I know how to do, I think, but I can't give her that. I can't confide in the same woman who stands outside of burning homes with bright lights and a microphone to ask the owners, huddling under borrowed blankets, how they're feeling about it. I can't confide in the woman who won't admit that her uncle's death may have affected her, yet knows with certainty that my brother's classification of oranges and clementines un-doubtedly did. Why should Alecia get to know who I am, when she doesn't even know herself?

"First of all, I'm not sick of being a doctor, I just wanted a change of scenery," I say. "I want to get more experience. Learn other perspectives on medicine."

Alecia considers this, lagging on the rim of her beer for sev-eral swallows. "How boring," she finally says.

We both look up to see our waiter setting down Alecia's steak-and-potato pie and my cold chicken plate, which is deco-rated with gobs of mayonnaise in the four corners of the square platter.

"Man, that was fast," Alecia tells him. "You're amazing."

"Cheers," he says, and winks, apparently no longer offended by our dislike of group sing-alongs.

"I think 'cheers' means thank you," Alecia says, after he walks away. "The Americanophile at the bar kept using it in that con-text."

Distracted by the mayonnaise, I scoop it onto my bread plate before it touches my chicken. "They randomly throw mayo on everything. They ought to warn you."

Alecia pushes a fork into her pie, sending a pocket of hot air into her face, which suddenly makes me salivate. My chicken looks icy, like it's been swimming.

"So," I say, risking a bite. "You left Ben over a simple word choice? Do you realize how nuts that is?"

Fanning her hands over her pie, Alecia waits until the steam clears to answer. "Holly, there are certain defining moments in every relationship. He never validates my causes. This frustrates me. But I don't expect you to understand."

I wonder what causes she could be referring to—fruit taxonomy?—but decide it's more important to establish how she found me and how long she plans on staying.

"So what happens now?" I ask.

"Well, I love your brother," Alecia says, "but I don't want to rush to get married right away just because it's the next thing to do."

"Or because you've already purchased the dress?" I ask.

"Right," she says, smiling sheepishly. "Believe it or not, I take marriage seriously. My parents are divorced. From what Ben tells me, yours should've been."

"My parents had their problems," I say, "but they were completely committed to each other."

"Come on. Ben says your parents fought constantly. He says everyone knew that when your mother left, she didn't plan on coming back. If there hadn't been an invasion, she would've—"

"My mother was not...some slut," I whisper, trying to defend myself against Simon's letter. *I'd like to believe that the woman who tastes of salt and sweat and sunscreen, who just spent the night on my squeaky twin bed, was the real Sylvia.*

"Who said she was a slut?" Alecia asks.

"And my father is far from a tyrant," I say.

"Oh, no, don't get me wrong. I love your dad," Alecia says. "I called him up to find out where you were. I knew he'd be cheerful about giving me your address. He's a blessedly oblivious man."

"Your pie is going to get cold," I say grimly.

"But sometimes he's just *so* out of it," she goes on. "I mean, God. Remember what happened at the funeral?"

I know she must be talking about the suit, the black Armani one that Jexy discovered hanging in the laundry room on the morning of the funeral. Dad didn't remember buying it, but, hell, the jacket fit perfectly and the pants could be hemmed later,

he told us after putting on the suit at Jexy's encouragement. When he put one of his work ties with it—the red one
decorated with stick figures of children holding balloons—Jexy
said, "No way, José," and replaced it with a silver-gray one that
happened to be hanging there as well. (Later Dad claimed that
he assumed Jexy had brought the suit with her, as if fashion de-
signers always carry extra suits for husbands of the deceased.)
We didn't discover who owned the suit until Thor Burnshack,
looking annoyed and uncomfortable in my father's blue blazer,
high-water khakis, and pediatric balloon tie, found us at the
church.

Still, there were worse fashion faux pas. Alecia Axtel was in a
little black cocktail dress. *Good thing I packed this after all!* And
Ubiquitous Vic wore flip-flops, despite that no one had stolen his
shoes.

Of course, no one looked more out of place than Mama. Jexy
had dressed my mother's body for the casket: she wore a springy
Ralph Lauren dress with a lavender Christian Dior scarf around
her neck. (No Prada bag or her cell phone, thank God.) I couldn't
go near the body. Not after I'd spent twelve weeks dissecting one
in anatomy. Mama wasn't in there anymore.

"I didn't even know Ben had a girlfriend," I say now, watching Alecia spear an onion from the middle of her piecrust. "It
was . . . weird."

"Is that why you ignored me?" she asks.

"I didn't ignore you," I say.

Alecia opens her mouth to say something, then seems to reconsider. "I remember your father walking home in the rain,"
she finally says, which makes me nod glumly. "It was so sad."

He skipped the burial, where we threw roses on her casket as
it was lowered into the earth. Instead, we passed him in our limo
on the way from the church. His head was bent down, and he
was sobbing.

"And he rebaked the Wheat Thins," I say, my voice growing
so thick that it's hard to take another bite of food.

"What?"

"Later, when all the neighbors and Mama's friends were at

our house for the wake. I went to get another platter of cheese and crackers and found him in the kitchen spreading Wheat Thins on a cookie sheet to put in the oven. Someone had left them out in the rain."

"Most likely me and Ben," Alecia says slowly. "I kind of remember eating crackers outside...."

And I kind of remember glancing out the bathroom window and seeing the two of you groping each other at the side of the house. It was revolting. Your hand was in his pants, and his hand was...

Luckily, the start of karaoke interrupts my thoughts. The man in the full-leg cast hobbles up to the microphone and leads the crowd in "The Gambler." His voice starts off timid, but they coax him into singing with conviction, until everyone's belting along. I feel like shouting out the words myself: "Know when to walk away and know when to run."

Instead, I raise my voice to ask Alecia what she's doing here.

"I don't know. It's just...ever since my uncle got shot...I need to know my family. I need to know them better than I knew him. I mean, sure, I know some of them. My dad. He's normal, and he makes a lot of money. But my mom is pretty loopy, living in Oregon. Did Ben ever tell you?"

I shake my head, but slowly, since I'm lying.

Alecia takes several gulps of Bass Ale before offering, "I don't even know what happened to her, or why."

"Well, if she's living in Oregon, why don't you fly out there?"

"I've been out there, but we just can't talk. I get the creeps when I go there. She lives in this filthy commune with a vegetable garden, and a tire swing out front. I don't know why exactly, but ever since her nervous breakdown, I don't feel comfortable being alone with her."

"Oh," I say with a nod. "So instead you came...all the way here."

"My aunt Roxanne lives in Britain. She's really the one person who knows—or knew—my mom and my uncle, and I think she can help me...I don't know, figure out my family. I guess it seemed like the right time to visit."

"So, ah...so..." I don't want to be rude, but I wonder why

her two fat suitcases aren't planted on Aunt Roxanne's floor. "Was she not home earlier?"

"Home? Well, I don't know her address. My dad didn't know it. She came over here fourteen years ago when she kidnapped my cousin from my uncle—the one who just died."

"Wait. She *kidnapped your cousin*?" I repeat. "Are you sure she's still your aunt?"

"Of course. She's still the mother of my cousin, isn't she? Unfortunately, Roxanne will get deported—no, arrested on sight if she shows up back in the States. It'll be nice to see my cousin, Di, again. We had a lot of fun before they took off," Alecia says thoughtfully. "We'd go on family road trips together and sing a lot of Cat Stevens."

"Wow," I say, still thinking about "arrested on sight." Grandmother raised us to live in fear of arrests, to always browse in stores very obviously displaying our intent to buy. Integrity was not the issue. We were told that getting caught with so much as a pack of gum could keep us from getting into our dream schools, and that, in turn, would cost us any hope of eventual happiness. "You don't have any idea what your . . . what Roxanne is doing now?"

"She was a fortune-teller in New York—I mean, a psychic. A 'spiritual advisor.' She gets pissed off if you call her a fortune-teller. I assume she's still doing . . . psychic things."

I stop chewing my chicken to ask with a full mouth, "Can she talk to dead people?"

"She'll pretend to if you pay her enough," Alecia says with a snicker. After a pause, she laughs again. I ask her what's so funny.

"I heard about your thing for Joshua Peter," she says, as if I'd taken to stalking the star of *Passing On*.

"I don't have a thing for him. He's just a guy on a TV show. And in case you were wondering, he's not why I'm here."

"Ben said he predicted—"

"Well, Ben's wrong."

In the corner, a dead-on Janis Joplin screams the lyrics to "Me and Bobby Magee," while a swollen cloud of silence hangs over our table and threatens to burst.

"Listen, I'm sorry about your mom," Alecia says finally.

Then why'd you make out with my brother in the yard? I want to ask. *Why'd you show up at all? Why didn't anyone remind me there's no such thing as stable when someone's critical?*

"Ben said you two were, like, symbiotic," Alecia adds.

"She was my mom. Not a tapeworm," I say, wiping my eye.

After I manage to finish my disappointing meal, Alecia walks me all the way back up the hill to pick up her suitcases. I call a cab to take her to the Royal Hotel so she won't be ambling alone in the dark. Then I tell her I'd better be getting to bed.

Back in my room I collapse on my mattress and put my ear up to the wall, just to see if Ed is in his room. But I can't hear anything, except the sound of Tracy Chapman's "Fast Car" coming through the opposite wall, from Marian's room. *What is Ed doing on a work night?* I wonder. *Where does he go? Does he have a girlfriend?*

I don't want to think about the orderly, though, no matter how good-looking he is, no matter how coincidental our remeeting. Instead I peruse the small stack of books sitting on my desk, the same ones I carried over on the airplane. There's *Synchronicity*—but I'm sick of Jung, sick of ESP and the importance of "falling together in time." And then there's my old friend *Ballet Shoes*. It's as if I grew up with the characters, Pauline, Posy, and Petrova. In fact, that's what I'll do with my first weekend in England, I decide. I'll explore London and find the house on Cromwell Road where I can imagine the fictitious sisters grew up.

Just as I'm opening *Ballet Shoes,* my mind drifts back to dinner with Alecia. *Ben says everyone knew that when she left, she didn't plan on coming back.*

I stare at the ceiling where the ladybugs flutter to and fro, and before I know it, I'm nine years old again, in the Murphys' kitchen across the street. I have just hung up the phone with Grandmother, after asking if my friend Jill can come back to our house to eat dinner.

"It's no problem," I say to both Mrs. Murphy and Mrs.

Fischer, another neighbor, who happens to be sitting in the breakfast nook having a cup of tea. "There's plenty of meatloaf."

As Jill starts dancing with glee—a tap routine without the tap, since she's in sneakers—Mrs. Murphy turns to Mrs. Fischer and says tragically, "Poor Will."

"Oh, no, it's fine," I say to the women. "He doesn't mind either." Dad won't mind because Dad won't be there. He has evening office hours on Thursdays.

Nevertheless, my remark makes both of them look at each other before smiling at me with pity, as if I'm just too young to understand.

"I feel so sorry for him," Mrs. Fischer says in a low voice, as Jill and I head out to the garage to ride our bicycles. "She left, and he's raising them all on his own."

"He's such a good father," Mrs. Murphy says.

My grandmother is raising us, you morons! I wanted to shout. But I had a feeling that wouldn't erase the pity in their eyes.

Did Ben really believe the neighbors? I wonder now. *And if he did, why say such a thing to Alecia, when Mama proved everyone wrong? She came back.*

I think of Alecia calling Ben "The Guy Who Wouldn't Smile" and wonder what other sad stories he might've said to win her over. That our grandmother didn't allow us to laugh at the dinner table? That Dad was angry for most of our childhood, and we didn't know why? Or maybe Ben spilled his more recent struggles. Before Alecia, before Mama was dead, he and I could spend hours on the phone lamenting how hard it was to find someone to love, and how hard it was to pursue a calling when no one would give you a chance. Then I remember how unusually peaceful Ben seemed standing at Mama's funeral and holding Alecia's hand. She had given my brother a chance, and Ben betrayed me by being happy. We were supposed to be lost together. Besides, did he have to fall in love with a woman so diametrically opposed to the values of our family?

Mama valued the theoretical little black dress, Holly, I hear my brother in my mind, and I know that he's right.

Mama probably would've stuck up for Alecia. *She's got the*

body for that dress. Let her wear it, she would've said to Grand-mother.

And to me: *Let's find you a dress that makes you look that good.*

Mama and I loved to shop together. "Just try it on," she'd say to just about anything, no matter how expensive. Unless it was during my stripes phase—which lasted for most of fifth grade through junior year of high school—then she'd say "Just walk away" if I approached another sweater or oxford, T-shirt or jersey that happened to have lines on it. Mama believed in outfits. One couldn't just buy a gray silk skirt—even on sale—without delineating specific plans on what it would be worn with. And if the only thing you could come up with was a white sweater, the answer was no. She believed in mixing and matching, and in bold colors like cherry red and marigold. She believed that you couldn't buy a little black dress to wear for a cocktail party that didn't exist, or for the boyfriend you didn't have, unless you looked stunning in it. Then she would buy the dress for you.

Closing my eyes, I listen to the walls for a while instead of my thoughts. Marian has finally put Tracy Chapman to sleep, but Van Morrison's "Moondance" is coming from Ed's room. I imagine Ed twirling me around in the moonlight. He dips me backward and hands me a rose. *No, not a rose, a balloon. One token balloon.*

It's the last thing I remember before falling asleep: letting it go.

CHAPTER 7

Code Blue

> "Question your conscience—no matter how strongly it tells you to act."
>
> —OXFORD HANDBOOK OF CLINICAL MEDICINE

Jet lag has caught up to me, making me feel nearly delirious as I plod back for day two in the trenches. I wonder how soldiers do it in war, get up every day and still move forward, not knowing what will take them down. I wonder how they ever fall asleep in the first place. Whenever I manage to drift off, it's never very restful, because I'm always making decisions in my dreams, struggling with chaos and misunderstandings.

At least the A&E is quiet when I arrive at 7 A.M. Marian is putting the tea kettle on a hot plate; Ed is transporting a middle-aged man in a wheelchair off to X-ray, and the Great Wall of Problems in the Fish Bowl has only one name on it, a "Gendry" labeled "Ankle Pain."

I'm staring at the marker board thinking that maybe this is worse, this quiet time, waiting for badness to happen—because goodness rarely takes place in an ER—when Mr. Danvers suddenly startles me from behind, booming, " 'What *is* the student but a lover courting a fickle mistress who ever eludes his grasp?' "

"A lover...courting..." I repeat, folding my arms across my chest.

"Truth. The fickle mistress. I quote Sir William Osler. Come," Danvers adds, beckoning me to follow him into his office. Just at the threshold he stops and calls to Marian, "Two cups of tea, if you would, my dear."

"Straightaway, sir," she replies, making me blink with disbelief. I'm imagining what the nurses would say if I ever ordered a cup of tea in the ICU back home. Shirley, who is known for exploding at physicians who get blood on her patients' fresh sheets, would probably prepare a scalding drink and pour it over my head. Wanda would laugh and say, "What is this, *Cheers*? Do I look like Diane Chambers?"

We sit down in the office and within moments Marian has not only brought us tea but a plate with poppy seed muffins on it. I've already eaten breakfast and am dying for a cup of coffee, but I want to be obliging, so I reach for a muffin when Danvers holds out the plate. Once Marian leaves, Danvers takes a small sip of tea and begins firing off questions on Osler, a professor at Johns Hopkins in the early 1900's.

Mr. Danvers asks what, according to Osler, are the four ideals a doctor should subscribe to. He prompts me: "The art of...?"

"Medicine?" I ask.

"The Virtue of...?"

"Chastity?" I suppose.

"The Quality of...?"

"Thought?"

"The Grace of...?"

"God," I say, which makes Danvers burst out laughing. I can't help thinking that in the United States there is an unspoken etiquette about asking questions or "pimping." Attending physicians can pimp senior residents and senior residents can pimp interns and interns can pimp medical students, but attendings never pimp fellow attendings. Maybe in Britain the hierarchy always goes back to age.

Calling me "young lady," Danvers elaborates: a doctor should learn the art of *detachment*, the virtue of *method*, the quality of *thoroughness,* the grace of *humility.* I ask if Osler is referring to the doctor/patient relationship in the art of detachment.

"No!" Danvers says. "The good student doctor detaches himself—or herself—from idle distractions of the commonplace world. An important ideal for anyone in this profession! There should be no love relationship to the young physician other than a love of learning."

At that moment, Ed knocks on the door, holding a mop and pushing a bucket with water in it. He asks if he can clean Danvers' office while things are quiet. *He's a janitor,* it occurs to me. *I have a thing for the janitor. What would people say? What would Eve say?* Most likely she'd call him "a crumb," her turn of phrase for anyone who isn't upper middle class or at least in pursuit of a graduate degree. If she was feeling generous, Eve would call him "colorful."

Mr. Danvers asks him to give us another moment and then says, "Now, Dr. Campbell, do tell us about yourself."

"I'm . . . I'm . . ." *Not currently dating anyone?* "From Maryland originally. I've been living in Pittsburgh the last three years."

"And what brings you to our fair city?"

So many things come to mind: I have to find my mother, have to find myself, have to see where the Fossil sisters lived, have to find out what it means to be a good doctor. But instead I say, "I thought it would be a great way to see new places."

"Ah. How unfortunate," Mr. Danvers says, standing up. "Next time tell us you're here to learn."

THE DAY PASSES QUICKLY, from casting broken bones and diuresing the congestive heart failures to oxygenating the pneumonias and medicating the migraines. Even Angus Bodley can't stay out of the A&E for one full day. He waits until nearly the end of my shift to show up—with chest pain, no less—as if to remind everyone of yesterday's scene. This time, instead of sending him for a stat CT, I schedule him for an outpatient stress test.

"Doctor, do forgive me, but I don't believe it's my heart," Mr.

Bodley tells me after I inform him of the plan. "It's my nerves that give me this pain."

"Have you talked to your doctor about this?" I ask.

"Who, my GP? He's gone and retired over five months ago. I haven't got another doctor."

"Well, sir, this is an emergency room. You need to find a doctor. You can't just drop in every time you feel anxious," I say, my voice giving away my impatience.

"No, of course not," Mr. Bodley agrees hastily, still fumbling with the buttons on his shirt, which he'd undone for yet another EKG. "It's just that you were so concerned about me yesterday."

That was yesterday, I think. *That was before Danvers humiliated me. That was before Alecia barged in.*

"No one has taken me seriously in such a long time," Angus Bodley continues. "And I thought...I just thought...perhaps you could be my doctor?"

"Sir, I can't be your doctor," I say, softening. "But I will help you find a GP. Now, what are we doing about your nerves?" I add, flipping through the chart.

I barely have time to explain the side effects of the antianxiety medication that I want to start him on and hand him his discharge papers when my pager goes off. This time it's for real: not a toaster fire in the cafeteria, not another chimney fire at Mr. Danvers'; it's a Code Blue.

Part of my role as the locum tenens, or as anyone who covers the A&E, is that I'm also supposed to "float" to the other ends of the hospital for any emergencies. It's funny that they call it "floating" when it feels like just the opposite, a violent sinking. Hospital crises rise up like whitecaps in the ocean, toss me around, tumble over my head, and pin me to the sand before I remember to take a breath.

Sister Gemma, the respiratory therapist, is already bagging the patient with 100 percent oxygen when I arrive on the second floor. Sister Gemma is eight months pregnant with her first baby. I can't help imagining what the little guy or girl hears inside her belly: lots of beeping and whirring from the ventilator, and gargling and choking from the patients, punctuated by intermit-tent suctioning. If I were that baby, I'd be terrified to be born.

"Does he have a pulse?" I ask from the doorway, still winded from running up the stairs. It's the first question I always ask, even before I know the story.

Sister Gemma feels his neck and nods. "He does."

Sister Renee gives me the lowdown: she came into his room to bring his meds and found him unconscious, unarousable, and hardly breathing. So she called the Code.

"He's full of crackles," Marian reports from the bedside, after listening to the old man's chest with her stethoscope.

I order IV Lasix and an arterial blood-gas kit. The patient is too unconscious to even notice when I poke the radial artery in his wrist. The blood that fills up the syringe looks blue instead of red.

"Venous?" Marian asks hopefully, looking at the sample. Arterial blood should be cherry red, rich with oxygen.

"It was pumping," I say, shaking my head.

We hook the patient up to the monitor on the crash cart and watch as his heart rate goes from very slow ... to slower ... into the flat line of asystole.

"Give him epi! We need epi!" I order, as the code team scram-bles around, handing off syringes and medication.

We watch as a blip appears on the heart monitor. I add an-other amp of epinephrine, a dose of atropine, and a third amp of epinephrine.

"He has a pulse again," Marian says.

"Third epi in," Sister Renee says.

"Where are the results of the blood gas?" I ask.

"The doctors always process their own blood gases," Marian says.

I blink. Not only have I never actually seen a blood-gas ma-chine (because the respiratory therapists usually just magically appear with the results) but I can't fathom leaving the bedside. "Forget it!" I say. The arterial blood was blue, and the patient is still not moving air. "Let's tube him."

Before I can even look around, Sister Gemma is reclining the head of the bed, and Marian is handing me the laryngoscope. That's right. We probably can't page "Anesthesia, stat!" here. I'm anesthesia, and lab support, and the EKG tech, and the doctor. Now is not the time to panic about the fact that I've placed more endotrachial tubes on dummies than real humans.

I lean over the patient, thrust his jaw forward the way I've practiced in the past, and attempt to push his tongue out of the way with the blade of the laryngoscope. Unfortunately, his dentures become tangled in the blade, as secretions fill his mouth.

"Get rid of the dentures," I order. "Suction."

Sister Gemma pulls out the dentures, tosses them aside, suctions out his mouth, and gives the patient another few blasts of 100 percent oxygen. Then she steps aside, and I move back in, thrust the patient's jaw forward, and tweak his tongue upward with the blade of the laryngoscope. This time I get lucky: the vocal cords are right there. I slip the tube in and hook it up to the CO_2 monitor, which lets us know we're in the right place—the trachea and not the esophagus. "We've got an airway," I say.

Frankly, I'm feeling pretty proud of myself. The ET tube is in place, the patient's got a heartbeat again, and if we can just get him down to the ICU, we'll hook him up to the ventilator just in time to head off to dinner. Another forty-nine minutes of this shift and then his respiratory failure becomes someone else's worry.

Only, the patient has to go and ruin everything by opening his eyes, bolting upright in bed, and trying to pull out the tube. I pounce on him, forcing him back down like a concert security guard wrestling a crazed fan to the floor of the stage.

"I thought he was full Code!" I say. "Full Code" means the patient wants everything to be done, from your basic buffet of heroic feats and extraordinary measures to futile attempts.

"He seems to have changed his mind," Marian says. "Do look."

I am looking at him. I am holding him down and looking at him. The patient is not interested in our saving efforts. He's kicking his legs, snapping his fingers, and pointing at the tube. Then he shakes his head. *No.*

"I can't take it out. I just put it in!"

I'm snapping at Marian, not the patient, but to the assembled Code team of nurses and respiratory technicians, it's probably hard to tell. Now that we've started resuscitating him, is it okay to stop? This is what he asked for in advance. Just a few moments ago his carbon dioxide level was so high that he was unconscious and barely moving air. Now he's awake and angry?

I let go of the patient but shout to make sure that he understands: "Sir, do you understand that you won't be able to breathe without that tube? You could die!" It's probably worse that he does. I should sedate him with some Versed, so I don't have to feel like we're assaulting him. "Get me two milligrams of Versed," I order, reaching for the chart.

"Yes, Doctor," Marian replies.

"He doesn't want Versed. He wants it out," Ed says from the doorway, obviously forgetting that he was paged "stat" because we needed more gloves, not opinions. I stare at Ed for half a second in disbelief, but he doesn't seem to notice. Juggling boxes of gloves in three different sizes, he's moving with purpose through the Code team, toward the bed, as if he'd encountered a car wreck that turned out to be his father.

"He's been hypoxic. Perhaps he doesn't know what he's saying," Sister Gemma adds.

"What's his name?" Ed asks, looking over my shoulder at the chart I'm holding. It's the first time it's occurred to me that I just put my fingers inside the mouth of a man whose name I don't even know. Then Ed shouts, "Mr. Swithen? James? Blink once if you want the tube out!"

"What are you doing?" I snap, partly because the goddamn orderly is not supposed to give any goddamn orders, and partly because anyone can see without using Morse code that this man does not want to be intubated.

"He blinked twice," Sister Gemma says.

"He blinked once, then he paused and repeated himself. He's being emphatic!" Marian says, sounding so emphatic herself that I think she's going to cry.

"He's got metastatic cancer," I realize, coming to a halt in the chart when I fall on the words "colon cancer" and "prognosis: grim." Tube out or in, this man is going to die.

"Get the wife in here! Where's the wife?" I shout as a harried blond woman appears in the doorway of the room.

The wife looks terrified as she peers around and seems to take in the entire scene at once: pregnant Gemma standing on a step stool, bagging Mr. Swithen; Ed clutching a box of latex-free gloves; Marian drawing up the Versed; and her husband pointing at the tube and jutting his thumb over his shoulder like an umpire, signaling "Out!" Then there's me fumbling with the chart. She looks at all of this and still pronounces:

"Please. Do everything you can."

So WE DO EVERYTHING we can. We make Mr. Swithen completely unconscious with IV Versed. We transfer him to the intensive care unit and hook him up to the ventilator. Then I give the patient's primary care physician a call to let him know about Mr. Swithen's change in status.

Instead of thanking me for responding to the emergency, the Scottish-sounding Dr. MacKinley bursts out, "Acht! Bloody hell!"

"Excuse me, sir?"

"Read the chart, did ye? The bugger was trying to die."

"Well, his wife wanted him to live."

"Doesn't matter what she wants! He's going to die. Should've let him go, really."

"Well, there was nothing documented about letting him go," I say, even though guilt is starting to suffocate me, and I'm feeling short of breath. Forget documentation, Mr. Swithen was practically screaming, "Let me go," and I still didn't listen. "That sort of thing should really be spelled out...for those of us responding to emergencies," I add between silent gasps.

"I should think his prognosis would've sufficed," Dr. MacKinley says.

"Well, I'll try to make his prognosis clear when I talk to the family—"

"Never mind that. I'm just coming."

But I can't wait for Dr. MacKinley to turn up, because "just coming" apparently means he has three more patients to wrap up in the office, and Sister Gemma has told me more than once that the family has assembled and is waiting for word. It's time to break the bad news.

Talking to the family after a patient's change in status may be the worst part of medicine, especially once a single member (e.g., the wife) has called in the rest of the clan, and they're waiting en masse for a pronouncement. Sometimes I feel like a messenger sent over from the opposing side of the war as I plod down the corridor toward enemy turf, aka the Waiting Room. It's not just that the family is looking for answers; it's that there's always at least one member looking for someone to blame. I imagine myself sent back to the ICU, my headless body strapped to a horse as if to demonstrate just how the family feels about what's happened to their loved one.

God, help me, I think, as the Waiting Room threshold draws nearer. I never know what I'm going to say or how I'm going to say it. Today when I open the door, six people, including the wife, stand up and surround me, making me feel like I wandered into a bad section of town and I'm about to be mugged.

First I introduce myself. Then I tell them what I know. I tell them Mr. Swithen is temporarily stable but critical. I tell them that even though he's on life support, there is ultimately nothing that we can do long term to support his life, since his colon cancer is running victory laps through his body. I tell them that they will have to use these next hours to ask themselves if he would want to live his last days like this, and if not, that they may want to consider weaning him from the vent.

"Cancer?" someone repeats. "What kind of cancer has he got?"

"Colon," I say, looking from face to baffled face. "You... didn't know?"

"We heard that there might be a tumor. We didn't know what kind. We didn't know it was serious," an elderly woman says. Everyone is nodding in agreement except for the wife, who is leaning on a younger version of herself—her daughter?—and crying. I'm not sure if she's crying because her husband is on the vent or because she's the only one who already knew he was terminal. I remember Mr. Danvers telling me yesterday that, unlike in the States, they never say the word "cancer" in front of the patient until it's certain. Did Dr. MacKinley forget to say the word, or did everyone choose not to hear it?

I tell them that it's very, very serious.

When I'm finally released from the waiting room into the fresh air of the corridor, the respiratory nurse, Gemma Hawkins, happens to be ambling by from the ICU. She keeps her head down and doesn't acknowledge me, instead just keeps waddling along toward the stairs, absently rubbing her big belly as if her unborn baby somehow distances her from the chaos that she just witnessed. Maybe it does, I think, watching her walk away and growing wistful for a second. *What do I have that distances me from the chaos that I witness? Nothing.* It occurs to me that as a woman, I'm supposed to bring people into this world, and that as a doctor, I'm supposed to keep people from leaving it. By these standards, I am a failure.

WHEN THE SHIFT COMES to an end, I stagger back to Parchment House and then trudge down the fluorescent-lit hall, which is quiet except for the sound of a woman's laughter in the kitchen. How is it that life in England is just as empty as it was in Pittsburgh? Only now my bedroom smells like mothballs. *Something has to change. Maybe even me.*

I pull on a pair of jeans and a T-shirt as the opening sequence of Tracy Chapman's "Fast Car" plays through the thin walls yet again. Marian must've just gotten home, too. It is apparently her theme song, which makes me wonder what kind of life she's led up to now and what she might be running from and *does she ever get sick of that song?* No doubt, it'll be in my head for the rest of the night. In fact, I'm humming the chorus as I make my way back down the hall: *"I-I-I had the feeling that I belonged; I-I-I had the feeling I could be someone. . . ."*

Cutting through the sitting room, past the horrible orange sofa whose foamy insides are coming out like a partially gutted animal's, I stop short in the kitchen doorway when I recognize the laughter coming from behind the swinging door.

"Hey! There's my elementary-school mate!" Ed says, grinning and holding up a beer in salute. "How's Mr. Swithen?" he adds, as if it's our old music teacher he's talking about.

"Alive," I say, only it feels like a retort.

"Elementary-school mate?" Alecia asks. She's sitting at the table. She's eating cheese and crackers. She will never ever leave me alone. "What are you talking about? What's he talking about?" she asks.

"We both had Mrs. Sandler for third grade at Misty Creek," I say in a bored voice, as if this is not what Jung was talking about in *Synchronicity*. "He sat at my table. What the hell are you doing here?" I add, trying to make my face appear more pleasant than my words, since Ed is watching and probably thinks Alecia is cute, probably thinks her bleached hair is sexy and glamorous, probably has no idea how annoying she can be.

"Waiting for you," Alecia says with a pert shrug.

"We sat at the same table?" Ed asks.

"Sure. Campbell and Clemens? We were alphabetical," I say, heading for the refrigerator. It occurs to me that, except for a premade salad (labeled "American Salad," as if the British would never be so lazy), I have no idea what food is mine after my dazed shopping expedition yesterday.

"The only Campbell I remember was a chubby kid who ate paste," Ed says, which makes Alecia cackle.

"That's because Nicolas Olzewski dared him to," I say, pulling out a bottle of ketchup from way in the back of the fridge, just because it seems to be in the wrong place. Ketchup should be in the door.

"Nicolas Olzewski. Wow. How do you remember stuff like that?" Ed asks.

I shrug, not in the mood to admit that I went to the prom with Nicolas, aka "Poor Nicolas," the guy who notoriously came in last at every cross-country meet. You couldn't help but feel bad for him—even the opposing teams would clap as he finished.

"So, is Mr. Swithen comfortable?" Ed asks now.

"Who?" I ask before realizing he's talking about the Code again. "He's paralyzed and sedated. I have no idea how he feels."

"The hospital sounds like a pretty exciting place to work," Alecia says in her news-reporter voice.

Ed swigs his beer and then tells Alecia, "Holly saved this guy's life today."

"I didn't save it; I prolonged it," I say. "It turns out he's dying, anyway."

"Are you a doctor, too?" Alecia asks Ed.

"I'm an orderly," Ed says. "I brought the gloves."

"I've been here two days and already I need a vacation," I say with a sigh, leaning on the counter, too overwhelmed to even think about what to eat.

"Good thing you're getting away this weekend." Ed smiles in a slow, evolving way and looks to Alecia for confirmation.

"She doesn't know yet," Alecia says. "You know, maybe I will have that beer."

"What don't I know?" I look between them, only Alecia is turned toward Ed, holding out her hand as if she wants him to throw her something: maybe a beer, maybe a rope.

"You guys are taking off on Friday for the Netherlands," Ed says, taking out a Sam Adams, cracking it open and handing it to her. "She booked the tickets."

"What about you, Holly. A beer?" Alecia asks, taking a sip of hers before sputtering on a cough.

"What's he talking about?"

"I did some research. It's where my aunt and cousin are now," Alecia says.

"The Netherlands?" I repeat, laughing in disbelief. It sounds like the River Styx should run through it. It sounds far-fetched and just plain far, considering I have a job *right here*.

"Amsterdam's supposed to be a great town," Ed says.

"Come on, Holly. Don't you want to get away for a weekend? I mean, this place is depressing," Alecia says.

"I like it here. It's quaint," I say, inhaling the dusty air. "Very . . . English," I add, coughing.

"Oh, go for it. Get out of Winchester. You'll have a blast!" Ed says.

I'm really beginning to resent Ed, beginning to resent the both of them. Why don't they go off to this Netherworld together, if they're so excited about it?

"When were you planning on going?" I ask, running my fingers through my hair. Except that my hand snags on the tangles; it feels like a math problem that will never be solved.

"Friday?" Alecia says.

"In three days? I can't," I say, reclaiming my fingers from my hair. "I have to work."

"You're not on the schedule," Ed says, and then adds, "Hey, does everyone know Maid Marian?"

"It's Sister Marian," says a small stiff voice from behind me. I turn to see Marian, whose pale, nearly translucent skin makes me think she belongs in a casket. Either that or she's going to look fantastic when she's eighty. When I shut the refrigerator, I briefly study the picture of the jollier version of Marian taped to the door. It's too bad about the diet, I find myself thinking. She seems to have shed her sense of humor along with the pounds. Only maybe it's not the weight. Maybe it's too many episodes of deferring to those in charge—bringing the tea or the Versed.

"Sister Marian," Alecia repeats. "How fascinating! I've never met someone so young with a calling to celibacy."

"I am a nurse. We're also called 'Sister.' "

"Oh." Alecia turns back around in her seat and shrugs, obviously no longer fascinated.

"Thanks for your help today," I tell Marian.

She looks baffled, as if no one ever thanked her before. "I didn't really have a choice, did I?"

"Well, you . . . everyone has a . . ." I'm so confused that I can't answer the question. Mr. Swithen didn't get a choice. He didn't pick colon cancer. When it counted the most, he didn't pick resuscitation either. But he got both.

"There's a phone call for you, Holly," Marian adds.

"There's a phone?" I ask, incredulous, which makes Ed chuckle as he sips his beer.

"Downstairs. Front hall," he says.

I leave the kitchen and run toward the phone, wondering if something's gone on with Mr. Swithen. He pulled his tube out? His wife changed her mind and allowed him to die peacefully? *Oh, please, please, somebody let him go.*

Instead, it's Ben, who tells me that my father gave him the main number to the hospital, and that somebody on the switchboard put him through.

"Is everything okay?" I ask. It occurs to me that if he's managed to track me down, there must be some sort of life-threatening emergency. Grandmother fell and broke her hip again? Dad really did electrocute himself this time?

"Alecia's gone."

Of course, I should have known better than to worry. Until this second, the idea of Alecia sitting in my kitchen didn't compute as an emergency for anyone but me. "Oh, yeah, I know."

"What do you mean you know?"

"She's here," I say, just as her laugh trickles from the vent over my head. I glare at the ceiling.

"Alecia?" Ben says, incredulous. "She's in Europe?"

"Where did you think she went?"

"I assumed she went to New York. Her note says, 'I went to visit my family for a couple of days. I'll call you once things have cooled down.' She's fucking *there*?"

"Apparently she has a long-lost aunt and cousin who live in the Netherlands. She wants me to help find them."

"Wants you to help find them?" Ben says, shouting. "They live in London! She and her cousin have been pen pals for years."

"Then what's she bothering me for?" I ask, annoyed. "What does she want from me?"

"I don't know what the hell's going on anymore. How long is she going to torture me over a goddamn piece of fruit?" my brother asks.

"Maybe it has nothing to do with the orange."

"It was a clementine!"

"Maybe it has nothing to do with any of that."

"Well, if she's going to be my wife, she can't just run off every time she gets depressed."

For some reason, Ben sounds like my father, making dictatorial proclamations from a position of having lost all control. It makes me wonder what really made Mama leave the first time: her desire to become a doctor, or her sense of being trapped in a role that she wasn't ready for?

"Listen, something else happened after you left," Ben says.

I imagine my father driving back from Home Depot, his car stocked with plumbing supplies, in particular a new steel pipe, which flies over the headrest and impales him when he slams on the brakes at a yellow light.

"I was reCalled," Ben says.

"By whom?" I ask, caught up in my reverie about being an orphan. *Two parents in two years. Good—*

"God."

"What?" I ask.

"God communicated with me," Ben says, with a laugh that I don't recognize—one that sounds half giddy, half possessed. "I'm not supposed to be a minister anymore," he says.

"You were *re*Called?" I finally understand. "You can't be reCalled!"

"I was in the library writing a paper and..." He chuckles, sounding sheepish now. "Suddenly I knew.... It's so hard to explain...the feelings that I had. It's like I woke up and knew I didn't have to do this. I've honestly never felt a more powerful connection to God.... I mean, except for that time that I was Called."

"Ben, don't you see what's happening? You're just depressed about Alecia running away. You're depressed because Mama's dead, and you never reacted. There's no need to drop out of divinity school." This speech comes out harsher than I intend.

"You're the one who's depressed because Mama's dead," Ben says. "You're the one who can't get over it. I mean, you didn't even—" He stops abruptly.

"I didn't even what?" I ask.

I didn't even come home right after the accident. I stayed to finish working even though someone could've covered for me. I wasn't with her when she died, only because I never expected she would die. I was as naïve as Mrs. Swithen, thinking that loving someone can make them survive, thinking that my father's presence would ensure she'd be given the best care. He was an orthopedist, after all, and Mama was filled with broken bones. I just didn't understand that sometimes it doesn't matter how many doctors are in the room. Death can still get its way.

"Forget it," Ben says now.

"Forget what?" I ask. But I'm glad he doesn't say more. It would be too hard to hear him say that I let my mother down when she probably needed me the most.

"Look, Holly, I do need to drop out of seminary," Ben says after a moment. "I've been confused for a while."

"But what about the Call?" I ask. "What about your spiritual responsibility? You were lucky enough to have a conversion experience. Now you're supposed to . . ."

"Invent that for other people? Well, I can't," he says.

For some reason, I really want him to believe in God and Jesus and the Miracles. I want him to believe enough for the both of us. Because if Ben's been reCalled, maybe I've been, too.

"Did you tell Dad?" I ask.

"Yeah, I told him. He seemed pleased, actually, seemed to think I'll have lots of free time to help him work on the house. He doesn't remember that they asked me never to come back to Habitat for Humanity after I installed all those doors backwards."

"What about Grandmother?"

"She asked if I could at least get a Ph.D. out of this. When I said no, she warned me that I could potentially turn out to be a Nothing."

According to Eve, turning into a Nothing was one of the worst things that could happen to a human being, next to getting arrested. Nothingness befell unmotivated, stupid people—often "the crumbs" who exuded the most school spirit, as if life didn't get any better after high school. As the senior class Spirit Award recipient myself, I've always been worried that Nothingness could happen to me, too.

"So, what are you going to do?" I ask.

"Hell, I don't know. I don't even know if I'm getting married. Maybe I will be a Nothing. Maybe I am a Nothing. It's strange, though. I've never dropped out of anything before."

"Yeah, there's been a scourge of that lately," I say wryly as another burst of laughter comes from the kitchen vent over my head. *What the hell is so funny up there?*

"So, can I talk to her?" Ben asks. "Is she there? Does she want to talk to me?"

From the sounds of it, Alecia probably wants to ride off into the sunset with Ed Clemens. "Um, yeah. She's...I'll get her," I say. "Hey, do you remember Edwin Clemens from Mrs. Sandler's class?"

"Who?"

"The kid that sat at our table? He came late in the year? And then he left three months later? And Mrs. Sandler cried, because he was her favorite?"

"I remember Mrs. Sandler," Ben says. "I don't remember her crying."

"You don't remember Ed?" I ask. "He was really popular."

"In third grade? No one was popular, Holly."

"Other children *gave* him balloons on Balloon Launch Day."

"Oh, wait, that kid. He's the one who smashed my Matchbox car! I'll never forget it. One day I was playing with my cars at recess—and you know, Mama was always warning me that I'd lose them. So the Balloon Kid comes up to check out my collection, and out of nowhere he stomps on my red Corvette. He just squashed it. For no reason! We weren't even having a conversation."

"Are you sure that wasn't Nicolas Olzewski?"

"No, it wasn't Poor Nicolas. It was definitely the new guy, the one everybody loved."

"Well, he's here," I say.

"Who?"

"Ed. The Balloon Kid. He lives in my dorm, only they call it a 'flat.'"

"What's he doing there?"

"He works at the same hospital I do," I say.

"That's really weird. Is he still a prick?"

"Um, it's really too early to tell," I say.

BACK IN THE KITCHEN, Marian is furiously peeling a carrot, and Alecia is tilting her head back and laughing so boisterously that she could be an entire TV sitcom audience.

Ed is saying, "Mikey was on the Life cereal box, and he was like forty years old. Last I'd heard he'd *died* eating pop rocks and drinking Coke."

"It's Ben," I tell Alecia.

"Here?" she asks, sobering up, her eyes growing wide. She even glances behind her, as if she's worried he might suddenly waltz through the kitchen door.

"On the phone," I say. It sounds like an order.

"Is he pissed?"

"Go talk to him and find out," I say, and stare at her until she steals herself from the seat and out the kitchen door. I feel like Mr. Danvers, with the power to move people with only a look.

"Who's Ben?" Ed asks, once she's gone.

"My twin brother. Her fiancé. The boy who ate paste."

Ed blinks a couple of times, looks puzzled, but doesn't comment on that. "I hope you don't mind. I stole some of your 'American Salad,'" Ed says, holding up the bag. "I love the way the veggies are all cut up for you."

"Did you maybe want a plate?" He's using a fork to spear the lettuce leaves, and if he's not careful, the prongs will go right through to his hand. I'm already imagining putting in the stitches.

"Oh, no, eating out of the bag is the best part," Ed says, smiling and crunching on a piece of celery. "It makes me feel like an astronaut."

"Really?" I put the proffered plate down and look at him curiously. "Do you remember Astropaks?"

"Astropaks?" he repeats. I watch as his eyebrows go from furrowed zigzags into arcs of recognition. Ed snaps his fingers and says, "Astropaks! Yeah! Now, that's a word I haven't heard in a long time."

We both start laughing. When Marian doesn't look up from her extremely engrossing carrots, I explain to the back of her head how at Misty Creek Elementary, Astropaks temporarily replaced the milk carton, and drinks were sold in tiny plastic bags.

Ed smiles, pushing some of his silky hair behind his ear. "Loved Astropaks. Had to get the straw in just right or the whole thing would explode. It's what they used on the space shuttle, you know."

"The whole gimmick never made sense to me, though," I say, digging through the pantry to try to come up with something I may have purchased. "*We* weren't weightless. We were just a bunch of little kids barely coping with gravity, and then they expected us to suck liquids out of bags? I think I was thirsty for all of third grade."

"Well, I was bummed, anyway, once they reinstated the carton. I knew I wasn't missing out on anything by leaving Maryland."

"Oh, you missed out on a lot," I say, thinking of three more years of balloon launches and field days and singing "Spread a Little Lovin' " in music class. . . .

"Did I?" Ed says, staring at me so intently that I have to look away—first from him and then from Alecia, who, apparently done speaking to Ben, is standing in the kitchen doorway again. I grab the first thing my hand bumps into: a five pound bag of sunflower seeds. Looks like I'll be enjoying seeds for dinner.

"Well, you two have a lot of catching up to do," Alecia says, folding her arms over her chest, eyes darting back and forth. "You know what it means, don't you? Remeeting after all these years? It's fate."

Ed only chuckles and says, "I don't know about that," while I can feel my face turning scarlet, from embarrassment this time.

(If Ben now has a minimum of six different laughs, I've been told that I turn four different shades of red.)

"What's for dinner tonight, Marian? A lettuce leaf and a single bean?" Ed asks, obviously trying to change the subject.

"Bugger off, Ed!" Marian retorts, shredding harder. The sink is filling up with so much carrot that she could be part of an assembly line for prefabbed American Salad.

"Oh, well. Might as well. I've got work to do." He shrugs and raises his bottle once again before ambling out.

"Thanks for the beer!" Alecia calls.

I wonder what kind of work that can mean. *What does he do in his room? Where does he go every night?*

When I realize Alecia's watching me, I give her a withering look.

"What?"

"You know what," I say, and then when she feigns confusion, I add, "Fate?"

"Holly, come on. He's hot. Don't pretend you can't see that. What do you think, Marian?" Alecia turns and asks. There's something about her poised eyebrows and expectant expression that makes her look as though she's missing her microphone. Marian, on the other hand, looks blank, as if she hasn't been standing by the sink during our entire exchange, whittling carrots down to the size of pencils.

"Pardon?"

"Do you think Ed is handsome?" Alecia enunciates.

"Oh, no. I suppose some might find...but he's...he's..." Marian is stammering so much that it's clear that she's imagined him naked. Her face is blooming with color. It's nice to see that she's alive.

"An orderly?" I ask.

"Divorced," she finally manages.

"Divorced? Really?" It makes me sad for a second to think we never knew what was coming, back in Mrs. Sandler's third-grade class: that Mama would be dead in twenty years, and Ed divorced by the age of thirty. It's probably better that we didn't know.

"And he left his new fiancée at the altar before coming here. She still calls every night, begging him to come home. He's a serial monogamist," Marian says, her pale blue eyes growing big and fearful, as if we should all lock our doors and carry sidearms.

"Now, if you'll excuse me," she says, leaving the kitchen, balancing her salad dish on top of her glass of water.

As the door swings shut behind Marian, I exchange the sunflower seeds for a box of fusilli, fill up a pot of water, and then set it onto the stove before turning the gas on. "So, what did Ben say?"

Alecia sits up straighter and looks indignant. "I really don't think that's any of your business."

"Oh, really? Well, are you going to tell me what you want from me, or is that not my business either?" I ask, folding my arms over my chest. The stove is popping and hissing.

"You have never liked me," Alecia says in a different tone than her Action News voice, yet the cameras might as well be rolling.

I think of a conversation I once had with my mother about how to handle patients that I just don't like. "You don't have to like everyone. You just have to treat them all the same," she said.

"I don't *dis*like you," I say now.

"You never returned my call," Alecia says. "I left a message on your machine one time."

"I told Ben to tell you that I was busy."

Alecia's face falls as if she's disappointed all over again. "He said you love shopping."

"Well, yeah, but..." *Not with you.* "You told him you were going to nominate me for *What Not to Wear*. For weeks I was terrified that the TV show hosts were spying on me with hidden cameras, and that at any moment I would be humiliated on national television."

My confession makes Alecia laugh, so I decide not to mention that I can't shop with anyone but Mama. I don't want to hear her laugh at that, too.

"You met us for sushi in kelly green drawstring pants and that baggy shirt that did nothing for your figure," she says.

"They were my scrubs! I had just gotten out of the hospital."

Alecia makes a face as if I still should've known better. "Look," she says. "How many people do you think I know in Pittsburgh? I moved there for your brother, and all my friends were back in New York. I just wanted a girlfriend."

Before I even realize I'm about to say it, I blurt out: "I saw you making out with Ben in the yard at my mother's funeral."

Alecia looks puzzled, as if she can't remember. *Was I at a funeral?*

"At the side of the house..." I say.

"I might've been comforting him," Alecia says.

"It looked a little hotter than comfort."

"Like you would know," she replies, and for a second I think that Ben has told her that I am somehow still a virgin at thirty. *What color is mortification?*

Alecia must have decided that she's given too much away, because she quickly changes the subject. "Holly, come on. Let it go, already. I need your help."

"With what?" I ask. "And what is this about the Netherlands? Ben said your cousin and aunt live in London. He told me you all have been pen pals for years."

"They moved from England to Holland about nine months ago. According to Di, Roxanne's 'psi' told them to go."

"What's 'psi'?" I ask.

"A hit of Roxanne's clairvoyance. You'll see when you meet her. She calls herself an 'energy clarifier.' If you want, she'll tell you what color you emit," Alecia says.

I see how she's trying to play into my former hope that the star of *Passing On* could tell me something true. But so far Joshua Peter hasn't gotten much of anything right, besides the coincidence of the letter "V." Ben is not getting married. And Mama's best friend is not dying of a "liver ailment."

"No thanks," I say.

"I can't go alone," Alecia says.

"You're a big girl."

"They aren't expecting me."

"Neither was I!" I say.

"Holly, it's been fourteen years since I last saw them. Fourteen years is a long time just to drop in."

"But why me?" I ask. "You and I don't even know each other."

"It's not for lack of trying," Alecia says.

"Why is it so important to you to be my friend?" I ask.

"You're Ben's twin! You're going to be my sister-in-law. I mean . . . probably," she says, taking a sip of her beer, or at least trying to. She seems surprised to find the bottle is empty, even studies the label for a second as if it contains some answers. Finally she says, "It's your first weekend abroad. What else do you have to do?"

"I'm already supposed to explore Cromwell Road on Saturday," I say, reaching for a lid to cover my water. Mama always called them "hats."

"Cromwell Road?" Alecia asks. "What's on Cromwell Road besides the Fossil sisters?"

I stop, mid-arc, as the lid hovers just above the pot. "What do you know about the Fossil sisters?" I ask.

"You know, from that book, *Ballet Shoes*. They aren't really sisters. They're orphans, brought together by an archeologist, Great Uncle Matthew. They lived on Cromwell Road."

"Holy shit," I say with disbelief, so startled that the pot cover crashes down like a cymbal.

"Who was your favorite?" Alecia asks.

"Posy," I say. "She was so driven to be the best dancer in the world."

"She was sort of pathological about it," Alecia says. "A little too obsessive for my tastes. But she did have red hair, just like you. I wanted to be Pauline. The movie star. I would have worn a killer dress to the Academy Awards. Pauline always had great taste in clothes."

"I wonder who'd want to be Petrova," I say.

"Petrova? No one," Alecia scoffs. "She flew airplanes!"

"She couldn't even dance," I say.

The kitchen is suddenly filled with silence, only it's the good, peaceable kind for a change, and it settles around us like fog until the pot begins to rattle. I tell Alecia that I still have to think about it, but I'm lying. If Mama hiked up volcanoes, dove under the sea, and fell in love, then I'm going to Amsterdam. I must make an adventure of my life.

CHAPTER 8

Travel History

> "The details of the travel history are very important, even if you cannot interpret them yourself."
>
> —OXFORD HANDBOOK OF CLINICAL MEDICINE

Despite my determination to leave for the airport three hours early, we get a late start. Alecia is unwilling to fully grasp the inconvenient location of Gatwick Airport—not just in relation to Winchester, but possibly to everywhere else on earth. Four P.M. somehow turns into four-thirty, and with a stop at Safeway, a late bus to the train station, and Alecia's overpacking, we don't make the train until 5:03 for the fifty minute ride into London. Alecia falls asleep as soon as we board, leaving me alone with my bewildered regret over coming on this trip. It's already a mistake. I feel like I am betraying my brother by aligning myself with Alecia. How did I let her talk me into this, anyway? Then I remember Gemma Hawkins absently rubbing her pregnant belly, and I decide that maybe this is what I have to do to distract myself from the chaos. *Keep moving. Meet new people. Explore.* Otherwise, it's just me negotiating the End of Life for my patients and their families, all the while feeling like I'm navigating my own.

I try to distract myself by reaching for one of Alecia's fashion magazines instead. Unfortunately, it seems all the articles are geared to an entire planet of people having sex but me. *Could I be asexual,* I worry, *doomed to reproduce by budding or binary fission?*

The fashion "Dos and Don'ts" are equally disturbing. Apparently, a "Do" is a model with "slim and trim" carry-on luggage, and a "Don't" is the disheveled lady handling extraordinary baggage: a huge purse, a backpack, a briefcase, and a body-bag-sized duffel. I guess a doctor with blood all over her scrubs would be a "Don't."

I begin to get restless as more people in the compartment light cigarettes. *Only twenty more minutes of pollution,* I tell myself. Then we still have to take the Tube from Waterloo to Victoria and another train to Gatwick. And I—*oh, God*—forgot my vitamins.

Alecia finally sits up from her nap, yawns, and offers me gum.

"I can't. I quit."

"Just say 'No thank you,'" she says with a sigh, unwrapping her own piece of sugary gum.

"I hope we still make the plane. It takes a half hour to get to Gatwick from Victoria. We'll never make the plane."

"Take it easy. We're fine," Alecia says, pulling the *Cosmo* out of the cloth flap in front of my seat.

"Everybody's smoking, and I forgot my vitamins," I say.

"Um, I know I'm not a doctor. I don't pretend to be a doctor," Alecia says. "But aren't we going to eat this weekend? Aren't we having food?"

"I thought so," I say.

"And aren't there vitamins in food?"

"Oh, forget it," I say.

Suddenly a guy wearing Buddy Holly glasses gets on the train. He makes me look twice, makes me think of Matthew Hollembee. It's not Matthew, of course, but just the glasses are enough to get me thinking. Is he taking call at St. Cate's tonight? Is he taking out one of the new interns? If so, would he tell me?

We have been exchanging e-mails ever since I discovered a computer in the hospital doctors' lounge. I update him on the clinical crises going on in my life—Mr. Swithen and the Code;

Mr. Bodley and his psychosomatic chest pain—and Matthew is usually quick to respond in a way that makes me feel like I did the right thing—or at least in a way that makes me laugh. In his last e-mail, Matthew wrote, *I miss you, Holly. Things are not the same without you here.* It wasn't exactly a Simon Berg profession of love and loss, but I felt strangely comforted to be missed by a man who is both decent and kind.

Will I ever meet another man like Matthew Hollembee? I wonder. *Someone with all of his goodness but just a little more spark?*

"By the way, Ed was into you," Alecia says out of the blue, as if she's tapping into where my mind is heading next. *What made her think of Ed all of a sudden?* I wonder, noticing that she happens to be turned to a page in *Cosmo,* which contains instructions on "How to Make Your Man Melt."

Just hearing his name gives me a funny aching in my abdomen. "What do you mean, 'into' me?"

"He said 'Well, she's just naturally beautiful, isn't she?' when you left to get the phone the other night."

"What a strange thing to say." In fact, I'm so baffled that I sit quiet for a while, wondering if Alecia's lying, wondering how to ask.

"God, what's the deal with the 'new' shape-up tips?" Alecia snaps in exasperation. "They show a girl wearing a flashy jog bra doing a push-up in three action photos, and that's 'new'? Every month there's a new *stretch* or a new *exercise* that we've all known about since sixth-grade gym." She slams the magazine shut and stuffs it abruptly away with the other one.

"Geez," I say. "What's the matter?"

Alecia sighs and folds her arms across her port-wine rayon blouse that seems a size too small, the way people on TV always wear clothes. She never hangs out in T-shirts, I realize.

"I'm afraid," Alecia finally says.

"Afraid? To see your cousin and aunt? Why?"

"Well, for one thing, they don't know about Uncle Gabe."

My eyes widen. "Nobody told them?"

"Who's gonna tell them? My mother, who's completely nuts? My grandmother, who's dead? I'm the only one left."

Suddenly I understand why she's come. Alecia is the messenger. She always brings the news. She can't do it over the phone. And I think I understand why she needs me there, too. It's not easy walking the corridor alone. Sometimes, on the verge of the Waiting Room door, you need backup.

"I'm also afraid to hear the truth about my mother."

"The truth about why she . . . got depressed?" I ask diplomatically.

"I have two theories." Alecia pauses and blows some blond wisps off her forehead with another sigh. I wait.

"Huntington's chorea," she says.

"You think your mom has Huntington's chorea?"

"I just read *Hocus Pocus* by Kurt Vonnegut." Alecia turns to look at me. "In the book the guy's wife spirals into a psychotic depression. She was normal when they married, right? But she degenerates around age forty into this creature with bad hair who jumps out of bushes."

"Did your mother often make jerking, dancelike movements?"

"Well . . ." Alecia considers this, biting her lips, which are neatly stained the color of bruised plums. "She was a really *bad* dancer."

"But did she make movements *involuntarily*?"

"Not really."

"And has anyone in your family before her ever had Huntington's?"

"Not . . . that I know of."

"I don't think you have anything to worry about," I say.

"Oh, okay, thanks, Doc," Alecia mutters.

I turn my head as if studying the rows of brick houses and spires of old churches springing up as we get closer to the city. The truth is, I'm still thinking about Ed calling me "naturally beautiful." Could he really have said such a thing? And if he did say such a thing, why use the phrase "naturally beautiful" instead of just "beautiful"? The only natural thing I can think of is a horse.

"When Ed said . . . what you said he said . . . what do you think he meant by that?" I ask.

Alecia stares at me and blinks.

"Natural as in...? Beauty as compared to...?" I ask.

"Oh, I get it," Alecia says, nodding. "You're getting it confused with the *bad* kind of natural beauty."

"Well, why would he say this to you?"

"Maybe he wants me to tell you," Alecia says, as if there's nothing more obvious. "I mean, he's single and you're single. Why not?"

"Doctors can't marry orderlies," I say.

"Are you worried he's poor?"

"Alecia, I'm poor. I've got loans on deferment. No, it's just... doctors give the orders that other people carry out. You can't take that kind of power play into a marriage."

"Why does it have to be a power play? What if you have a mutual respect for each other?"

"Oh. I... forgot about mutual respect," I say. "But what if I know more than he does? Guys don't like that. It destroys the male ego."

"Holly, something tells me he could teach you a thing or two," Alecia says, looking amused. "Besides, marriage should be the last of your concerns. Why not have a fling while you're living abroad?"

"I can't do that," I say. "I don't... fling."

"Why not? I mean, *God,* Holly, I've known Amish people who've been having sex sooner than you—and they're riding around in buggies pulled by horses."

"Alecia," I say wearily. "You don't know any Amish people."

"What if you knew it would be the most memorable sex of your life before you went off to your safe little life and marriage?"

"Are you talking about you and Ben now?" I ask.

"This is about you, Holly. Try having some fun for a change."

You don't know me, I suddenly think. *You don't know that the only way I can get out of bed every day is to tell myself that one day I will be larger. Not fat, just spiritually larger. Someone who understands the purpose of life and death, understands the purpose of practicing medicine when you can't heal anyone. Someone who's not afraid of being Nothing.* As loosely connected images are floating across my mind—including the sight of my feet touching the cold tile floor in the morning and the vague feeling that joy lies somewhere beyond the battle of the day, Alecia leans over and speaks.

"Let go."

"Let it go?" I ask, thinking of my dream the other night and my one token balloon.

"Let yourself go. At least long enough to believe that someone thinks you're beautiful."

THERE'S NO MORE TIME for conversation, since the train from Winchester has pulled into Waterloo station. We hustle, me balancing my backpack and two Safeway bags, and Alecia with her wheeled suitcase, over to the escalators to descend into the Tube. The expansive circular ceiling makes me feel like a cricket, getting sucked into the stomach of a vacuum cleaner. In fact, the buglike sensation doesn't end for most of the ensuing ride, because the Blue Line is packed, and we stand the whole way.

At Victoria station, Alecia and I mill around outside the ticket booth, arguing over whether to pay extra for the Gatwick Express versus the regular commuter train. Just as we both realize our plane is taking off in seventy-five minutes and decide to pay for the faster train, we look over and watch the Express pull away.

"And when is the next train?" Alecia asks, as she pays for our tickets.

"Fifteen minutes," the man in the booth replies. "Thirty minute ride."

"Which leaves us a solid..." Alecia does the math, "thirty minutes to get to our flight."

"A solid thirty minutes," I repeat, stunned.

We thank the ticket man and move toward the empty tracks in silence. I put my groceries down to ease my aching arms and join Alecia by the yellow platform line, where she stares at the empty tracks. I stare, too, as if a boat has just sunk right in front of us.

"Fuck!" Alecia finally exclaims. "This is always happening to me. I'm always missing planes!"

"You miss *planes*?" I ask. "Planes take off without you?"

"The last three times I've flown," she says.

"You pay for tickets and then ...?"

"And I don't get to the airport! I was actually supposed to beat you to England, but once again ..."

"You miss *international* flights?"

"This is an international flight," Alecia says.

"Isn't Gatwick the airport where you have to take the shuttle to the other terminal?" I suddenly remember. "We'll never get to the other side in time."

"Why do I do this to myself?" Alecia yells up to the sky. "Why did you have to make Gatwick Airport so inaccessible?"

"Hey, now," I say uneasily. "Stay behind the yellow line."

She backs away from the platform edge, then tips over her suitcase so she can flop onto its side. Her jeaned legs straddle the tweed square like it's a magic carpet she wishes would carry her off. Her luggage is so sturdy and wide that it occurs to me that, for once, someone is carrying more baggage than I am.

"Why do I travel like this? Is it the risk? The quick pulse of excitement and loss? I lost my job, and I can't go back!" Alecia says, in a voice that sounds like a wail.

"Your job? But I thought ..."

"My sabbatical? Ha! I was leaving for leverage! If they wanted me to track down bad news, I wanted them to pay me more. I mean, God, the stories were making me sick—gunshots, rapes, bear violence—"

"I saw that one!" I realize, remembering her in the red suit, standing in the woods. "How are the campers now?"

"Dead." She turns to stare at me. "Still dead. What part did you see?"

"I remember your suit ... looked good," I mumble. "I can't wear red like that."

Alecia takes in a deep breath and looks at the ceiling again. "Nothing that I do matters."

"Of course it does. The news is important."

"Don't patronize me."

"I'm not! People live for the news," I say.

"Which is so sad," Alecia says bitterly. "Nobody cared about my uncle. They cared about the story."

"So, why can't you get your job back?" I ask, throwing down my pack and sitting on the floor of the station next to her, not worried about scuffing my old jeans.

"Because they filled it!" she erupts again. "They filled the position with some girl who's right out of college. They made her a reporter, and they're paying her less than they paid me! It's a 'good move for the station.' " She hugs her knees and cries into them. "Everything sucks. I'm unemployed. I'm unengaged. My mother's psychotic. And I probably have Huntington's chorea!"

"Come on," I say. "Is your mom really psychotic?"

"Are you kidding?" Alecia pulls her wet face up from her knees to stare at me again.

She tells me about the time at the mall when she was fifteen and cutting school. Wearing a Madonna-in-*Desperately-Seeking-Susan* outfit that included five neon jelly bracelets and a smoking cigarette, Alecia looked up to see her mother. Maddie appeared raggedy and unkempt and was unsuccessfully hiding behind a pole while using a pair of opera binoculars to spy on Chick-fil-A.

"Spy on Chick-fil-A?" I ask.

"It's a fast-food restaurant that serves nuggets and waffle fries," Alecia says.

"Right, but who was she watching?"

"The food handlers, I guess," Alecia says with a shrug. "Maybe she was getting up the guts to order. Or maybe she had a thing for one of the cashiers. I don't know."

Alecia tells me that after she stomped out her cigarette, she waited for her mother to sense her, and when she didn't, Alecia finally called "Mom!" Her friends thought she was being uncool for shouting, but she had to do something to make her mother stop hiding behind a pole, which was even more embarrassing since everyone had recognized her. When her mother still didn't turn, Alecia yelled, "Maddie!" and watched openmouthed as the wacky lady with the binoculars turned and scanned the length of the food court. When the lenses finally stopped on Alecia, Maddie lowered the specs, turned on her heel, and ran away.

"Did she know it was you?"

"I was fifty feet away from her! I'm her daughter! And she had binoculars! Yes, she knew it was me."

"Did you ever confront her?"

The Gatwick Express is finally returning to the station. Its headlight approaches in seeming slow motion.

"No way! It was all too weird. I went home and told my dad what happened. I told him I cut school—left out the cigarette part—that I saw Mom and that she was spying on the fast-food court. Dad looked right at me and said, 'She's crazy, you know. She's absolutely crazy.'"

We both stand up to receive the train, which stops in front of us and decompresses with a loud hiss. I feel like the train, weary without getting anywhere.

Struggling with our baggage—a *Glamour* fashion "Don't"— we climb on board and slump into seats across from each other. Unfortunately, no one else comes and joins us in our compartment, so I can't ask which terminal Transavia Airline is located in. But a ticket collector is bound to come through.

"So," I say, once the train starts moving, "what was your other theory? Besides Huntington's chorea?"

"Antigovernment militia group."

My eyes widen. "You mean now? Out in Portland?"

"She lives in this environmental-activist, man-hating commune and writes health-food cookbooks. It wouldn't surprise me if she turned out to be a terrorist."

"Geez Louise!"

"Of course, this is all just worst-case scenario."

"Yeah . . . hey, look!" I'm drained, but trying to sound hopeful when I see an Indian woman pushing a drink cart through the far end of the compartment. Consistent with the speed of the train, the lady in the sari is moving at a languid pace, and several minutes seem to pass before she makes it from the opposite end to where we're sitting. She speaks just enough English to make it clear that she's never heard of Transavia Airlines, but she'll find out about the shuttle.

"She's not coming back," I say as we watch her wrestling with the drink cart and the steel compartment door.

"Well, we've got thirty minutes to get to the gate once we get there. Maybe it's only a five-minute shuttle ride," Alecia says.

I start laughing. It comes over me like an abrupt surge of weakness, accompanied by the sensation of imminent diarrhea. At least the train is finally pumping along with speed, and we aren't suspended in that dreamlike, laggard state anymore.

"Are you okay?" Alecia asks.

I keep laughing, crying, and nodding, saying, "I've never missed a plane."

"Well, maybe you'll bring us luck. Maybe the plane will be detained by a needed repair."

"A repair? Geez, maybe." I wipe my eyes, sobering up at the thought. I can't help imagining a repairman like my father, a man who likes to tinker with problems rather than fix them.

"We have to make it," Alecia says with sudden renewed resolve. "I can't put this off."

"Sure . . . well, if the plane works . . ." I say, preoccupied by the image of a mechanic duct-taping the airplane engine.

"Roxanne'll know. She'll know what's going on with Mom."

"Because she's a psychic?" I ask seriously.

"Because they were sisters-in-law! Because until Roxanne ran off with Di, we were all pretty close."

"Why did she kidnap Di?" I ask. "Was she afraid she wouldn't get custody?"

"My uncle Gabe fell in love with someone else. Roxanne never really got over that."

"Did he marry the other woman?"

"Eventually, once both of their divorces came through. Roxanne couldn't deal with it—sharing her daughter with the guy she still loved, who no longer loved her back. So, she wasted a lot of time trying to get even, and nothing really worked until she took off for England."

"How'd they let her stay here without a visa?"

"Got married when she arrived."

"Are you serious? How'd she manage that?"

"She'd had an affair with Clyde, a British actor, in New York the year before. More revenge stuff. Never really worked."

"Aha!" I say, as though the plot to a soap opera just revealed itself to me.

Alecia hears it in my reaction. "I feel a little self-conscious disclosing the psychopathology of my family."

"It's interesting that you consider this woman part of your family," I say. "I mean, she kidnapped your cousin. Your uncle must've been devastated."

"Di's a big girl. She could've come home once she turned eighteen, but she never did."

"And she doesn't have any idea...about...that he's...?" I can't say the word. If Mama's still not dead to me, then Alecia probably doesn't have to believe her uncle is either.

Alecia shakes her head as her face drops into an expression of uneasiness, and my own digestive system seems to turn over at the same instant.

"Uh-oh," she says with a swallow, as she moves her feet to the floor.

"Uh-oh what?" I ask, even though I can feel it. The train is slowing down again.

"Tie your shoes and get ready to run," Alecia says. "We're at Gatwick."

CHAPTER 9

Palm Readers

> "The Philosophic Hand: This shape of hand is generally long and angular with bony fingers, developed joints and long nails. People with such a type are, as a rule, students. . . . Such people love mystery in all things."
>
> —LIBRARY OF HEALTH, 1927

The tall, skinny Amsterdam flats seem pulled down to the cobblestone streets like a colorful Hollywood backdrop. Wooden boats are parked along the lengths of canals like props, and gray clouds swell overhead to complete the surreal image. Even the trolley cars trundling past appear to be the whim of an unseen director shouting, "Action!"

"Now, *this* is Amsterdam," I say to Alecia as we walk in the daylight drizzle.

Last night, I wasn't so sure. It was one in the morning when we got off at the deserted Monkespoork train station, whose exit was underneath an overpass decorated with graffiti. Standing nearby was a Real Life Shady Character smoking a cigarette. (Unfortunately, the sari lady, who returned and gave us directions that miraculously delivered us to Transavia Airlines one minute from departure, never reappeared on the Netherlands train from Schiphol Airport.) Alecia peered around our surroundings with interest, as if the spray-painted cement contained lines of Dutch poetry, and then wheeled her suitcase over to ask the Shady Character for directions. I stood where I was, backpack strapped on and a grocery bag balancing from each hand like the scales of justice. Hadn't she ever been taught not to consult overpass trolls? And didn't I *tell* her all the taxis were back at that Central Station?

The Shady Character didn't speak English and didn't seem to understand Alecia's hand gestures for the Hans Brinker Hotel (I didn't either), but once his cigarette caught fire, he accompanied us down a gloomy street empty except for two burly shadows at a bus stop.

"See those guys across the street? Thugs. Those are thugs, Holly. But they won't bother us. Not when *he's* with us," Alecia told me, waving a finger at the leather-suited guy.

I looked around at the wide intersection farther ahead, where the brick buildings looked blue in the silent, flashing lights of several parked police cars. We seemed to have approached the scene of a recent shooting.

"I thought Amsterdam was supposed to be like Venice," I muttered before adding in a low voice, "And do you have to roll that thing?" I didn't need to whisper: Shady Character probably couldn't make out anything beyond the rumble of Alecia's suitcase wheels.

"What's the difference if I roll it or carry it?" Alecia asked. "Either way, we could get mugged."

As it turned out, the stranger must've understood Alecia's bizarre mime for the Hans Brinker Hotel after all, because he ended up leading us right to it and even pointed out the entrance. We thanked him profusely, and yet he still followed us right into the lobby and even watched us while we checked in. The man might've even tried to bunk with us if Alecia hadn't realized we were supposed to give him a tip. I let her handle it as payback for nearly getting us killed.

ALECIA THOUGHT she had made us reservations at a real hotel, but the Hans Brinker turned out to be a youth hostel. After brushing my teeth in a crowded communal bathroom and sleeping in a stuffy room full of bunk beds and other women, I was more than ready to check out this morning. Breakfast consisted of toast and Mueslix in the hostel cafeteria—I kept looking for the gruel. Then Alecia put her pajamas and toiletries in my backpack and stored the rest of her junk in a huge metal locker inside the lobby. Finally we set off for downtown Amsterdam, which is where we are now. Already I can feel it: today will be better than last night. Today we will find Roxanne.

Alecia doesn't look up from the map she's studying, just tells me to look out for a sign that says "Leidsplaat."

I try to be helpful, circling around to find the name of the perpendicular path and canal but can't. "It's above a coffee house, you said?"

"That's what Di said. The Sky Fish Coffee Shop." Alecia wipes a few raindrops off her city map.

Amsterdam is lovely, I decide, even in the rain. Every now and then, bicycle tires zipping through puddles kick up more water. The cyclists wear jeans and jackets in colors of mourning, but ring their handlebar bells like cheerful birds. I'm actually feeling cheerful myself.

"Will there be a sign of a palm out front? A giant handprint?" I ask, nearly skipping.

"There's just a flag with a big fish covered in stars," Alecia says. "I told you. Roxanne's not into advertising."

The flag overhead bears a painted black symbol covered in pinpricks of white, like a fish-shaped, cookie-cutout of a night sky. Above are the words: "Tattoos and Fortunes! Second Floor!" It's located on the corner of a skinny cobblestone alley, next to a Thai restaurant and right across from a used-book store called "Sister Betty's Banned Books," presumably owned by a lapsed nun or an English nurse.

Through the window of the Sky Fish, warm yellow light glows as groups of people linger over giant mugs of coffee. From the street, the Sky Fish atmosphere makes Starbucks Coffee back home seem as sterile as an OR.

I point to the wet, whipping flag overhead and remark, "I thought she didn't like to advertise."

"Must be new management. Roxanne gets offended if people think she's a fortune-teller. She was an internationally ranked psychic. Believe me, she'll tell you that within the first ten minutes that you meet her."

"Well..." I hesitate. "Did you want to get some coffee first? Or should we go right to the second floor?"

"You know that coffee shops around here are where people go to smoke pot, right?"

There's a pause. A strange cross between "I know" and "I knew" escapes my lips, so that I involuntarily mew.

"Uh-huh. Sure you did," Alecia says with a nod. "Let's go."

The thick smoky air of the Sky Fish smells like wet leaves in the fall. A pink-haired girl, amazingly wearing twelve barrettes in her close-cut 'do, stares at a cartoon on the TV in the corner. A waitress stops to point out the stairs to us before explaining to a group of stoned Americans that they have to keep ordering coffee if they want to stay and roll the next joint.

The room at the top of the narrow stairs greets us with light and a jangle of bells. Its pale wood floors are empty except for a glass counter displaying various designs of colorful tattoos. Psychedelic music emanates from a wall speaker and seems to pulse in time to the swirling colors of a spinning optokinetic drum, which, for some reason, is positioned on the glass counter, where a mirror in a jewelry shop might have been.

From another room, a guy appears. His blond hair, gelled into deliberate points, makes him look like a prickly cactus. His tight black turtleneck makes his gaunt cheeks look even more hollow.

"It's forty-two guilders if you're here for your fortune," he announces in perfect English.

"We're here to see Roxanne," Alecia says.

"Oh, Roxanne. She's *loong gone*. Girl had to *fleeeee*." The man makes pairs of fingers stampede across the table as if they are two little people running for their lives.

"What do you mean, flee?" Alecia asks.

"Can you say *deported*? Can you say *international incident*? Can you say *sent back*?"

"What? That can't be!"

"You're right!" the man says, breaking into a laugh. "She's just no longer with us. Lost her touch. We had some complaints." He shrugs a bony shoulder. "We had to let her go."

Alecia's eyebrows furrow. "Roxanne hated the tattoo parlor, didn't she?"

"Loathed it. *Loathed it.* And the bit about the 'fortunes' which made it sound so 'stop-n-shop.' You know, Roxanne and her 'aesthetics.' She reads *energy,* doesn't create 'predictions on order.'"

"So did she leave to set up her own psychic network . . . of the Netherlands?"

"Of course she did. She's Roxanne. Set up her very own little gig. With all the right aesthetics. Located in her own home, in the middle of nowhere, and without a *single* advertisement out front," he says, sharping on the word "single." Then he lowers his voice and narrows his eyes, adding, "So you tell me how connected she's been."

"I think they're getting ready to move back to England," I say, feeling strangely compelled to justify Roxanne's departure from the scene of Amsterdam.

"Oh, well, they better move. With that daughter of hers? Roxanne needs to get her out of here fast!"

Alecia swallows. "Who, Di?"

The man purses his lips and makes a silent whistle, rolling his eyes. Gesture finished, he snaps to attention simply by improving his posture. "I'll draw you a map."

"Oh, I have one." Alecia steps forward to place the city map of Amsterdam neatly on the counter.

"She's not on *that* map," he says, scoffing. "As usual, Roxanne is in a world of her own."

It takes him ten minutes to finish sketching out the elaborate path to take, complete with drawings of trees, windmills, and moving landmarks, like cows. None of the street names leading to her place is labeled, but it turns out Roxanne lives only three miles from town. How lost can we get?

"And that's what I tell the taxi driver?" asks Alecia, after studying what he's written. "I say, 'Left at the second weeping willow tree after the windmill on the other side of the Keirke-straat canal'?"

"Taxi driver? This is a bicycle map. I wouldn't know the best route by car," the man says with disdain. "You want to go by car, get a real map."

"O-okay. Thanks," Alecia says uncertainly, folding his piece of paper into her pocket.

"Tell her Guy said, 'You don't have to wear that dress tonight,' " he calls after us. "Tell her."

GUY DREW a good map. We pedal along on our rented bicycles in the pouring rain, passing tulips and fields of steadily twirling windmills. Fifty degrees on a June day, the cold rain on my face makes me feel light and clean.

"Now, the reference to the Police song..." Alecia says, squirming in the hood of her black poncho, which she tied too tightly around her face. "Was he saying my aunt's a whore?"

"Maybe he just likes the song 'Roxanne,' " I say, forcing my-self to look away from her so I won't laugh at the rain gear I in-sisted we rent along with the bicycles. It seemed so funny to me: renting a poncho, like renting a down jacket on a ski vacation.

"Why did he act like Di's been running wild?" Alecia asks.

"I'm sure we'll find out," I say. We're getting closer to a small cottage, where smoke spirals up from a chimney and a cow munches on the front lawn.

"How am I going to tell them about Uncle Gabe?" she asks after a moment.

Pedaling along, I think about how much bad news I've bro-ken. As far as Alecia's concerned, we are nearing the threshold of her Waiting Room. But I don't know Gabe or Roxanne, and the little I do know—their love, their affairs, their breech—is being rapidly whisked away between the wind and drizzle and the cir-cle of my feet. For the first time in a long time, I am leaving bad news, and maybe myself, behind. But I can't say that to Alecia, not when she keeps glancing my way, waiting.

"Maybe they already know," I say, for lack of better advice. "After all, Roxanne is a psychic."

"So she says." Alecia sighs.

We bicycle by the tiny brick cottage, where, out front, a little fellow works on his garden in the rain. The old man waves his hoe in greeting.

"Did you see that?" I say with glee. "A little man wearing yellow wooden shoes! He was tending his tulips, in yellow wooden shoes!"

"Hold on a second, I think that's the bridge." Alecia points to the upcoming canal bridge, which has arching metal balustrades. "Oh, my God, it's just like that painting of Van Gogh's!"

"Did he visit here, or something?" I ask.

"*Van Gogh?* Are you kidding? He's Dutch."

"I thought he was French."

"That's disgraceful," Alecia says in disbelief. "He's absolutely Dutch."

"Are you sure?" I ask skeptically.

SHE OPENS THE DOOR while we're still parking our bicycles, either because she feels our presence or because she just looked out the window; I'm not sure which. Standing on her front steps, Roxanne calls out like a blind woman, "Could that be . . . Alecia?"

"Roxanne!" Alecia says. "Should we lock up these bikes? They're rentals!"

"This ain't New York, honey," Roxanne replies.

"Of course not," Alecia says, suddenly becoming giddy. She lets go of her bike without putting down the kickstand and runs toward the steps with her poncho-covered arms outstretched, looking like a crow in flight.

I hang back to pick up the toppled bicycle and to gingerly fish Alecia's fallen purse out of the bushes. Then, after grabbing my Safeway bags from my own bicycle basket, I make my way to the front door, where aunt and niece are embracing for the first time in fourteen years. I feel a little ridiculous.

Roxanne steps back to open the door so we can get in out of the fading rain. She doesn't look like the bandanna-clad, fake-beaded gypsy that I imagined. Her red silk dress is decorated with gold stems that loop into green buds or full-bloom purple petals, reminding me of butterflies bursting from caterpillars. "And this would be?" she asks.

"Oh, this is..." Alecia seems perplexed about the best answer.

"Holly," I say.

"Holly," Alecia agrees.

"Hello, Holly," Roxanne says emphatically, giving my shoulder a squeeze. Her hair is long and black, which only makes her blue eyes more shocking. "And look, you brought us groceries from America! Safeway, no less!"

"Oh, well, it's just... I like certain foods..." I say lamely, suddenly wondering why I bothered to carry it all this way. "It's actually just from England," I say, as if that makes it much more reasonable.

"And Alecia, your hair got so light," Roxanne says with such aplomb, I can't distinguish sarcasm from true amazement. She shuts the door behind us.

"DI'S BEEN EXPECTING YOU," Roxanne says as we sit in the kitchen drinking tea from dainty blue-flowered cups—china apparently left to her by the famous psychic Olga Worrell. The house smells like Thanksgiving, warm and almost buttery. "She's been soaking the raisins in cognac ever since she realized you were coming."

"She's been waiting for me specifically?" Alecia asks. "Or just someone from out of town?"

"She said you. She actually thought it would be you and, well..." Roxanne nods in my direction. "Alecia's mother, who, incidentally, has red hair."

"Auburn," Alecia says. "She has auburn hair. At least, she used to."

"What color is it now?" Roxanne asks.

"I wouldn't know," Alecia says.

"You wouldn't know? You don't see your own mother?"

"She's in Oregon."

"For God's sake, Alecia! Oregon is still America! Go visit her. I would visit your mother, but I would be arrested!"

"Portland's supposed to be a fun town," I offer, and Alecia glares at me. I feel as if I am Ed, earlier this week, roping me into going on this insane adventure.

I decide to keep my mouth shut and look around the kitchen instead. I notice a quote in calligraphy by Ralph Waldo Emerson on the far wall: "What a pity that we cannot curse and swear in good society! Cannot the stinging dialect of the sailors be domesticated?" Over the stove a framed cross-stitch orders: "No Unsolicited Sorries." There are posted words by Emily Dickinson: "They talk of Hallowed things aloud—and embarrass my Dog—" but I don't see any dog. Just next to the shelf of china is a child's painting of a girl riding an elephant with a bouquet of balloons in his trunk—Diana's childhood effort?

"So why would you guys think Mom and I would pop in for a surprise visit?" Alecia asks, looking into her tea. "After, what, fourteen years?"

"Di has the idea something happened to Gabe," Roxanne says, no longer glib. In fact, she's staring at Alecia, waiting for her to look up again. And so am I.

"She said she saw him in a dream. He was coming to say good-bye," Roxanne goes on.

Alecia just nods and keeps looking down, until she finally asks, "When was this?"

"Sometime last April or May. She hasn't seen him since. But she's convinced..."

Roxanne waits. I start to stare into my own tea and am perplexed by the molten things floating in it.

"Yeah, he...there was...some guy went crazy..." Alecia says as the tears start to come out of her eyes. "Uncle Gabe was coming to visit me in Pittsburgh. He'd never visited before. But he was giving a lecture at Pitt—or maybe he set it up to see me and meet Ben, I don't know. I'd told him I was getting married, and he wanted to take us out to celebrate. But he never made it." She starts to weep.

"Oh, God, honey. Oh, God," Roxanne says. She reaches over and hugs Alecia. They sit rocking for a while as Alecia cries into her shoulder. Roxanne isn't crying at all. I swirl my tea in circles.

Finally, Alecia sits back and blows her nose. "So I guess that's why I'm here. Plus, I missed you. Any chance of you moving back to the States now?" She laughs a little maniacally, as if there's a sob still hovering just a chuckle away.

"Actually, we are moving, but just back to England," Roxanne says. "Next week."

"Next week?" Alecia snaps her head up and glances around from wall to covered wall. "Are you ready?"

Roxanne looks puzzled. "Psychologically? Sure."

I snicker, drawing attention to myself.

"Now, Holly, you two are friends from . . . ?"

"Don't answer that, Holly," Alecia says. "She's the psychic."

Roxanne leans back in her seat, staring at me with those bright blue eyes under very tense brows. She turns to examine Alecia, then looks back to me. "But I *am* sensing you're friends," she finally says, as though one of us said otherwise.

"Well, friends how?" Alecia says.

"Certainly not by choice," Roxanne says. "And the only people who aren't friends by choice . . . are family." She obviously doesn't like the sound of what her own voice is saying. Roxanne considers what she's said, picking up her cup of tea and letting it hover near her mouth.

She's engaged to my twin, I think.

"You're involved in a conflict . . . it involves someone you both love?" Roxanne puts the teacup down.

I stare at her, but she isn't looking my way.

"Well, yeah," Alecia says. "I'm . . . engaged to her twin brother."

"Engaged?" Roxanne grabs Alecia's left hand, apparently searching for the ring, but Alecia's not wearing my mother's emerald today. In fact, she hasn't been wearing it since the night she showed up on my doorstep. Did she lose it? Did she leave it in a hotel safe back in England? I wonder. All I know is, I want the ring back. It should've been mine.

"We haven't set a date," Alecia says.

"You broke up," Roxanne says instead of asks.

"I don't know what we did. I just left. It's complicated. He's got all these issues. Too much baggage for one person to deal with."

I'm grateful that Roxanne doesn't play customs agent to the secret pockets of Ben's brain; instead she merely says, "Perhaps your own baggage is too much for you to deal with."

"Yeah. I don't know. Maybe." Alecia sounds skeptical. "So what's up with Di?" she adds.

"Well, she's been talking about going back to school to get a degree in psychology."

"You don't sound happy."

"Oh, it's my bias," Roxanne says. "Every shrink or 'clinical psychologist' that I've met has been a little bit fruity." I must look perplexed, because she looks my way and elaborates, "A nut ball. A quack."

"Roxanne!" Alecia says, laughing with disbelief. "You're a fortune-teller!"

"What's your point?" She turns toward me. "I used to consider myself a psychic until we moved here. I was *internationally ranked*. Alecia knows that. She's insulting me."

"I'm going to go pee," Alecia mutters. She gets up from the table and leaves the kitchen without even asking for directions to the bathroom.

"First door on the left!" Roxanne calls.

I feel uneasy about being left alone with this woman, and I'm not sure why. It isn't as if she can steal me, like she did her own daughter.

"So, you're not a TV reporter like Alecia, are you?" Roxanne asks.

Shouldn't you know? I want to ask, but instead I find myself saying, "No, actually, I'm a doctor." Suddenly the room feels very small, the air too hot, and I want to leave.

"Your mother was a doctor, too?"

I choke and sputter on my last swallow of tea. I'm coughing on my own reflux, anxiety, and the sudden hope that Roxanne will give me what I want. What I was hoping to find out from the star of *Passing On* the day I dragged Ben to Chautauqua. *Does Roxanne know my mother? Is she okay? Am I okay? Is Alecia's uncle okay? Are we all okay?*

Instead of answering her question, I blurt out, "Do I have a color?"

Roxanne is startled. "A color? An aura? Well...sure."

"What's my color?"

"Your color"—she hesitates again—"seems to be yellow."

"Is that bad?"

"No. It's just that I don't know what it means. I'm picking up a lot of interference. In fact, everyone seems to project yellow lately. A rather sallow glow. I've been meaning to get that checked out."

"Why didn't you know we were coming?" I ask.

"Oh, Di knew. Di knew about Gabe. She knew you were coming...."

"But you didn't sense anything?" I ask.

"My psi has been off," Roxanne admits. "Even before the shenanigans with the new management over at Sky Fish."

"Alecia told me that psi is the source of your intuition?" I ask.

"Oh, no. Psi is just the experience of knowing things. A rush of energy. Clifford is my source."

Alecia is back from the bathroom, grimacing at the topic of discussion. "Oh, geez," she groans as she slumps into her chair.

Roxanne reaches out and takes her hand. "Honey, I love you. I'm so glad you're here."

Alecia folds her arms across her chest and gives a cool shrug, but the corners of her mouth turn up.

"So, you were mentioning your...you were mentioning Clifford?" I ask, a sheepish grin forming on my face.

"Clifford, yes. My spirit guide," Roxanne says. "We all have them. You just have to know how to keep an open mind, so you can tune in to what they're saying." Roxanne nods to Alecia, adding, "This little girl could be a psychic if she wants. It's in the blood. All you have to do is pay attention. That's all I do. I pay attention."

"How do you know his name is Clifford?" Alecia asks doubtfully.

"He introduced himself," Roxanne says.

"Can you read my palm and tell me my future?" I ask, forgetting that Roxanne never supplied predictions on order.

"I can't tell you the future. But I can give you my impression about an energy I pick up."

"Where are you going?" Alecia demands, instantly annoyed when she realizes Roxanne has beckoned me to get up from the table.

"The other room. Sometimes I need to wall off a little space so that I can read people better."

"Since when do you need a wall? You used to pick up things about people walking down the street in Midtown Manhattan."

"I'm not as sharp as I was back then," Roxanne says. "Now I need candlelight and a little silence."

"Oh, sure. Make it into a show," Alecia grumbles. "Just like Joshua Peter and *Passing On*."

We cross the hall into the dimly lit living room, where several Oriental rugs are piled on top of one another, and every corner and wall of the room is filled by another piece of furniture: end tables, corner tables, sofas, chaise lounges, a recliner. Roxanne chooses the old-fashioned parlor sofa, and we both sit down. I offer my hand.

"Both hands, please," Roxanne says. "I don't understand palm readers who don't examine both hands. It's silly not to read them both."

Uncertainly, I glance down at the hands holding mine, when I notice it: a lesion on the back of her wrist. It looks like a red spider but not a tattoo. It's not supposed to be there. My smile fades.

Roxanne's eyes are still shut, but not tightly. "Well, now. Let's see. What am I getting... what does Clifford want me to know...."

I'm staring at the bright red dot with streamers, the red star on her arm.

"First of all," Roxanne begins, "you don't see things correctly. You are bursting with love to offer and yet... you've never seen anyone in love. You don't know what it looks like."

Am I allowed to protest? Certainly I've seen people in love before.

"You've seen *other people* who you believe are only *imagining* themselves in love. But you don't want to imagine yourself in love. It scares you—*Oh,*" she says, almost tragically. "You were abandoned as a child."

"No I wasn't," I say, trying not to sound as indignant as I feel.

"You were separated from one of your parents—hang on." She pauses, straightens. "A healing light just came and touched your eyes."

I hold my breath, Roxanne's spider nevus forgotten. *Mama!* I see her all at once. We're driving in her green MG on a spring day when the magnolia blossoms rain down along the road, and she's blasting Jackson Browne, and we're belting, "Doctor My Eyyyyyes!"

"Get a new pair of glasses. Look around you," Roxanne says.

"Figurative glasses or actual new lenses?" I ask.

"Maybe you need new lenses," she says, willing to accept the idea.

I swallow, thinking of Matthew. "Buddy Holly glasses?"

"Honey, I can't see specific frames. I'm not an ophthalmologist."

My mother's lecturing voice echoes in my head: *Opticians help you find frames, optometrists can fit you with glasses, but only ophthalmologists do surgery.*

There is silence. Roxanne rubs her thumbs deep into my thenar eminences, as if giving me a hand massage.

"Oh, dear," she says suddenly, her eyes fluttering open. Something about their incredible blue makes me feel like the lights are back on in the room.

"Something bad?" I ask.

"Well, I don't know." She releases my hands and points to the lesion on her wrist. "You're worried about this."

"Oh!" I'm surprised. "Well, I just...have you had that mark since you were pregnant?"

"With Di, twenty-five years ago? God, no. This was recent. Within the last year."

I reach over and press the red sun on her skin to watch it blanch at the center. "Do you have a lot of these?"

She pushes up the sleeve of her splashy dress so I can see the pattern of spiders stringing themselves up her arm.

"It's only on my right arm and shoulder, not on the left," Roxanne says.

The stars form a constellation in the distribution of the superior vena cava blood supply.

"Do you drink at all?" I ask.

She tells me she used to drink socially, back when she had a social life. Now they don't even keep wine in the house. "Unless you count cognac. But that's just for soaking raisins," she says.

I don't pursue what that means. "Have you been tired lately? Or lost weight?"

"Well, I'm always tired. And no more than...ten or fifteen pounds," Roxanne says slowly.

I reach over and take both her hands in mine to examine. There isn't erythema of her palms or signs of Terry's nails consistent with liver disease, but the creases in her lifelines are pale when her palm is stretched flat, indicating anemia.

"May I...?" I ask, reaching up to peer at her conjunctiva, which looks almost pale, and her sclera, faintly icteric. The light is too poor to be certain. "You may have a touch of jaundice. It's hard to tell."

"Jaundice," Roxanne says. "You think that's connected to why everyone's aura looks yellow?"

"I'm not really familiar with that correlation, but it might make sense," I say, willing to accept the idea. "You've had episodes of easy bruising or bloody noses lately?"

"Yes! Bloody noses!" Roxanne says with interest, as though

this is a game, and I just produced a stop-n-shop fortune. "Within the last two weeks, I'd say . . . How many times?"

Roxanne seems to be waiting for *me* to come up with a number. "Three?" I suggest. "Three bloody noses?"

"Exactly!" She hits my knee. "I told you anyone can access their psi."

"I was really just saying any number. . . ."

"Isn't it amazing how much you can tell about someone's whole history and future just by looking at them for one instant?" Roxanne goes on.

"I was just guessing three. . . ." I trail off, uneasy in her electric gaze. She doesn't want to hear that it could be serious, doesn't want me to tell her to see her doctor. She already knows.

"Yeah," I say seriously. "It is amazing. It's almost scary."

"Hello? Mom?" a girl's voice calls from the kitchen. "Who's here? Did you check the turkey?"

"Come, come!" Roxanne says enthusiastically, jumping up from the sofa to lead me by the hand across the hall. Apparently, the discussion is finished.

In the kitchen Alecia is nowhere to be seen. Instead there's only Di going through my Safeway bags, looking perplexed. "What are these Go Aheads?" she wonders, and then puts my box of low-fat cookies onto the counter when she sees me.

"Oh," she says.

"Those are my—"

"Wait! Nobody say a word!" Roxanne holds up her hand to silence her daughter and me. She turns back to me. "Now. Tell me what you see."

"Just by looking?" I ask slowly. Di has very dark hair in braids, fair skin, and in her overalls looks like she's about sixteen, even though I already know she's twenty-five.

"Just by looking," Roxanne agrees, her eyes sparkling with devilish delight.

Clearly this must be Roxanne humor. "She's pregnant," I say.

Pregnant is an understatement. The way her belly sticks out in her overalls, she looks like a clown preparing to set free a couple of helium balloons.

"I mean, can you tell if it's going to be a healthy baby?"

"Can *you* tell if it's going to be a healthy baby?" I ask. "I mean, Diana looks healthy," I add, feeling funny about shortening it to "Di" before we've been introduced.

"It's Diotima," Di says in a delicate voice that matches her classic beauty. "My name's Diotima—like the Wise Woman from Mantinea."

"Ballbuster to Socrates," Roxanne says.

"His instructress in the art of love," Diotima adds.

Of course her name is Diotima. Despite the pregnancy, there's something about her six foot height that makes her look like she ought to be holding a torch, wearing a diadem, with her black braids flapping out from underneath.

I'm about to introduce myself as Holly, her cousin's future sister-in-law, but before I can open my mouth, Alecia is screaming from the doorway of the kitchen in a high-pitched frenzy I didn't realize she's capable of.

"You're *pregnant!*" she shrieks.

"You're *blond!*" Diotima exclaims.

CHAPTER 10

Pregnant Pauses

"Four or five seconds may not seem like a very long pause, but it is long enough to make the naïve interviewer very uncomfortable.... Extremely skilled interviewers can leave up to 20-second pauses when asking about prior imprisonment, sexual matters, or other taboos...."

— THE ART AND SCIENCE OF BEDSIDE DIAGNOSIS

'll never forget the day Gabe and I met," Roxanne says later, over dinner.

The raisins and cognac, it turns out, are not elements in a psychic's voodoo potion, but instead ingredients in Diotima's turkey stuffing, an amazing concoction of cornbread, sausage, spiced apples, and swollen raisins. Treating us like Thanksgiving guests, she prepares the turkey, basting it with butter, twice-bakes the potatoes, drizzling them with cheddar, and dresses the salad in apple-cider-bacon vinaigrette.

"I thought I was doing your mother a favor, Alecia. It turned out to be a blind date at Penn Station, New York. Maddie needed someone to pick her brother up at the train station, because she couldn't get out of work in time. It never occurred to me that it was a setup. Though I do remember thinking, 'Hasn't he ever heard of a taxi?'"

"How'd you recognize each other at the train station if you'd never met?" I ask.

"We were both supposed to carry fruit. I brought an orange

and stood by the clock tossing it up in the air, trying to be all care-free and casual, until I dropped it and had to go scrabbling around on the floor for it. Right as I straightened up again, there he was, tall, dark, and clean-shaven, stepping off the escalator. We made eye contact. He waved his banana."

Di is smiling. This is the love story of her parents, I'm realizing. It must be a subject that's never mentioned around here. And yet, when she heard the news of his death, she took it so well. She didn't cry either. I wonder if this is because if you see people as always alive—I mean, actually see people who've passed on—there's nothing to be sad about. They may be out of reach, but for Di, maybe her father is closer than he has been in a while. Either way, she didn't break down like I expected. She just kept cooking. And now I just keep eating, not out of politeness or even shyness over bringing out the contents of my Safeway bags. I just can't imagine sitting at the table spreading jam on my loaf of stale French bread. I want to hear stories; I want to be part of the feast.

"I still can't believe you were ever friends with my mother," Alecia says.

"Well, this was in the olden days, honey, before she got so strange," Roxanne replies.

"But remember the trip to the Grand Canyon?" Di pipes up, suddenly animated. "Aunt Maddie was fun then."

"God, I'll never forget her behind the wheel of that Winnebago. She swerved all over the place, but she'd always remember to signal," Roxanne says, wiping her tearing eyes.

"And the appliances were just raining down on us," Alecia says.

"That's probably why most people don't bring them camping," Di says.

"A *toaster* fell on my head," Alecia recalls, and the three of them erupt into hysterics.

I chuckle at their glee and check my salad bowl for signs of leftovers. Two lettuce leaves and a piece of bacon remain. I spear the bacon.

"God, are we done?" Alecia finally groans as Di gets up to start clearing.

She reaches with her free hand for my salad bowl, and I surrender my fork. "I just can't finish."

"I hope you saved room for banana cream pie," Di says.

"Banana cream pie?" I repeat like a stuporous drunk. "Wow."

"So, was that a labor of love, or what?" Alecia asks. She's resting, chin on hand, across the muslin tablecloth that's splattered with grease and sprinkled with crumbs.

Di runs water in the sink over the dishes and realizes belatedly that she's being addressed. "A labor of love?" she asks. "The dinner? The pie?"

"That baby," Alecia points to Di's denim belly.

"They were mutually deluded," Roxanne says, making me wonder if she believes in love at all now that she's been spurned. And is that why I'm always so cautious—I'm just afraid of rejection?

"If Di says it was love, then it was real," Alecia says.

We watch as Di shuts the water off and goes to the refrigerator to pull out a tin of ground coffee. "Of course it was real," she says simply.

"What exactly is love again?" I ask, accidentally slurring from the greasy aftertaste in my mouth. I'm thinking of Matthew Hollembee and how Roxanne said I may need a pair of Buddy Holly glasses. Could I have walked away from love without knowing it? Is it possible to find a statistically significant relationship without ever taking a chance? I wonder. Did I just "accept the null hypothesis" without even doing the experiment?

Diotima stops scooping spoonfuls of coffee into the machine. "According to Plato, Love is the son of Zeus and Poverty, born on the birthday of Aphrodite. That's why Love will always adore the beautiful, and will always be poor but strong. He isn't fair or ugly but is the medium in all things. Love handles all the conversations between mortals and immortals."

"So who's the father?" Alecia asks.

"Vincent van Gogh," Roxanne says.

"Mom," Di says, pouring water into the coffee machine.

"Is his name Vincent?" Roxanne asks.

"Yes," Di says.

"And is he not a self-proclaimed *artiste*?" Roxanne points at the oil painting on the far wall, the one of the girl riding a pink-toed elephant with balloons coming out of his trunk.

Di sighs, snapping the coffeemaker lid shut louder than necessary. "You know very well his name is Vincent Oorsprong."

"That's right. Vincent Little Pecker."

" 'Oorsprong' means *little spring*!" Di yells.

"My mistake," Roxanne acknowledges, as if it had been an honest one. "I'll tell you one thing. I never knew that Van Gogh was Dutch. I always thought he was from Arles."

She looks at me and winks.

AS THE COFFEE COZILY PERCOLATES, I watch Di whip up the topping for the banana cream pie, a meringue made out of egg whites, vanilla, cream of tartar, a dash of salt, and a cup of sugar. The electric mixer is broken, so Di works hard, turning red and concentrating as she beats the ingredients from nondescript goop into a cloud of fluff.

"About our family," Alecia says from where she sits at the table. She and Roxanne apparently aren't interested in watching the spectacle of the developing meringue. "Do we have a history of people who dance funny?"

"I can only tell you about Gabe. He had no sense of rhythm. He was an abominable dancer. Only marginally worse than your mother."

"Did he ever dance involuntarily?"

"It all looked pretty damn involuntary," Roxanne says. "You just don't come from dancing stock, honey."

Diotima looks up from her frenzied whisking. "Some of us dance. Some of us ballroom dance."

"You got that from my side, kid," Roxanne says.

Until Alecia mentioned dancing, I'd forgotten about her fear of having inherited Huntington's chorea or her mother's breakdown. Now I'm ready to digress on the topic of ballroom dancing and this Vincent Oorsprong.

"Does Mom...hate the government?" Alecia asks.

"Maddie? She's not a fan of Republicans in office, if that's what you mean," Roxanne says.

Alecia sits back from the table. "Well, I had some theories."

"About Republicans?"

"About Mom! I did visit the Oregon commune once," Alecia says. "I never wanted to go back. She's living with a bunch of crazy women who probably all had nervous breakdowns before leaving their husbands and children. One night I woke up hungry and went to get a snack downstairs. It was three A.M., and Mom was standing in the living room, flashing the lights. At first I thought she was sleepwalking, but she was perfectly awake! She said she'd noticed her neighbors flashing *their* living room lights, so she figured she might as well answer, even though she didn't speak Morse code or anything. The only neighbors she has are a few miles away, so I thought for sure she must be hallucinating, but when I looked out the window, I could see that she was right. The house sitting way down in the valley really was flashing its lights."

Di spreads the meringue over the creamy pie, chunky with bananas, pops it in the oven, and starts wiping down the counters. I sit down again while we wait for the meringue to brown.

"Alecia, about your theories..." Roxanne says.

"Then Mom suggests, 'Let's establish a pattern and see how they answer.' So she flashes the living room lights three times, and then they flash three times."

"Alecia, you do know—"

"So I'm thinking, who does this? Who flashes their living room lights in the middle of the night just for fun? Surely people who build bombs and leave them on bridges or in tall office buildings or at the—"

"Did she ever tell you that she's a lesbian?" Roxanne asks.

"What?" Alecia is startled.

Di stops sponging the counter.

"Who are we talking about?" Alecia asks.

"Your mother. Maddie is gay!"

"When did that happen?"

"She was always gay."

The coffee is ready, steaming out of the lid. Di begins putting cups and saucers onto the counter with only the slightest clink.

"She knew when she married my father?" Alecia asks.

"She'd had one serious relationship with a woman before she met Frank. But she said that she wanted children and a more conventional lifestyle."

"Oh, yeah. Because she gave me that," Alecia mutters.

"She tried hard to love your father. But they just weren't a good match. Your mother can be flighty, but she's a brilliant poet. Frank never appreciated that about her. He just kept making more money. I sound like I'm blaming him. I'm not really. He's charming and has good intentions. But he..." Roxanne opens her mouth to say more but then shuts it. "You want to ask me something."

Alecia shrugs. "No."

"Yes, you do. Tell me what you want to ask."

A silence passes that grows progressively uncomfortable. We're suspended in time, like at a traffic intersection when it seems like everyone's got a red light. *Who's supposed to be going?* I wonder, *And who exactly are we obeying here?*

I wish Di would at least create a diversion by pouring the coffee and taking out the pie, just so Alecia doesn't feel pressured to speak.

"I'm a little confused," Alecia says finally. "Why was Mom standing in the living room flashing the lights at three in the morning?"

"Honey, some things I just can't explain."

"I FEEL REALLY BAD about your stomach," Di says later as she comes into the living room carrying purple flowered sheets and pillows on the fundus of her enormous abdomen. She's obviously used to the extension of her body, or at least is handling it well, I decide after watching her deftly pop the sleep sofa out from its hibernation. In the five minutes she disappears in search of another blanket, I curl up on the bare mattress in the fetal position.

"I feel bad you're so sick," she adds, coming back in the room with a comforter.

My GI tract, usually a perfectly balanced intestinal milieu of gut bacteria and digestive enzymes, does not have the absorptive capacity to handle the rich dinner I consumed. Distending under the volume of trapped gas, my rebelling gut stretches the nearby peritoneal pain fibers, causing me to double over.

"It was a great meal." I wince and then realize Di is waiting with the fitted sheet. "Oh, here, I'll move...." Slowly I sit up, clutching my belly, so that the pregnant girl can finish the job.

"Are you sure you don't want some Pepto-Bismol?" she asks, whipping the sheet so it hovers, slowly floats in descent, and then settles onto the mattress.

"No, no. I'll feel better soon, really," I say, making a half-hearted effort to tuck in one corner. For someone with a decreased functional residual lung capacity due to her pregnancy, Di isn't terribly short of breath. I wonder if she rides her bike the distance into Amsterdam to visit Vincent or if they're taking Lamaze together.

"So, this Vincent Oorsprong," I say.

"We broke up." Di throws the pillows on the head of the bed.

"Oh."

"Over a month ago."

"Oh."

"Here's more blankets if you get cold."

She turns around just as another shooting pain hits me in the gut. The way I call after her sounds more like a groan than a question. "Who's... delivering... your baby?"

Di stops and slowly faces me again. "What?"

"Who's... delivering... who's your doctor?" I gasp, doubled over. My stomach makes an ominous sound like a tidal wave reaching shore.

"I don't have a doctor. Are you going to throw up?" Di adds, concerned. She even reaches for a trash can.

"I'm fine. Really, I'm fine," I say with a wince. "When are you due?"

"The baby?" Di looks down at her belly thoughtfully. "I don't know."

"You don't know?" I repeat with disbelief. "When was your last menstrual period?"

Di glances up and then laughs as if I've said something embarrassing. "I really have no idea!"

She leaves me alone, and I slump onto the sofa bed, trying to comprehend how gas pains apparently don't even touch labor pains. *How the hell is Di going to cut that baby loose?* I wonder.

It makes me think of my mother having to push out two babies in one shot, and I don't know whether she was lucky or cursed.

Alecia comes into the living room, slouching over to join me in the sofa bed. It looks like she doesn't want to talk but she can't contain herself. "It *reeks* in here," she says.

"Sorry," I mumble.

I'm not sure if I should ask if she's okay. I don't know how to make her tell me she isn't. So I keep talking instead. "I was just asking Di about when she's due, and she didn't even know. She looks like she could deliver at any second, and she hasn't made any plans!"

"Uh-huh," Alecia grunts, pulling the sheets roughly toward herself.

"Do you think she'll see a midwife or go to a hospital?" I ask. "Is she taking prenatal vitamins?"

After a moment comes Alecia's gruff reply. "I really don't know."

"What about Roxanne? Would she ever see a doctor? Because she should have some liver function tests and an ultrasound."

"Fuck that," Alecia says, rolling over to face the wall. "My mom's a lesbian."

CHAPTER 11

The History

> "What a patient gives you is a mixture of hearsay...innuendo...legend...exaggeration ...and impossibilities. The great skill in taking a good history lies not in ignoring these garbled messages but in making sense of them."
>
> —OXFORD HANDBOOK OF CLINICAL MEDICINE

Parchment House is quiet when I return from the train station Sunday afternoon. Exhausted, I collapse onto my bed and rub my eyes, still thinking about Alecia. When she left me in London, she got out of the taxi and slammed the door so hard, I almost wondered if we were in a fight I'd forgotten about.

"You're okay from here?" Alecia asked, unfolding the handle on her little wheeled suitcase.

"Well, yeah, but...what about you?"

"What about me? I'm done. I found out what I needed to know," she said, a comment that puzzled me because, as far as I knew, she still had no idea why her mother left her.

"Are you going home, then?" I asked stupidly.

"Home? Ha! No, definitely not." Alecia started to walk away, dragging her suitcase on its side like it was a stubborn child.

"So where are—what should I tell Ben?" I blurted, trying to make her wait. I'm still not sure why I cared so much that she was leaving. Before she showed up on my doorstep, I was ready to make a life abroad by myself. Now I feel like a game whose pieces are shaken up or lost.

"Tell him I went shopping," Alecia said before turning and stalking off, leaving me alone to pay the taxi driver and find my train from Waterloo station back to Winchester. It felt strange to watch Alecia disappear into the crush of people on the London sidewalk. I had the disconcerting sensation that I would never see her again.

It's only four in the afternoon, and I have the dorm to myself, but it's too noisy in here for even a nap. Ladybugs skitter around the light shades and daredevil in flight to the window. The water pipes—previously only knocking in eerie, low thuds—begin emitting unexplainable high-pitched vibrations. Cathedral bells clang down in the valley, and someone's car shifts gears up the street.

What if it was a mistake letting Alecia go? I think. What if she needed someone—her future sister-in-law...or a friend? *Dear God, don't let her do something stupid,* I pray, turning on my side in bed to stare at the wall. Though I'm not sure what I'm afraid she'll do—buy a two-hundred-quid pair of leather boots that she can't afford, or a tacky scarf decorated with aquamarine Trojan horses? It occurs to me belatedly that it's the first time in over a year that I've prayed to God and not my mother.

Suddenly the phone rings: a double ring so shrill and so startling that I bolt from my room, as if participating in a fire drill. Alecia is probably calling to tell me the dimensions of her expensive London hotel room, probably relaxing on a queen-size bed, surrounded by bags of new clothes and shoes—the fruit of rampant retail therapy.

"Holly?" comes my father's voice over the line. "That you?"

We haven't talked since a quick conversation a week ago, when I called to let him and Grandmother Eve know I arrived. I tell him that it's me, that it's good to hear his voice, and that I just got back from the Netherlands.

"I got to meet Alecia's cousin and aunt," I say.

"The Netherlands? What about England?" Dad asks. "Who's Alecia?"

"The woman Ben was living with," I say. "Remember? His fiancée?"

For once, I am not aggravated by my father's forgetfulness. I've spent so long blaming him for being emotionally absent and even paranoid—paranoid that Mama never loved him when she came back, paranoid that she would leave again. It occurs to me now that maybe Dad withdrew just to protect himself.

"Oh, that Alecia," Dad says. "I didn't know you two were close."

"We're not."

I wait. Static fills the line, making me wonder if my father is navigating through traffic. Before I can ask if he's on his cell phone, Dad asks, "Ben tell you that I bought a boat?" It's interesting the way he can so easily leave a reaction behind. Maybe that's why his favorite place to call from is the car: he needs to think just long enough for a light to turn green.

"No, he—what kind of boat?"

"A sailboat! It's completely dilapidated!" Dad says. "I'm going to restore it myself. You should see the thing. Looks just like Noah's Ark."

A gruesome image flashes in my mind: animals, two of every kind, drowning inside this wooden wreck. The barking and neighing, clucking and oinking reach an unbearable crescendo until the muffle of water covers their heads.

"Your grandmother, of course, doesn't approve," Dad adds.

"Have you ever done anything that Grandmother approved of?" I ask.

"I married her daughter," Dad says after a moment. "She approved of that."

"But you weren't Catholic," I say.

"I still think she liked me," he says thoughtfully. "I didn't intrude on their relationship. Another man might've come between them."

"What do you mean?" This is the first time anything like this has come out of my father's mouth, though ever since Mama's death he's been much more inclined to ruminate on the past. It's as if he keeps reliving it to see if he could've made it any better.

"Eve always told Sylvia what to do. When we got married, she told both of us what to do." He laughs but doesn't sound happy. "Still not sure why we let her stay in charge of so many things."

"So, it was Eve's idea that Mama should go away to medical school?"

"Oh, no," Dad says, sounding emphatic. "That was all your mother. Eve didn't want her to go any more than I did. She even flew down to the island one weekend and tried to guilt Sylvia into coming home."

I think of Simon's letter. *But maybe the real woman is the one who looked terrified when the dean's secretary interrupted our Heart Sounds tutorial to say your mother was coming.*

"I don't remember a single time Grandmother wasn't with us," I say to my father. "Except when you dropped us at Grammy Campbell's farm for the weekend, and she made us drink warm goat's milk and eat sugarless cherry pie."

"That was the time," Dad says a little too cheerfully.

"Well, if you wanted Mama to come home so badly, why didn't you go down to bring her back?"

"I did. Eventually," Dad says.

"Why don't I remember that?" I ask.

"You were little. And you had your grandmother. Two cheeseburgers with fries and a large Coke," he adds, and it takes me a second to realize he must be at a drive-through. "Yes, the Meal Deal. *The Meal Deal!*"

"Dad?" I ask.

"One second, Holly. Can I pull around?" he shouts.

Permission to pull around granted; my father's attention returns. "What were you saying?"

"You were telling me what happened when you went down to get Mama."

"Was I? Well, she wasn't happy with me. And I was pretty upset with her. Actually, Holly, it's not something I really feel like remembering." His chuckle sounds sad. "The funny thing is, I had everything to be mad about, but she was the one who got furious. As usual, your mother never made much sense to me. Hang on. I think I have four pennies."

"Did it ever occur to you that she was always angry because you never listened to her?"

"Yes. There you go. Is there ketchup in the bag?"

"You didn't listen to her!" I repeat, shouting.

"But what was she saying?" he asks.

"Listen to me!"

"Besides that."

There's a pause filled with honking and chewing, until finally I say, "I really don't know."

"Well, that makes two of us," Dad says.

AFTER HANGING UP, I head back upstairs and pace the four-foot capsule of my room a few times before taking Simon's letter out of my money belt. I want to peruse his handwriting again for some sort of clues. Did my father meet Simon Berg when he went down to the island that October of 1983? Had Dad found them together? Then I remember that Simon's letter was written the summer before, when Mama was still trying to end her relationship with him.

You said on our last night that we couldn't let this happen again and that, for the sake of your children, you had to go home and repair your marriage. It seems to me that your marriage was over a long time ago.

Mama must've listened to Simon—or to her normal heartbeat—because apparently, if Dad had anything to be mad about, it was that her affair with Simon continued until the invasion that sent her home. It was that Dad must've surprised her and Simon together. Suddenly I want to talk to someone who can tell me the truth—Jexy maybe, or even Simon himself. But instead, I resort to the only witness whose phone number I have: my grandmother.

With each ring, I find myself cringing, only because Eve doesn't know how to walk to the phone; she always runs, knocking over lamps and tripping over rugs in the process. Thankfully, she picks up without breaking her hip this time.

"Holly!" she says, celebrating my voice for just a second until her voice turns direct: "What's up?" With Grandmother, there are no pleasantries to discuss; life, from her point of view, is just a series of problems to be solved. At times like this, it's almost a relief.

"Who was Sylvia Bellinger?" I ask.

"Oh, darling," Grandmother says with a sigh. "You're forgetting her already?"

"I remember Sylvia Campbell. I never really knew Sylvia Bellinger."

"Well, she was so bright," Grandmother begins in her storybook voice, and for a second she could be talking about a fairytale character instead of my mother. "She was valedictorian of her high school at sixteen; she skipped two grades—"

"I know all that," I say before she can get to Mama's SAT scores. "What was she like on the island?"

Grandmother gets quiet for a moment. "How do you mean?" she finally asks. "She was herself. She was Sylvia."

But she couldn't have been Sylvia, because Sylvia didn't scuba dive or hike volcanoes or make love with a man who wasn't my father.

"When did you go down there?" I ask instead.

Eve tells me that it was February 1983. The dry season. My mother had been gone for six weeks.

"Well, what was it like?" I ask.

Eve sighs, apparently, like my father, remembering something she doesn't really want to. "It was very, very brown. And hot. There were rows of spindly, dead trees lining the road from the airport. And the cows in the pasture looked sickly—you could see their ribs. And the locals were black. I never expected the blacks to look so black. When I mentioned this to Sylvia, she got annoyed."

"I can't imagine why," I say, thinking about my grandmother as Simon described her, *looking ready for tennis in that pink sundress with her perfectly hair-sprayed helmet of blond hair.* She must've been so out of place.

"Sylvia was annoyed a lot, that visit," Grandmother goes on. "You know, we had always been so close, but there was a distance there. She was the sweetest child, such a lovely temperament. Then there was this new, angry Sylvia."

"What was she mad about?"

"Oh. Everything."

I wait. When Grandmother doesn't volunteer more, I ask if she met Mama's friends.

She sighs again. "Yes, that Jexy girl was there. Wearing next to nothing. She was peculiar. And there was Victor, of course. He and I had quite a chat over lunch. He knew all about the politics of the school and of the island." Grandmother recollects what she ate: callaloo soup, which was a lot like spinach. She remembers dropping a knife at lunch and how seven stray dogs attacked one another, trying to eat it. "Sylvia said the same thing happened to her one day when she dropped a pencil."

"Who else did you meet?" I ask.

"Well, there was the Giant and the Oriental fellow," Grandmother says, apparently meaning Thor and Ernest. Her voice turns dark. "Then there was the Jewish man."

"Simon Berg?" I ask.

"Was that his name? I can't remember," she says.

But you remember what you ate. You remember there were seven dogs, not six.

"What was he like?" I ask.

"Smooth," she says with disdain. It's the same voice she usually reserves for discussions on Bill Clinton, as if the former president had once attempted to seduce her. "He showed up at lunch," Eve says, adding that he came through the tangle of dogs on the ground just to shake her hand. " 'You have a wonderful daughter, Mrs. Bellinger,' he said oh-so-smugly."

"What was he smug about?" I ask.

"I don't know, but I didn't trust him." Eve says that later when she asked Sylvia about him, my mother got very testy. "She told me that he wasn't just Jewish, he was half Indian. She seemed to be trying to shock me. 'Indian?' I said. 'Didn't he know to put that on his application? He could've gotten into any U.S. medical school.' "

Not an American Indian, my mother told her. An India Indian.

"Hindu!" Grandmother said.

No, Sikh, my mother said.

"Shouldn't he be wearing a turban?"

Sylvia said that he must've left it at home with his yarmulke. Then she snapped, "Jesus, Mother!"

"It was the first time I had ever heard your mother swear," Eve says now, sounding sad.

They ate dinner at Grandmother's hotel, the Holiday Inn, which had a restaurant sitting right beside the ocean on Grand Anse Beach. The candlelit terrace was completely empty except for the waitstaff and the sound of love songs playing over a loudspeaker. Eve said that she embarrassed my mother by asking for "bottled water, no gas." Sylvia immediately started guzzling her tap water as if to prove she was one of the locals now.

Grandmother informed my mother that my father was devastated and that he wanted her to come home. My mother got angry, saying that he knew when they met that she wanted to be a doctor. He knew when they got married that she wanted to be a doctor. Why was he acting like she just sprung this on him? And why couldn't he come and say these things himself instead of sending an ambassador?

Eve reminded her how busy my father's orthopedic practice was.

"Oh, I know all about it," Mama said, sounding bitter.

Eve explained that Will never expected her to leave the country just for this. She reminded my mother that she had two children at home who needed her.

"Had she forgotten?" I ask.

"She hadn't forgotten," Grandmother says. "But she seemed to think that it was Will's turn. She had done everything for eight years, and now she wanted him to step up and be a father. And she knew that I was there to pick up the slack . . . although . . ." She trails off.

"What?" I ask.

"Oh. Sylvia was just angry. I'd never seen her like that. She said hurtful things."

I wait.

Finally, Grandmother says in one breath, "That I'd been running her life forever. Running her marriage. That she didn't even need to be there. She even thought that, when she didn't get into medical school, I *told* her to have children right away."

"Did you?" I ask.

"Holly! Your mother made her own choices!"

"She resented Ben and me," I say.

"No, Holly. Your mother loved you. She just wanted it all. She refused to believe that she couldn't have it all. When the medical schools didn't let her in, it only made her more determined."

I think of Simon's letter: *You were already a rumor, even before I got involved. "Did you hear she left her husband and children behind to do this?"* How could I have believed for so long that her leaving was acceptable? How could I have made her calling into mine?

My grandmother tells me how she told my mother to come home.

"You're not safe here," Eve said. "These people are communists."

Sylvia replied that their waiter was probably high, and Eve was worried that he might be a communist?

Grandmother told her what she'd learned from Ubiquitous Vic: that the prime minister had overthrown the last government, that he hadn't held an election since he came into power by a coup d'etat, that Prime Minister Bishop was "close friends" with Fidel Castro.

Sylvia asked what Fidel Castro had to do with her. And what about her dreams?

Eve replied that she could follow her dreams—just at home. She told my mother to apply to University of Maryland a few more times. She told my mother that she could be a nurse or a physician assistant. But these options only seemed to make Sylvia even more mad, and she started to cry. Eve reached out across the table, took her hand, and told her not to worry. "The Lord makes Good out of what the Devil has wrought."

Sylvia told her not to be so dramatic, that she did have friends there.

"Which is what I was afraid of," Grandmother says now with a sigh.

"You were afraid of Mama's friends? Or just Simon Berg?" I ask.

"Why do you keep bringing him up?" Grandmother asks, irritated.

"Mama was in love with him," I say. It feels strange to say it aloud to anyone, to admit it even to myself.

"Oh, no, Holly," Grandmother says. "She may have had a crush, but it was nothing she would've acted on. She wasn't like that. Your mother was *never* like that."

You keep saying I'm not like this, Simon wrote. *Not like what— happy?*

"It was so hard to say good-bye," Grandmother says, sounding thoughtful now. "She seemed to know things between us were going to change, but she was determined to stay."

Even without my grandmother saying it, I know that things were going to change, because it was the first time Sylvia hadn't obeyed her. In fact, Grandmother probably didn't like Simon Berg not because of the threat he represented to my father, but because of the threat he became to herself.

Grandmother tells me how, on her last morning on Grenada, she was out taking a walk. Because of the traffic on the windy, single-lane road, she ended up in a ditch, trying to avoid passing "reggae buses" and the Grenadian men, who, instead of whistling at women, liked to hiss. All of the hissing felt like snakes crawling up Eve's spine, and keeping her head down, she walked faster and faster. Suddenly Sylvia appeared, looking out of breath and sweaty. She'd found out from the hotel clerk that Eve had gone walking alone, and my mother had run to save her.

They grabbed on to each other at the same time. "I don't want you taking this road," each of them said, nearly in unison, and my grandmother saw tears in Sylvia's eyes.

Then my mother took my grandmother's hand and led her back to her hotel. Sylvia told Eve that she was okay with this road, even if Eve was not.

AFTER HANGING UP with my grandmother, I head back to my room and collapse on my bed, feeling further apart from my mother than I have since she died—even since I found Simon's letter. Did she leave simply to break away from her own mother's domination? But how could Mama be so selfish when we needed her? The fact that she can't answer my questions depresses me even more.

Suddenly I remember my shortwave radio, a gift from Ben when he heard I was going abroad. Usually, fiddling with the dial only produces signals of people speaking in foreign languages, but even that would be better noise than my thoughts right now.

I set it up on the windowsill. Initially, the radio only picks up static and high-pitched alien sounds. Then Led Zeppelin unexpectedly erupts from the small speakers. For a moment, I'm afraid to move, as if "Fool in the Rain" is an outer-space transmission bouncing between satellite, radio antennae, and myself. A second later the drums and whistles sequence explodes, and I let the music ease the shaking inside me. I spin in circles, do quick steps, and flail my arms. "Whhhoooaaaa" and "Ooohhhh" Led's voice sings, and I moan in unison, dancing around the tiny square of my room.

The music slows down again, but I'm still belting, "I got no reason to doubt you bay-by, it's all a terrible meh-hess..." when a voice from my bedroom doorway interrupts me.

"Holly?"

I turn and scream, not a ladylike yelp of surprise either; it's one of those outbursts usually associated with horror movies.

"You scared me!" I shout at Ed, shutting off the music. "What are you doing here?"

"I live here," he says, smiling.

"It's Sunday!" I say, still breathing heavily from my dancing and general mortification.

"I live here Sundays, too," Ed says, unfazed, apparently used to bloodcurdling salutations. He's wearing jeans and a T-shirt that make his brown eyes look gray. He looks fantastic.

"Wow. You've got a great voice. Gonna have to get you singing with the band sometime," Ed says.

"Oh, I don't think...what band?" I ask, still catching my breath.

He tells me he's the lead singer and guitarist for the Purple Tongues and even invites me to hear them play next weekend at the Café Boheme in Soho. Ed grins at me and adds, "Big Zeppelin fan?"

"Well, I like some songs. Usually, I call him by his full name. Or just 'Led,'" I say. "Real fans probably call him 'Zeppelin.'"

"It's actually a band. Not one man," Ed says, moving into my bedroom, which, as I've said, is the size of a closet. The way he advances toward me makes me flash back to seventh grade and my first boy/girl birthday party. Ed was long gone by then, probably playing spin the bottle in some other closet in some other state. Probably actually kissing the girls instead of saying, as Nicolas Olzewski said to me, "Let's not and say we did."

"See. Real fans probably know that..." I say loudly, nervous that he's getting so close. Ed doesn't seem to notice and begins investigating my desk, even picks up the picture of Mama grinning.

"Your mom?" he asks.

I nod, feeling invaded and hoping he doesn't ask me any questions about abandonment or affairs.

"You look just like her," Ed says instead.

"She's dead," I say.

"How long?" he asks, without sounding grave.

"A year last April."

"Oh, man. You're still so close to it," he says knowingly.

"Is your mom dead?" I ask.

Ed looks puzzled, as if he can't make the link in the conversation. "Um. No."

"That's good," I say, suddenly wanting him to get out of my room.

He notices the picture of my parents, Ben and me at my medical school graduation. In the photo, Ben's arm is wrapped around me.

"Your twin?" Ed asks.

I nod.

"So what's the deal with Alecia?" he asks, putting the picture back.

"Alecia? What about her? She's shopping in London. And she's engaged. What else do you want to know?" I ask, folding my arms across my chest.

"I dunno. Like, what's the deal with your brother? Why isn't he here?" Ed asks. "And what's the deal with you two?"

"What do you mean?" I ask.

"Are you friends?"

"With Alecia? Yeah, we're friends," I say, deciding right then. "Definitely. Why?"

He shrugs again. "Just curious. She came across as very . . ."

"Pushy?" I suggest.

"Single."

"Well, she's not! No, she's not. She's definitely still with my brother," I say. It feels like a declaration. "Unless you count leaving the country as a breakup."

"Worked for me," Ed says with a shrug.

"So I heard," I say.

When Ed looks puzzled, I add, "Marian said you have an ex-wife, and an ex-fiancée who you left at the altar to come here."

"Ah. Good old Maid Marian. She lurks around corners, listening to my conversations, and then rushes back to her room and blares Tracy Chapman's 'Fast Car.'"

"But only before quiet hours begin," I say, which makes us both laugh. Finally, I'm starting to relax. *You are standing in your bedroom with a gorgeous man who smells fantastic,* I remind myself.

After a moment, he looks my way as if studying me intently and asks, "You want to make sauce with me?"

"Sauce?" I repeat stupidly.

"Yeah. Did you eat while you were gone?"

"N-no... What kind of sauce?"

"Any kind we want. I was thinking of standard tomato."

"I've never made sauce. It comes in jars. From the store. But I guess... that would be all right," I say slowly.

"You gotta find out what you're missing," Ed says, and I follow him out of my room and down the hall toward the kitchen. As we move past the horrible orange sofa in the sitting room and into the warm kitchen through the swinging doors, the realization comes over me that Ed showed up at a very good time. Perhaps there really is a God who, as Ben says, doesn't give out stones when his children ask for bread. He gives out bread and sauce and handsome men who know how to cook.

So we make sauce. Or, actually, I watch Ed make the sauce, watch as his muscular arms swirl in circles when he wipes off the counters before pulling out the ingredients: garlic, onions, crushed tomatoes, herbs and spices, honey and even chocolate. I realize I'm salivating—both for food and maybe even for him.

"So where'd you learn to cook?" I ask, snacking on some of Marian's leftover carrots, while Ed expertly dices onions next to a burning candle, which he says makes the onion fumes less toxic.

"I taught myself. My mom is a terrible cook and I really liked to eat, so I figured I might as well learn," he says, sniffing and wiping his hair off of his eyes with the back of his hand. The onions are so sharp, my eyes are starting to sting from across the room.

"My mom was a fantastic cook," I say. "She made homemade bread every Sunday. And the best mashed potatoes and Yorkshire pudding. I was never inspired to learn."

"That's okay. I can teach you," Ed says. "It's like doing a lab experiment."

"What does your mom do?" I ask.

"What, career-wise? Retired gym teacher."

"Oh," I say, watching him pour the onions into a skillet with olive oil.

"Your mom was a doctor, right?" he asks, stirring the sizzling onions around with a wooden spoon.

"Yeah, why?"

"You sounded polite when I said 'gym teacher.' "

"I was just thinking about how much I hate dodgeball. In seventh grade I just stood there with my arms hiding my developing chest and allowed the balls to pummel me in the head," I say. It occurs to me that maybe I keep having seventh-grade flashbacks because Ed makes me feel as awkward as a thirteen-year-old again.

"So what happened to you after you left Maryland?" I ask as he crushes the garlic in a contraption that looks like it could make Play-Doh hair, but which is apparently called a "garlic press."

As one hand jiggles the onions and garlic on the skillet, Ed jams the other hand into the pocket of his worn jeans and gives a brief summary of the last twenty-one years since I saw him: he moved from Maryland to Marengo, Iowa, a little town in the middle of the prairie. His father worked for an agricultural company and was finally relocated to Des Moines when Ed was fifteen. Ed married his high school sweetheart—they were Prom King and Queen, of course—and they went off to Iowa State together, until Ed dropped out of school to make music.

"So, you started college but never finished?" I ask. "Did you hope to be famous?"

He laughs. "No. Didn't care about that. It was all about the music."

"Huh," I say.

Ed chuckles as he pours the crushed tomatoes into the pot. "Seems strange to you? That I wouldn't finish school?"

"Well, yeah," I say. "If you got in, and you were doing well . . . I guess I think education is important."

"And you think there's only one kind of education." Ed is not asking me; he's telling me.

I remember Alecia saying, *Ed could teach you a thing or two,* and say, "No, there's more than one kind of education."

"Yeah? Like what?" Ed asks, licking the wooden spoon.

"Well, like, there's...the School of Life. And the School of Hard Knocks," I say, which makes Ed laugh out loud.

"What about you?" Ed asks. "Did you know you wanted to be a doctor way back in Mrs. Sandler's class?"

"I guess so. I've always been afraid of death since I was little. I think I had the false impression that if I became a doctor I would have this—this weapon"—I wave around an imaginary light saber—"to slay...bad things with."

"Like Beowulf did," Ed says.

"Right. Or like a Jedi knight. So, when I applied to University of Maryland, and I didn't get in, I felt like Yoda himself was telling me I wasn't good enough. I could just imagine this little, shriveled green man linking his arm through mine: 'Holly, not everyone should try to use the Force.' When I got in off the wait list after all, I was only going because they said I couldn't. I just wanted the sword, like a possession."

I clear my throat, embarrassed. "Now, of course, I really want to help people."

Ed seems to be laughing at me, so I ask, "What?"

"I'm sorry. You just sounded so reverent when you said 'Yoda himself.'"

ED's SAUCE IS THE BEST I've ever tasted. We sit at the kitchen table by candlelight and eat pasta off of the same plate, because all the rest are crusty. I feel like Lady and the Tramp.

"So, what about your brother? He a doctor, too?" Ed asks, expertly twirling linguine on a fork. I can't help noticing how clean his nails are despite his rugged-looking hands.

"My brother is in between jobs. He thinks he's been reCalled from seminary."

"ReCalled? What does that mean?"

"He quit," I say, wiping my mouth with a paper napkin, hoping there aren't any herbs in my teeth.

Ed leans back in his chair and puts a hand in his pocket, somehow a gesture of thinking, the way other men might rub their chins. "Seems like the greatest thing to be into your religion, if you've got one. There was a guy in my college fraternity, Fred Leibowitz, only Jewish guy. He used to eat matzo and leave a mess of crumbs behind, and everyone knew it was him, because he was the only guy who ate matzo. Seemed so cool to me to be that distinctive. Like, if I even left my *crumbs* behind, people would know it was me who'd been there."

"Is that how you got interested in music?" I ask before sloppily forking more pasta into my mouth. A noodle hits me in the chin.

"Why, because my music is...crummy?" Ed looks at me from the corner of his eye.

"No!" I say, but since my mouth is full, it sounds more like "Moh!" Once I'm done swallowing, I add, "I mean, did you get into music to make yourself distinctive?"

"Mmmm, no. I didn't really know how to be distinctive. So I started eating matzo, just to confound people. Whenever they'd find my mess, they'd try to blame Fred Leibowitz, but I'd tell them proudly it was me."

I snicker and then admit, "My brother Ben's kind of worried about being distinctive. He's afraid he'll end up as a Nothing since he can't figure out what to be."

"Nothing's not so bad," Ed offers. "Ever read the *Tao Te Ching*?"

"Um...I don't think so. What's it about?"

"Following the way to the Ultimate Reality."

"What's the Ultimate Reality? The same as God?"

"It's nothingness. You know, mysterious, wonderful nothingness."

"How can nothingness be good?" I ask.

"You gotta be quiet, calm, lighthearted. You strive for nothing and everything comes to you."

"*Everything?*" I say.

"Yeah." Ed chuckles, shaking his head. "Whatever 'everything' means."

"So how do you strive for nothing?" I ask.

Ed shrugs. "By not striving."

I stop chewing to consider this. *How will anything get accomplished? How will anything come to me? If I don't strive, how will I ever get control of my life?*

"How do you know all this?" I ask instead.

"You mean 'cause I'm a college dropout? I was a theology major. Still like to read the stuff," Ed says, leaning forward again to reach for the sauce.

I watch him cover the plate with another mound of red sauce and think of him working as an orderly to pay the bills to make music, and realize how wrong I was about him. I imagine us on the playground as nine-year-olds, remember Edwin Clemens letting his fistful of balloons go.

"It's your philosophy, isn't it?" I say, watching him twirl out another forkful of pasta. "You strive to be nothing . . . I mean, you actually *don't* strive to be nothing, you just are nothing. . . ." I'm getting carried away with excitement.

Ed laughs, but not wryly, as he takes a bite. "You have a funny way with a compliment."

"I'm trying to say you're really good at just *being,*" I say.

"Yeah," he says with a nod, and his silky dark hair slips loose from behind his ear.

Over the flickering candle, we look back and forth in a silence that has become strangely shy with smiles. In the middle of the plate, our forks accidentally touch.

"Oops," I say.

Ed laughs. "You're not good at it, are you?"

CHAPTER 12

Wimbledon

> For you will be invincible
> and vulnerable in the same breath
> which is the breath of your patients...
>
> — "Gaudeamus Igitur," John Stone, MD

I am fixated on lesbians," Alecia says.

It's Saturday, one week later, and we're sitting in the bleachers of Wimbledon after standing on the famous "queue" for two hours. Alecia keeps pronouncing it *queuille* with a French zing, while Di insists, "It's Q. Like the letter." It turns out I shouldn't have wasted any energy worrying about my future sister-in-law, because Alecia called the night after Ed and I made sauce to tell me that she was okay, that she would be moving in with Roxanne and Di as soon as they set up their new flat in North London later that week. Apparently they were flying in from Amsterdam, flying despite Di's pregnancy. When I pointed out to Alecia that it was her cousin's third trimester, Alecia replied, "Well, no one really knows for sure when she's due." It was as if by pretending Di didn't look nine months pregnant, they would keep her from delivering on the airplane.

I guess it worked, because now the three of us are here, though not without much coaxing from Alecia. She had to bribe Di to come out, promising to buy her a pair of Cat Lady sunglasses this morning. (Given the weight of her enormous abdomen, Di isn't in the mood for tennis in the heat.) I was inspired to pick up a less pointy version of the same, so here we sit, sweating in our mysterious shades on either side of Alecia, who searches the stands for women in love.

"Everywhere I look I see them," Alecia says, pushing her Jackie Onassis frames onto her nose. "Those two women hugging good-bye in the street this morning? Lesbians. In the Tube, there was a girl checking me out. People probably think *we're* gay since there aren't any men with us."

I don't see how we could be mistaken for lesbians, the way we keep fighting about which male tennis players are cute. Kipp Linus is playing Mike Marlin, and we haven't heard of either, though apparently Marlin is expected to play Andy Roddick later.

Di offers, "Most men get really excited by the idea of two women getting off on each other."

"It's my *mother,* Diotima! Everyone gets sickened at the thought of their own parents having sex, and now I have to imagine Mom and the other women in that commune doing whatever it is they do with one another."

"God, Alecia. Lower your voice," I whisper, checking my pockets for a pair of sunglasses to hide in, until I remember I'm already wearing them. Between Di complaining that we aren't seeing any good tennis players, and Alecia's tirades about her mother, we're turning lots of heads in the stands around us. "Is it really that important?" I ask.

"Important?" Alecia says, swallowing hard. "My mom married my dad, and she knew she was gay! If she had been true to herself, I would never have been born."

"The only thing Aunt Maddie ever wanted was a baby. She wanted you," Di says.

"How would you know? You weren't even born yet," Alecia grumbles.

"I still don't see why it matters," Di says.

"Because, Diotima, I didn't grow up with two mommies," Alecia says bitterly. "I grew up with a daddy and a mommy. A mommy who never once acted like she wanted me, so don't give me that crap about her wanting a baby. She couldn't wait to leave me."

"How old were you when she moved to Oregon?" I ask as people around us start clapping. Apparently Marlin just out-volleyed Linus for a point.

"Eighteen," Alecia says, giving a halfhearted noiseless pat on her leg.

"Eighteen," I repeat, turning from Kipp Linus—who's in the middle of double-faulting—to stare at her. "Weren't you in college?"

"I hadn't left yet!"

"Can we go now?" Di asks.

"We just got here," Alecia says. "We have to watch one match."

"I'm dying of heat, and neither of them is even famous!" Di says.

"I thought you *wanted* to come today, Di," Alecia says. "You said when you woke up you could breathe better, like a big weight just dropped down off your lungs."

I mop the side of my sweaty face on the short sleeve of my T-shirt and sigh.

"That was this *morning,* before it got so hot. Before we waited so long in the queue," Di says. "It's just too hot to be here, but I can't go home to all that mess! Mom's idea of unpacking is doing a box a day. *I* can't handle all those boxes myself. I'm too fat.... Okay, Kipp Linus is downright ugly!" Di suddenly says. He's just smashed another ball right into the net.

"Look, you want me to unpack your things? Just ask! I'll help you tonight," Alecia says, as if that solves everything, including the current temperature. She turns to me. "So, how's your suitor?"

"My what?" I say with a jump.

"Your suitor. Ed. The divorcé? The orderly?"

"I haven't seen him since yesterday's shift," I say, pushing my sleek shades up on my nose and pretending to be engrossed in the blond girl who ran out on the court to grab a stray ball. "How do you think you get to be one of those ball kids?"

"I bet you have to be really good at the shuttle run. I *sucked* at the shuttle run," says Alecia.

"So, who's this guy?" Di asks, struggling to lean forward and look across Alecia at me. "Is he English?"

"He's from America, and he's gorgeous," Alecia says. "Holly just thinks he's not good enough for her."

"That was before I knew he had a band," I say, and then turn to Di and add, "He sings in a rock band called the Purple Tongues. He started it himself. He's very passionate about music." I sound like I'm giving his résumé. I sound like a reporter. I sound like an ass.

"So does he like you?" Di asks.

"Yes," Alecia replies before I can. "He said she was naturally beautiful. And Holly thinks he's incredibly hot, but she's paralyzed by her approach-avoidance conflict with men." She folds her arms across her chest and studies me. "This is about your parents, you know."

"I'm sorry, I thought Di wanted to be the psychologist," I say.

"It's all about control," Alecia says. "Your mother may suddenly die. Your father will live in his private world that doesn't include you. But nobody is going to change Holly Campbell. Holly Campbell will maintain control over her own life and feelings."

My mouth gapes for just a moment. I want to tell her that she's completely wrong, but I'm afraid it might be true.

"Don't you ever want to give up a little bit of your battleground?" Alecia asks. "Look, it's exciting when a man gives you that *look*. Let him be intrigued. No one's been intrigued by you before, and you forget you're a woman."

I don't answer right away, feeling indignant. *No one's* found me intriguing? Should I inform her that Matthew Hollembee was extremely intrigued by me, thought I was hysterically funny when I wasn't even trying to be, which, come to think of it, used to annoy me. I actually just got an e-mail from him yesterday saying he was coming into town to visit his mother in two weeks and that he wanted to meet me in London. I'm still not sure what might happen with Ed, but maybe it doesn't matter—after all, Matthew and I are just friends.

"If you happened to fall into bed with him, it wouldn't be leading him on," Alecia says.

"Who—Matthew?" I ask, startled.

"Ed," Alecia says. "Who the hell is Matthew?"

"My ex-boyfriend," I say. When she looks confused, I add, "The guy who took out Ben's appendix."

"Buddy Holly? He was your boyfriend?" Alecia sounds doubtful. "Anyway, we're talking about Ed. It wouldn't kill you to loosen up. You act like passion is an infection. Just keep tucking it away in your sterile sandwich Baggies."

"Leave her alone," Di says.

"What about you? You're the approach-avoider," I say. "You thought you could get married, and then when things got tough, you bolted. And now you want to give me tips?" I slump back against my bleacher seat. "And for your information, a sandwich Baggie is not sterile."

"Can we go now?" Di asks again. "I'm really not feeling well."

"I didn't leave because of Ben. I needed to find my family," Alecia says.

"Well, why don't you let him know what's going on?" I say. "He doesn't deserve to be ignored."

Alecia nods, slowly. "You're right. He doesn't." After a pause, she asks, "But what if I don't know what's going on?"

"Tell him that," I say.

"If I don't get some shade soon, I'm going to pass out," Di says.

"Di, we can go if you want," Alecia says. "Just tell me 'We're leaving' and I'll leave."

"We're leaving," Di says.

"Oh, *come on*!" Alecia says. "Let's get some lemonade first. Then tell me how you feel."

*　　*　　*

WE SETTLE ON a picnic table in the sun, drinking our overpriced lemonade that took forty-five minutes to buy. Alecia slurps hers down while urging me to go stand over by the practice courts, where she thinks she saw Andy Roddick warming up. She's hoping we can meet him.

"I'm pretty sure he's already dating a model or an actress," I say.

"He might have other pro-tennis-playing *friends,*" she says.

"You're still engaged, aren't you?" I ask, but Alecia doesn't answer my question.

"Kipp Linus is dating the model Serenity Fields," Di says. "That's the only reason he's in this tournament."

"Serenity Fields," Alecia says. "You should name the baby Serenity. I was supposed to be named Serenity, but Mom apparently looked at me for the first time in the hospital and knew I was much more of an Alecia. Can you believe that shit?" She tosses her empty cup in the direction of a trash can.

"Hard to believe," I say.

"Aren't you going to pick that up?" Di points to the plastic cup on the ground. "You can't just litter."

"Are you kidding? That lemonade cost me six quid! I *paid* to litter." Alecia holds on to her lower abdomen. "Oh, man. I've gotta pee, but look at the size of that line. Di, I know you have to go. Pregnant women are always peeing."

"By the time I got up there I could go, but I'm not standing in line for an hour."

"Tell you what: I'll wait in line for both of us," Alecia says. "You two keep enjoying your lemonade, okay? I'll give you the signal when I'm close."

Alecia walks off toward the bathrooms. The line looks about as long as the queue to get into Wimbledon itself. We watch as she tries to get closer than she's supposed to be, until several women point her toward the back. Even from the picnic table, I can easily lip-read her reaction when Alecia finally realizes the end of the line is thirty yards away: *No fucking way.*

I look at Di, who smiles uncertainly.

"What the fuck was Mom thinking when she didn't name me Serenity?" I ask, mimicking Alecia.

Di chokes and sprays a mouthful of lemonade all over me.

"I am so serene," I say. "Last week when I was meditating—"

Di breaks into a scream of hysteria.

"Last week when I was meditating I swear I was on the verge of knowing the Ultimate Reality when *some fuck* came and stood in my sunlight."

Di is laughing and crying and wincing and gasping. "Ow—oh—ow—don't do that to me."

"I explained how I was one step away from becoming a Holy Light, so he could do me a favor and *fuck off*."

"Aaah," Di says, doubling over, which makes me laugh, too. Only Di seems to have lost all control, hysterical to the point of writhing in pain. "Owww. Oh, God. I wet my pants," she says, wincing.

I stop laughing. "Di, did you wet your pants or did your water break?"

"Well, I don't know. How should I know?" Her eyes widen in terror. "Ohhh, no."

Alecia walks up, dramatically rips off her sticker that says "I queued at Wimbledon," and tosses it to the ground.

"No way in hell will I wait in a line that long! This whole queuing thing is overrated." She seems to notice something is wrong when Di doesn't bother her about the littering. "Hey, what's the matter?"

"Holly thinks my water broke!"

"Well, did it?" Alecia asks.

"I don't know! I don't know! It was just a trickle, it wasn't a gush. . . ." She cringes. "Except it keeps trickling. I gotta get up—help me up."

"Holly—what is that—a trickle but not a gush?"

"In the movies it always bursts like a huge water balloon," Di says, staggering away from the picnic table.

"Holly, you're the doctor—what do you think?" Alecia asks.

"Well . . ." I hesitate. It's been so long since I've delivered a baby. "In the movies it always bursts like a huge water balloon."

"I was laughing," Di says hopefully. "I was laughing and—"
She suddenly winces, holding her belly while leaning on the

fence of the practice courts. Finally, she gasps, "I don't—want people staring at me."

"Nobody's staring, you've got the sunglasses on," Alecia says. She turns to me. "So, what do we do?"

"Count how far apart the contractions are," I say.

"What about the—the trickling," Alecia asks, making a face.

"It's possible that she just peed. She was laughing," I say. "Di, have you ever gotten contractions before?"

"Well, yeah, but not like this. Not in my back and pelvis. I can usually walk them off."

"All right, let's walk. Let's shake it off," Alecia says, clapping her hands together like a boxing coach.

We begin walking. Approximately three minutes later, Di grabs the fence again and moans.

"Di, do you feel the baby's head?" Alecia asks.

"The baby's head!" she says in dismay, as though the thought is too daunting to handle, as though she is having a moment that I had as a first-year medical student flipping through the gruesome pictures in my embryo book on fetal mishaps. I saw a ghastly photo of a hairy ball protruding through some orifice and when I looked at the caption, it read: "Normal Birth."

She starts crying.

"Di, calm down. Are you still trickling?" I ask. Once she nods, I make my pronouncement: "Let's just assume she's in labor and go to the hospital."

It's a slow journey weaving through the crowds of Wimbledon, especially since Diotima doesn't want a scene and refuses to allow Alecia to shout, "Woman in labor! Coming through!" Out on the street a wonderful policeman spots Di wincing and holding her pregnant belly. He immediately helps us catch a taxi, butting ahead of all the people who are already waiting. The whole moment, led by the British bobby's kindness, reminds me of *Ballet Shoes,* when the policeman helped the sisters hail a taxi after Pauline first became famous. It occurs to me that we could be the Fossil sisters. Alecia would be Pauline, after Pauline spent a few years being a Hollywood prima donna. I could be Posy, if Posy had been driven to be a doctor. Diotima could be the misfit

Petrova, if Petrova ever got knocked up by one of the members of her flight crew. We could be the Fossil sisters gone bad.

WE HAVE MORE TIME than I realized. The registrar at London University Hospital doesn't even come to consult with us until after Di has been examined by a midwife named Rosie, who turns out to be from Trinidad and speaks with a lilt that relaxes all of us, even Di. After Rosie finishes the sonogram, she hooks Di up to the fetal monitor to get a thirty-minute tracing. Alecia goes to search for a pay phone to call Roxanne, while I wait with Di in a room of other pregnant women connected to thudding monitors. I have the claustrophobic sensation that we are all trapped inside a big womb, especially when the beating hearts synchronize. It makes me imagine the way Ben and I used to be tangled together inside Mama's belly, which only reminds me of how far apart we are now.

Finally the registrar comes behind our curtain, wearing glasses that magnify his brown eyes into quarter-size chocolates. "All right, chaps, how's it holding up?" he asks, extending a hand to introduce himself as Dr. Windmill.

"Windmill?" I ask.

"Windfield," Alecia corrects me.

"*Wing,* all right? Wingfield," he says.

For some reason, just hearing the newfound "wing" in his name makes Alecia and me say, "Oh!" with high-pitched approval. It makes him sound so celestial and pure. Di probably would agree if she weren't in the middle of another contraction.

Wingfield asks who's been following Di during her pregnancy, and rather than admit that she has not seen a doctor, she points to me as she huffs and puffs out the pain.

"I'm just the family friend," I say, holding up my empty hands to show I had nothing to do with the fact that she probably hasn't taken her prenatal vitamins. "I mean, I'm a doctor, but we just met. . . ."

Wingfield nods and then asks us to step out of the holding area so he can examine her cervix, behind the curtain.

Out in the hall, Alecia taps her foot on the tile floor and folds her arms across her chest. "God, I hate hospitals," she says with a dramatic sigh.

"When have you been in a hospital?" I ask, making her stare at me.

"You never watched me on the news?" Alecia asks. "Ever? Because I reported 'Live' almost every night from outside of Presbyterian. Car wrecks, shootings, drownings—when the Easter Bunny from Robinson Town Centre got whipped and beaten by those religious fanatics?"

"Standing on a curb outside is not the same thing as visiting a hospital," I say.

"Close enough," Alecia says, tapping again.

Finally, Dr. Wingfield beckons us to follow him back into the room of monitors, behind Di's curtain. As we watch, he spreads the paper strip out to read the last fifteen minutes of fetal activity, then looks at Di, who's sweating and grimacing in pain. "Jolly good," Wingfield decides, refolding the strip into neat squares and placing it back onto the monitor. "All right, chaps. Not worried a'tall. She's three cm, fifty percent effaced, minus two station, all right? And sono showed baby was vertex. I'm happy with the fetal heart tones, all right? Good variability, all right? No decelerations."

"What's he saying?" Alecia asks me.

"The baby's fine. The head's down, and the heart rate is good. Her cervix is this wide"—I hold my fingers open in a V—"and this thick"—I spread my other fingers about two centimeters apart. It's been a while, but I can still speak the obstetrical language.

Alecia makes a face, as if she hadn't asked for such a specific translation.

"The chap is doing all right, all right?" Wingfield says.

"When you say 'chap,' do you mean it's a boy?" I ask.

"P-permit me, if you will, my habit of speech. I do use 'chap' generically, all right?" He looks among the three of us. "You want a surprise, do you?"

"Surprise," Di says, still squeezing the armrest of her chair.

"Well, surprise it is. I'll be handling the delivery instead of

Rosie, all right? Baby looks a bit big per sono, but nothing to worry about, all right? Just something the midwives aren't trained to handle."

Rosie pulls back the curtain then, and for a moment I think she wants to protest, but she is actually just showing Roxanne to where we are.

"Mom!" Di exclaims.

Roxanne is wearing a snakeskin-patterned, nylon fuchsia dress that makes her skin look even more jaundiced, or just extremely exotic.

"Excuse me, you are...?" Roxanne asks the registrar.

"Dr. Wingfield." He holds out his hand.

"Windfield?"

"*Wing*—Wingfield," he says.

"Oh," she says brightly.

"Just telling the chaps, all right, baby's big. Not too big. Nothing sinister, all right? Just something I like to handle myself, all right? Now, basically, we send our para zeros walking, all right? First baby won't come willy-nilly. You go walking, young lady," he tells Diotima, disconnecting her belly from the fetal monitor. "Chap's head can drop more, and it'll help dilate her cervix, all right?"

"It's a boy?" Roxanne asks.

"Generic term," I say.

"Why don't you know what the baby is, Roxanne?" Alecia asks with a smile that looks almost challenging. "You're the psychic."

She's sick, I think. *And she's using up all of her energy trying to pretend that she's not.*

Instead of answering Alecia, Roxanne looks at me with curiosity, as if I've just spoken aloud. Then she turns back to Dr. Wingfield and asks what he means by "chaps."

"Just a habit of speech, all right?" He smiles and then points behind him. "P-permit me, if you will... Other patients are waiting for me."

"We'll catch you later," Alecia says agreeably as he ducks out from behind the curtain.

"Who is he, Rain Man?" Roxanne asks.

"Help me up," Di says. "We gotta help the chap drop down."

WE DEBATE BABY NAMES out in the hall as we walk. After ruling out popular names like Ashley, Britney, Bryana, and Madison, without much discussion, it's difficult to come up with a name that doesn't arouse a large association with a person one of us already knows.

"Avoid names of cities and states," I say. "Savannahs and Dakotas are usually adorable kids who spend far too much time in emergency rooms, fighting off their rare childhood diseases."

"Lucy?" Alecia suggests.

"And Skye," I say. "Another bad omen. The saddest cases are always named Skye."

"Danielle," Roxanne says. "I've never met a Danielle that I didn't like."

"Larissa," I say. " 'Larissa' means laughing, and you were laughing when you went into labor."

"She'll grow up to be a slut with a nickname like Gummy," Roxanne says. "I knew a Larissa who was *notorious* for leaving her chewing gum behind when she gave blow jobs."

"If it's a boy he'll be named Maximilian," Di says.

"He'll be a dictator!" Roxanne says.

"Well, that's better than a slut called 'Gummy,' " I say.

"Max-a-one-in-a-million," Di says.

"Is 'Serenity' out of the question?" Alecia asks.

"What are the chances anyone in our family would be born serene?" Roxanne asks.

Di begins groaning and crying. As another pain grips her belly, she leans against Roxanne. "I feel like my body isn't my own!" Di says in despair.

"It's not your own, kiddo," Roxanne replies.

The thought startles me. Of course, I'm surrounded by evidence of this every day at the hospital, when people's bodies no longer obey them, except I refused to believe it. Di's swollen body seemed just a result of her actions. Suddenly, I see how Diotima can be as much a guest in her own flesh as the baby is.

"If it's a girl...it'll be..." Diotima struggles to speak. "Petrova."

"Petrova! Like...Petrova Fossil?" Alecia asks.

"Petrova couldn't dance or anything," I say.

We watch as the contraction lets go. Di relaxes and straightens, exhaling in relief. After wiping her brow, she replies, "Petrova flew airplanes and could fix cars. I'd love to be able to do that."

In Di's private labor suite, we spend the night next to her bed, waiting and checking, waiting and checking. It makes me feel like we're a group of people stranded at the airport after a canceled flight, impatient for our airplane. In the wee hours of the morning, Dr. Wingfield still insists the baby won't arrive willy-nilly, even after I yell down the hallway, "She's crowning!"

"Do not allow her to push," he says from twenty feet away. A woman screams from the open doorway he's standing near. "P-permit me, if you will—another delivery is imminent. Rosie will inform me of the progression at your end, all right?"

It doesn't matter if it's not all right, because he disappears with the close of a door that muffles the unseen woman's cries. Luckily, Di has an epidural percolating and is far more in control than the drama at the end of the hall. When I walk back into the room where Di waits in stirrups, Rosie is already breaking down the foot of the bed. Roxanne, wearing a blue paper gown, is telling Di, "Honey, it's *here*. Not much longer," while Alecia struggles into the blue shoe-covers, nearly tripping into the cart of shiny, sterile instruments.

"Okay, Wingfield's...on his way," I say. "As soon as someone else delivers..."

"Baby's gonna fall right out, doncha know it?" Rosie says. She points to the box of sterile gloves by the sink. "Get washed up," she orders. "You gonna catch it, Docta'."

* * *

I GET A FEELING, when it's all finally happening about ten minutes later, that being a part of a smooth birth is like riding the flume ride at an amusement park. Granted, it's the little chap who's really traveling the canal, but in the midst of the big arrival it's easy to forget exactly who's being born.

And once the head is free, the baby slips out like a boat flying down the water ride, literally splashing in blood and fluid while everyone's screaming and laughing and crying and I'm just trying not to drop him.

"Feet up, feet up, all right? *Other feet up!*" Dr. Wingfield insists from the doorway as I accidentally tilt up the head.

"Clamp de cord, clamp de cord," Rosie chants as she calmly uses the blue bulb to suction his mouth and nose. He squinches up his face and starts wailing.

"Happy birthday!" Alecia shouts. Everyone weeps freely but me. My heart beats wildly as the little guy squirms and twists in my shaking hands, but I can't let him fall. For just this second, he is mine.

Meanwhile, the heart monitor on Di's empty belly sends out a cacophony of static transmissions that sounds like a celebration— like the planets and stars rumbling in joyous agreement.

I hold the baby so Di can see he's attached, just until Roxanne uses the scissors to cut the umbilical cord and set him free. Then Rosie collects the soaking wet, grimy boy to dry him off, and suddenly the ride is over.

It is 7 A.M. on the seventh day of the seventh month of the year when nine pound, nine ounce Max-a-one-in-a-million backstrokes into the world.

CHAPTER 13

The Whispering Wall

"Preoperative care. Do not rush the patient to theatre."

—OXFORD HANDBOOK OF CLINICAL MEDICINE

After arriving on the one o'clock train from Winchester to Waterloo, London, I decide to go about sightseeing in a systematic fashion, starting farthest out on the Central line, then working my way into the center of town from St. Paul's Cathedral. In the two weeks since Wimbledon, I've been dreaming about its Whispering Gallery, which Matthew Hollembee told me about: the part of the cathedral where if someone speaks faintly near the wall, murmured sounds will be transmitted 107 feet away to a bystander on the opposite side. It's this kind of magical scenario—a gallery of whispers—where I can imagine tuning in to some celestial frequency.

But unfortunately, I won't be seeing Matthew today, despite the fact that he's in London for the week, despite that we were supposed to meet at Trafalgar Square at ten o'clock this morning. After working the overnight shift, I meant to take a twenty-minute power nap and accidentally woke up three hours later. *Maybe it's a sign,* I think now, as the Tube pulls into Cannon Street station. *Maybe I'm supposed to be with Ed.*

Getting out of the Underground, I walk halfway toward the Tower Bridge before I realize I'm going in the wrong direction. To avoid getting more lost, I walk up to a trench-coated woman pushing a stroller and ask her how to get to St. Paul's. She points to where I just came from and tells me to walk on until I reach Ludgate Hill. "Look for the dome. You can't miss it," she says.

She's right. It's hard not to notice the golden cross perched at the very top of the awesome arena, and beneath it an impressive circle of a building with stone columns, which reminds me of pictures of ancient Greece. The cathedral is so big that once I get close, I can't fit more than a pitiful swelling of the dome in the square viewfinder of my camera. Finally, I give up and plan to buy a postcard that will do it justice.

Walking up the steps to get to the front entrance, I find myself saying a small prayer as I pass through the columns. *Meet me here, God. Meet me.* It's not as if I'm expecting an epiphany like my brother, Ben, has experienced, but it would be nice to feel, well...*something*. I think of Matthew talking about truth lying in the space between things. That's what I'm hoping for: to be convinced of just one true thing.

"RICK, YOU'RE GONNA HAVE to speak louder than that if you expect me to hear you!" says a large American woman with obvious irritation. She's thirty feet away from me, but by Whispering Wall physics, her voice transmits right to my ears. We're sitting 259 steps up inside St. Paul's dome, above the organist, above the choirboy rushing in robes, above the buzz of the tourists, a perspective where everything below looks graceful and hushed.

"I'm losing you, Rick! Shout if you have to!" she hollers.

I'm just starting to appreciate the absurdity of straining to hear the walls talk when there's no one in particular to listen for when a German voice says, "Hello? Hello? Das dis ting vork?"

Glancing around self-consciously, not seeing the sound's source, I say, "Yeah, it works. The wall works."

"Where are you!" the Arnold Schwarzenegger sound-alike asks with glee.

"O-over here." I wave my arms over my head. "Underneath St. Basil's statue. Now, where are you?"

"I am here! I am here! Do you see?"

My eyes scan the great circle of the dome until I find a blond guy waving from far across the chasm on the other side. I start laughing. This is a new twist to a pickup: eye contact from 107 feet away.

"I am Johannes from Germany!"

"Hi, Johannes. I see you, Johannes!" I laugh and wave.

"Holly," a deep voice says from over my right shoulder, which makes me jump, especially because when I turn, there's no one there.

"Yeah?" Only it occurs to me that I never said my name. "Me?"

"You," the voice in my left ear replies. "It's me, Holly. Turn around."

I glance behind me, but I don't know where to look, and all I hear is: "Halloooo!" from Johannes again, transmitting from the other side of the dome. "Are you still there?"

"Johannes, I'm getting another call. I have to go."

"Holly, I'm on the other side. Just stay there and I'll come to you."

"Wait, where are you?" I ask, practically hugging the wall, but it refuses to answer. There's a pause long enough to make the surrounding murmurs sound like static.

"Holly."

This time when I turn to look over my right shoulder, Matthew Hollembee is standing there.

So overcome by amazement and relief, I gasp loudly and even punctuate it with a squeal.

He lunges for me and claps a hand over my mouth as he grabs me in a hug around my waist. "This is a cathedral, Holly. You can't scream in a cathedral!" But he's not angry; he's smiling and laughing and as soon as I nod that I'll be quiet, he releases his hand-muzzle from my mouth. I give him a hug. It's a tight hug, too. I don't think I've ever been so happy to see a familiar face— or his face.

"What are you doing here?" I whisper.

"I told you. Every time I come home, I must see the cathedral. What are you doing here?"

"I'm ... being a tourist."

"But you never showed up at Trafalgar Square!"

"I overslept," I say. "I had no way of reaching you."

"But I rang you three times this morning! No one answered."

"I sleep soundly when I've been up all night," I say sheepishly—sheepish because I can't get the smile off my face, which doesn't seem right for an apology. "If I'd heard the phone, I would've picked up. If my alarm clock hadn't died, I would've been there...." I trail off.

Luckily Matthew is smiling, too. "So whatdaya say, bay-bee?" he finally asks. "Can I take you to the top?"

Given his dead-on American accent, it's hard not to think he's cute.

THE NEXT 368 STEPS aren't so easy. Trying to keep up with the myriad schoolchildren, we start out at a bounding pace, until about halfway, when we deteriorate into graceless trudging. Finally, thighs burning, we make it, stumbling out into the wind, flying high on the third largest dome in the world. London spreads out in miles of church spires and Gothic buttresses and triangular rooftops.

"We're so bloody high!" one of the children screams as he scrambles closer to the view.

Matthew and I follow him to the edge to see the Thames winding through the city landscape. The river runs somewhere beyond the clock-face atop a golden structure.

"Hey, there's the other Big Ben!" I say.

"The *other* Big Ben?"

"Growing up, I always thought Big Ben was the clock in downtown Baltimore," I say, digging into my pocket to take out my list of sightseeing plans. "Now I can cross that off."

"Cross it off? From this distance?" Matthew sounds baffled. He takes the paper out of my hand, his eyes darting over the items. "Well, we can cross off everything from up here. Tower Bridge, Westminster Abbey...Cromwell Road—is that for the Victoria and Albert Museum?"

"A museum? No. I just have to see the road. It's where the Fossil sisters lived."

"Whoever they are," Matthew says. "You realize that you could've accomplished all your sightseeing on the plane?"

"I didn't think of it at the time," I say, reaching out to reclaim my list. But the wind rips it from Matthew's hand, and we both watch as it flaps away like a suicidal bird.

"You littered!" one of the schoolboys says, pointing.

"That's not litter, it's my To Do list!" I say.

"I do apologize—it just flew out of my hand," Matthew says, straightening his glasses into slightly crooked.

The scrap of paper whips to-and-fro, rising with a gust of wind. An airplane circles so close it seems like its windshield will soon be decorated with my carefully spelled-out plans for the day. *How quickly something becomes trash once it's let go,* I think.

We stand in silence, watching one dark rain cloud roll toward us in the middle of all that blue.

"Gosh," I say, "I feel so close to the weather."

Matthew looks at me and, after a snicker, erupts into noisier giddiness. Soon I can't help joining in. We stand there, the two of us at the top of the world, laughing our heads off at the weather.

WE TAKE THE TUBE from St. Paul's to Trafalgar Square, where we were supposed to have met five hours ago. Matthew wants me to see the lions, and besides, they were on my list, even if the list is now joyriding several hundred feet over London.

"So what's going on at St. Cate's these days?" I ask as we rumble toward our destination, lucky enough to have claimed seats next to each other.

"Ah, let's see. The ICU nurse, Surly?"

I smile, knowing he means Shirley.

"She quit smoking, so she's even more of a pest. Wanda has a new man, so her fingernails are painted with purple hearts. Mary Worthington is considering suing the hospital because she worked two hours over the new eighty-hour workweek. That sort of thing. Basically, everything is the same. Except I'm only starting to get used to it without you there. I do miss popping 'round the corner in the ICU and seeing you standing there."

"Well, I miss you, too," I say. And I do. Working in the A&E at the Royal County Hampshire Hospital would be so much more enjoyable if I had a friend like Matthew to bounce things off of instead of making decisions by myself. Ed is definitely a friendly face, but we can't exactly "talk shop." Besides, I forgot how easy it is to be around Matthew.

"This is by far the second strangest thing that's ever happened to me," I say. "Running into you like this, in the middle of London?"

"Only the second strangest thing?" Matthew says with a laugh. "What was the first?"

"Oh, well, there was this guy who went to my elementary school . . . for three months," I say. "He works at my hospital in Winchester."

"Ah," Matthew says, without much reaction.

Suddenly, I'm relieved to be here with Matthew and not Ed. *Thanks, God. Way to orchestrate,* I think. I'm not sure where all this reverence for holy intervention is coming from—the London architecture or sheer loneliness?

"Is this the strangest thing that's ever happened to you?" I ask.

Matthew thinks for a moment. "It's probably the fourth strangest coincidence."

"Fourth?" I say, slighted. "What was stranger than me?"

"Every time I travel, I run across someone I know. In Florence, it was a girl I'd known from a summer theatre camp in Oxford. In Köln, Germany, I saw my old nanny. Once in the Tube, I was reunited with my friend from high school. It's actually in accordance with the Law of Large Numbers," Matthew adds with a shrug. I must look confused because he goes on to explain that by employing the statistical principles of probability, for any average person, a coincidence can happen at a rate of once a month.

"So you were expecting to see me," I say. "Did someone tell you that I'd be at St. Paul's Cathedral today?"

"Yes, Holly. It was all set up. I waited at the wrong spot for nearly two hours and then only pretended to run into you." Matthew laughs. "I take it back. There is no one stranger than you are."

As SOON AS WE SURFACE from the Underground, I remember the main attraction and shout, "Look at the lions!"

They aren't real, of course, just huge black lion statues perched as majestically as C. S. Lewis' Aslan, the golden lion who sacrificed himself to save Edmund's sorry soul. They're so overwhelming and gorgeous that I break into a run that stirs up flocks of pigeons. Behind me, I hear Matthew repeating, "Pardon" and "So sorry," and for a moment I think he's apologizing to the birds, not the tourists feeding them.

"Your apple," he says, catching up, handing me a bruised golden delicious secured in plastic protection, which had dropped from my backpack. "No knickers for lunch today?" he adds with a grin.

"Just food," I say, flushing and turning to face the black lion, who looms over a fifteen-foot drop.

Matthew stares at the lions, too, before asking, "Shall we?"

"Shall we what?"

"Climb the lion," he says.

"Climb the—I can't get on him! He's two stories high."

"Easy peasy. Kem on," Matthew says, gently pulling on my elbow. "I'll be your spotter."

I'm in need of much more than a spotter. Once we scale the platform where the lion rests, it's obvious there's no way to get onto his back without a springboard. How does Matthew expect to protect me from the surrounding cliff if I overshoot? The lion sits like a purring peninsula, jutting out over a sea of cement.

"I'll give you a boost," Matthew says, folding his hands

together to demonstrate his method of propelling me. "You just get a proper hold on to his back."

"A proper hold? I'd need a harness with pulleys! Maybe a net!"

"I won't launch you."

"You said 'boost.' That means launch." I look around helplessly. "Aren't there any smaller lions anywhere?"

"No, no, no. You'll get on this lion!" Matthew says.

"*Are* you getting on him, or what?" a voice inquires from behind me. We turn to see a woman in a spaghetti-strap tank top, wearing khaki pants with enough pockets to sustain life on safari: pockets for food, for canteens of water, for guns and tranquilizing ammunition, as if she has designs to shoot the lion into submission instead of climbing it. "My boyfriend's waiting to take my picture," she informs us around a mouthful of purple gum.

"There are three other lions here," I say.

"Kem on, Holly," Matthew says, nodding his head toward the lion's wide, magnificent back. He's holding up his fingers, laced together.

"What if I get stuck up there?" I ask.

"*Pardonez moi,*" a greasy-hared man says. His prominent, unshaven chin seems to cut into our huddle more than his voice. "Are you climbing him? No?"

"Yeah, either get on or get out of the way. My boyfriend's got the camera set up down below," Safari Pants starts again.

"There are three other lions here!" Matthew snaps.

All of the surrounding attention is suddenly making me panic. "Okay, I've seen enough," I say. "It was nice to get this close."

"Vhat is zee problem?" the unshaven man asks.

"She's afraid of falling," Matthew says.

"It's a big drop to the ground," I add, pointing to the pavement below, where, amongst all the pigeons, a gorgeous man in worn jeans seems to be taking my picture. His hair isn't dark enough to be Ed's, but, after looking twice at his nice shoulders, I stand up a little straighter and try to get the worried expression off my face. Then it occurs to me that maybe he's a photographer for the *Glamour* fashion "Don't" section, and I slouch again.

"Take a look around," Safari Girl says, chomping indignantly on her purple wad. "Everybody's climbing on. Nobody's getting hurt. If people got hurt, they'd put up signs."

"Is very simple," the Frenchman says, taking my arm. "You take *te main*. You put it in his..." He stops, looking confused. "Wait a moment."

Matthew and I lock eyes—his are twinkly, mine feel nervous.

"You take *te main,*" the man says, taking Matthew's palm, "and put it in her *vie*."

"In my...*what*?" I ask, horrified, when the only "v" word that comes to mind is "vagina."

Matthew bursts out laughing, but I'm growing weak. I have a feeling it's too late to go home now. Everyone is going to make me hop on this lion.

"You take your hands—you put it in each other's lives, okay?"

"Brilliant!" Matthew says, still laughing. "Good man."

" 'Specially zee woman. Put your hand in his life. He won't let you fall."

I keep my hand to myself, but do use my foot to push off Matthew and climb up the tail until my own legs are wide-open scissors on Aslan's back.

"I made it!" I yell. Various people standing in the rack of birds below glance up at my triumph and have to be jealous that they aren't up there, too.

"Coming behind!" Matthew says a moment later, scooting toward me.

"Ca va bien?" comes another voice.

"Everybody wave at my boyfriend!" Safari Pants says.

So we wave at the boyfriend.

For the second time in one day, I'm thankful to be here.

AFTER WE'VE BEEN UP there long enough to annoy the people waiting, Matthew holds my hand to help me off the lion and then keeps holding it as we walk through the babble of people and cawing birds.

"So, what's that over there?" I ask, pointing to the palace with great columns, across from us. Having Matthew along is much easier than getting out the guidebook.

"The National Gallery."

"It wasn't on my list," I say. "But should we go in?"

Matthew stops walking and adjusts his glasses once again, but doesn't, I notice, take his other hand back from mine. "Listen, Holly, I'm rather late for an engagement."

"Oh." I'm so disappointed that I feel wounded. I miss Matthew, I realize. I miss him terribly, and he lives in Pittsburgh, and this was my only chance to see him, and I blew it. "Will I see you again?"

"I do hope. I'm here for a few more days. Could I come up to Winchester?"

"Well, you can, but I'm working these wacky shifts right now while people are 'on holiday.' "

"Well...would you want to come along right now? My mother is staying at the Connaught. I should be meeting her for tea..." Matthew looks at his watch "...fifteen minutes ago."

"Oh," I say, starting to smile. "That would be lovely."

WE TAKE THE TUBE from Charing Cross to Bond Street, switching lines at Oxford Circus. By the time we surface from the Underground, Matthew is pulling on my hand, practically running, because we're over forty-five minutes late.

"Why does your mother stay at a hotel if she lives here?" I ask, out of breath as I jog next to him, the vitamins in my backpack rattling around like maracas.

"She loves to make a holiday of visiting my sister—shopping, shows, and whatnot. Mum still lives outside of Aylesbury, but my sister, Charlotte, is in Earls Court."

I know better than to expect to see Matthew's father at high tea today, considering he's been dead for at least ten years.

Mr. Hollembee used to ride his bicycle the twenty miles from Aylesbury to Oxford to teach physics, and one morning he was hit by a car. He came home for a nap and never woke up. Blood had filled up his skull and pushed down on his brain. It was one of the first things Matthew and I ever bonded about back in the States. I'll never forget the amazement I felt. *Someone else has a dead parent?* It felt like such a relief, neither one of us remembered to be sorry for the other.

"Here we are, then," Matthew says as we round the corner of Carlos Place and I catch my first glimpse of the tall building. A bellman in a black top hat and green tails stands outside, guarding the door like a henchman to the Queen of the Leprechauns.

"*This* is the hotel?" I ask, breaking into a walk, hoping to avoid the bellman's scrutiny. He's watching us draw near, making me feel like we're storming Buckingham Palace. "I can't go in there."

"Just keep your hands in my pants, and we'll both be fine," Matthew says under his breath. I laugh, feeling giddy and weak as I let him pull me up the stairs, past the Lilliputian who is insisting he wants to help us, and past the well-dressed people in the marble lobby who are milling beneath the crystal chandelier. We keep sailing until we reach the foot of the impressive mahogany staircase near the front desk, but it's not the concierge who stops us. Instead, it's a white-haired woman in a royal blue dress who grabs Matthew by the arm.

"Darling, really!" the woman scolds him. "I told you I had a schedule! Now I'll be late to collect Edward from the nanny, and your sister will be all in a bother!"

"I forgot about your schedule when I ran into my friend," Matthew says. He smiles in my direction as if that's supposed to be an introduction.

"Nobody explained that there was a schedule," I say, and then extend my hand to the older woman, apparently his mother. "Hi, I'm Holly."

"The American, are you?" Mrs. Hollembee barely musters a squeeze before letting me go and turning back to her son. "She's not as I imagined. You said she was fair. Like Grace."

Grace Allingham, I realize. Matthew's last serious girlfriend, the one he broke up with before coming to the States for residency.

"She is fair," Matthew says. "Fair-skinned."

"I believe you said blond."

"I never said blond, Mum."

"Well, it's really nice to meet you," I say a little louder.

"Lovely to meet you," Mrs. Hollembee says, sounding wan as her eyes drop to survey my jeans and sneakers before coming back to my face. Her inspection makes my heart race, makes me wonder if I actually remembered to put on a pair of pants this morning after I took off my scrubs.

Mrs. Hollembee turns to Matthew and asks if she can have a word with him in private.

"No," he says.

"Well, we can't possibly stay here and have tea," his mother whispers. "She's not even dressed for the lobby."

"Oh, I'm really sorry. I can go," I say, pulling back, only Matthew isn't letting me. He's holding on to my hand, even tighter.

"You're fine, Holly. We can sit by the bar. Back corner," he says, giving me a squeeze. Once again, I let him lead.

TEATIME PASSES PAINFULLY. The three of us hunker down at a small corner table, which has a long tablecloth to hide my jeans but is unfortunately too intimate to hide the rest of me. I do my best to be forgotten by leaning back in my high-backed Victorian chair, which successfully removes Mrs. Hollembee from my peripheral vision but does nothing to stifle her shrill voice. Besides, from my particular position in the chair, the transfer of treats from plate to mouth becomes increasingly difficult. My T-shirt is quickly covered in a blanket of crumbs, but that doesn't stop me from reaching for more and more off the silver tray—for tiny sandwiches made of cucumber and smoked salmon, for dense scones full of raisins and mini-piecrusts filled with creamy custard and fruit. It is, by far, the most luxurious meal I've had in

ages and makes me wonder why I've been eating so healthfully—
so boringly—for so long. *For God's sake, it's not as if I've had my
first heart attack.*

"What about you, Holly?" Matthew asks, and I realize I've
been so purposefully engrossed in the condiment options—jam
versus honey versus clotted cream—that I seem to have missed out
on a conversation about books. Apparently we are discussing our
favorite authors. Of course, I suddenly can't remember any book
that I've read in the last ten years, other than *Ballet Shoes*. But by
the way Mrs. Hollembee is leaning forward in her stately chair
with one eyebrow raised (How does she do that?), I somehow feel
more is expected of me than an elementary school reading level.

"Um..." I pick up my tea and take a sip of it, racking my
brain for someone Ben might've read. He was the English major.
He's read everything. "I'm into American literature," I say, only
because that was Ben's passion before he replaced it with Jesus
and then Alecia and then... whatever it is now. I put down the
teacup and decide. "I love Wordsworth."

"Wordsworth, the poet?" his mother asks.

"Yeah. I love his..."—I mime something small and square,
like a book or a trap for a small animal—"collection of poems."

"Wordsworth is British!" Mrs. Hollembee erupts. By the volume of her exasperation, it occurs to me that maybe she wants to
make a scene.

"Well, Whitman's American," I say, replacing my imaginary
book with my real cup of tea. Wrapping my fingers around it, I
hunch forward as if huddling around a very small fire. It's no use
hiding now.

"Oh, *darling,*" Mrs. Hollembee says, only she seems to be
pleading with Matthew rather than me. Her pained laugh grates
on my ears. It's hard to believe she gave birth to such a wonderful person as Matthew. "Americans are so egocentric," she says.
"They think everyone and everything famous must've come
from America."

With a look, I send Matthew a telepathic message. *Don't say
anything about "the Other Big Ben."*

His mother asks me how I have the time to be a doctor.

"The time?" I repeat, setting down the cup of tea. My hands feel instantly cold and jittery, so I pick it up again. "It's just... what I do."

"That's right. I suppose that's why you aren't married and don't have children. How old are you?" Mrs. Hollembee is starting to remind me of my grandmother Eve: *The truth is never mean; it's just the truth.*

"Thirty. But my mother had two children and raised us despite being a doctor. It can be done," I say.

"Her mother even went off to medical school for a few years, didn't she, Holly?" Matthew says, choosing another salmon sandwich off the platter. "Holly was in kindergarten at the time."

"Third grade," I say, but it sounds like a mumble. "But my mother was only gone a few months. She was back before we knew it. It was like she was never gone."

"And who took care of you?" Matthew's mother asks quizzically. That eyebrow is doing tricks again.

"My grandmother. And my father," I add hastily. "He was... fantastic, and supportive of my mother's dreams and... well, it all just kind of worked out." I'm smiling so hugely that I should be on a commercial for tooth-whitening strips.

"Well, your family is the exception. Most physician relationships do end in divorce. Haven't you read that, Matthew?"

"Yes, Mother. But Holly and I are not even dating," he says. "Why must you keep nattering on about it?"

I'm strangely disappointed by Matthew's hasty dismissal of our relationship as being nothing more than friends, which doesn't make sense, since I broke up with him. Maybe I assumed that his feelings for me would stay the same. Maybe I'm just desperate for someone to want me. But at this moment, my longing feels very Matthew-specific.

"I am merely making conversation, Matthew," his mother says now. "I find statistics interesting."

"So does your son," I say, remembering the beginning, our beginning—when Matthew intended to disprove the null hypothesis, eliminate chance, and claim a statistically significant relationship.

Matthew smiles at me.

Mrs. Hollembee looks between us but only asks, "More tea?"

"CONVERSATIONS WITH MY MOTHER are like standing in baggage claim long after everyone else has picked up their suitcases and it's clear mine is never coming in. I can watch the leftover pieces circling round and round, but they'll never be my own," Matthew says later, as we're walking toward Hyde Park from the hotel. "I do apologize. I should've never subjected you to her," he says, wrapping an arm around me.

"Oh, she's nothing compared to my grandmother," I say.

"Really?" Matthew sounds hopeful.

"Well, no." I can feel the tears welling up in my eyes. "I hated it when she compared me to your ex-girlfriend."

"Who, Grace?" Matthew asks. "Oh, Mum has never quite come to terms with our split."

"And I hated it when she was grilling me about my mom."

"She doesn't understand that women in medicine can be good mothers, too," Matthew says.

"My mother had an affair," I blurt out, just like that. It's the first time I've ever admitted it aloud to anyone. Grandmother might've believed that Sylvia was capable of an extramarital "crush," but I could never have convinced Eve of the whole truth—not when she holds such a fixed notion of who my mother was supposed to be. Unlike my grandmother, Matthew won't disagree.

"When?" he asks.

"Twenty-one years ago. In medical school. I read an old letter from her boyfriend." I keep my head low and wipe my eyes before Matthew can see that I'm crying. We keep moving down the sidewalk, moving forward.

"Why does it matter now?" he asks, reminding me of myself asking Alecia why it matters if her mom happens to be gay.

Just as Alecia can't admit the truth about her own mother, I can't either. The part that hurts the most is that she wasn't around.

"She's my mother. And she's...supposed to be perfect." I know that sounds naïve so I add, "I mean...everybody slips up...."

"Except for your mother?" Matthew asks gently.

"She's supposed to...do what's right," I say, my voice catching on an embarrassing sob. I stop walking and cover my face.

"Perhaps she had reasons. Perhaps she was lonely..." Matthew says.

"That's no excuse," I say, remembering how alone I felt when Mama never came home, how I read *Ballet Shoes* over and over again in my room. It wasn't just because she gave the book to me; I read it because it was about orphans who fashioned themselves into a family, and I was desperately missing the most important member of my own.

"*I'm* lonely!" I say now. "That's part of life." Though ever since Max's birth, I can't help thinking that with the amount of suffering it takes to separate people from one another, maybe we aren't really designed to be this alone.

"You can't be that bad off. You speak the language, after all," Matthew says.

I could really let myself go and cry forever if it weren't for his earnest voice making my weepy shakes turn into chuckles. Besides, when Matthew pulls my wet hands off my cheeks, I can't bear to let him see my contortions of despair, which, according to my brother, resemble a human face melting.

"It's called a handkerchief," Matthew says, watching me stare at the silky cloth that he's just placed in my palm. I feel as if I've been invited to blow my nose on one of his ties. "Go on. Use it."

"How is your new hospital?" he adds, once I finally get up the nerve to honk into the white hankie.

"It's the same, you know?" I say, wiping my nostrils over and over to be sure they're absolutely clean. "I mean, it's different because I have to do my own blood work and run blood gases and place IVs and do EKGs...but yet it's the same. I'm still me."

Matthew laughs. "Who did you expect to be?"

"I just thought...if I left, I'd be a better doctor. But I'm still falling short. Every single day. I try to listen more," I say doubtfully, thinking of Mr. Swithen wanting his tube out, and Ed saying I didn't listen. "But I can't say that I am a good doctor. What do I do with this?" I add, holding out the soiled handkerchief.

"Keep it," Matthew says. "Please."

We reach the street corner and look in opposite directions for traffic until I notice the instructions painted onto the road: "Look Left!" I do so, thinking how grateful I would be if the correct decision were always this obvious.

"What is a good doctor, I wonder?" Matthew asks once we're on the opposite curb, heading down a bike path that meanders toward an oak tree. Its graceful branches dip down and reach up again, like a person trying to tell a very complicated story.

"A good doctor loves everybody, even if she doesn't like them," I say. "She has the power to heal, not just to observe and temporize."

"So...Jesus, perhaps?" Matthew says.

"Yeah," I say, slowly smiling. "He was probably a good one."

Matthew smiles with closed lips and turns to look at me. His expression, probably amusement, makes me feel jumpy, just from the sheer force of his gaze. "Know any other good doctors, do you?"

I think for a bit about Osler, who, according to Mr. Danvers, said there should be no other love relationship to the young physician than the love of learning. *Osler probably wasn't very well rounded,* I decide, shaking my head.

"Well, for what it's worth, I'm glad you're still you," Matthew says.

WHEN WE REACH the hub of the Underground, Matthew says, in front of everyone, "Listen, I've got two tickets to see *Buddy,* the story of Buddy Holly's life."

"Oh," I say.

"I can see I've put my foot in it," Matthew says, hands in his pockets as we complete the stairs. "Ruined a splendid day by inviting you to a play."

"No, of course not," I say. "I'll just have to check the date."

Music is playing down the corridor of the Tube, and we near a guy singing, "I don't wanna talk about it . . . How you broke my heart." He could be Ed on his acoustic guitar, only he's more unkempt and certainly not as ruggedly handsome. It occurs to me that Ed could be a bum playing his guitar in a subway, and I'd still want him to touch me.

Matthew doesn't look my way as he wryly says, "I haven't told you the date."

I find myself babbling, "Listen, I'm sorry, I can't commit right this second. It's just that I'm adjusting to this new hospital, and I've got this new baby—"

"You do realize he's not your baby?" Matthew asks.

"Well, I know," I say. "But my aunt's got something wrong with her liver—actually, she's not even my aunt, is she? And I do like Buddy Holly's music, but frankly, I just don't want to relive that horrible plane crash again!"

"I'm sorry, but—the plane crash?" Matthew says, sounding both exasperated and amused. "You weren't even born when he died!"

"Didn't you see *La Bamba*? It's Ritchie Valens' life story. And you know, Ritchie and Buddy were on the same plane—it was a really traumatizing movie."

"Well, as long as your reluctance to go is simply about your overwhelming grief for Buddy Holly and not at all to do with me," Matthew says.

"Maybe it's silly," I say slowly as a smile forms on my face. *Maybe it's absurd. A charming Englishman wants to take me to the theatre, and I'm hung up on a subway musician?*

My Jubilee Line train comes in, headed for Green Park so I can switch for the train toward Holloway Road just to see if the baby (who's not really my baby), and the aunt (who's not really my aunt), and the almost-sister-in-law (who may be my friend) are home. Matthew will be off on the District Line to have dinner with his sister in Earls Court. He's looking at me funny again, and I wonder if this is the face of disappointment or confusion.

"I'm sorry that I'm such a mess right now—" I start, only before I can finish the apology, Matthew kisses his finger and holds it up.

For an instant, I don't move. *What's he trying to say with the raised pointer finger? I'm number one?...I've scored a point?... Touché?*

Something makes me kiss my own pointer. He reaches out. We touch, just like in *ET*.

Our fingers don't light up when it happens, but something in me does. I remember the way his lips are soft and capable. I remember why I trust him. I remember that until you cry in front of another person, you're never really naked, which is what I was today.

"Mind the gap," orders the unseen voice of the Underground, and I pluck my finger back, as if it's at risk of getting hacked off.

"I'll e-mail you," I say, and hop aboard the Tube just before its protective doors slam shut.

CHAPTER 14

Acute Confusional State

For after you learn what to do, how and
when to do it
the question will be *whether* ...

— "Gaudeamus Igitur," John Stone, MD

I am falling in love, I think, nearly a week later. Not with Ed or
even Matthew, but the little boy in the ER who is patiently letting me examine him. He's a five-year-old asthmatic who came
in short of breath after he was playing in the dusty attic. He
reminds me of Di's baby, Max, skipping ahead a few years—
the same wispy hair, the same big, wondering eyes. Only, my
patient's lips are bluer than Max's, which is just a little disturbing.

"Rorrie is such a good boy," I say, rifling his blond hair and returning my stethoscope to my neck.

"He usually is, when he can't breathe," his mother replies.

I tell her the plan—that I'm going to start him on a nebulizer
treatment and give him his first dose of steroids—when I hear
shouting from outside the curtain. The ambulance has arrived.
They're bringing in a patient who's "been down" for forty-five
minutes in the field. I cut my speech short so I can give Marian
quick instructions on Rorrie before running over to help out the
Code team of paramedics and nurses who've assembled around
the body.

"The chap was having dinner with his friends when he choked, proceeded to turn blue, and eventually dropped to the floor. Partygoers attempted the Heimlich but were unsuccessful. When we arrived, he was asystolic," the paramedic reports, and then looks at his watch. "He's been asystolic for at least forty minutes."

He also adds that the patient has had five amps of epinephrine, four doses of atropine, and is now on two vasopressors, medications that are barely providing him with a blood pressure. The medics have been doing CPR since they scooped him up from his dinner party. In fact, the fat medic is working so hard to make his compressions forceful that he's growing winded and sweaty. I hope we don't have to resuscitate him next.

"Any history of heart disease?" I ask.

"Not that we know of."

This should be easy, I think. All I have to do is check to make sure that there is a flat line in more than one lead on the patient's EKG. Once I can confirm that the asystole is truly accurate, I can pronounce him dead.

We do exactly that.

"Does anyone object to me calling it?" I ask, moments later, looking for a clock on the wall for the time of death. The medic up near the head—the sweaty one—is looking at me with confusion, and for a second I think he doesn't know my American slang—that "calling it" means game over, the patient is out. Only, maybe he isn't.

"Hold on—just a moment!" the medic huffs and puffs. "I believe—we've got a pulse."

"No we don't," I say in a low voice.

"He has a pulse, Doctor. He definitely has a pulse," the other EMT pronounces, the one whose hand is feeling for the femoral artery in the patient's groin.

I move toward the body to examine it myself. His eyes aren't reactive, and his fingertips are blue, but the chest wall is still warm, and underneath, a heart is beating with pumps so powerful that my hand moves up and down. *Here it is again, the fireworks finale.*

I give Sister Gemma vent settings so she can hook the endotrachial tube to the ventilator, then I rip off my gloves and beat it toward the Waiting Room. I will not repeat the same mistake that I made back in the States. This man was dead for forty minutes before he rolled into my ER, and just because he is temporarily alive doesn't mean it's going to last. I'll talk to the family and encourage them to withdraw life support. I won't let Death have the last laugh.

"Room 11 is quite tight," Marian says, grabbing my arm before I can make it out of the Fish Bowl. "The little boy? He's done his first nebulizer treatment."

I turn around and follow her back to Room 11. Rorrie is really tugging now—his little chest is heaving up and down, making me wish I could lay a hand on him and it would stop. "Start an hour treatment of Albuteral," I say. "Put him on a continuous pulse oximeter and give him oxygen. Has he had his steroids?"

Marian shakes her head. "It hasn't come up from pharmacy."

"Then go to the pharmacy and get it," I say, and then tell the mother that I will be back to look in on him again.

In the hallway, I sail past Mr. Despopoulous, my confused and confabulating homeless patient with Wernike Korsakoff syndrome—the permanent result of a brain ruined by alcohol. I should probably send him back to his room, but my mind is whirling as I try to remember if there is anything else I should be doing for the little boy, when I open the door to the Waiting Room.

Twelve people stand up as soon as I enter the room. With some relief, I note that no one is cracking their knuckles or drawing switchblades. They all look appropriately worried sick.

"Hi. I'm looking for the family of—" I stop. I can't think of the patient's name. I never found out the patient's name. He was just a body on a gurney. *Oh, God. Help me.* I look at my pager, as if it went off. "Please excuse me," I say, backing out with a small nod.

Shutting the door behind me, I turn and bump smack into Marian, who is racing toward me.

"The pharmacy hasn't got Orapred," she whispers.

"What's the guy's name?" I ask.

"I dunno. Room 11!"

"Not him. The Code."

"Mr. Bodley. Angus Bodley," Marian replies.

"Got it," I say, sailing back to the Waiting Room door. "Oh, give him IV decadron or solumedrol. Whatever steroid the pharmacy has. Just hurry up," I add.

Only, Marian is standing there, blinking. "You want Mr. Bodley to have decadron?"

"No! Rorrie! The little boy!" I say, snapping my fingers. "Oh, and should that guy be in a room?" I add, pointing down the hall toward Mr. Despopolous, who is shuffling toward the main exit in his hospital gown. As Marian rushes after him, I find myself, once again, crossing the threshold of the Bad News Terminal.

"I'd like to speak to the family of Angus Bodley," I announce. This time only four people stand up and make their way toward me: an elderly couple, a man whose stomach is about to pop the buttons off his oxford shirt, and a brunette about my age.

Just as I open my mouth to give them the prognosis, it occurs to me who Angus Bodley is. He's our "frequent flier," the one who shows up weekly with chest pain. My first patient here in England, the one who I tried to send for a stat CT scan without even examining him. It's Angus Bodley with the "bad nerves," who hasn't been back since I gave him an antidepressant. I didn't even recognize him.

"Did he choke to death, then?" the older man asks, after I've opened my mouth to speak and nothing is coming out. I feel like I'm choking myself.

"We watched him turn blue. He was laughing and eating and suddenly...he wasn't doing either," the gray-haired woman adds, breaking down into sobs.

I think of Grandmother Eve, all of a sudden, and her constant warnings of danger associated with laughing at the dinner table. *She was actually right.*

I tell them what I can: that when Mr. Bodley arrived, he'd been without a heartbeat for forty-five minutes, that even though he has a heartbeat now, he's been down so long that he has no meaningful chance of recovery. His brain hasn't gotten enough oxygen.

"But how could this be?" the stuffed shirt asks. "He was finally getting his ducks in order. Got the new job, made up with his daughter." He points to the brunette, who gives a faint nod. "He was even getting on better with Lucy."

"His ex-wife," the elderly woman adds, blowing her nose.

"He was finally not a nervous wreck anymore. And now this," the man finishes with disbelief.

"I'm very sorry," I say, and I mean it. Somehow I'm sure that something I did led this to happen—or more likely, something I didn't do. "You're going to have to ask yourselves what Mr. Bodley would want if he could speak for himself."

"Do everything you can," says the old woman, a declaration. "The medications, the breathing tube—everything. But absolutely no life support."

"Ma'am, mechanical ventilation is life support," I say. "He's already *on* life support."

"No more poking and prodding—right, Louisa?" says the older gentleman as he nudges Bodley's daughter.

"What, specifically, do you mean by poking and prodding, sir?" I ask, eyebrows furrowing, thinking of the thick-lumened catheter coming out of Mr. Bodley's neck, the smaller IV sites on his arms, the accordion of the vent going up and down, filling his lungs with air.

"No shocks," the man says gruffly. "And no pounding on the chest. I've heard that they can break ribs when they pound on the chest."

It's a little too late for—

"But don't you remember how many ribs he broke when he fell down the elevator shaft? He broke nearly every bone in his body, and he still survived!"

"Granny, that was thirty years ago," Louisa says.

"My son is a survivor!" Granny declares. "How many heart attacks did he have?"

"None at all," Louisa says. "There was nothing wrong with Dad's heart."

"Perhaps I'm remembering James," Granny says, looking puzzled.

"Which one of you is the patient's decision-maker?" I ask.

"I am," the young woman says with clarity. "My father would have never wanted to be on life support."

Leading the family back from the Waiting Room toward the A&E, I feel like a hearse at the head of a gloomy processional. As we meander past Triage and the Fish Bowl, patients and staff alike seem to be checking us out, and I'm almost relieved to pull back the curtain to Room 10 and shepherd the family inside, away from the scrutiny. But once we're in the room with the body, I'm almost afraid to look myself. Angus Bodley seems so different now, the way he's lying so still and staring at the ceiling, his pasty chest rising and falling on the ventilator, his limbs growing bluer by the minute. He looks like a dead body, not a man terrified of dying. It's hard to believe that this could really be the one person I vowed to help.

After the family gathers 'round to say their farewells, Sister Gemma turns off the whirring ventilator, and I slip out the endotrachial tube and tell the family that it won't be long now. Then I respectfully bow out and head toward the Fish Bowl, where Ed is labeling a urine culture.

"You okay?" he asks when he sees me.

"Yeah, I'm just..." I shake my head, wondering what more I could've done. Wondering if I somehow made this happen. After all, I'm the one who gave him the antidepressant that gave him his life back so that he laughed and choked.... "Mr. Bodley choked and suffocated and had a cardiac arrest."

"Did he die?" Ed asks, wide-eyed.

I look at my watch. "It won't be long now. I'm not even going to get him a bed."

Marian is coming out of Room 11, which reminds me of Rorrie, my little asthmatic. I go to check on him, and thankfully his wheezes are finally starting to break. His cheeks look pink and he's not working so hard to breathe. I tell his mother that I want to observe him for at least another half an hour, pull the curtain shut, and spin around, almost tripping in a puddle of bright red blood on the floor. Shuffling away from the accident is Mr. Despopolous, who's not even bothering to hold his oozing head wound. He probably doesn't remember the bar brawl that led him here, or the fact that he's bleeding internally as well.

"Has the blood arrived from the blood bank?" I ask Marian as she walks by me, charting something on a clipboard.

"It's just coming," she replies, without looking up. "And Mr. Bodley just put out 500 cc's of urine."

"I've got to sell all those TVs," Mr. Despopolous says.

"You don't have to sell anything. You have to stay in bed," I order, grabbing his arm and pulling him back to his own gurney.

"I'll take care of it," Ed says from the doorway, just as I'm pressing a wad of gauze onto Mr. Despopolous' head.

"This guy?" I ask, clapping the patient's hand on his own head to hold the gauze before I make an escape. For a brief moment, I even consider taping his hand there—and maybe taping him to the bed while I'm at it.

"The blood on the floor. Hey, got plans for tonight?" Ed adds, just outside the curtain, as I'm trying to get back to the Great Wall of Problems. I stop walking and pretend to listen, just so that he isn't compelled to shout after me. He mentions his band, that they're playing in London, and that he wants me to go. "Don't worry—I'll get you home early. At least before sunrise." Ed winks.

Still distracted by Mr. Bodley's baffling urine output—*he's not supposed to be making urine, he's supposed to be going into multisystem organ failure; he's supposed to be dying*—I rub my temples and tell him that it doesn't matter when I'm home. I'm not working tomorrow.

"I think we all have to make an appearance at the Disaster Drill," Ed says.

That's right. I almost forgot. There is a "Major Incident" scheduled for tomorrow. The A&E will be filled with actors pretending to have been mangled by a bomb in the Tube, while doctors, nurses, and students have to pretend to save them. I wonder what the orderlies will be called on to do.

"Well, I'd love to hear your band," I say, and then recall

belatedly, "Oh, but I have plans." It's Matthew Hollembee's last night in England before he heads back to the States. "In London, actually. I'm seeing a musical about Buddy Holly's life."

"So come by afterward. We're not far from the Strand," Ed says, leaning on the handle of his mop. I realize that's exactly what I want to do: see him gripping a microphone for a change rather than a mop.

"I guess I will."

"Shall I get Room 10 a bed?" Marian asks, coming toward me with a clipboard. "His vital signs are stable, but he's still completely unresponsive."

I peek behind the curtain before approaching Mr. Bodley, who is surrounded by the same circle of family members, holding vigil. I check his vital signs on the monitor, which are normal, and touch his chest, which is warm. Now what?

"It won't be long now," I say to the family before ducking out again. Outside the curtain, I tell Marian to give him time. "No sense in carting him upstairs only to turn around again."

The only thing is, after I send little Rorrie home on his steroids and Albuteral, and long after I give Mr. Despopolous two units of blood for his gastrointestinal bleed and staple his scalp laceration, Mr. Bodley still isn't dead.

"Dr. Campbell, may I please have a word with you?" Mr. Danvers asks in a low voice, just as I'm trying to lead my confused alcoholic patient back to his curtained corner of the A&E once again.

"Mr. Despopolous, you need to stay in here," I order, giving him a gentle push behind his curtain, feeling like a magician trying to stuff a jack back in its box. "You're being admitted."

"How long do you intend to occupy Room 10 with your body?" Danvers asks in a low voice.

"As long as it takes. He's not dead yet. I told the family that once we pulled out the breathing tube he'd die within minutes."

"Not with a brain stem infarction, my dear. He could linger for quite some time in a persistent vegetative state."

"Anybody want to buy a TV?" says a voice from behind me.

Goddamn Mr. Despopolous. "I got quite a showroom back here. Wide screen. Flat screen. Plasma TV."

"No, thank you," I say, only because it's no use trying to convince the man that he does not work at some British Circuit City.

I heave a sigh then realize Danvers is still waiting for a better answer. "Okay, okay. I'll tell them I was wrong. I'll get him out of here."

"Why not tell them you simply do not know when he's going to die?" Danvers asks.

I blink. This is an approach that had not occurred to me. "Tell them . . . I don't know," I repeat.

"Dr. Campbell, do you really believe that you are in control of his dying?"

This is something that had not occurred to me either. "I guess . . . not," I say, expelling a breath of air that I must've been holding. "But shouldn't I act like it?"

"That, my dear, is the American way, which only leads to false expectations. When you pretend to be God, you inevitably let people down."

I nod slowly.

"Get him upstairs and focus on comfort," Danvers says, striding away from me. He turns back moments later. "Oh, and Dr. Campbell? I expect to see you at the Major Incident tomorrow."

I tell him I won't miss it.

AFTERWARD, I MAKE my way back to Room 10, where I talk to the family and I tell them the truth, which is that I don't know exactly when Mr. Bodley is going to die. And they amaze me. They aren't indignant. They nod with understanding, as if they never expected me to know exactly when, because who could?

BACK AT PARCHMENT HOUSE, Ed's bedroom door is open and Sublime is playing, so I know he's got to be here somewhere. When he's not in the kitchen or living room, I head into the basement, where the laundry machines are. Unfortunately, it's completely empty except for the sound of clothes churning in the wash. Just as I'm about to turn and go, a composition book lying on top of the dryer catches my eye. Without thinking, I pick it up and start flipping through it, thinking of *Harriet the Spy* and secrets.

The first thing I see are verses, lots of verses, and music notes. "Purple Tongues of Fire" is written on the inside cover. *Ed's a songwriter,* I realize. At the same moment, I know that I shouldn't be looking. But I have to.

The first few tunes aren't so impressive. There's one called "Girl No More," which seems to be written from Humpty Dumpty's point of view, before his topple from the wall. There's one called "Prairie Fire" about wanting to be buried in a flat field, possibly Iowa inspired, and a song called "Lips, Generous Lips," which turns out to be a sappy ballad—"When Sarah Smiles/ I'm having my first memory/ My hollow parts collapse/ She fills me with eternity"—thankfully not about someone's labia. I glance at a tune called "Band Geek," which is actually kind of cute:

> Could I be your band geek in leather?
> Could I be a member of your clan?
> Could I get to play you like no other?
> Hey, trumpet girl, I'm a faaaaan!

I evaluate what I'm learning: Ed had obviously been married to someone, not a girl but possibly an egg (named Sarah), who left him all cracked and broken and in want of a proper burial. *Did she cheat on him?* I wonder. What about the other woman, the one he left at the altar before coming to England? Was she the trumpeter? If Ed has a thing for band geeks, could he be into medicine geeks? As if in answer, my fingers stop turning pages on a song called "Code Blue."

> We met in the Fish Bowl
> To hand off the Code Pager

Which sounded, just as you
Touched it.
My heart froze, then leapt
You were holding it now.
Your eyes grew with panic
Do doctors go to Code Reds?
You asked.
Only to learn to use
A fire extinguisher,
I said.
We stayed in the Fish Bowl.
You, anxiously anticipating
The inevitable but true
Code Blue.

My heart drops and rises with terror and excitement. It's beating so fast and so hard, I feel like I've got an engine inside me. The basement stairs thump with footsteps, so I shut the notebook and take flight for the door.

"Hey," Ed says.

"Hey," I say, breathless. We're sharing a very small space in the musty stairwell. I could reach out and wrap my arms around his neck and pull him to my mouth. But I don't.

"Whatcha up to?" he asks.

"Looking for you. I needed directions... for tonight. To the bar."

"Think you'll really come?" he asks, grinning.

"I wouldn't miss it!"

"Well, if you show up after ten, you will miss most of it. But that's okay. Still be cool to see you there."

Ed gives me directions, but I barely hear what he says. Nodding over and over, I am trying to remember exactly what the poem said. *My heart froze, then leapt, you were holding it now.*

BACK IN MY BEDROOM, as I sift through jeans, cords, T-shirts, and button-downs in my closet, I realize that I have nothing intriguing to wear. There's the brown sweater dress that Mama and I bought together on our last shopping spree—the "Last Dress," I always call it. But I want something sexier. I want a little black dress for the theatre.

The sound of acoustic guitar, Tracy Chapman's "Fast Car," emanates from the opposite wall.

"Marian?" I call before rapping on the thin divider between us.

Tracy's voice is lowered a few notches before I hear Marian's: "It's not yet quiet hours!"

"I know, I know. Can you come here for a second?"

There is a pause long enough to make me wonder if she heard, then she appears in the doorway, her arms folded across her chest and a look of defiance on her face.

"What do you think of this outfit?" I ask, stepping backward.

"Sorry?" Marian says, clearly baffled.

I explain my predicament: that I'll be going out tonight, first to a restaurant, then to the theatre, and then to a bar. "Is this okay?" I ask, gesturing to my jeans and brown button-down shirt.

Marian doesn't answer, only looks suspicious. She even glances around my room, as if there might be hidden cameras.

"Maybe this is fine," I say, which makes her green eyes widen.

"You can't wear jeans," she says. "Not to the theatre. They won't let you in the door!"

"Perfect!" I exclaim, relieved to at least have a nugget of honesty thrown my way. "I'll take off the jeans. I mean...not yet," I add, when Marian seems to be backing away.

"And the shirt makes you look as if you're a cowboy," she says.

"Take your pick!" I say, pointing to my closet.

Marian approaches it slowly, wearing the same tense look she always has on at the hospital. "All right..." she says with a weighty sigh, after surveying the shirt selection. "But this won't be easy."

*　*　*

WHEN IT'S ALL OVER, I'm borrowing Marian's black stretch pants to wear with my black V-neck shirt that seems to have shrunk in the wash. After showering, I try a few different combinations with my hair—bun, ponytail, braid—and settle on loose and curly. I put on some lipstick from a half-melted tube that I've been carrying in my purse since my medical school graduation, the last event that I wore it to. Then I look at my watch and grab my purse. I have to catch a train to London.

FOUR HOURS, one dinner, and a musical later, I find myself in the Underground with Matthew once again. Riding the Tube, we do our best to keep our composure, discreetly tapping our toes beneath our seats and glancing everywhere but at each other. His reflection in the window across the aisle gives him away, still bobbing his head. We step onto the platform, humming beneath our breaths but snapping freely. Heading for the stairs, Matthew and I look at each other and finally burst into song, Buddy Holly's "That'll Be the Day." We belt our way out of the Underground and dance ourselves to Carlos Place, singing all the way to the Connaught Hotel.

"That'll be the day—ooo, hoo... That'll be the day..."

Just as we're nearing the entrance, Matthew abruptly stops walking and reels me in with the hand he's holding, as if we're dancing. "Holly Campbell, you are stunning in black."

"Well, thank you very much," I say, stepping back from our dance, accidentally colliding with the bellman who's trying hard to direct us through the door—either that or bar our entry. The small man recoils as if I am a bus running a curb and he narrowly missed getting mowed down. "Sorry!" I say.

"What room?" the concierge asks, jumping to his feet as we stumble past toward the cherry staircase, whose curving, glossy banister may've been carved by Michelangelo himself.

"Two-eighteen," Matthew calls, jangling his keys.

"Two-eighteen," I add gleefully. When we're farther up the stairs, it occurs to me to wonder aloud if Matthew is sharing a room with his mother. He assures me that he is not.

*　　*　　*

"So, it's your last night, huh?" I ask, accepting a glass of champagne that Matthew has just poured from a bottle that was waiting on ice. I have agreed to come up for a nightcap, even though it's already ten o'clock, and I should be on my way to Soho. I never meant to see the inside of Matthew's room tonight; it was not in the plan. But I never expected to be having such a good time, and I hate to say good-bye.

"It is, indeed, the end of my visit," Matthew says, sitting down on one of the yellow armchairs across from me. The room is so enormous that, at the far end under the picture windows, there is a plush sitting area.

"Here's to…" Matthew starts, holding up his own glass before he seems to notice that I've already downed half my glass in a single gulp.

"Sorry," I say, laughing sheepishly as I let him fill up my glass again. "Small glasses. Unlike the rest of this place. Can I explore?" I ask, jumping up from my seat.

"Darling, you can do whatever you would like," Matthew says, looking at me so intently that if I were sober, it would probably make my heart flip. As it is, I've had quite a bit to drink with dinner, and the champagne is already fizzing in my head. I feel wonderful. I ought to get drunk more often.

"Look at this place!" I say, pointing to the crown molding on the ceiling, the gold chandelier, the cherry furniture. I open up the TV cabinet after feeling its glossy finish and then keep wandering over to the luxurious bathroom, whose floor is marble and whose bathrobes are white and fluffy.

"Does the paper come to your door every morning?" I ask, going over to sit on the bed, where I can't help bouncing up and down. I have never seen a bed so big. It reminds me of a gymnastics pit, where ten girls can simultaneously practice backflips without crashing into one another.

"Every morning," Matthew says, and then smiles at me. "You look happy. I love it when you look happy."

"What size bed is this?" I ask, holding up my glass for another refill on champagne.

"King, I suppose," Matthew says, sitting down next to me to pour with a steady hand.

"No, it's bigger than a king. It's megalomaniac," I say, and then hold up my champagne flute to make a toast. "Here's to Buddy Holly."

"To Buddy Holly," Matthew says quietly, even though his glass is across the room and he has nothing to toast with. His mood, or maybe just his face, has turned strangely serious. I want to go back to when we were singing and dancing in the Underground.

"I love Buddy Holly!" I declare, making an emphatic gesture with my arm, managing to spill most of my fresh glass of Dom Perignon all over the bedspread.

"Do you?" Matthew asks, reaching to take the glass away from me. "Even after you didn't really want to go?"

"Sometimes I just need a little convincing," I say.

Matthew looks at me, and suddenly we're kissing. First his lips are on my lips, his tongue on my tongue, and his hand is on my face, and before I know it, he's laid me backwards and put his leg between my own legs and is grinding against me. Meanwhile, his lips and hands are navigating my face, my neck, my breasts. God, it feels good. It feels better than good.

I can't stop kissing him back. It's like the champagne: it feels wonderful. But when he lies right on top of me, and I can feel his erection between my legs, I remember I have somewhere to be.

"I'm in the wet spot," I say, struggling to sit up.

"Wet spot?" Matthew repeats, out of breath.

"Where I spilled the champagne."

As Matthew tries to maneuver us over, I manage to get out from underneath him, sit up, and straighten my shirt.

"I think I better get going. It's late."

"You're leaving? Now?" Matthew asks, looking disheveled and wounded. I realize his glasses are off and that without his glasses, he looks amazingly handsome. "I thought you weren't working tomorrow."

"There's this disaster drill in the A&E. I have to get up early. And you have a flight to catch."

"Right," Matthew says, blinking. "Right." He looks down, fumbling for his glasses. "Why do you run from me, Holly?"

"Matthew, you're going back to America *tomorrow morning,*" I say.

He shakes his head and heaves a sigh. "Of course, you're right. It just seems..." Matthew sighs again. "But you're right. Absolutely."

I let him walk me back to the Tube, but I won't let him see me all the way back to Winchester like he wants to.

"Are you certain you'll be safe?" he asks. "You're not even sober."

"I'm fine," I say with a smile, and then reach up to touch his cheek because he looks so concerned. "You be safe. Okay?" I kiss him one more time and then head into the Tube.

"You're making a mistake, Holly," Matthew calls after me, and for a second I think he's on to me—that if I were really going to Waterloo station I'd be picking up the Victoria Line and not the District Line for Soho.

"A mistake?" I ask, turning slowly around.

"About you and me. You're making a type two beta error."

"A what?" I've had too much to drink to remember my statistics.

"A beta error. The worst kind. You have failed to reject the null hypothesis, when the null hypothesis is false. You are saying that Holly Campbell and Matthew Hollembee are merely a random, chance pairing."

I blink. I could've sworn alpha errors were the worst kind, but I can't remember why.

"People *die* from beta errors," Matthew says. "Smoking related to lung cancer? Lord, no. No relationship there. Let's not jump to any conclusions."

"So, that's what I'm doing? I'm saying there's nothing here, when in reality there is?" I find myself grinning. "I'm saying we're not statistically significant...but we are?"

Matthew moves toward me and takes my face in his hands. "We just need some outside power to convince you that if there is something significant, you will be able to see it."

"And what is power again?" I ask sleepily.

"One minus beta," he murmurs, kissing my forehead one last time before waving good-bye.

When Matthew smiles I try to memorize the directions of his teeth. Then I turn to the real map of the London Underground, the one that will take me to Ed.

SOHO IS A MERRY SECTION of town. People overflow from pubs and onto the sidewalks. They hang out, laugh, drink, and generally mill around Frith Street and up Old Compton Street. It's like wandering into a block party.

Outside Café Boheme, a haphazard crush of loiterers wait, but I stagger ahead of the crowd and coax the bouncer to let me in by insisting I'm there with the bachelorette party ahead of me. The tiara-wearing bride-to-be contests this, but luckily, as two girl-friends are holding her up, she appears too wasted to be reliable.

After weaving through the crowds of drunks, doused with their beer, annoyed by their glee, I move toward the sound of music. In the corner of the bar, Ed stands alone, strumming on an acoustic guitar and singing a soulful version of a Madonna song. Since he doesn't notice me across the crowd, I approach when it's over and tap his shoulder.

"Holly!" he says, the light of his face switching on as he finishes snapping his guitar case shut. Ed kisses my head, even steps back to take in the black stretch pants. "Wow."

"I heard you singing 'Like a Virgin,' " I say, trying not to slur. "I was in the mood for Madonna."

"Thanks," Ed says, smiling and nodding. "But it was 'Like a Prayer.' Never really thought of doing 'Like a Virgin.' "

We both start laughing.

The Purple Tongues have apparently wrapped up for the night, and he tugs on my elbow to move us away from the next band setting up. The bachelorettes are already screaming for "Sweet Caroline."

"Who're you here with?" Ed asks.

I say myself.

"You need a beer?"

After I nod yes, I remember, *Not really,* but he's gone.

I try to find a place in the bar to stand that doesn't already have a person in it. Even a place to lean would be handy, and I spin around, searching for a patch of wall. The rest of the room trails after my head.

Ed reappears a few minutes later with a tall Guinness for himself and only a half pint for me. "Figured you didn't really need a beer," he says.

"Are you saying I'm drunk?" I ask with a laugh, but Ed only smiles and ushers me back to a table surrounded by two chairs and a bench against the wall. The chairs are filled with abandoned coats, so we scoot onto the bench, like two lovers snuggling into the same side of a booth.

Ed leans in close and even puts a hand on the small of my back.

"How was your show?" he asks.

"Lots of fun. How was your show?"

"Lots of fun." He grins.

The bachelorettes are belting so loudly that they're overpowering the band. It sounds more like cheerleading than singing.

"I saw your poem," I blurt out.

"My poem," he repeats, so expressionless, so neutral, that I imagine that it wasn't his poem, but Marian's. Maybe Marian is secretly in love with me. Or maybe I misinterpreted the whole thing. Maybe it was all about a doctor waiting for Mr. Bodley to choke to death and code.

"Were you snooping?" Ed asks.

"No, I just was in the basement, doing laundry. Actually, I

wasn't doing laundry," I remember. "I was looking for you, and I happened to see ... this page...."

"In my notebook, which was shut."

"Well, I thought it might be a book of songs that you might be working on...."

"It is a notebook of songs. That's still private."

"I guess ... that would be," I say. "I'm sorry."

Ed studies me. I study him, study his lips. He retreats back into his beer—peering into it, then taking a gulp—and sets his glass down.

"So what'd you think?"

"Of ... the song?"

"Any of them."

"Oh, great. Fantastic. Of course, I don't read music, so I'm not the best judge.... Who's Sarah?" I ask.

Ed stares at me.

"I read your song called 'Sarah Smiles.' "

"That would be Hall and Oats. Mine is called 'Generous Lips,' " he says.

"Is she your muse?"

Ed chuckles, shakes his head. "She was my wife."

"So, she's your ex-wife now, right?"

Ed leans in so close that I think he's going to kiss me, but instead he says in a low voice, "I'll say this much, just to set the record straight: Sarah's dead. But I'm not going to play that card."

"Play ... what card?" I ask, trying hard to swallow another mouthful of Guinness. After the champagne, it tastes like bitter brown bread.

"The young widower thing," Ed says. "I'm only telling you because Maid Marian got it wrong."

I can feel my eyebrows furrowing. "I'm sorry, but ... is the young widower thing a typical hit with the ladies?" I ask.

Ed looks at me. "Well, yeah. Sympathy sex. At the drop of a hat."

"You let women sleep with you ... for charity?" I ask.

He nods his perfect head, smiles his lovely lips. If only he would stop moving them. "Been known to."

So Marian had it wrong when she called you a serial monogamist. "So, is it true? Is your wife really dead?"

"You think I'd lie about something so awful?" Ed asks, looking horrified.

"Well, I don't know…" I say slowly, imagining him surrounded by throngs of women who are completely captivated, if not charmed, by his pitiful tale of woe. "What'd she die of?" I ask.

"Breast cancer," he says automatically. A little too automatically, I think.

"How'd she die?" I ask.

"Respiratory failure," Ed says. "But the doctors called it 'DIC.'"

I consider this for a second. Disseminated intravascular coagulation, a very bad thing to have, a certain death. But Ed works in a hospital. Maybe he only saw a woman like this, used her for a case study. "What were the exact circumstances of her death?" I ask.

Ed coughs on his mouthful of beer and sets down the glass. "You don't believe me?"

I narrow my eyes.

"Most people just take it at face value that if your wife… She ended up on a ventilator, okay? Blown up like eight times her original size." Ed spreads his arms wide. "Like when the Stay Puft Marshmallow Man takes over the city in *Ghostbusters*? She was that big and that white. They couldn't get the blood into her fast enough when she went into DIC. On one side of the bed the blood transfusions would pump, while on the other, her own blood was pouring out from a post-op drain, hooked to a suction canister on the wall. The nurses kept changing it. Her dad wouldn't stop begging them to do whatever they could, to keep going, to bring her back. He just felt guilty because he was trying to finish his twelve steps of Narcotics Anonymous and couldn't make amends if she was unresponsive on the vent. But I had the power of attorney. We got that settled early on, after the diagnosis.

So I told them to stop. Stop everything." Ed makes a motion with his hands that reminds me of an umpire signaling *safe*.

"And we all went into the room and they turned off all the monitors and the switches of the ventilator, and it was like watching a factory being shut down. All the whirring just stopped. And then it was over." Ed looks at me and wipes a tear from his eye. "Christ, are you satisfied?"

"Ed, I'm sorry," I say, scooting closer, rubbing his back, his arm. "I never meant to invade your privacy."

He stares at me. "Sure you did."

"Well, I'm sorry I made you say so much. I'm sorry I read your notebook. I'm sorry about your wife."

Ed looks back down into his beer again, swirls it around, and then asks me what I think.

"Of your story? It's terrible. It's sad," I say.

"Not that. My song," he says. "The one about you."

My mouth opens up to speak, but nothing comes out. In fact, I've stopped breathing. "I . . . it was . . . amazing."

Ed starts kissing me in the most natural swoop—a lean of the shoulder, a tilt of the head, the faintest positioning of his chin—and suddenly our lips and tongues are swirling and touching . . . until Ed stops and looks uncertain. "Maybe this is a bad idea."

I grab him by the T-shirt collar and pull him back. I don't want to hear anything. All I want is Ed Clemens, right now.

Finally, the hard bench and table's edge combined with the kaleidoscope of people, music, and flashing lights seem to be an extraneous and uncomfortable background, as extraneous and uncomfortable as our own clothes. "Are we both thinking the same thing?" Ed says, his lips still pressed against mine.

"Yes," I say.

We don't move except for our hands . . . our mouths. . . .

"Should we leave?" I ask.

He takes my hand from the back of his neck and puts it in his lap. "Let's go home."

CHAPTER 15

The Morning After

> "From a psychodynamic standpoint, a most important part of the interview occurs as the physician and patient part company...."
>
> —THE ART AND SCIENCE OF BEDSIDE DIAGNOSIS

When I wake up Saturday morning, my left eye feels like a fork is stuck in the socket. My open mouth is laminated in drool to my mattress, which has escaped its fitted sheet, while my shoulders are contracted up near my ears. After taking a moment to sip some water and pop a paracetamol, I fall back asleep.

The next time my eyes blink open, I can see very clearly. The window curtains are partially drawn back to show a stab of light. The phone rings, my bleep bleeps...and I made out with Ed, it occurs to me suddenly. *Ed and I*...

I fumble around on the floor to recover the bleep, which summons me to the Accident and Emergency department, baffling when I'm not working a shift today. I hobble to the window to peer at the valley of Winchester whose stone houses and churches dot the green hills. It would be peaceful if there weren't sirens blaring from somewhere in the background. *Ed and I snogged,* I try to comprehend. But along with the sirens, the phone keeps ringing downstairs.

Outside my room, the hallway is empty except for Mr.

Despopoulous. Instead of a hospital gown, he's wearing blue scrub pants, a white T-shirt, and a hospital bracelet. Instead of my sexy black outfit, I'm wearing blue scrub pants, a white T-shirt, but no bracelet.

"Mr. Despopoulous? Should you be here?" I wonder aloud.

"I had to sell all those TVs," he replies, walking away from me with such purpose, I decide it's easier to let him be the imaginary entrepreneur of my dorm rather than deal with getting him back across the street to the hospital.

The lounge is littered with newspapers, crusty breakfast dishes, and a World Religions textbook soiled with coffee. *Marian is going to have a fit,* I think. It appears to be a room besieged and abandoned after some sort of disaster, but was probably just Ed's breakfast.

Disaster. It hits me as I am leaving the lounge, heading downstairs toward the ringing phone. There is a Major Incident being acted out in A&E that morning. The sirens are coming from ambulances filled with actors covered in fake blood, while the paramedics only pretend to revive them. I shake my head to clear it of the notion of the real patients escaping and reach for the incessant telephone in the front hall.

"Holly? Is that you?" my brother asks.

"Ben! You're alive," I say, only my voice sounds too rusty for cheer.

"I'm alive," he says. "Are you? You sound terrible. Rough night at the hospital?" Ben asks.

"N-no," I say, thinking, *I was all over Ed, and then suddenly I wasn't. Suddenly, he was insisting that I'd had too much to drink and needed to be put to bed.*

"Are you all right?" Ben asks.

"Yeah," I say, rubbing my head. "Sort of. I don't even know. I'm a little hungover."

"Did things go well with Matthew?"

"Matthew?" I stand up straighter.

Footsteps thump down the stairs, and I turn my back and cradle the phone closer to my ear, trying to blend in with the wall. It seems to work. The front door slams moments later and, glancing out the side windowpane, I can see Marian, looking tousled and rushed in her nurse's outfit, running from the building like there's a fire. I don't have the voice to tell her to settle down, to remind her it's all pretend. Then I remember, she probably knows. This is Marian, after all.

"I ran into Matthew at Whole Foods in Pittsburgh last week," Ben says. "He mentioned that he'd be visiting you."

"He was visiting his mother, not me," I say, pacing back toward the only chair in the front hall—a metal one with a green cushion someone must've swiped from the kitchen, a relief to sink into. "What about you? Where the hell have you been?"

Ben says that he spent the last month on a retreat, planting vegetables and weeding at a monastery outside of Virginia.

"Chanting?" I ask.

"The monks did. I kept a vow of silence."

"What made you go?" I ask with a yawn.

"I needed a break. I was very strung out before I went away... couldn't sleep. Couldn't eat. Whenever I closed my eyes, all I could see was crushed newspaper."

"What does that mean?" I ask, rubbing my eyes.

"I don't know what it means. It was just there. In my mind. Crushed newspaper kept filling my head, suffocating me. It was just all that shit Alecia kept reporting on the news every day. I'd close my eyes and see my hands, trying frantically to smooth the newspaper out, but it was too crumpled. The only way to win the battle to fall asleep was to get the image of a cool, glossy stone in my head. Only, after Alecia left, it got so hard to find the stone. I could just see my hands working, and smoothing, and I'd get short of breath. It was really sort of a horrible way to fall asleep every night."

I close my eyes, feeling a wave of nausea washing over me. "When did this start?"

"Last spring. After Mama died. Then it got worse after Alecia's uncle got gunned down and she left. Except it wasn't...." Ben sighs. "It's like I didn't even care about Alecia. I cared, and I didn't care. I was so screwed up. She's been a different person since the day her uncle died. She kept pushing and pushing me away. I was beginning to feel like tuna fish."

"Tuna fish?" I ask, forcing myself to swallow an equally fishy taste in the back of my throat.

Ben reminds me of his theory about tuna fish, one he developed back in high school. In places where food was prohibited— like the library, or particular classrooms—anyone could get away with their quiet bagels, pretzels (if he chewed slowly), and even sandwiches. Almost every kind of sandwich could slip by, except tuna fish. Tuna fish was crossing the line. Even people who loved it in other settings stood up from behind study carrels with wrinkled noses and an edge of disgust to ask, "Is that *tuna fish*?" In fact, sometimes you got the same reaction from people in the dining hall, who, fond of it otherwise, just weren't in the mood. Tuna was the all-around barge-in. Tuna kept calling, long after you tried to give him a hint.

"How can she make you feel like tuna fish?" I ask. "Alecia's your fiancée, not a one night stand."

"Is she my fiancée? We haven't spoken in four weeks," Ben says.

I don't know how to answer that question, so I tell him how to find Alecia instead. "She's staying with her aunt and cousin. She has a phone number now."

"She knows how to reach me," Ben says.

"You've been in a monastery for a month," I say.

"Is she still wearing the ring?" Ben asks.

"She's not," I say. "We'll have to get it back."

"We?" Ben repeats.

"It's Mama's ring."

"Mama doesn't own things anymore, Holly," Ben says bitterly. "It's my ring. My life. My problem."

"Ben—" I say before stopping abruptly. I want to tell him everything: about Mama falling in love with Simon Berg, about how she forgot about us and refused to come home. But I can't. If the ring is his problem, maybe the letter is mine. "I have to go. I just . . . have a disaster to take care of."

"Are you sure you're okay?"

"When did I say I was okay?" I ask.

BEN AND I MAKE PLANS to talk again later, and after hanging up, I stagger back upstairs to my room. Passing by Ed's door makes me wonder if he's still asleep. *Something happened last night. But why did it suddenly stop? We were practically undressing in the hall when he pushed me away.*

I can't stay trapped in my dorm room trying to paste together snippets of memory. Instead, after showering, putting on fresh scrubs, and drinking a bottle of water, I slink down the road toward the hospital and slip in the side entrance so I can head upstairs to the Nightingale Wing.

"How is he?" I ask at the nurse's station.

Sister Renee looks up from the chart that she's writing in and then seems to startle when her eyes focus on me. "Still with us," she says.

"And the family?"

"They've gone to lunch. Pardon me for saying so, but you look awful, Dr. Campbell," she adds. "Are you all right?"

"I'm fine," I say, going into Mr. Bodley's room.

The man looks much like he did yesterday, still flat on his back, mouth sagging open, eyes fixed and staring at...what? The ceiling? Or has he transcended this body? Is he looking at himself from somewhere up above—looking at both of us right now? Does he wish I could make him die any faster? I pick up his limp hand and squeeze, but he doesn't move a muscle, except of course his heart and his diaphragm, which keep pumping and expanding. At least he looks comfortable.

"Sorry, Mr. Bodley," I whisper. "Sorry I let you down."

If I really came to England to become a better doctor, where did I go wrong? It occurs to me that I have to truly help one person before I go home, or I will have failed.

Relax, kiddo. You've got time. You're not leaving yet, a voice says in my head. Only it's not Mama this time. It's Roxanne.

There she is, her black hair in complicated knots on her head and her silk dress falling off one of her shoulders. Her skin and eyes are glowing yellow, making me wonder how I could have let her get away with this blatant neglect of her own body in this last month? She has to be given an ultimatum about seeking treatment. I will help Roxanne, even if it pisses her off.

Going back down the hall from the Nightingale Wing, I'm starting to feel relieved until I see Ed coming toward me. He stops walking for just a second, then starts moving again. His eyebrows are knitted in apprehension. Forget tuna fish in the library; this is like carrying tuna fish into the OR.

"How're you feeling?" Ed asks, nearing me. The corridor is empty except for a candy striper pushing a tea cart at the far end.

"A little ill," I say.

"When you never showed up this morning for the disaster, I told Danvers you've got the flu. I feel really bad," he adds.

For a second I think Ed means the fact that I'm sick. Then I remember that I haven't got the flu and there was no disaster, except maybe Ed and me. How could I have thrown myself at this guy, just to be humiliated?

"You'll be happy to know nothing happened," Ed says.

"Nothing happened?" I repeat. "So glad to know that, to you, nothing happened." My voice comes out louder than I intend.

"Holly."

"Glad to know that kissing me in a bar, and in the street, and on the train didn't mean anything—"

"Dr. Campbell, what, pray tell, are you doing here?" comes a booming voice down the corridor. It's Mr. Danvers coming toward us with his white coat-cape flying behind him.

"Hello, sir," I say. It seems easier than trying to explain myself.

"You look positively peely-wally," Danvers says. "Do go home." Before I finish nodding, he turns to Ed. "Did you find the old X-rays, then?"

"Working on it," Ed replies, and then waits until Danvers is safely around the next corner before pulling me into the stair-well. Once the steel door latches shut, Ed puts his hands on my shoulders and faces me. It makes me sad that I'll never be able to kiss those perfect lips again.

"Holly, of course it means something," Ed says. "I'm just not looking for anything serious. Just because I want you doesn't mean I should have you when I can't follow through."

"But you want me," I say.

"God, yes," Ed says nearly breathlessly, which makes my heart freeze, then leap. "But I just got out of something seri-ous . . . I mean, really serious . . . and I can't . . . do that again." Ed finishes this confession with a sigh.

I nod, slowly, wondering what I really want or need. The only thing I can come up with is being touched by him over and over.

"I don't even know what I'm looking for," I say. "I don't know what I would want you to follow through on."

"You'll figure it out, Holly," Ed says, dropping his arms to lean back against the wall. "Believe me."

Feeling defeated, I slump against the wall next to him.

"So that's it, then, huh? Just . . . one moment in time?" I ask. "As opposed to several isolated moments in time?"

"Several isolated moments in time would add up to a relation-ship," Ed says.

"Or an affair," I say.

Ed turns to look at me. I'm so mixed up that the wall could be the floor right now and we could be lying on it. "What's the dif-ference?" he asks.

"I'm not sure," I say. "But you're right. We should never re-peat what happened last night. It's the most sensible thing to do."

Ed leans over and finds my lips with his own. The kiss is so intense that it makes me drunk all over again. It's definitely not a kiss good-bye. It can't be.

"What was that?" I ask, after he pulls away.

"I don't know," Ed says, grinning. "I wanted to see you smile again."

And I am smiling. Once we part, I smile myself out of the stairwell and smile myself down the hallway and smile myself into the bright sunlight of the afternoon. It's only when I'm outside in the blinding sun that I realize I just told a lie. I want something so serious that it's holy. Denying the relationship is like being a doctor without seeing disease. How will we ever see the truth in the space between us?

CHAPTER 16

Breathing Lessons

> "No tonic invigorates so well as a few, deep, full inspirations of pure, cold air."
>
> —THE LIBRARY OF HEALTH, 1927

Roxanne picked the place on Tottenham Court Road called Chez Suzette, where nobody appears to speak French except for the sultry recording artist on the speaker overhead. The restaurant is a little dark, a little trendy, while outside it's a gorgeous September day, where the sky is come-get-me blue and the leaves are just beginning to turn. After the waitress shows me to a table, I sit in the dimness and start to wish I'd suggested a picnic in Hyde Park.

"Sorry I'm late," Roxanne says moments later, bustling toward the table, juggling several shopping bags, her purse, an infant car seat, and Max, who's swaddled in a blanket with his head poking out like a bouquet of flowers. When I jump up to take the squirmy bundle in my arms, I can't help inhaling him. He's like a hot-milk cake.

"I didn't realize I was babysitting this afternoon. Di has some clients today, and Alecia is working at Waterstones. Here—let's put him in his car seat," Roxanne adds. "He'll be fine."

"Waterstones?" I ask, holding on to Max for just a second

longer. He's so much heavier than when we first met in the delivery room, so much pudgier, a real baby boy, not about to slip away. I stare at him in my arms with his sleepy blue eyes and wonder how my own mother could've ever put learning medicine ahead of me.

"The bookstore. Alecia's a cashier. Only she's calling herself a bookseller."

Our waitress approaches wearing platform sneakers, skin-tight bell-bottoms, and a nose ring. She seems perturbed that we want menus.

Stooping down to put the baby in his seat, I ask what sort of clients Di has.

"Insane ones, who pay her to wax off their pubic hair. She's working at a day spa. You look fantastic, by the way," Roxanne says with a smile. "When did you start wearing lipstick?"

"Oh, about four weeks ago," I say, turning red.

Roxanne's eyes widen. "You've met someone."

"Well, sort of," I say.

"Sort of!" she repeats. "You're in love."

"I wouldn't call it that," I say, grinning.

Roxanne scoffs, then asks for my opinion, white or red?

"What, *wine*?"

"You don't drink?" she asks, picking up on the horror in my voice. "But it's after noon."

"Roxanne...you've got jaundice," I say, feeling the anxiety ridge my forehead tectonic plating into a Grand Canyon of concern. "You're yellow."

"Oh, come on! So, I'm a little sallow. Relax, Doc."

"Roxanne." My voice is stern. I didn't want to have to get into this so soon, but if she's going to be knocking back the drinks, it'll have to be now. "Why don't you come see me?"

"I'm seeing you now."

"Seriously, Roxanne. Drop by the hospital where I work. We'll do blood work. We'll get an ultrasound. Ultrasounds don't hurt."

The waitress is back and looking annoyed when she almost stumbles over the car seat next to the table. She asks if we'd "like that somewhere else," as if Max were a pile of coats. When Roxanne tells her we'd like *him* right where he is, the waitress blinks as though not understanding. It must be the blank expression on her face that makes Roxanne speak slowly when she orders one carafe of chilled Chardonnay, two glasses. I don't protest, figuring I'll have to drink as much as I can to save her liver.

"So, you don't trust me," I say, once our anorexic waitress has clomped away.

"I don't trust doctors," Roxanne says, searching the menu for a moment. "It has nothing to do with you. Why the hell are we talking about me, anyway? Who's the lucky guy?" she adds.

"He's . . . an orderly," I say, feeling my face heat up. "And he's in a band."

Roxanne laughs. "How wonderful. How long has this been going on?"

"A couple of weeks."

The waitress puts the wine on the table without bothering to pour or even ask if we've decided on lunch. Roxanne fills our glasses and then holds hers up, though she seems to be studying me more than making a toast. "You're in love," she says. "You're glowing."

"Oh, I barely know him," I say, clinking my glass against hers before taking a large gulp of wine under her scrutiny. The Chardonnay is light and fruity and refreshing. "You can't call it love when you barely know someone."

"Of course you can," Roxanne says, waving my thought away.

I'm wary of such a pat, cinematic label to the complex feelings bursting all over me, and insist, "Everything takes time. I have to rule out conflicting issues, like lust."

"Oh, Holly," Roxanne says with a laugh. "The rest of us just fall in love. For you, it's a diagnosis."

Our waitress is back, sighing as she takes our orders. Roxanne chooses a cheese and spinach quiche, while I go for the salad Niçoise. For some reason the waitress caps her pen and clips it to her top just as I'm elaborating, "No anchovies, dressing on the side."

"The weird thing is, I met him once before," I say. "The guy? A long time ago, when we were nine. And now it's just so strange that we ended up next door from each other. Does that have any sort of cosmic significance?"

Roxanne thinks for a minute. "No. But it's a nice coincidence." She must see the disappointment on my face, because she adds, "I mean, hell, everyone you meet is important. Does it mean you'll end up with this guy? No. But don't listen to me. Psychics never know who you're going to marry, and if they say they do, don't believe them. Your mother says as long as he's not an optimist, you're okay." Roxanne considers this, as though she's been fed the words without the time to think about them. "Interesting. I've always mistrusted the perky and upbeat myself."

"My mother says . . . ?" I say, and then look around. "You see my mother?"

"I have." Roxanne nods. "Only I didn't realize until you and I met who it was that Clifford kept bringing around."

"Clifford."

"My spirit guide."

Oh, yeah. Him. "Is she happy?"

"How can she not be?" Roxanne asks, as if everyone's happy when they're dead. *Because I'm not with her,* I think, but don't say this aloud. Besides, I already know the answer to that: Mama doesn't need me to be happy. She already knew how to be happy without me.

Then it hits me: my mother was probably not railing against the optimists.

"She doesn't mind if I marry an optimist," I say grimly. "It's op*tome*trists that she has a problem with. Ophthalmologists always do."

Roxanne laughs, pours us both more wine, then leans back and suggests, "Your mother was something of a control freak, wasn't she?"

"No."

"Sometimes," Roxanne says.

"Never," I say, forcing down a swallow of sickening aftertaste. "Just incredibly proud."

"You have such separation anxiety," Roxanne says.

"She's dead," I say, putting down my empty glass harder than I intend. "Doesn't that count as separation reality?"

When Roxanne cocks her head to look at me, I can't help wondering if Clifford is filling up the pause in her head. "You're angry at her," she says finally.

"That's silly," I say. "She's not even here to be mad at."

"That's exactly why you're angry. Because she died."

"No, actually." I shake my head, annoyed. *What the hell kind of spirit guide is he?* "I'm angry because she left me when I was eight. I'm angry because she was apparently in love with someone other than my father."

Roxanne's eyebrows lift into arcs of surprise.

"My mother was completely selfish," I say.

The food arrives, my salad complete with dressing and anchovies, which I don't bother to send back, too overwhelmed with a sense of defeat from my last comment. *My mother is selfish. My mother is myself.*

Roxanne doesn't even try the quiche, just leans forward and whispers, "I'm glad you know the truth about her."

I look up from the jungle in my bowl and stare at Roxanne.

"If your mama wasn't perfect, maybe you don't have to be either."

But I don't want to screw up like she did. I don't want to betray the people I love.

"You're so afraid of making a mistake," Roxanne says. "That's why you won't let yourself fall in love."

I consider that for a minute before slowly agreeing. I'm so afraid of picking the wrong words, the wrong actions, or worst of all, the wrong person. Maybe that's the best way not to screw up: you simply never choose.

It's all too depressing. *Mama screws up, and I'm supposed to embrace it?* I shake my head and pick up my fork to get to work on my salad, stripping away anchovies, all the while thinking, *I shouldn't be here. I can't even remember why I've come.*

"I know why you came," Roxanne says.

I stop picking the yellow eyeball of egg from its white to look up. "To England?"

She nods. "And you know why, too, even though you think you don't." I swallow air, unable to look away from her blue-and-yellow-eyed gaze. Finally, Roxanne says, "You want to lose your mother."

"No, I—that is exactly the opposite—"

"The *ache* that is your mother. You won't always ache like this."

I'm momentarily speechless, confused. Do I want to lose Mama? As soon as I stop aching for her, she's gone, gone, gone, back to the Dryads in Narnia or the Elysian Fields or whatever heavenly place that she inhabits.

Roxanne stops raising her wineglass en route to her mouth, as if on the verge of a toast. "You came here because you're search-ing for love."

"No," I say, starting to get annoyed by her assumptions. "I wouldn't have left the country for that. My odds were better in the States. I even had a boyfriend!"

"A boyfriend?" Roxanne raises a quizzical eyebrow. "Did you consider him that before you dumped him and left the country?"

"Actually, I did!" I say, even though I'm lying. I didn't know what we were; I was too busy denying my feelings for Matthew.

"So, why did you leave him behind?"

I shake my head, feeling something fizzing behind my eyes. "I just wanted to get out of Pittsburgh."

"There are closer places than Winchester, England," Roxanne says. "Tell me, were you sleeping with this guy?"

"Matthew?" I cough on my wine. "Oh, no. I didn't let it get that far." I put down my glass. "If you eliminate sex, you can judge the other person for who they are. You can walk away when you know you're better off alone. Sex screws up every-thing. It's like CPR for bad relationships."

"But that's why it's so wonderful!" Roxanne exclaims with such gusto that people at other tables can probably hear her. "Aaaah, the make-up sex," she celebrates, a little too loudly, which makes Max stir in his car seat. I rock it with my foot so that he'll fall back to sleep again.

Make-up sex reminds me of my parents. I can't help imagining Mama coming home for the summer after spending a semester in Simon Berg's squeaky twin bed. Presumably, she fell right back into bed with my father, because they were downright lovey-dovey for the first time Ben and I could ever remember. We all went to the beach that summer, and best of all, we went without Eve. Nobody else made our decisions. We stayed up late and slept in late, and our parents let us eat fried dough and ice cream on the boardwalk every night. We were all happy at exactly the same moment. Had it ever happened since?

"Oh, Holly," Roxanne says, "I'm not talking about coitus, penis-in-vagina. That doesn't interest me. Well, it does," she adds. "But I mean falling in love with all its attached vulnerabilities. Before now, you wouldn't have known love if it knocked the glasses off your face. Now you're ready." She spears a piece of quiche crust, smiles as she takes a bite. "You're coming outside yourself. You want to hold someone else's life in your hands."

I look at Max. I stop objecting for a moment.

"You wake up every morning thinking the best is yet to come. But you came here because you believe you have to go out and find the best. You're too afraid to let it find you."

I nod with a small noise that sounds more like a catching sob than a chuckle. As I'm quickly wiping my eyes, Roxanne reaches over and touches my arm. She tells me not to worry so much.

"How do you know all these things?" I ask.

"Oh, you know everything about me, too."

"I do?"

She nods.

I sample another mouthful of the wine, as if it'll supply me with answers or the guts to say them aloud. "I know you're insecure even though you pretend not to be."

"Well, of course. Aren't we all? You can do better than that."

"I know you've never loved anybody except for Di."

She's not protesting but not agreeing either.

"Including your husband," I say. "Di ranked higher than he did."

Roxanne looks thoughtful, then nods.

"I know you'd rather be a pleasantly confused but beautiful old lady than a wise old hag."

"Ooooo—yes." Her face turns gleeful. "And you know … ?"

"And I know what?" I ask.

"You know that I'm dying."

BACK AT PARCHMENT HOUSE, I sit alone in the kitchen having a bowl of cereal for dinner. I can't stop thinking about Roxanne and our conversation—and about my mother, too. It doesn't matter if I'm angry at Mama, because I can't get her back. Her leaving then and now can never be made right. And it doesn't matter if I want to help Roxanne. Something bad is going on inside her, something that can't be stopped. I can't take it away; the most I can do is find out what it is—like my past, or rather, Mama's past.

"Hey, woman," Ed says, coming into the kitchen. "How's it going?"

As soon as I look up from my Cheerios to see Ed—shirtless Ed, muscular Ed—I can't remember what was just troubling me. It's so hard not to stare at his pecs. I think of telling Alecia that I don't have flings, and it occurs to me that all I want right now is to fling myself into Ed's arms. Instead I make myself stay seated and ask how his concert went last night.

Ed chuckles as he grabs a Mountain Dew out of the fridge. "Wasn't quite a concert. Played in a bar. But thanks for asking." He reaches out to touch my cheek, and I can feel it turning red.

Just then Marian materializes like the ghost of a dead nurse from behind the swinging door. She sees it all, I know: his hand caressing my face and my shy smile. She can probably see right through to my tingling insides.

"What's up, Maid Marian?" Ed asks with a grin, taking back his hand.

"There is a dress code for the dormitory," she says, keeping her head down as she heads to the fridge, as if Ed is completely naked and not wearing scrub pants.

"Sorry. Guess I never read my handbook," Ed says, looking amused by her discomfort. He turns to me and asks, "Got plans right now?"

"No plans," I say, smiling back.

"So, come with me. I gotta give you something," Ed says. "Later, Marian," he adds as I follow him out of the kitchen.

Suddenly, I don't give a damn what she knows.

As soon as we're alone in his room, Ed clicks the lock on the door, and strides toward me, pulling my T-shirt over my head to kiss my neck in one fluid motion.

"What did you have to give me?" I ask with a startled laugh, a question that only gets answered with kisses as Ed takes off my bra and unties the knot of my scrub pants, which drop to the floor. *Oh. Oh, right.*

It's only after I'm lying on his bed that I start to hesitate. "Um..." I say, sitting up.

"Relax. Lie down. It's just a massage," he says. "In fact, roll over. Come on, roll over. You deserve it."

I flip onto my stomach, catching a glimpse of the picture in the frame on his nightstand. A pretty girl with blond hair—and not his wife, as I imagined, but his ex-fiancée, Nicky. It took a lot just to get him to cough up her name. "Nicky, why do you care?" he finally said, all in one breath, one night last week. *Forget about her. She's history and you're not,* I think, burying my face in the pillow so I don't have to see her face.

"Can you breathe like that?" Ed asks. I can hear his hands lathering up with lotion. And once I turn my head toward the wall, I inhale the scent of lavender.

"Fine," I say, stiffening as I feel his hands moving up my back.

"Relax, will you?" he says. "This is supposed to feel good."

Di does this for a living, I tell myself. *On strangers. Before ripping off their pubic hair.*

"Breathe," Ed says, rubbing my neck.

"Okay," I say, holding my breath.

"No, really. You gotta let go. You carry everything with you. You can't find a space for all your baggage, so you just keep adding more and holding it all in."

"So, how do I let go?" I ask.

"Breathe," Ed says, massaging my rhomboids, my trapezius muscles, my lattissimus dorsi.

"Breathe," I repeat. "That's so New Age-y."

"Breathing?"

"Well, it's popular," I say.

"You hold everything in. Breathe deeply, in and out, and let the corpse go."

"I'll try that," I say, meaning later.

"There is no *try,* only *do,*" Ed says in a high-pitched incantation.

"Thanks, Mr. Miyagi," I say wryly.

"Mister who?" he asks.

"*Karate Kid,* right?"

"That was the word of Yoda himself. Thought you'd recognize it," Ed says.

Without thinking, I laugh and feel my insides open up, from the top of my head to my pelvis. I keep laughing, and breathing, and laughing and breathing, as my bones creak apart, and my muscles grow soft, and my rib cage expands along with my filling heart. All the while, Ed's hands keep working and smoothing me out, as if I am bread dough just waiting to rise in the oven. With the next exhale, I let it come out as a moan.

"I'm making you better," Ed says.

And I believe him.

Which is why, when I finally roll over, I know it's time. Yes, it's definitely time. Ed's pants and boxers must go—he must get thrillingly, completely naked. I don't care if he's an orderly or a witch doctor, a shaman or a quack. I am thirty years old, and it's time to be healed.

CHAPTER 17

Single Blind

"If the subject does not know which of the two trial treatments she is having, the trial is single-blind."

—OXFORD HANDBOOK OF CLINICAL MEDICINE

I t is 8 A.M. on Thanksgiving Day when I return to the A&E from the second floor after pronouncing a patient dead, yet another of the responsibilities of "floating." Since the attending physicians are generally at home and asleep, the emergency room staff is expected to go wherever an inanimate body lies and name it dead or alive. Sometimes it's hard to tell.

"Well, Dr. Campbell," Mr. Danvers says with a smirk as I get to the Fish Bowl. "Was the patient dead this time?"

Considering the A&E director has just arrived at the hospital, and I'm ending my shift, someone must have told Danvers what happened. It's true, Mr. Alameda was pronounced dead twice since Sister Theresa, the Nightingale nurse, originally reported that the patient ceased to breathe around 6:45 A.M. On my first visit to the bedside, I wove my way through eighteen family members holding vigil, took the stethoscope out of my pocket, gently placed it on his chest, and listened for heart sounds. It seemed awfully quiet in there, though it was hard to tell with all the sniffles in the room. After flashing a light over the patient's nonreactive pupils, I turned and announced to the family that he'd passed on, but was interrupted by Mr. Alameda, the deceased, taking a noisy gasp of air.

"Shortly," I said. "He'll be passing on shortly." I felt more like a flight attendant describing an imminent connection at O'Hare than a doctor.

The second time Mr. Alameda ceased to breathe was around seven-thirty in the morning. Sister Theresa must've waited to be absolutely sure, because by the time I climbed the stairs to the second floor and found myself in the patient's room, Mr. Alameda was mottled and blue, and his edentulous mouth looked like a bird beak frozen mid-squawk. His chest was silent. He was, without a doubt, completely and thoroughly deceased. The only thing making noise in the room full of people was my stomach.

"That was him, was it?" one of the grown children asked after the disgraceful howl made by my gastrointestinal tract. It seemed to announce that life rumbles on toward pancakes and coffee no matter who dies. I informed the son that it was actually me, that indeed Mr. Alameda had passed on this time.

Forcing a weary smile, I say to Mr. Danvers now, "He's gone this time. And so am I."

"Get some rest, then," my boss says as Marian writes another Chief Complaint, Vomiting Blood, on the Great Wall of Problems and hands him a clipboard.

The cycle continues, I think, giving Danvers the code pager so I can leave. That's my favorite thing about working the night shift, somewhere between handing off the torch of responsibility and sinking into bed, when I walk home in the morning mist just as other people are starting their days.

Only, this morning there will be no time for a nap. This morning, Ed and I are off to Roxanne's to celebrate Thanksgiving.

BACK AT THE DORM, I shower and then dress up for the occasion, feeling torn between dressing warm—the first snowfall was just this week—and dressing sexy. I settle on the Last Dress (my chocolate brown sweater dress) and high leather boots.

There's a knock at my door, and I open up expecting Ed but finding Marian instead. She tells me there's a call for me downstairs and then disappears into her room so quickly that I feel contagious.

"Happy Thanksgiving!" Dad says when I pick up the phone in the front hall.

I wish him the same and then ask if it's cold there (it is), and if he's having turkey (he isn't). My father is from Illinois, which means that, unlike with Grandmother, it's okay to talk about the weather and holiday dinner menus, elements of conversation that Eve finds superficial.

"We're having Boston Chicken," Dad says. "I couldn't make the effort to cook, what with the counter missing. Besides, we don't even have a dining room table!"

I briefly entertain the image of men wearing panty hose on their heads and slipping out our back door with slabs of Formica. "What happened to everything?"

"The counter—gone," Dad says in a voice that tells me he's been remodeling the kitchen and it won't be done for years. "The table, I gave to Roberta. She needed one. I had no idea my new one would take six months to come in. How do they expect you to live without a table for so long? The chairs looked so pitiful and lonely that I spread them out, faced them different ways."

"Why don't you take your table back from Roberta until the new one arrives?" I ask. I have no idea who Roberta is.

"It's Thanksgiving! I can't do that! She has guests over. She even wanted me to stop by to mingle with the neighbors, but I'm not going over there when half of them are suing me!"

"Who's suing you?" I ask, just as Ed comes down the stairs, handsome in his olive green Shetland wool sweater. His face lights up when he sees my sweater dress, and the way he sambas toward me makes me feel sexy, makes me think of Simon and Sylvia making love on a dock. Could I ever be that carefree?

"The township is suing me," Dad says. "They think the boat in my driveway brings down the value of all the other houses in the neighborhood. They say it breaks the covenant laws of Columbia. Covenant laws! We can't have weeping willow trees, aboveground pools, or rotting ships on our own property! Apparently we signed a divine pact. I knew we should've moved to Annapolis."

"So I take it you're not inviting all the neighbors over for your infamous bean and lamb dip?"

"Over my dead body will I serve them bean and lamb dip ever again!" Dad says.

Ed gives me a sign for "wrap it up" by twirling his finger in the air. That, or he knows Dad has lost it.

"Oh, hang on," my father says before I can end the conversation. "Pick up the other—press 'Talk,' Eve—"

"Holly, is that you?" My grandmother's voice sounds shrill over the telephone wire. It's hard to believe we're an ocean apart when her voice crackles like a nearby fire.

"Yes, Grandmother," I say as Ed starts rubbing my shoulders from behind.

"How's it going over there?" she asks.

Ed pulls my hair out of the way to start kissing my neck, and I say, "It's going really well."

"Is it?" Eve says, sounding surprised. "Well, I can't say the same thing for your brother. He's having a terrible time. I don't know what prompted him to drop out of seminary."

"Um..." I say. The way Ed is pressing himself against me from behind, I can feel his erection through my skirt.

"Holly?" Eve asks, but I can't answer because now Ed is turning me around to bring his hand up under my skirt. "Ben is thoroughly miserable. He has no direction. He's been mowing lawns for people. When it snows, he plans on operating a plow. He went to Duke for this?"

"He misses Alecia," I manage to say, pushing Ed off me, mouthing, *It's my Grandmother*.

"Who?" Grandmother asks.

"Alecia. The woman he was engaged to." I point to Ed and then point to the nearby chair. *Sit. Heel.*

"Oh, I'm sure he's over that. He's better off without her," she says. "But your father. Your father has succumbed to the Internet. He's met a lady friend."

"Eve, I'm still on the line," Dad says.

"Have you met a lady friend, Dad?" I ask. Ed is holding up the train schedule.

"She's a sailor who lost her husband to cancer. Met her in a chat room," Dad replies.

"She could be a teenage boy, for all you know!" Grandmother erupts.

"She owns a boat on the Chesapeake Bay," Dad says, sounding triumphant.

When I tell my father to go for it, that he deserves to be happy, my mind shifts back to Simon and Sylvia once again. Is it possible they deserved to be happy? I wonder, thinking of Simon telling her to listen to her normal heartbeat. *But she forgot about you,* I answer myself. Maybe Sylvia should've gotten what she wanted. But not Mama.

HALF AN HOUR LATER, we are riding the train, Ed and I, on our way to Roxanne's house. It seems a good time to tell him my plan.

"I want us to go away together," I say.

"We are going away. We're on a train," Ed says.

"This doesn't count. I want a weekend."

"A whole weekend?" Ed laughs with apparent disbelief. "Where is this coming from?"

I shrug and tell him I don't know, even though I know perfectly well. It's Mama's affair with Simon. Whenever I read his letter, I find that I am less disturbed and more intrigued. *If I don't write it down, I won't believe it happened. But it was real. The stars moved. And you and I fell in love.* If only Ed and I could get completely away, outside of our real lives, something magical will happen to us, too. Of course, it doesn't occur to me until right this second that we already are outside the realm of our real lives—I am living in a dorm for a year and having my own secret affair with the orderly.

"Where do you want to go?" Ed asks.

"Anywhere," I say, and then add, "Cornwall."

"Why Cornwall?" he asks.

"Why not?" I say. I don't mention that I've already done the research, that I've found us a cottage to rent on the edge of a cliff with an amazing view. We can have it for a long weekend and it's not much money.

"If we do go away, are you going to let me do you all weekend long?" Ed says, wiggling his eyebrows as he puts a hand between my knees. "Every second?"

I slap him away but not hard, and only because I don't want him feeling me up on the train.

"You want to shag me, eh?" I say with a smile.

"I'd shag you right here if you'd let me," he says.

"Why do you want me so bad?" I ask, trying for coy, though I know he'll never say what I want to hear: that he's in love with me. That the moment he saw me, he forgot everything he'd ever learned, that he wanted to learn me instead. Still, I'd settle for *You're sexy, you're beautiful, you're hot.*

Instead, Ed shrugs and says, "I think it's doing you some good."

I sit back in my seat, so dumbfounded that I'm actually smiling. "What the hell does that mean?"

"I'm making you less uptight. If you spent a whole weekend in bed with me, you'd be really chilled out."

I'm blinking with such disbelief that I could start screaming or laughing. "That's it? That's why you want me?" I ask. "Oh, keep talking, baby. This is so hot."

"I'm serious! I bet that getting laid is making you be a lot more open to your patients and their problems...." Ed trails off, possibly silenced by the dumbfounded look on my face. *Could this be any further from love?* I think.

"So you want...to help me..." I say slowly, "be a better doctor?"

"Kinda. Yeah," Ed says.

"Wow," I say, and suddenly I want to cry. But not on his

shoulder and not even in front of him. It seems easier to turn the whole thing into a joke. "You're really turning me on. I'm wet."

"Tickets, please," the conductor says with a frown.

THE ASSEMBLY LINE IS ALREADY WHIRRING at the counter when we walk in the front door. Roxanne bastes the turkey, Alecia mashes potatoes, and Di pours pumpkin batter into a piecrust. The whole house smells like butter and gravy and allspice.

"Everyone, this is Ed," I announce, feeling just a little bit proud. I've never brought my boyfriend home for the holidays. Even if this isn't really my home. Even if Ed isn't really my boyfriend.

"We *know* Ed," Alecia says.

"I don't know Ed," Roxanne says as she wipes off her hand with a towel before giving him a Charmed-I'm-Sure kind of handshake. In her clingy purple rayon dress, once again Roxanne manages to make jaundice look pretty good, like the spray-on bronze that people pay for.

I point to the blond, roly-poly creature in the baby swing near the kitchen island. "And that's Max."

"Well, hello, Max," Ed says, crouching on the floor to start making cooing noises at the baby. "Can I hold him?" he asks, and when Di nods her okay, Ed takes the bundle of baby, raises him up to his own face, and gives him an Eskimo kiss. When Max rewards him with a smile, it seems to overwhelm Ed. He nuzzles the baby and makes gobbling noises on his cheeks. It's not just me. I look around the kitchen and realize we're all mesmerized by Ed's instant infatuation. It occurs to me that I'm jealous of a four-and-a-half-month-old who is not even mine.

"I'm Max's mother," Di says with a wave, before I can wake up enough to introduce her. "Di."

"Hello, Di," Ed says, giving her a dazzling smile. He tells her that he's heard all about her, and that Max is the most beautiful baby he's ever seen.

"Isn't he, though? Unfortunately, no one thinks he's mine

with his blond hair," Di says. "Vincent looks equally alien," she adds with a sigh.

"Vincent?" Ed asks.

"Alien?" I add.

"I mean Aryan. Did I say 'alien'?" Di realizes with a sheepish giggle. "He *was* kind of weird-looking. He had this mop of blond hair and a monkeyish mouth."

"And you want to get back together with this guy?" Roxanne asks, wielding a butcher knife, though I'm not sure what she plans on dicing. "Vincent Little Pecker?"

"Mom. Let it go. Please," Di says.

"Well, I would, but you keep bringing him up." Roxanne turns to explain to Ed and me that Max's father wrote Di a letter. "He's *'very sorry'* for treating her like shit back in Amsterdam."

"He's only twenty-four, which is about seventeen in girl years! He can't really help it if he's immature."

"Why are we still talking about the letter?" Alecia asks. "I thought we were letting it go."

"He's a Nazi," Roxanne says.

"He's not a Nazi," Di says, and then adds thoughtfully, "He's not motivated enough."

"Ed, do you like artichokes?" Alecia asks, setting down the potato masher.

"Love 'em," he replies, moving to put Max back in his swing.

"Do you know how to roast them?" she adds.

"I can follow a recipe," Ed says.

"Can I help?" I ask, feeling left out.

"Yeah," Alecia says, opening the silverware drawer. "You can set the table."

"Oh. Great," I say.

LATER, ONCE WE'RE WAITING for the turkey to finish and the homemade bread to rise, I sit on the back step with Ed, watching him smoke. He's never actually done this in front of me before, though I've certainly smelled the evidence, usually after he's been performing. Still, it's disturbing to actually see him breathe in the toxic fumes, like watching people on reality shows chow down on human remains for a chance to win a million dollars.

"I like your family a lot," Ed says, blowing a smoke ring. "Feel like I could hang out here forever."

"They're not quite my family. But they sure like you," I say, trying to keep the grimness out of my voice. *What did I want?* I wonder. *For them to hate him?* Then I realize it's like being stuck in Mrs. Sandler's class, when Ed was the only kid to make our teacher cry as she presented him with the giant, laminated farewell card. Maybe I'm worried that they like him better than me. Or maybe I do want them to hate him, for not loving me like he should.

"Having a good time?" he asks, blowing another smoke ring.

"Yeah... I just... feel kind of mellow."

"Mellow," he says, "or melancholy?"

I smile in spite of myself and lean on him. When he puts his arm around me, I try not to inhale the sickening scent of tobacco smoke.

The back door opens and Alecia pokes her head outside to tell me someone's here for me.

"For me?" I ask as a pair of Buddy Holly glasses on a familiar face steps into view. "Matthew?" I realize, rising to my feet, letting Ed's hand slip off my knee. The way my stomach floats up into my lungs, it's suddenly hard to catch my breath.

"Hullo, Holly," Matthew says, looking sheepish and just a bit nervous. His brown hair is windblown and missing its part, and his down jacket has a small hole on the left breast. He's seeping feathers.

"How did you find me?" I ask, moving inside to give him an awkward hug—praying I'm not covered in the scent of Ed.

"Your brother, Ben." Matthew looks around at everyone who's watching him and says, "Sorry—I hope I'm not disturbing...."

"Not at all," Roxanne says with a smile, over by the kitchen island. "You want a drink?"

When Matthew shakes his head, Alecia steps forward and offers her hand instead. For some reason, she almost looks sly as she tells my ex-boyfriend that they already know each other. "From St. Catherine's ER?" she says. "I was with her brother when you took him to the OR that night last year."

"She used to have black hair," I say, when Matthew seems to be blinking instead of responding.

"Ah, yes," Matthew realizes. "The reporter. Channel Four, is it?"

"Alecia Axtel, taking action for you!" she says, smiling and putting her hand on her hip. The way Alecia poses, she could've worked for *Playboy* rather than the news.

"I haven't seen you on the telly for a good while," Matthew says.

"That's because she works at Waterstones now," Di pipes up, coming toward us as she wipes her hands on her apron. As she introduces herself to Matthew, Di doesn't even seem to notice that Alecia's scowling at her.

"What about Ed?" Alecia asks, cocking her head to the side. "Has Matthew met Ed before, Holly?"

This time it's my turn to narrow my eyes. Does she have to be such an instigator? When Matthew looks over my shoulder, I turn to see that Ed has followed me in from outside.

"Hey," Ed says sleepily, even though we haven't even had the turkey yet.

"Hey," Matthew repeats, reminding me of a pilgrim trying out American Indian phonetics.

When I ask Matthew if he's in town for Thanksgiving, he says, "Well, it's not our thanksgiving," and then adds for everyone's benefit, "My mother's been in hospital. But she seems to be all right now." He steps forward and asks in a lower voice if I'll take a walk with him, is there time before dinner?

I turn around and look at Ed, who only shrugs. "Go for it," he says. "I'm content."

*   *   *

Outside, the sky seems to have grown darker, along with the ground. The sidewalks on Lorraine Avenue are covered in black clots of snow, which seems to be rotting instead of melting.

"How are you?" Matthew asks, hands in his pockets.

"I'm good. Um...yeah," I say, thinking that I can't stand the smell or taste of Ed when he's been smoking. "Actually, I don't know how I am. More important, what happened to your mom?"

Matthew briefly tells me that she had a small heart attack—is doing well after her angioplasty—and then launches into another subject with more urgency.

"It was awfully strange, when we saw each other last. I mean, it was lovely to see you, apart from the end, which became incredibly awkward. I didn't know if I'd succeeded in telling you what I wanted to tell you."

"Listen, I want to be honest," I say. "I've kind of been seeing someone."

Matthew blinks. "You're seeing someone. A psychotherapist?"

"No!" I laugh. "I mean, a guy. I've been hanging out with... this guy. I probably should've mentioned him in my e-mails."

"Hanging out," Matthew says, and then scratches his head. "You're in a relationship?"

"It's not a relationship," I blurt out. "I don't know what it is. I just wanted to be open about it. Since you're standing here in front of me, talking about what happened last time."

"You have feelings for this...guy?"

I think about Ed telling me that getting laid is helping me be a better doctor. "I don't want to," I say.

Matthew laughs, laughs so hard he appears to grow weak. It's only after he's sat on the frozen curb with his face in his hands that I realize his laughter has turned into groans. "Why am I here?" he asks.

"Your mother," I say.

"Which does not explain why I have chosen to barge in on your family at Thanksgiving."

"Hey. I always want to see you," I say, squatting next to him and reaching for his arm. "Why do you think I write you all the time? You're my friend and I—"

"Friend," Matthew repeats, sounding grim.

"Well, you are."

"You're not sleeping with this guy, are you?" Matthew asks suddenly.

I hesitate. "Well..."

Matthew groans and holds his head again, until it snaps back up. "It's not the guy at the house?"

"We went to third grade together," I say.

"But he was...I mean, he didn't even..." Matthew trails off. "If you two are...together...does he care that you're out here with me?"

I shrug. "Well, you saw him. He's fine with it."

"Asshole!" Matthew says.

"No, you're not."

"I mean him."

"Well, he's...comfortable with himself, I guess. He's not really threatened by anything or anyone."

"Does he care about you?" Matthew asks, and when I can't answer right away, he adds, "Why would you ever settle for such a thing?"

"I'm not settling for anything. I'm just confused." I watch him get up off the curb to walk away. "Where are you going?"

"I just don't know what to think at this moment," Matthew says. "I don't know what to think about you."

"About me?"

He doesn't answer for a moment, just stands there, apparently searching for the words, until finally he shakes his head. "I want you to be happy. At all costs. But how can you be happy...?"

"I'm not perfect!" I shout suddenly, feeling tears invade my eyes. "I thought that was okay."

"It is all right. It's absolutely fine," Matthew suddenly decides. "This has nothing whatsoever to do with me."

"No, it doesn't!" I say, wiping my face.

Matthew opens his mouth and then seems to reconsider. "I really must go."

"That's it? You just stopped by to chew me out, and now you're *leaving*?"

He nods solemnly and then reaches for the top button of his coat, which is already closed. "Good-bye, Holly."

It doesn't take long for me to get back to the house. Outside, I find Roxanne sitting on the cold steps and staring into the dark.

"Roxanne? What are you doing out here? It's freezing."

She looks up at me and answers with only a blue and yellow gaze. She isn't even wearing a coat.

"Roxanne?"

"Thinking," she finally says.

I sit down next to her on the front step and decide I feel like thinking, too, but aloud. "Things with Ed are going nowhere, and now Matthew hates me. He hates me!"

When Roxanne doesn't answer, I glance over her, noticing for the first time the purple bruises that have erupted all over the skin of her hands. I study her neck, which is decorated with another mark—a bluish splotch with scratch marks—like she's recently been given a hickey or escaped strangulation.

Roxanne must feel my inspection because she looks over to ask pointedly, *"Yes?"*

"What? Nothing." I keep the worry out of my voice. It's quiet, except for the sound of Ed and the girls laughing inside the house. *Ed and the girls. He'd probably be happier dating one of them.*

"You'll be happy to know that I finally saw a doctor," she says.

"You did! Roxanne, that's great," I say, until the look on her face shuts me up.

"There is a very large, inoperable 'shadow' in my liver that appears to be of the cancerous variety. There are also spots on my spleen, and some on my diaphragm and lung. Six months, if that."

Here we go, I think, sucking in a deep breath like the next parachutist getting ready to jump. On an airplane at a couple thousand feet above the ground, we're all suited up with gear, taking the reckless plunge one by one: Mama with her pulmonary embolism, Mr. Bodley with his asphyxia, now it's Roxanne's turn. Only, what am I doing on the plane, afraid of heights and flying?

"Do they know what the primary cancer is?" I ask.

She shakes her head. "They're speculating liver, but the cells from the biopsy are . . . what's it called when you can't really tell?"

"Undifferentiated?"

"Right."

Badness, I think. *Badness all around.* Who cares if Matthew hates me or Ed won't go away with me? Roxanne is going to die. But I have to be positive. "Roxanne. Six months is an average."

"I know that. Some people live *less* time."

"What about chemo?" I say.

"They said it wouldn't improve my survival time. It just improves the histology of my liver. What the hell do I care about how nice my liver cells look on a slide at my autopsy?"

"Roxanne, let's say chemo doesn't improve the outcome of ninety percent of people who try it. That still means ten people in one hundred live longer than six months. You could be one of those ten!"

She shakes her head. "I've got karma problems. I've broken nearly every Commandment."

"You haven't stolen—" I start.

"I stole my daughter, Holly! I stole my daughter simply because I was pissed off at her father and didn't want to give him the satisfaction of knowing her. I've cheated, I've lied."

"You haven't killed anybody," I say.

"But I've *seriously* thought about it," she says with weary bitterness.

"Roxanne, why does this disease have to be your fault? Everybody's got bad karma!"

"I don't know; I don't know." She sighs heavily. "I think I've been sick up here for a while," she says, tapping her head, "and I just didn't know I was sick down here, too. But they're somehow connected. I mean, it's not like I was amazed to find out or anything."

I don't like the thought of someone giving herself her own cancer. That means maybe I have cancer, too, maybe Ben does, maybe Dad, maybe Alecia. . . .

"Have you *ever* been amazed before?" I suddenly wonder. It occurs to me that an occupational hazard of being a psychic would be a lack of general amazement, like always knowing about your own surprise party in advance.

"No . . . I . . . can't say that I have," Roxanne says slowly.

I try to think of the milestones of amazement that might be tainted if I'd been born with a strange gift of premonition. Certainly it would still be neat to see places I'd only dreamed about? Certainly *birth* would still qualify as something profound? "Did you know what Di would be like before you met her?"

Roxanne shrugs. "I knew she'd be a lot like me."

I can't get over it, never being amazed. Such uninspired apathy would amount to a small life, one that I'd never associated with Roxanne. With all her undaunted wisdom, she seems to have lived colossally.

"I'm not telling everyone yet," she says. "I'm telling you because you already know."

"Okay."

We sit and stare at the bleak evening sky.

"What made you go to the doctor?" I finally ask.

"Shopping," Roxanne says grimly. "I pretended to go looking for Christmas presents, but really I was just looking for more clothes to perk me up. A woman wearing too much hairspray coaxed me over to a cosmetics counter by saying they were giving away free moisturizer. It sounded perfect, like a good, cleansing rain—moisturize my life away! And I went to the counter and was holding up one of those hand mirrors when I finally saw myself. I hadn't bothered to really *look* in a long time. Well, you know how they can do those aged composite photos of people?

One year ago, I had men telling me I looked like a blue-eyed Cher. Then I see this—this ghoul staring out at myself—wrinkled yellow skin and eyes, craggy hair—it was like an aged composite photo of the Devil. And I was so horrified that so much could have changed in one year—that I could be so sick—that I dropped the mirror. It shattered into bits."

"Roxanne, that's seven *years* of bad luck," I say.

"I know," she says, hugging her knees. "If only."

CHAPTER 18

Aequanimitas

> "The first essential is to have your nerves well in hand. Even under the most serious circumstances, the physician...who shows in his face the slightest alteration, expressive of anxiety or fear...is liable to disaster at any moment."
>
> — "AEQUANIMITAS," SIR WILLIAM OSLER

If this were *ER,* we'd be having a party right now," I say, flipping a chart shut. "We'd be eating good food and listening to funky music. There might even be a cowboy with a broken finger who would teach all how to line dance. We wouldn't be just sitting here at four o'clock on Christmas Eve, waiting."

"Are you kidding?" Ed says, wincing as he drives another staple into the ceiling with a staple gun. "If this were the show *ER,* you'd have to handle a smallpox outbreak *and* a school bus accident *and* a roller-coaster collapse, all on Christmas Eve."

He removes his hat to mop his sweaty face the way construction workers do in the hot sun on a steel beam, stories above the city. Only, Ed is standing on the desk of the nurses' station, and his hat is red felt with a white pom-pom. "These decorations won't be coming down for a while," he says, surveying his array of hanging Santas and gold ribbons.

"Nice work," I say, reaching around the poinsettia on the counter to grab another gingersnap.

"You going to be at Alecia's tonight?" Ed asks, stooping to jump down off the desk.

Just as I'm puzzling that over—*Didn't I invite him three weeks ago?*—the back door to the A&E opens with a bang and a scream. I turn to see the medics wheeling a young woman who's screeching and wailing. She looks surprisingly, well, *alive* for a change.

"What the hell is going on?" I ask, tossing the cookie aside to walk briskly toward the action. At a quick glance, she's neither bloody nor covered in smallpox, but she *is* pregnant.

I find out the story as they push the gurney inside a curtained corner: thirty-one-year-old female started having contractions a few hours ago after her water broke; now they're every two minutes and she's complaining that she has rectal pressure.

"I'll get a bedpan," Marian says.

"I'm going to have the baby," the woman screams, *"right now."*

"Okay, just try to calm down a second," I say, pulling on a glove with a snap and reaching for some lube. "Lie back and let me check your cervix."

The woman is anything but calm. She's writhing with so much pain, it's hard to even get her to open her legs. Once I do push up her skirt and put my gloved hand inside her, there's no cervix left to feel. The baby's head is taking up the vagina.

"Forget the bedpan and get the ob kit," I say. "The head is right here. Don't push yet," I order, just as the woman gives another glass-shattering scream and pushes.

The head pops out, just like that, faceup, between her legs. It hovers there like a blue ghoul.

"Stop pushing!" I say, frantically trying to untangle the umbilical cord from around the baby's neck. The cord won't budge. "Get Danvers," I say to Marian. "No, get me hemostats and scissors. And suction. Then get Danvers!"

"I'll get Danvers," I hear Ed say from somewhere behind me.

My heart is firing like a machine gun, and my hands are shaking. There's no time to weigh the pros and cons: I have to act now, but as soon as I cut the umbilical cord—*Clamp*—the baby loses its oxygen supply—*Clamp*—so I have to get it the hell out, but if the shoulder gets stuck—*Snip*—it won't be able to take its first breath, and it could die or be brain damaged from the lack of oxygen. With the swipe of the scissors, I unwrap the tight cord, tilt the baby's head down, and the shoulder slides out like a miracle before the rest of the baby. It's free!

I'm trembling as I lift the blue baby from between its mother's legs. It's not crying. It hasn't even made a sound.

Then, a bright flash goes off, temporarily blinding me as I carry the baby over to the incubator.

"Boy or girl?" the new father asks, camera up to his face, though he appears stricken, as if he just shot a gun and not a picture.

"It's a girl," I realize, looking for the first time. After passing a suction tube down the baby's nostrils and rubbing a knuckle on her chest, I reach for a face mask. It's not until I hear the woman starting to cry that I tell Marian to massage the mother's uterus and deliver the placenta. Finally, just as Mr. Danvers blows into the room in his white coat, the baby makes a sound—a pitiful, catlike whimper, but a sound.

"Is she . . . crying?" the mother asks, suspending her own tears for just a second.

"She's starting to," I say, passing the suction one more time to try to get the meconium out of the baby's lungs.

"Congratulations!" Danvers booms, shaking the hands of the young couple.

"She had a nuchal cord," I say. "Meconium aspiration."

Danvers looks over my shoulder at the baby, who's turning pink and starting to wriggle, before pronouncing her "lovely." He moves back toward the bed and tells the parents that we'll be observing her in the neonatal unit, and that she'll be evaluated by the pediatricians. "But congratulations. She's looks absolutely perfect."

"Oh, thank you! Thank you so much!" both of the parents gush.

"Well done," Danvers says in a low voice before leaving.

It is, I realize, my first "well done" since I came to England.

*　　*　　*

Out by the Fish Bowl, I'm trying to wash my hands but I can't stop dropping the soap.

"Good thing this isn't the baby," Ed jokes, picking the bar up off the ground.

"Right," I say, feeling so weak I could collapse with relief.

"So, are you still going to Alecia's tonight for dinner?" Ed asks.

I nod, still shaking, and trying to take deep breaths. I try to tell myself that this wasn't a school bus accident or a roller-coaster collapse. It was just a complicated delivery. But is the baby going to be okay? Did her brain get enough oxygen during those critical moments? It will take time to know.

"I might be a little late. She asked me to bring the tree," Ed says.

I look up from my soapy hands. "Bring the tree?"

"Yeah. I saw her the other night at my show. She said that they still don't have a tree."

"Alecia came to your show?" I ask, squeezing the soap, accidentally sending it flying again. "Were you playing in London?"

"No, Aylesbury," Ed says with a chuckle, stooping on one knee to reach up and offer the soap again. "She came out to the Hobgoblin when we were doing a set. Took the train and everything."

"She's quite the fan," I say.

"Guess so," Ed says with a shrug. "Hey, why don't we meet there, okay? Let everyone know I'll be late, but I'm coming."

"Sure," I say, baffled. *Alecia took the train an hour to Aylesbury? He's bringing the tree?*

Two hours later, bent over in the freezing wind, I walk the blocks from the Tube stop at Holloway Road toward Roxanne's house. I want to call Matthew right now to tell him about the baby, to tell him that I finally did something right, and she still might not be okay. But we haven't spoken since Thanksgiving, and he'd probably hang up on me if I did pick up the phone. Right now, some form of precipitate is falling, and I touch my cheeks with my hands, trying to decide what it can be. Not cleansing like rain, not holy like snow; it's grittier and more substantial and almost hurts.

Wearing a long black dress decorated with red orchids and drinking a glass of something alcoholic, Roxanne opens the door to 55 Lorraine Avenue. The living room and kitchen are dark, and she quietly shuts the door behind me. Neither of us acknowledges that it's Christmas Eve, that the precipitation is sleet, and that she's probably turning yellower by the swallow. To become a doctor is to feel responsible for people I don't know how to be responsible for. If Roxanne wants to destroy her already failing liver, I'm too weary to play the part of educated nag.

"Where is everyone?" I ask. "Can I turn on the lights?"

"Where is everyone. Excellent question. Alecia is finishing her Christmas shopping. Di and Vincent Oorsprong are moving back to the Netherlands."

"What?"

"Before I answer that, would you like some Scotch?"

"Okay."

She pulls a crystal cup out of the cupboard, fills it with ice from the freezer, and explains how Di has been in touch with Vincent again. "She said that he's coming to town, and he wants to marry her. They're going to elope. Maybe they already have by now."

"That's what she said? 'We're going to elope'?"

"She said she was meeting with him to talk." Roxanne hands me the glass and adds, "But I found a *Brides* magazine stashed under her bed."

"Roxanne, people don't elope in big, poofy bridal gowns. He's just back to woo her. She's excited by the idea of marriage."

"No! Not to him! Not to a pipsqueak, immature boy who didn't want to speak to her after she got pregnant. He's a loser! She doesn't realize that. Add some water," Roxanne orders as I begin coughing from the Scotch.

"How do you know she's even planning on living in Holland?" I manage to gasp. "Did she pack?"

Roxanne stares at me, as I'm filling my glass at the sink. Then she touches her finger to her lips, points at me, and abruptly leaves the kitchen, apparently to go ransack Di's room for more evidence. In the light of the electric candle in the window, I stand by the counter numbly drinking my watered-down Scotch, thinking about the newborn baby girl and thinking about Matthew. *Please, God, let her be okay. Let her be healthy. And let him forgive me.*

"It's so fucking cold out!" Alecia yells, slamming the front door behind her. "Can't we destroy the ozone layer any faster?"

I stare at her coming toward me, thinking of train rides to Aylesbury, thinking of the Hobgoblin, thinking of her and Ed getting it on.

"What's going on?" Alecia demands, hitting the kitchen light switch. "You're drinking iced tea—it's freezing!"

"Oh, no, it's whiskey—I mean, Scotch."

"Didn't anybody start dinner? Where's Di?"

"Vincent Oorsprong is back in town."

"Vincent Little Pecker?"

"Her backpack is missing!" Roxanne calls from the other room. "Some of her clothes, her red turtleneck, her green cords—"

"She's probably wearing them," I say. "Roxanne thinks Di and Vincent eloped."

"Well, what are we gonna do about Christmas Eve dinner?" Alecia asks, moving to examine the contents of the fridge. "I can't cook."

She's so unbelievable, I think. *Grandmother was right. Ben is better off without her.*

"I heard that you asked Ed to bring the tree," I say, folding my arms across my chest. "When was that?"

"What? Oh, sometime last week. He told me you'd invited him to dinner, and I told him he could do us a favor.... Should I defrost something?" Alecia asks, opening the freezer. "What about this honey ham?"

"Where would you have seen Ed to ask him to bring the tree?" I ask.

Alecia turns and stares at me, then her eyes start to widen. "What's the matter with you? You think we hooked up?" she realizes.

"Well, why else would you take an hour train ride just to hear a mediocre band?"

"Christ, Holly, I was bored! I thought I'd go to a bar where I might know someone instead of drinking alone, like some people do around here. He's a nice guy. He's a hot guy. But I'm not interested."

I don't answer, just narrow my eyes and make a face. *Yeah, right.*

"Believe me. I don't want him," she says, and then adds quietly, "I want Ben."

"What's that supposed to mean?" I ask, irritated. "You still love my brother?"

"I've always loved him. I just thought we needed a break." She shrugs. "I've called him a couple of times. Somehow, he's never there."

She looks so honest that I can't help but believe her. Reluctantly, I say, "He misses you, too."

"He told you that?"

"I know him," I say. "He doesn't have to tell me."

Alecia seems to be thinking this over, while from the other room, I can hear drawers opening and closing and closet doors slamming.

"I would never do that to you," she finally says, which makes my eyebrows furrow. "Ed," she adds. "I wouldn't go after your boyfriend."

"He's not my boyfriend," I say with a sigh, looking at my feet. *I don't even know what I'm doing with him, except that I can't bear to think of never spending the night in his bed again.*

"Well, whatever he is. I would never go after some guy that you're into. Okay?" Alecia says, a little louder this time. "Geez," she adds, "I thought you'd know that about me. What kind of person do you think I am?"

I look up. "Why do you care what I think of you?"

"Because, you're...you know...one of my best..." Alecia hesitates. "You're a Fossil sister."

ALECIA AND ROXANNE DECIDE to call Di on her cell phone; meanwhile, I peer out the window at a passing car. Its tires are scrabbling on the treacherous road. It's not until the headlights slide past that I let go of the breath I'm holding. I have a nervous feeling inside that something is going to happen tonight.

"It's ringing!" Alecia says, just as Di, struggling with several sacks of groceries, opens the front door. Her green cords and her red sweater are no longer missing: she's wearing them.

"Oooo...I've got a call—somebody help me with the bags... can one of you..." Di says.

Watching her slam the door against wind and sleet, I wonder how she managed all of this on the Tube. Luckily, she keeps a tight hold on Max, who's resting on her left hip. "Di! You're back," I say.

"Yeah. Can somebody...?" The plastic jug of milk hits the welcome mat but doesn't break open.

"What did you tell Vincent Oorsprong?" Roxanne demands.

Di looks startled and seems to forget the ringing cell phone in her hand for a second.

"I told him he was an idiot," she replies simply, and then flips open the lid to her phone. "Hello?"

"It's me," Alecia says, from across the room. "What's for dinner?"

WE SURROUND THE KITCHEN ISLAND and watch as Di gets started on the main course for Christmas dinner: homemade pizza. It isn't until she's worked all the ingredients into a doughy consistency that she describes the scene: Pret A Manger for lunch, chicken on tomato basil bread, he paid. There were no tables free, so they sat on freezing cold benches outside and ate with chattering teeth. Vincent didn't come prepared with the diamond ring after all (too worried he'd be charged duty to transport it into England), but he did bring Max an outfit, sized for a newborn, not someone nearly six months. Vincent was obviously intrigued by his son, delighted that they shared the same straw-colored hair and apple cheeks. He even fed Max some of the chicken that fell out of his sandwich onto his sweatshirt—Max's first experience with meat. Vincent said he'd been working Diotima's old job at the coffee shop below the Sky Fish and was saving lots of cash since he could smoke all the pot he wanted for free. He'd even found a more affordable apartment in the Red Light District, so for the first time, Vincent had no financial obligation to his father. In fact, if Di would just agree to return to the Netherlands that night, they would—Vincent, Di, and baby Max—have a decent place to live as a family... that is, just as soon as he got rid of Stefanie.

"Stefanie?" Roxanne repeats. "*Guy's* sister Stefanie?"

Di doesn't look up from the cutting board, just kneads the dough with fingers that are as delicate and as strong as her voice. "That's the one. Vincent has been living with Guy's younger sister. *Romantically* living together," she adds, pulling on the dough, which has grown elastic by now.

"Stefanie has a *very large* overbite," Roxanne says, with such animosity that I'm glad I suffered through braces.

"She knows all about me," Di says. "She was planning on moving out once I arrived. Vincent and Stefanie *both* think it's the right thing to do—for us to try to be a family. Stefanie even volunteered to babysit, which Vincent thought was really generous."

Roxanne's fists are clenched and her head is shaking, but I'm glad she doesn't chant her usual line about Nazi pricks.

"But that's not even the disturbing part about lunch," Di continues as she transfers the dough to the mixing bowl she's coated with olive oil. "The disturbing part came after all that, when Vincent asked if he could legally change Max's name. None of the Oorsprongs were really partial to calling him Maximilian, and even Stefanie said it was a bad name, so for the past seven months, Max's Dutch relatives have been calling him 'Hebert.' Hebert Oorsprong."

"Son of a bitch!" Alecia says.

"That's when I told him that not only was Maximilian going to stay Maximilian, he was going to stay in England with me. I told Vincent he was a jerk and didn't deserve to have anything to do with Max. Then I told him to excuse us, because we had to finish our Christmas shopping." Di runs water over a paper towel and wrings it out. "And I stood up, and I walked away, and Vincent was yelling my name, pleading with me to come back, or at least wait up. But I hugged Max even tighter and just tried to get away." She unfolds the towel like a surrender flag and places it over the dough.

"Oh, sweetie," Roxanne murmurs. Di has started to sob, and Alecia offers another paper towel in lieu of a tissue. I try to look away from Di but I can't. I stare at her—as she wipes her damp hands instead of her wet eyes—and feel like I'm spying on her soul, until it occurs to me that maybe I'm looking at the reflection of my own. The front door bangs open from the wind.

"Make way for the Christmas tree!" Ed bellows.

Di stands up straighter, takes a deep breath.

"Come on—move the recliner! Let's go! Let's go!" he orders, easing a four-foot fir tree—its large bulb mounted in a wheelbarrow—backward into the house.

I'm the only one who reacts swiftly enough to move the furniture. Alecia leans on the counter, saying, "Let me get that," but not moving, while Di adds, "The thing is, Vincent said he's not going home without Max. He threatened to come by with the police tonight. He said he's going to find a way to bring the baby home to Amsterdam."

"Well, he can't do that. Max is an English citizen. It's just that simple," Roxanne says.

"What's up, ladies?" Ed asks, setting down the wheelbarrow to peer around the living room.

"Max's father came to claim his son," Alecia says.

"And rename him," I add.

"Di sent him packing," Alecia says.

"Nobody's gonna take you away, are they, Mr. Snugglesticks," Ed says, coming toward the baby in Di's arms. Max smiles in his little red jumpsuit and kicks his happy legs before reaching out for Ed.

"I feel so stupid," Di says, still holding on to her son. "I can't believe I thought he'd actually change for me. I guess I just wanted a life."

"What are you talking about? You have a life. You have Max," Alecia says. "Who wants eggnog?" she adds, holding up a bottle of rum to spike it with.

By the skeptical expression on Di's face, it isn't the answer she's looking for, so I offer, "I'll babysit Max anytime I'm available."

"Me, too," Ed says.

Di squeezes Max even tighter. "Oh, no, I *love* Max. I love him. And I'm breast-feeding him, so it's not like—like I could just take off—not that I'd want to." She sighs. "I just don't quite know where I'm going now. I thought once he was born I would know my whole life's direction."

I think about Mama and wonder if, when she had us, we were supposed to fill up some void in her life, only we came up short? But where did this void come from? Are we all born with the same sense of being incomplete?

"The Wise Woman from Mantinea said we should strive to be pregnant souls," Di says. "I always loved that expression. Really creative, virtuous, wise people have a pregnant soul, so they don't have to have babies to be eternal. They fill themselves up."

"I'd like to be a pregnant soul," I say, and when my eyes meet Di's, she looks almost grateful, until the sound of a motor gunning to get up the curb and into the driveway makes her stiffen.

"Are you guys expecting anyone else?" I ask, going to the window.

Roxanne is right behind me. "It's Vincent!" she says. "Lock the door."

"Is he alone?" Di asks, cradling Max's head against her chest.

"You want me to tell him to get lost?" Ed asks.

"Wait a second. I thought someone said Vincent was a pip-squeak," I say. "This guy is tall."

The stranger in the yard raises an arm in greeting. He must have seen us hovering by the bay window in the flickering candlelight. Suddenly, hope and fear start beating in my chest—could it be Matthew? Would he consider giving me another chance—at friendship or more? I can't help hoping his mother had another heart attack, and he came home for Christmas after all!

Despite Roxanne's protestations, I rush to open the door, except that Matthew isn't standing there—and neither is Vincent.

"Surprise," says a sheepish voice.

"Ben?" I realize. He's carrying a big navy sea bag, slung over one shoulder like Santa Claus.

"Hey, Holly." He takes off his hood, revealing his red hair. "Merry Christmas."

I'm so amazed that it takes me a second to grab him in a hug. As soon as I let go, someone gasps from over my shoulder, and Ben stands up straight and gulps. "Hi."

"What are you doing here?" Alecia asks.

"Merry Christmas," he says.

"What are you doing here?" she asks again.

"I came to give you this," Ben replies, fumbling in his coat pocket with shaking hands. We watch as he pulls out a clementine and sets it down on the counter like a small, bare heart.

Alecia covers her eyes, not moving for a moment, and then lowers her hands, crying and laughing at the same time. She stumbles—either tipsy from the rum or tipsy from the sight of Ben—toward him, and they grip each other.

I stare at the fruit on the counter, wondering if either one will name it—an orange or a clementine? That's when it occurs to me that maybe the truest love shows itself between people like this: laid out but unnamed. Suddenly, I feel so alone. When will I ever be able to lay my fruit out on the table?

* * *

CHRISTMAS EVE AT ROXANNE's house is much different from Christmas at my own when Mama was alive. For starters, in Columbia we didn't eat pizza for dinner, we always ate a standing rib roast. And we didn't open all our presents the night before, we only opened them Christmas morning, wrapped and tagged "From Dr. Claus." Christmas Eve was a time for Mama to dust off the Bible and quote passages pertaining to the holy birth, but Diotima prefers to read aloud from *Great Dialogues of Plato,* concerning a holy death:

> "And at last, when the bonds by which the triangles of the marrow are united no longer hold, and are parted by the strain of existence, they in turn loosen the bonds of the soul, and she, obtaining a natural release, flies away with joy."

In Columbia we sang carols, but we never actually rocked around the Christmas tree (and we never bought trees you could actually save and plant). On Lorraine Avenue, Ed plays the guitar and we all belt Creedence Clearwater Revival.

Ben fits in right away, a good thing, considering that when Roxanne asked him how long he was staying, he said, "Indefinitely." He is self-effacing: "I do landscaping," he says, without even adding: "But I went to Duke." Maybe Ben knows he's welcome here and doesn't have to prove himself. Instead he shares the recliner with Alecia and puzzles with her over the *Where's Waldo?* book that my father sent. "Do you think they'd ever put out a picture *without* Waldo in it, just to fuck with us?" he asks. If Ben is auditioning for a role in this family, he's already got the part.

"Look at Max, Holly! He really loves that frog!" Diotima says, as he sits on the floor, shaking the stuffed frog with the bell inside it. Di and I shopped for Max's gift together, testing out different toys on him, but it was hard to distinguish what he liked—he was happy with almost everything. Then we figured out that the best way to determine his favorite toy was to gauge how much he cried when we yanked it away.

"Save your bows!" Roxanne says, collecting the paper ribbons instead of the torn wrapping paper at our feet.

"Why, Mom? Why do we always have to save them?" Di asks.

"In case there's a war, and we can't get bows," Ben says.

I study the picture my father sent me of a Black & Decker power saw and ask grimly, "So, this was donated to the Campbell household in my name?"

"Yeah. I got a massive grill that you could tow behind the station wagon. If I move back home, I can even use it," Ben says.

"That is the worst gift-giving system I've ever heard of," Alecia says. "Your dad buys what he wants for himself and says it's for you?"

"Well, we got the *Where's Waldo?* book to share," Ben says.

"I'm disappointed," I say. "I thought I was getting Noah's Ark."

"Come use one of our boats, Holly," Alecia says, taking me seriously. "My dad has another house up in the Finger Lakes. It's fantastic in the summer—we can go waterskiing!"

" 'One of our boats,' " Ben repeats. " 'Another house.' Has anyone else ever seen their everyday, meager shack? It's like a replica of the White House. The first time I went there, doves just rose up and flew away from the silver Porsche in the driveway, like we were watching a commercial."

"They weren't doves, they were crows. And they shit on the car." Alecia is laughing. "I've been trying to convince Di she should come visit us in New York sometime. I mean, she's allowed to go back, right?"

Roxanne looks tense, either from the general strain of the night or from Alecia's proposal. She doesn't respond to the suggestion, just holds up the yellow cashmere sweater I gave her and says, "Perfect with my skin tones, huh, Holly?"

"You could give Di a shopping list of things to bring back, Roxanne," Alecia says. "It'd be so much fun."

"Mom, I already told her, I'm not going," Di says, cradling

Max and the stuffed frog. "Not right now. Not when Max is so small."

"Now's the perfect time—he can't even walk yet. He's so portable," Alecia says. "Right, Roxanne?"

"Is this my cue for acting like I don't care?" Roxanne asks, putting down the cardigan.

"Why *do* you care?" asks Alecia.

"Because I'm sick, Alecia. Because I don't know what's going to happen to me," Roxanne says.

It's completely silent except for Max chortling at his own milk bubbles.

"I really need Di to be around right now," she adds.

No one speaks. It's as if someone hit the pause button on Christmas. It occurs to me that Di and Alecia have been acting like they don't know, even though Roxanne's been jaundiced since we met last summer. Maybe it's like Di's pregnancy: they watched her grow larger every day and still didn't expect Max's arrival.

"I have cancer. And it's spread. And that's why I'm yellow," Roxanne says.

"What kind of cancer?" Alecia asks.

"The bad kind," Roxanne says.

"Oh, Mom," Di says, starting to cry.

"Now, see, this is why I didn't tell you before," Roxanne says, reaching over to grab her shoulder. "But it's all right. It's okay. Even if I'm not okay, you're going to be okay. Come on, let's get back to presents."

Nobody is saying anything. Nobody's moved. "Somebody say something. Please," Roxanne says.

Wiping her face on her sleeve, Di struggles to get out her next question. "Did they give you...a..."

"An expiration date?" Roxanne suggests. "Six months. If that. Listen, I want to get back to Christmas. It may be my last one, and I don't want to waste it talking about me. Now, there's one more present left. Is it for me? Well?"

Thank goodness for Ed, who jumps to check before anyone has even glanced back at the tree. Digging around the canvas bag of roots, he grabs the last wrapped box and reads the tag. "It's for Holly!"

IT'S A SHINY BLUE CASE with gold lettering that spells "The Box of Stars." Only after I've already unwrapped it do I notice the card. "Merry Christmas," it says and, "Matthew."

"How'd this get here?" I ask, holding up the card and looking around.

"He asked me to bring it and save him a couple of stamps," Ben says.

"Is he your best friend now?" I ask, trying to ignore the guilt lurking around my conscience. *Oh, Matthew. I treated you so terribly, and you send me a gift?* "When did you see him?" I add.

"He took out my appendix," Ben says, as if that explains everything.

Roxanne watches as I open up the box of stars. "It has cards inside, see? Poked with holes of different sizes to represent the constellations," she says. "That way you can learn the patterns at home and take it with you to the sky."

The box also contains a corresponding book of myths and legends, and I pick it up to feel the pages, imagining Matthew shopping for it. How could he not hate me, when I was so cruel? Maybe I shouldn't have told him about Ed and I sleeping together. I think of Grandmother saying, "The truth is never mean; it's the truth," and now I know how wrong she is. My father never got over the truth about Mama and Simon.

We clear off the coffee table, light candles, and choose our cards. Diotima picks up Ursa Major, the she-bear placed in the sky by Zeus to protect her and her unborn child from Artemis. Ben gets dealt Bootes, bear keeper, who herds them around the poles, while Alecia reaches for Draco, the dragon (" 'Well known for vigilance and sharp vision,' thank you very much," she reads). Ed grabs Orion (" 'The most beautiful man in the world, according to legend,' hey!"), and Roxanne snags Delphinus, the dolphin.

" 'Sacred Fish, according to the Greeks,' " Di reads.

My card says I'm looking at Capricornus, the mountain-climbing goat-fish, whose paper-cut holes glitter with points of light. In the biggest spaces, I can see the rippling fire of the candle, just like in the brightest stars. I try to memorize the shape of the constellation, its goat mane and horns, the flip of its fish tail. But I know it's useless. I'll get outside, dazzled, unable to name anything.

I look up in the darkness of the living room to observe everyone else studying their hand. Ben, the prodigal boyfriend; Ed, as uncomplicated as a triangle; Alecia, ferocious and loving; Diotima, Wise Woman from Mantinea. None of them is paying attention anymore to the book of myths that explains what they're seeing, but each wears a look of intensity: *Will I recognize it when I see it?*

Even Max, without a card, is in a trance of concentration, pointing and staring in amazement at something invisible. Can it be the lamp that thrills him or the chair? Or something else entirely? If truth is the space between things, how much does Max really know? I begin staring at the spaces in the room myself, looking for Mama, and wondering if I'm making eye contact with the truth without even knowing it. I'm reminded of Matthew again, how he's managed to save the night without even being here. *Why didn't I treat him like the gift that he is?*

Finally, my gaze falls back on Roxanne, whose brilliant blue eyes smile at me from over her card. It suddenly feels like Christmas.

CHAPTER 19

Engine Trouble

> "The human body is like a very beautiful piece of machinery whose engine is of the finest and most delicate construction; and if wrong or poor fuel is used to feed it...it will soon...develop what the skilled mechanic would call engine trouble."
>
> —THE LIBRARY OF HEALTH, 1927

don't know what to do," I say.

It's six o'clock on a dark, January night, and we're rolling along at 60 mph headed for Wales. The only trouble is, we're not supposed to be headed for Wales.

"Choose a gear," Ed suggests.

In some unconscious desire to reverse the previous five minutes—which involved searching for the M4, attaining the M4, and learning we needed the M5—I attempted a downshift from fifth to fourth but somehow hit reverse instead. The car answered with a grind of indignation, then repeated this several times as I tried third then fourth then third. Nothing would engage, so now we're sailing along in the dying wind of neutral.

"Try fifth," Ed says. "Try *something*."

Miraculously, the car accepts fifth gear at 45 mph, and I careen to the right of the two-lane highway to the sound of honking and collapsing air—a veering noise I tend to associate with high-speed fighter jets narrowly missing a collision.

"Easy, buddy. Try the fast lane," I mutter, watching the crazy driver swerve ahead of me again.

"This *is* the fast lane," Ed says, strangely tight-lipped. "Think *opposite*." He glances behind us.

"Police?" I ask.

"No. Just the transmission," Ed says.

He decides we'll somehow return to the M5 via the "back roads," so I obediently put on my blinker and move into the left-hand lane. I refrain from pointing out that it might be difficult to follow these so-called back roads considering he forgot to pack the map and has refused to let me stop and buy one.

Silence is starting to fill up the car like an airplane cabin depressurizing. I look down at the stick shift in confusion, wondering if I'm supposed to be manipulating it. *Oh, yeah. Still in fifth.*

"What's the use in having a navigator if he can get completely overridden by the pilot?" Ed asks.

"You said we wanted the M4!"

"In order to pick up the M5."

"You didn't *say* that. How am I supposed to know what *this* means?" I say, wielding my index finger in a violent poking motion.

"It means, 'There's the M5.' It means, 'Go there.'"

"But you didn't *say* it. Then you try to send us the *wrong way* on the M4, back to *Swindon*."

"So we could recircle the roundabout and merge with the M5."

"I was positive we didn't want Swindon. We just *came* from Swindon."

"So you decided we'd see Wales instead."

"It sure as hell sounded better than Swindon."

Ed snickers with exasperation, while I sit quiet for a moment, wondering where the compromise is. It seems silly to apologize when I feel dignified for shaking him off.

"So, you happy now?" Ed asks.

"Why—because we're going the wrong way?" I snap.

"Because we're going away."

"Thrilled," I say, clenching my teeth, trying to remember

how we got here. Ah, yes, it was nearly two months ago during Thanksgiving dinner when Ed seemed to change his mind about traveling. He was showing me how to unwrap the roasted artichokes leaf by leaf to get to the center. Everyone watched as he scooped out the heart, dipped it in butter, and fed me, saying he'd go wherever I wanted him to. It occurs to me now that maybe he was just basking in Di and Alecia's attention and wanted to bestow some of it on me.

"Hey, come on. This is funny," Ed says now.

I grip the steering wheel harder and remind him that I almost got us killed back there.

"That's okay. Gives us something to talk about," Ed adds with a grin, tucking more than a strand of my hair behind my ear. It feels like a clump.

Of course, I forgot a brush. My first weekend away with a man, and the most I can do is run my fingers through my hair and tie it up from my face in a scraggly bun. The idea of bringing out the sexy black negligee that I bought seems absurd when we'll probably end up at a youth hostel tonight. The fact that I brought a bathing suit is even sillier, when there's snow threatened on the moors. It occurs to me now that every book I've read concerning the moors involves people bracing themselves against chills and battling consumption. Nobody sips lemonade on a warm veranda.

"Who cares if we never get to Cornwall?" Ed asks with a carefree laugh.

Easy for you to say, when you didn't pay for the cottage.

"I mean, it's almost like someone's playing a joke on us!" he adds, suddenly dissolving into fits of glee as we pass yet another unreadable road sign, positioned just outside a streetlamp's cone of light.

I keep driving through the darkness, looking for a place to turn around.

"What's the point of having a light exactly three feet from the sign?" Ed asks.

When I realize he's actually waiting for me to respond, I give him a Courtesy Smile.

"There we go! At last! She smiles!" Ed says.

I give him a Courtesy Laugh, too, knowing he'll never pick up a difference.

WE END UP SACRIFICING our first night in the cottage by staying in twin beds in a ramshackle B&B outside Dartmoor National Park—not ideal, but at least we finally ended up in the right direction. Early the next morning, we take off for Porthcurno in the pouring rain. Unfortunately, the weather doesn't improve down to the Cornish coast. Wind bucks against the car, and the sky intermittently wrings itself out in torrents of rain. After stopping for tea in the town of Mousehole—Ed can't come *this* far without trying a pork and apple pastie—he encourages me to buy a warm hat since we've planned to go hiking. The only hat we can find is brightly colored in red and blue stripes and stands a foot off my head, à la the Mad Hatter. Heathcliff would've avoided Cathy had she worn it.

As we fly around the shady, rainy lanes stretching toward Porthcurno, I finally start to relax, just knowing we're almost there now. Outside the car window, trees with green mossy trunks and flailing arms look like goblins. Ed weaves the car around another bend, then skids to an abrupt halt.

"Are we all right?" I ask, when he pulls up the emergency break. "Should I drive?"

"We're here," Ed says. "This is Porthcurno, baby."

"Oh," I say as drops thicken into streams against the windshield. It's hard to appreciate the view in the pouring rain. A shack perched on a grassy swelling hovers in gray mist across the road. "Boy. We have to get out of the car now?"

"Come on," Ed says, undoing his seat belt to grab his wide-brimmed Indiana Jones hat from the back.

"Are you sure we can't park in there?" I ask, pulling on my brightly colored cap.

"That's not a garage, Holly. That's the cottage you rented. Check out the mailbox."

"Oh…" I say, trailing off, realizing its true. "I thought we were staying somewhere on the other side of the hill."

"There's nothing but ocean on the other side of that hill," Ed says before looking over and chuckling. "I'm sorry, but you just look ridiculous in that hat," he says with a grin.

UNFORTUNATELY, THE BEST THING I can say about the shelter that I've rented is that it vaguely reminds me of Abraham Lincoln's birthplace, which we visited on a fourth-grade family vacation. The air is chilly, the wood floor dusty, and an iron stove sits in the center of the room, probably the only source of heat.

"You all right?" Ed asks, over by the stove, where he's begun to stack dry wood inside.

Still standing with my arms folded across my chest, I peer around with trepidation. *I'm freezing,* I think, but instead blurt out, "The lamps scare me." The bases of each light are statues of winged cherubs playing a variety of stringed instruments, while the shades are stained various hues of yellow. Matthew would call them "beastly."

"It's like someone urinated on the shades." I point at the baffling yellow streaking.

"I bet it's just the natural aging of the lamps." Ed pauses. "I hope."

Tentatively, I move to sit on the hard wood bench in the corner, then opt for the bed instead, which creaks and strains under my weight and sends up a puff of dust and feathers, making me cough.

"That bed looks really old," Ed says from the stove. "Did this place come with any history? Can we find out who lived here before?"

I cough—trying to clear the fossilized bedbugs from my airways—and debate whether to flip back the lumpy duvet just to make sure there's not a skeleton under there.

"I got no information except for 'charming' and 'ocean view,'" I say.

Ed preoccupies himself with making the fire. Crouched on the floor, he controls the smoke that's hovering over the wood by blowing on it. For a moment, I'm mesmerized by the way he encourages the thick air to make the logs start crackling orange. He seems to be demonstrating physics and magic all at once.

"Here we go," he says at last, standing up with his hands on his hips.

I stare at him staring at the fire and think that he has never been as fascinated with me as with the blazing spectacle in front of him right now.

Ed turns, grinning. "I should probably tell you. I love fire."

You love fire. You love Max. You will never love me.

"Come here," he says, so I go and sit by him on the dusty floor. Just feeling the touch of his arm around me makes me sigh with relief, and I lean my head onto his broad shoulder, thinking how good he smells when he hasn't been smoking.

"So, now that you've got me here, what do you want to do?" Ed asks.

"Did you ... bring any books?"

"A few," he says with a shrug.

"Are you hungry?" I ask.

"For you," he says, kissing my neck as he leans me down on the floor and crawls on top of me. I can't find my smile— Courtesy or otherwise—imagining my two options: sex on the hardwood floor, or sex in a swamp of musty feathers.

"You're not breathing," Ed says, shifting his weight to the side. "What's the matter?"

"Do you ever think you could give this relationship a chance?" I blurt out all in one exhale.

"Holly ... I think you're really cool. ..." Ed stops and laughs. "But what exactly do you want?"

I want you to be madly in love with me, the way Simon was in love with Sylvia. "I just want a chance. I mean, you won't open up at all."

"Neither will you," he says, running a hand up between my thighs. When he figures out that I'm serious, Ed sighs and sits up. "What do you want to know?"

"Well, for starters, who is this Nicky girl that you left behind?" I ask, struggling to sit up. "Why did you dump her?"

"She wanted to get married."

"And you weren't ready for marriage," I say.

"Right."

There's a long pause. I wait, staring at him. "And?"

Ed sighs. "*And* I figured, what are the chances that I'll ever find someone like Sarah again? You only get one great wife in your lifetime. Some people get 'em at the end, some for their very first shot. So, ever since she died, I kind of gave up on the inside. Dated around. Then Nicky joined in the band when our drummer quit—and we were hanging out twenty-four/seven... I mean, I basically moved in with her, without all that official We're-Moving-In-Together! kind of hype. So, I thought I could go through with it."

"And you proposed," I say.

"Sort of," Ed says. "I mean, it was her idea, and I said I could do it, then we went and got a ring. I gave it to her right there in the store."

"In the store?" I repeat. "With everyone watching?"

"It wasn't a giant production or anything. I said, 'Here.' "

"Oh, God," I say with a groan.

"So she made all these plans, and the more plans she made, the more I knew I couldn't do it again, and I finally told her so." He nods, slowly, watching the fire hiss and pop as another piece of wood catches the flame. The cottage is starting to feel cozier as the glow from the fireplace gets brighter. "Unfortunately, that was the day of the wedding."

"And that was right before you came here?" I ask.

"Well, yeah. I had no place to go. I was living with her at the time. Had to pack all my stuff and get the hell out. And the band took her side, wanted nothing more to do with me. So I bought my ticket for England." Ed looks at me. "I don't like to talk about it because it makes me feel like shit."

"Well, it should," I say.

"Thanks." He nods before asking, "What about you? Who's the guy who showed up at Thanksgiving?"

"My old boyfriend," I say slowly, eyebrows knitted. I'm thinking of this pathetic Nicky girl not getting the picture. This is a man who gave her a ring and said, "Here." *This is a man who just told me You're cool, but...* "He's actually one of my best friends," I say as an afterthought. "Or he was."

"See, that's nice. You're still friends. Why can't more people be friends after it's over?"

"Well, they can be when one doesn't break the other's heart or completely wreck her self-esteem," I say, thinking about Matthew again, wondering if I really blew our friendship for good.

"You think we'll be friends when this is over?" Ed asks.

"I think...this is over," I say slowly, and then turn to look at him. "Isn't it?"

His eyes open wide. I appreciate, once again, the yellow speckles in his brown irises. "Already?"

"Well, what's the point? What are we doing here, anyway?" I ask. I can't help thinking that being alone must still be better than being with someone who doesn't love me. Besides, how can I be lonely again now that I've got Roxanne, and Alecia, and Di—even Max? Ed called them my family, and maybe he's right.

"You invited me. To the end of the earth. And I came." Ed nudges me. "You don't want to wait to break up until the end of the weekend? Until after we try out Grandma's bed?"

I stop smiling.

"Holly—joke," Ed says, shaking my shoulders. "I don't care about that. I mean, I do, but I wanted to come on this trip."

"Yeah?" I look at him and his perfect profile. It's okay that it will never belong to my offspring.

"Yeah." He nods. "I like you, believe it or not."

"I like you, too," I say, puzzled.

"Except when you ignore my directions," Ed says, and then laughs. "Hell, don't look so serious. It's okay to smile. And laugh. And *breathe*."

I nod.

"Now would be fine."

I exhale and stop. He waits. "And again."

I inhale and stop. He waits. "Breathe, damn it."

We both start laughing.

"Wind," Ed says. "You need more wind."

CHAPTER 20

Buying Time

> For the patient will live
>   and you will try to understand
> For you will be amazed
>   or the patient will not live
> and you will try to understand
>   For you will be baffled
>
> —"GAUDEAMUS IGITUR," JOHN STONE, MD

show up for lunch at Lorraine Avenue on my day off, the last Saturday in February. Alecia is holding a section of the newspaper when she pulls open the front door, while Di stands at the kitchen island, snapping string beans. The house smells like an Italian restaurant.

The place has changed remarkably in just the last several weeks since New Year's. Cereal bowls now nestle with vomit bowls in the dishwasher, grocery bags contain diapers for Max and Depends for Roxanne, and the refrigerator is stocked with IV bags of normal saline alongside red, yellow, and green peppers. But it's not just the accessories of illness that make the place feel different. It's the tension.

"Who's he talking to?" I ask, pointing at Ben on the cordless. The way he's pacing back and forth makes me think he's talking to Grandmother. She must be appalled that not only has Ben been sharing a bedroom with his girlfriend since Christmas Eve, but that the Duke graduate is now working at Starbucks.

"It's your dad," Alecia says, which doesn't explain the pacing.

"How's Roxanne?" I ask.

"The same," Di replies, which means not good. She stopped eating more than a few bites last week. Now all she seems to do is sleep or throw up.

Ben hands me the phone, so I can hear my father wish me a happy birthday—a day early. Just hearing his voice suddenly overwhelms me with homesickness. I can just imagine where he's talking to me from: the den, on the soft leather couch, beneath a sketch of my mother as a child. She's looking serious under red braids, like a person who's got far too much expected of her.

"Do you feel any older?" he asks.

"Actually, yeah," I say. "What about you? Do you feel older knowing your children are turning thirty-one tomorrow?"

"Unbelievably decrepit," Dad says.

"I miss you," I say, realizing it as my mouth is forming the words. "I wish we were there."

"I wish you were here, too. I could use your help packing. Did Ben tell you that I'm moving?"

"You're moving?" I repeat, so that my brother, who seems to be engrossed in the comics once again, will look up at me. Ben nods and shrugs, as if this isn't something to be upset about.

"I can't live in a town with such arbitrary covenants, where a person can't keep a boat on his own property," Dad says. "I'm looking for a house on the water, near Annapolis."

"When is this happening?"

"As soon as I can put the kitchen and plumbing back together and sell this house. I'm drowning in twenty years' worth of clutter. It's funny the way you each erected a shrine of cardboard boxes to hold your place when you left home. It's like living in a storage closet."

He adds that he's been surprised to find out how empty our boxes actually are. "Or at least, there's nothing important in them. For example, your box marked 'personal.' It was filled with T-shirts! Only T-shirts, Holly!" Dad says with a laugh. "Since you haven't worn them in years, can I give them to Goodwill?"

"Dad, I'm saving them to make a commemorative quilt of my life."

"A commemorative T-shirt quilt," he echoes. By the sound of his voice, he can't imagine the blanket of memories that I'm envisioning.

I stop for a second and wonder myself. Ben used to tell me that I was one of those people whose memories were always better than the actual experience. Like with Mama going away. Until I found Simon's letter, it had never seemed that bad. Sure, it wasn't easy, those months of tense silences punctuated by my grandmother's shrill commands or my father's screaming fits where he'd throw pots and pans—never at anyone, just to make noise. But I always remember Eve's No-Laughing-During-Dinner Rule, and how that always made us want to laugh. It's not actual distortion, I just forget what to emphasize. But now I don't know anymore. Maybe a bunch of T-shirts sewn together would look just as ugly as Mama running away and having an affair.

But I want to see my house again, the house that my mother last lived in. I don't care what happened there.

"Does this moving business have something to do with the woman you met online?"

Ben puts down the paper and stares at me. I can tell by his face: this, he didn't know.

"Who, Carly? No. This is about me getting on with my life," Dad says. "I can't wait here forever."

"Wait for what?"

"For Eve to let me go. For you kids to come home. For all I know, you and Ben will stay abroad forever. I'll be lucky to meet my grandchildren one day. They'll probably have English accents."

The idea of having children with English accents reminds me of Matthew Hollembee and how he never responded to my thank-you card or my follow-up e-mails. "Dad, be realistic," I say aloud. "We're coming home eventually."

"Well, when you do, I'll be in a slightly different location," he says. Only there's something about my father's voice that's changed, as if it, too, is coming from a different location.

"You're happy," I say.

There's a pause. He must be startled by my diagnosis.

"Maybe I am," Dad says slowly, as if afraid to admit it aloud.

"You sound happier than you've been in ages—happier than when Mama was alive," I say. "Are you sure it doesn't have to do with this Carly?"

Carly? Ben mouths.

"Maybe it is Carly," Dad says. "Or maybe I'm just done worrying about when I'm going to lose your mother again. I wasted a lot of years, Holly, waiting for the worst. I loved her too much, I think."

"There's no such thing," I say, just as the call-waiting beep sounds. "Oh, Dad, hang on—someone's clicking in."

On the other line is a male voice, deep and stern yet so modulated, he could be reading from a telemarketer's script. "Hello. This is Alecia Axtel's father. May I please speak to her?"

When I tell Alecia that it's her father, her eyes widen and she shakes her head, making me wonder what she's been up to. "Tell him I'll call him back," she says.

"If you would kindly tell her that it's an emergency," her father says, in the same disconnected tone.

"I'll get right off, Mr. Axtel," I say.

After saying good-bye to my father—telling him he'll see us sooner than he thinks—I hand off the phone to Alecia just as the doorbell rings. Ben reaches the door first. "O . . . kay," I hear him say as he steps out of the way so a woman can enter. "Sister Lavinia," Ben says to Di and me.

"Home health sister," Sister Lavinia adds. She has frizzy hair under a cap, pudgy cheeks, and two pairs of eyebrows: a carefully tweezed black pair and another red-brown set penciled in above. She looks like the sort of woman who would be into crystals or feng shui.

"Where *is* Roxanne?" I ask.

"Back in her room," Di says, only it sounds like a warning.

"Can somebody tell her—" Ben starts.

"I'll go," I say.

*　　*　　*

WILL I EVER BECOME immune to the sound of retching? I wonder, standing outside Roxanne's master-bathroom door as she sits on the toilet and puts the official "Vomit Bowl" in her lap to use. Her primal noises make me feel helpless and out of control, make my own stomach lurch.

Di is a better person than I. Di usually rubs Roxanne's back during these bouts, but the best I can offer is to retrieve the Vomit Bowl and rinse out its painfully achieved puddle of gastric juice. Roxanne finally groans, signaling a temporary end, and I exhale my own sigh of relief.

In a slow-motion dance of shifting, shuffling, and steadying, we maneuver her and the IV pole back to bed. Roxanne sits, still attached to my arm, and then untwists herself to lie back. Just in time, I get the pillow under her head and she closes her eyes. I stare at her skin, so yellow it's nearly neon. Next to the white sheets and blankets, she's practically glowing.

"Roxanne? Sister Lavinia's here," I say before she can fall asleep again. These days, that's all she does anymore.

Roxanne opens an eye but doesn't speak. Plastic tubing snakes from under her T-shirt and connects to a bag of green fluid strapped to her leg.

"Roxanne? The home health sister—" I say.

"Sure. Whatever."

"She's got two sets of eyebrows—I think you'll get a kick out of it."

Roxanne blinks. "What?"

"She's shaved off one pair of eyebrows but they're sprouting back. Then she's drawn on another pair in brown pencil.... Oh, here she is!"

Sister Lavinia is standing behind me, so I quickly excuse myself, embarrassed to have been caught.

Joining the group again, I find Ben juggling an armful of Max, while Alecia has gone into the bathroom to finish her conversation with her father.

"He likes it better when you hold him upside down," Di says, adjusting the flame on the stove. I can't wait to see what she'll cook up next. The scent of oregano and garlic and sweet sausage is already making me hungry.

"Upside down," Ben says.

"Yeah. Flip him over," Di says with a nod, moving the skillet of beans over the flame.

"Hey, Holly, how 'bout that Sister Lavinia?" Ben asks, and then adds in a whisper, "Was it me, or did she have two sets of eyebrows?"

I give my twin a look as if to say I hadn't noticed and then add, "Roxanne seems really depressed."

"Well, that's because she *is* really depressed. Wouldn't you be?" Di asks.

"What's with that drain, Holly?" Ben asks. "That bag coming out of her side? What's it do?"

I explain how her liver cells, infested with cancer, can't do their usual job of handling bilirubin, and as it builds up in her system, Roxanne will grow more and more lemon yellow with a hint of lime. But with the miracle of the liver drainage bag, the bile gets skimmed off the top of Roxanne's failing system.

"So, if the bag keeps working, it'll save her, right?" Ben asks.

It's too hard for me to say that at some point the bilirubin will get too high, that she'll become incoherent and nonsensical and will eventually peter from a coma into death within a matter of a few weeks. "It's palliation, Ben, not a cure," I say instead.

"Okay, can we please stop talking about this?" Di says loudly, pacing back and forth the length of the kitchen tile. Her hands are trembling.

"I'm sorry, Di, I just…don't know what's going on," Ben says, still flipping Max back and forth upside down. Max, as usual, is happy and laughing, oblivious to the strain in the room.

Alecia comes out of the front-hall bathroom, hangs up the phone, and stands there for a second, blinking.

"Is everything okay?" I ask.

"My mother tried to kill herself," she says. "They found her this morning."

"Aunt Maddie?" Di asks, covering her mouth. "Oh, my God!"

"Oh, babes," Ben says, holding out a hand, but Alecia recoils before he can reach her.

"How'd she do it?" Di asks.

"Drug overdose. They pumped her stomach." Alecia shakes her head and folds her arms across her chest. She looks like she wants to punch someone. "And Daddy wants me to catch the first plane home, so I can visit her in the hospital."

"I'm going, too," Ben says.

Alecia stares at my brother. "Well, let me know how she's doing, because I'm not going!"

"But it's your mother," he says. "She almost died."

"By choice," Alecia says, enunciating as if he's mentally challenged or just deaf. "She left me. She flew all the way across the country to get away from me, and when that still wasn't far enough, she tried to kill herself. Why the hell should I go visit her now?"

"She must be really depressed," I say, which only makes my twin glare at me: *You think?*

"We can't tell Mom," Di says in a whisper.

"I don't care who knows, and I don't care what anyone thinks. I will not go back," Alecia says, as if she's still having a conversation with her father.

"We just can't tell Mom," Di says. "It'll only make her worse."

The buzzer on the oven goes off, making all of us jump. "What's that?" I ask.

"Lunch," Di says.

WE SIT DOWN at the table with plates of lasagna, only no one is really eating anything, and I feel a little self-conscious for digging in. Is it okay to have an appetite when Roxanne is lying in the other room and can't eat? Is it okay to chow down when Alecia's mother attempted suicide? The clock over the table ticks out the seconds.

Sister Lavinia walks into the kitchen holding sheets splattered with a body fluid I can't identify. We all stop chewing.

"I've spilt betadine all over the bed," she explains. "Where are your linens kept?"

Since Ben is too busy looking nauseous, I hop up from my chair to find Sister Lavinia a fresh fitted sheet from the linen closet. It bothers me that she's still wearing her wool cap inside the house.

"Did she leave a note?" Ben is asking when I return to the table. Max grunts so that Di will keep feeding him applesauce.

"She left a whole goddamn notebook," Alecia mutters. "Apparently I was mentioned once, but not by name."

I can't help wondering what sort of grim thoughts her mother's notebook cataloged, which then gets me thinking about Mama. If only she had left behind a diary! Although, would I really want to read what my mother might have written about us? After all, according to Simon, she was only "acting" in her marriage. Was she just pretending to love her children, too? Then I remember Grandmother saying that Mama loved us, but that she wanted it all and was determined to get it. Maybe her going had nothing to do with Ben and me. And just maybe, if she really loved Simon, her coming back had everything to do with Ben and me.

"Oh, we forgot the champagne," Di suddenly recalls, only seconds before her gaffe seems to register on her face. "For Holly and Ben's birthday."

"Another time," I say.

"Yeah, maybe next year," Ben says.

"Oh, no! Let's celebrate!" Alecia says, dropping her fork. "I mean, my God, I have loads to be happy about! My mother tried to kill herself! Maybe next time she'll succeed!"

Alecia pushes back from the table and goes to unload the contents of the fridge—first the milk, then the cider, then the leftovers—apparently searching for a bottle of champagne. "You guys can't bring me down. This is my celebration!" she says, and then gasps when Ben, who has followed her into the kitchen, lays a gentle hand on her shoulder.

"Hey," he says.

"Where the hell is it?" Alecia asks, agitated.

"Champagne? I meant I forgot to buy it," Di says.

"You'll regret it if you don't go home," Ben says. "You need to see her."

"I need to see her?" Alecia repeats, her eyes flaring with disgust. "Can you honestly say that seeing your own mother in a casket was a nice way of wrapping things up?"

My brother looks startled, and when he opens his mouth to speak, nothing comes out.

"Yeah, I didn't think so," Alecia says. "That's how I feel about visiting my mom on a psych ward."

Thankfully, Roxanne hobbles down the hallway, cutting the conversation short. She's hunching over the IV pole like it's a cane. Roxanne nods politely, obviously trying not to pay attention, as Sister Lavinia talks about her own mother's "battle with cancer."

"Did you need help with the door?" Ben asks, as if Lavinia's arms are full, as if we live in a castle behind a massive wooden bulwark.

"Aw, no. Enjoy your meal. I can see myself out," Sister Lavinia says. "But if I can use your loo first?"

Alecia jumps up to lead her to the bathroom, but I have a feeling she's just trying to escape.

Roxanne winces in pain as she struggles to sit down. "Guys, happy birthday."

"How about some lasagna?" Ben asks, hopping up to fix her a plate.

"I'm really not that hungry," she says in nearly a whisper. "How was your father?" she adds, just as Alecia gets back to the table. Alecia and I look at each other, unsure which father Roxanne is talking about.

"F-fine," I say, and then glance at Alecia, who sits back down and then proceeds to move bits of meat around on her plate. "He just called to wish us happy birthday."

Ben sets a plate down in front of Roxanne, and we all watch as she takes a bite of the lasagna with trembling hands. Her teeth start to chatter. "I think . . . I think . . ."

"Roxanne? You okay?" I ask.

She drops her fork and pushes back from the table. "C-c-c . . ."

"Cold?" I ask, and then order, "Ben, get a *blanket*."

"C-c-couch," Roxanne manages to say, and I grab her shoulder to walk her to the sofa, as Di pushes the IV pole while holding the baby in her arms. Refusing to let me support her, Roxanne collapses, shaking and shivering and contracting with rigors, onto the couch. We cover her with a pink fuzzy blanket and then call out for Alecia's blue comforter. Under her igloo of blankets, Roxanne chatters.

"C-cold. So c-col..." she mumbles.

"Should I get Sister Lavinia?" Ben asks, as the toilet flushes down the hall.

"Holly's a doctor, Ben," Alecia snaps, tucking the blanket around Roxanne's arms.

I feel Roxanne's legs for signs of a cool, clammy periphery, but she's warm, so warm. A rash, the first of the petechiae, has already erupted on her ankle. A hit of bile must've gotten into her bloodstream.

"She's septic," I say.

"Perhaps I should check her pressure?" Sister Lavinia suggests timidly, appearing behind the sofa.

"Yeah, get a pressure. And somebody call nine-one-one."

"Do they dial that here?" Ben asks. "Nine-one-one?"

"Just get an ambulance," I say, looking around for my black bag.

Roxanne mumbles something like *green smell* before her eyes roll back into her head. I rub her sternum with my knuckles. "Roxanne. Roxanne, are you with me?"

"Sixty over palp," Lavinia says as the blood-pressure cuff hisses in release.

"What's that mean?" Alecia says.

"Her pressure is low. Really low. She needs access. Start an IV," I tell the nurse, reaching over to check for a pulse in Roxanne's groin. It's tachycardic but there. I run to get my doctor's bag from the kitchen as Ben, holding the phone, yells out for our address. Everyone starts answering at once; Di and Alecia argue over the best directions, while Sister Lavinia struggles to place the peripheral IV line.

"I'm afraid I can't seem to get it started," she shrills moments later. "She's a difficult stick."

"Roxanne—come on, Roxanne," I shout as she shakes and moans.

"Fifty over palp," Lavinia checks her pressure again.

I snap open my black bag, take out the central-line kit.

"What's that?" Alecia asks, terrified.

"Access," I say, peeling it open, unfolding the sterile blue cloth containing the kit. "Shit, I forgot gloves," I realize, and for a second I'm paralyzed until Sister Lavinia slaps a pair into my hand. I knew she was here for a reason.

Like a mad scientist, I choose my needle from the kit and then, with shaking fingers, use my other hand to feel for her pulsing artery. *Don't want to hit that. Go medial. Find the vein. Stick it in. Go.* The syringe splashes with maroon blood. "We're in," I say. *Who's we? Me, God, all the angels, hallelujah.* I thread the guide wire, *Come on baby, come on baby,* then the dilator. "Scalpel," I say. Sister Lavinia hands it to me. I make a small incision to open the skin more. Roxanne's thighs are swimming in blood; it's all over the sofa, ruining the plaid. "Do we have a blood pressure?" I ask, pulling the dilator off and threading the line. I snake out the guide wire and pick up a saline flush. "We've got blood return."

Yet they're all still standing there, staring, dumbfounded, as if a bomb went off in the living room.

"Hang the fluids and squeeze the bag! Let's get her legs up, up, up."

When the paramedics finally arrive to take Roxanne to London University Hospital, the fluids are running, her pressure has returned, but I'm still sewing the goddamn line in place, tacking it to her skin with a needle and thread, the same stuff regular people use to attach buttons to shirts. The fine blue thread keeps getting caught on my clumsy thumbs. It seems like an omen. I'll never be able to tie a knot.

CHAPTER 21

Lightness and Strength

"But not withstanding this diversity in form, the general plan constantly kept in view by the Divine Architect has been the central idea of combining lightness with the greatest possible degree of strength."

— THE LIBRARY OF HEALTH, 1927

Ben and I wait to smile until her eyes flutter open.

"How long have you been standing there?" Roxanne asks.

"Five—ten—fifteen minutes, tops," Ben says, clutching the rail of her hospital bed.

Her forehead crinkles in annoyance. You should've woken me, she says. We weren't going to wake you, we insist. Well, you *should* have. No, Roxanne.

We go back and forth like this, wasting another valuable chunk of time—valuable because she doesn't seem to be in pain, she isn't freezing cold, and she's apparently lucid once again.

"So how're you doing, Roxanne?" Ben asks cheerfully.

Her eyebrows furrow in annoyance. "Oh, gee, fine, thanks. Ben, could you excuse us?"

Relief washes over Ben's face and smoothes out the sand of nervous fear. "Sure, yeah, I'll just be...I'll grab something to eat...I'll look for the others."

As IV antibiotics infused round-the-clock last night, Alecia slept next to Roxanne's hospital bed while the rest of us stayed late and arrived early. Di has gone to forage for coffee.

"I don't think I've ever been better," Roxanne says as the door shuts behind my brother. Miraculously, she's been given a private room, which they usually save for the critically ill or highly contagious. But the privacy is nice.

"How's the bag? Is it draining?" I ask, checking the plastic receptacle attached to her bed. "Hey, great. There's a lot of green stuff in there."

I'm not just trying to say something nice. It feels like we're all physically connected to the bile-collecting bag and entirely dependent on its drainage.

"Barbaric, isn't it?" Roxanne says. "I didn't know medicine hadn't advanced beyond the four humors."

"Well, the bag will be clamped off soon," I say.

The oncologist explained yesterday that if the liver and small bowel would just start properly communicating by the plastic catheter they'd inserted, then the unwieldy bag could be replaced by a small cap.

"Hooray," Roxanne says dryly. "It'll get capped off, I'll go home to my bed, and you can invite Sister Lavinia over to inject saline mixed with *bile* right into my bloodstream again."

Apparently, the nurse, in an attempt to clean out the plastic tubing, had not known to gently irrigate.

Roxanne looks miserable, her face gaunt and jaundiced, her eyes sunken and hollow like a prisoner in a concentration camp.

"So...how're you doing?" I ask.

She tries out a pitifully weak snicker and then stops and winces.

"Your liver hurts?"

"My back," Roxanne says. "See what's on my back. Is something pressing there... or *jabbing* me?"

I wrap my arm around her shoulder and pull her forward to inspect her skinny back; the spinal cord shows off each individual bony prominence. For good measure, I inspect the pillow, too. Both are devoid of sharp objects, so she must be suffering from referred diaphragmatic pain.

Tentatively I reach out and touch her bare yellow skin, as shyly as the first time I touched Matthew Hollembee's hand a long time ago. "Where? Here?"

"To the left...yes...*there,*" she says. "And dig your hands in."

I don't dig too deeply. She seems too fragile for that.

"How do you think Di is doing?" Roxanne asks.

"She's okay."

"Will you talk to her?"

"Sure, but...I think she just wants to talk to you."

"She *can't* talk to me. I mean, she can and she can't. The dynamics are different now. I can't..." Roxanne frowns. "Comfort anybody."

"You don't have to," I say, still rubbing her back.

"That's good enough, honey."

Gently, I help her lie back and meet the pillows. The way she sighs with relief makes lying down seem as taxing as a hard run. "I didn't expect this so soon," Roxanne says in a whisper. "I want to be Joan of Arc about this whole thing, but deep down, I'm such a wimp about pain."

"You are *not* a wimp, Roxanne. You're one of the strongest people I know."

She sighs and tells me she hopes hell feels better than this.

"Stop talking about hell," I say, knowing she really means it.

"I'm a hypocrite, Holly, and it's the hypocrites who end up there. I don't follow any of my own rules. Like the Closet Commandment: Thou shalt give something away when you add something new? When we fled the United States I didn't even have enough *suitcases* for all my clothes. I had to check *green garbage bags* at the gate—and there I am, trying not to draw attention to myself."

"Roxanne, nobody ever went to hell over a bunch of clothes. Besides, we're all hypocrites."

She holds up her arm to point.

"What do you want? Something to drink?"

"On the night table. See that magazine? Alecia brought it to me."

It's an installment of *Outside* magazine; the cover exhibits a picture of a Tour de France cyclist blazing down a mountain under the caption "He Beat Cancer and the World."

"I used to sleep with that guy," Roxanne says.

"Lance Armstrong?" I say, startled.

"The other guy. Not so famous." She means the corner snapshot of a man hiking a snowy cliff wearing a puffy ski jacket and goggles. "One of my New York clients—a Wall Street man who wanted me to predict how his stocks would do. He turned fifty-five and climbed Everest. He's got an article in there, trying to inspire us baby boomers to go out and *live*. Seize the day . . . ha." Roxanne opens her eyes, not smiling. "My world has *shrunk* to the size of the bed I'm lying on. Don't tell *me* how to live. Tell it to the thing that's eating me."

"Roxanne, you've got time. Septic shock is . . . a setback," I say, "but it didn't get you yet. We've still got plenty of memories to be making."

"And that Beating-Cancer propaganda just infuriates me!" Roxanne ignores me. "Like all you need is the right mind-set, and you'll be cured. He *beat cancer*. He told cancer to *kiss off*. Why can't they just say he *survived*? Isn't that enough of a miracle? Do they have to play him up as a *winner,* making the rest of us feel like the losers as we crawl into our graves? I mean, they don't say Otto Frank *beat* the Holocaust, they say he survived it. They don't imply that his wife and daughters and everyone else who got gassed were just missing a positive attitude."

"Roxanne, stop. You're not crawling into your grave yet. Take your life in manageable increments of time," I say, something that Mama used to tell me when I was overwhelmed with getting through the next day. "If hour by hour is too long, go for fifteen-minute blocks; if fifteen minute—"

"Nobody can live a life by the minute," Roxanne says.

"We'll seize tomorrow," I say. "You'll get off IVs. We'll go shopping."

"Shopping for what? Moisturizer?" she asks. "I can't ever leave the house again. People will stare at my jaundice and my bile bag."

"We'll go to a cosmetics counter. We'll tell them you tried their self-tanning lotion, and you're really disappointed in the results."

She stares at me, blinks, and then gives me my birthday present: a loud and genuine laugh.

For all the clarity imminent death brings to those sharing its radius, it also stirs up a fog of disbelief that it can actually be unfolding right in front of you, that we are helpless against it. Somehow, in all this haziness, a deep belly laugh seems like the only solid thing in the room. We grip it, this golden brick of giddiness, and then pass it back and forth between us.

"Oh, Holly," Roxanne says, still shaking with the aftershocks of a good chuckle. "You're a great doctor."

"No, I'm not," I say, sobering up. "I hate it."

"Since when?"

Since you started suffering. Then I remember, *Since I started suffering.*

Before I can answer, Roxanne says, "Your mother's legacy is such a burden to you, isn't it?"

"You mean her affair?" I ask.

"Medicine," Roxanne says. "She gave up everything to be a doctor. She was willing to risk her life and her family for it. But you're different."

"I was thinking about quitting, right before she died," I say. "But then I never got to tell her and now...I don't know what I want to do."

"Your mother visited me the other night," Roxanne says. "She says don't be afraid to look under the hood."

"The hood?" I sit up straighter. "Like...of a car?"

Roxanne shrugs.

"H...O...O...D?" I spell.

She nods and says, "Whatever that means to you."

I imagine myself standing before an exposed car engine loaded with all of its baffling devices—metal and springs, tubing and wires, all of it undecipherable.

"It means nothing to me...nothing at all..." I say, worried. "Should it mean something to me?"

"Eventually."

"How'd you know it was her?" I suddenly wonder.

"She looks just like you."

Noticing her blue-and-yellow eyes are glazing over, I say, "Roxanne, talk."

"I feel like I'm being punished."

"But you're *not*. I know you're not. Everyone who lives long enough will get cancer."

Roxanne's eyebrows furrow, and she answers in a low voice, "The point is, I haven't lived long enough."

"I know," I say.

"I have to rest now," Roxanne says.

IN THE HALLWAY, I'm surprised to find Ed sitting on a bench and holding Max, who's fallen asleep on his shoulder.

"How'd you know I was here?" I ask, accepting a hug from his free arm.

"Di called the dorm," he says. "Wanted to know if I'd take care of Max tonight, so she and Alecia can camp out here at the hospital."

"Oh. Oh, right," I say, shaking my head, both disappointed that he's not here for me and relieved all the same. What I really want is to walk around the corner and bump into Matthew again, just like at St. Cate's.

"She's been so bummed out," Ed says.

"Roxanne?" I ask, thinking what an understatement "bummed out" is.

"No. Di." He shakes his head. "Hate to see her looking so sad."

I turn and stare at him.

"Listen, Holly, I know we're not together anymore, but..." Ed says, and in the pause that follows, I steel myself against his next question. He's going to ask me if it's okay if he's in love with Di. It's going to be painful, but not as painful as Roxanne's dying.

"Is it okay if I go with you guys to Skye?" Ed finishes.

"Skye?" I repeat.

"Roxanne wants to take a trip to the Isle of Skye. I'd like to go, too, but only if you're cool with it."

I blink. I have no idea what he's talking about, but I'm pretty sure this is a vacation that Roxanne won't be taking, unless "Skye" is a euphemism for heaven. "Sure, Ed. You can go to Skye," I say slowly.

"You hangin' in there?" Ed asks, stroking the baby's back so comfortably that Max could belong to him.

"Well, yeah. I'm not the one dying," I say.

But when I move down the corridor to find my brother, I feel dazed and incomplete, as if half of me is still in the room with Roxanne, lingering like pockets of air from her lungs, in and out, in and out.

BEN AND I TAKE the Tube toward Charing Cross to hang out in bookstores—belatedly remembering the bookstores won't open until after lunch on Sunday—and then walk over to Kensington Park instead. It seems like we should commemorate the day, however melancholy. Sunlight hides behind a sheet of clouds so that even though it's late morning, it looks like dusk. Everything below the cirrus blanket has the kind of golden hue that always makes me feel like I'm acting out a memory.

To let myself cry in such cold weather seems tantamount to peeing in my pants: temporary warmth that will leave me freezing to death.

"I'm terrible around sick people. I always say the wrong thing. I don't know how you do it," Ben says.

"I say the wrong thing, too. I say the wrong thing to *healthy* people."

"Thank God I didn't finish seminary. I would've had to spend time at the hospital, laying hands on people."

"They would've expected you to *heal* them?" I ask.

Ben smiles and says, "No, Holly, that's your job, remember?"

"Oh, yeah..." I say.

"My duty would be to bless people," Ben says. "And anoint them before they died."

I stop walking to fish for a scarf in my knapsack, thinking how blessing and anointing sounds a lot easier to me, especially if the person is already dead. *How badly can you screw that up?*

"Do you believe people can ask for healing, and it works?" I ask.

Ben shrugs. "Maybe. Maybe not. Weird miracles do happen."

I relive the bloody moment of inserting the triple lumen catheter into Roxanne's groin last night, the way I got the vein on the first stick, the way the wire advanced without even a catch. It was like magic, the kind I could've used back in Pittsburgh, when I was taking care of Clara Storm.

"What?" Ben asks, as I stand there, holding the scarf instead of tying myself up in it.

"Just thinking about last night. Just thinking that I believe in magic after all."

"Holly, that wasn't magic. You're a doctor, and you saved her life."

"Ben, I didn't save her life—she's still dying!"

We reach the frozen pond, where ducks squawk noisily, looking for bread, and where a young couple giggles as they wrestle with each other. I watch as the guy picks up his woman to dangle her over the water's edge. Only it's ice, and she'll be more liable to end up with a cracked skull than wet clothes.

"I don't know what to pray for," I say, trying to ignore their giddiness. "Do I pray that she'll recover, when I know that she won't? Do I pray for her to go quickly, so she won't suffer? I mean, geez, I don't even know how to pray anymore. Sometimes I think believing in God is like believing that Mama was perfect."

Ben looks puzzled. "Why does Mama have to be perfect for you to believe in God?"

"She doesn't, it's just—I don't want to get duped again. It turns out my whole life is a lie—or at least my childhood."

"We had the same childhood," Ben says.

"Oh, yours is a lie, too," I say, and then stop walking to tell my brother the truth about Mama, about what she was doing those seven months she spent without us.

Ben nods, looking not surprised but not happy either. "I kind of figured Dad was paranoid for good reason. And when Jexy and I had lunch in New York one time, I asked her point-blank, and she answered the question."

"But why didn't you tell me?" I ask.

"Because you didn't want to know the truth. And I didn't want to spoil things for you."

It's strange that we're talking about our mother and not Santa Claus. Was Sylvia Campbell really so fictional?

I ask Ben if he remembers when Dad went down to get Mama.

"Of course I remember," he replies. "Grammy Campbell made us drink warm goat's milk. She could've chilled it first."

"And pasteurized it," I add grimly. "Was Dad depressed when he got back?"

"Well, yeah. Don't you remember? She'd refused to come home. The day he got back, I heard him banging things around in the kitchen and telling Grandmother that they'd be getting a divorce. But then the invasion happened about a week later, and she came back, and I never heard him mention it again."

I am starting to remember. I was in the cafeteria when Nicolas Olzewski came up to Ben and me and said, "Did you hear that we invaded Grenada?" I thought he meant we were adding it on, like Hawaii. It seemed like that would make Grandmother happy, because now Mama could say that she graduated from a U.S. medical school. But Ben said that if we invaded, something bad must've been going on, and that Mama might be in danger. Together we cornered the cafeteria monitor to see if we could go to the front office to use the phone and call our father. But Mrs. Richards said the United States went in to "save the American medical students," and that "we won," and it was "all over now." She told us there was nothing to worry about, and that we should follow everyone out to recess. So we did. That night at dinner, my father told us that the invasion just meant that Mama was finally coming home. Which seemed interesting because Dad had just gone down there to bring her back but had returned alone. It was as if he'd gotten so fed up that he'd commissioned an army to go and get her.

"She forgot about us," I say. "As soon as she left, it was like we didn't exist."

"Holly..." Ben shakes his head. "God doesn't forget about us."

I consider that for a second, folding my arms across my chest, until a sheepish smile forms on my face. I tell my twin that for a seminary dropout, he's awfully preachy.

"You brought it up," Ben says.

"Why did you drop out?" I ask, as we start walking again.

"I just didn't want to be a minister anymore. I still don't. Maybe I was never officially 'Called,' " Ben adds.

"Yeah, well, maybe you're just a little too hung up on 'official,' " I say. "You think God's going to give you a purpose and then notarize it?"

"Maybe not," Ben agrees, putting his chin down into his jacket as the wind blows. "But look who's talking," he adds, giving me a shove, which makes me smile.

"Roxanne says Mama's legacy is a burden," I say. "That if I don't like medicine, I can still get out."

"What would you do instead?" Ben asks.

The question makes me feel like a contemporary of Galileo who has just found out the world is not flat, that we don't get to the end and fall off. And yet, the truth doesn't make me feel any better. What am I supposed to do with this big, round planet, when my whole existence was predicated on the fact of its flatness? "I have no idea," I say, daunted.

"I thought you loved medicine," Ben says, reminding me of myself when I tried to convince him to still be a minister despite his apparent reCall.

"When was that?" I ask.

"That week you spent being the camp doctor at Kon-O-Kwee. You sounded really happy."

He's right. I was happy three summers ago, before Mama died. I had just gotten out of the ICU where every night I was breaking someone's ribs during a Code before breaking bad news to the family. I went from the fluorescent lights and sick building air of St. Catherine's to Camp Kon-O-Kwee, where, for seven days, the most serious thing that I treated was home-sickness. There was not one conversation about death. It was bliss.

"So, be a full-time camp doctor," Ben says now.

"I can't live at a summer camp all year-round. I'd have to eat Beefaroni for lunch and listen to Britney Spears on the loud-speaker every single day."

"So, be a pediatrician."

"But I like adults, too," I say. "I like talking to people and hearing their stories."

"I don't get it," Ben says. "Why have you just spent the last few years in the hospital, when it depresses you?"

"I have to be able to recognize and manage a crisis," I say.

"I think you've got that covered," Ben says as we keep walking down the white gravel road. "So, if you decide to stay a doctor, I guess you'd have to go back and be trained in family practice?" he asks.

"Oh, God, no. That's what I did my residency in," I say.

Ben smiles.

"Oh, right," I say with a chuckle. "You think I should actually try that before I quit?"

"It's just a thought," Ben says.

"Mama told Roxanne to tell me not to be afraid to look under the hood," I say. "Whatever that means."

"The hood," Ben repeats. "Like, the Grim Reaper's hood? His cloak of death?"

"God, I hope not! You think this means I'm gonna die?" I ask.

"You are going to die, Holly," Ben says. "There are no sur-vivors."

"Oh, yeah," I say.

In silence, we walk along the road, until finally Ben puts his arm around my shoulder and says, "If we leave the park now, we can get lunch and then go to the British Museum right when it opens."

"What about Roxanne?"

"We'll be back at the hospital before dinner. It's got Egyptian mummies, Holly."

"Can we see the mummies before the ancient books?" I ask.

"Well, I don't know. It's my birthday, too, you know."

"So, here we are. The big three-one," I say.

"Yeah. Look out," Ben says with a sigh. He turns and looks at me. "We can see the mummies first."

CHAPTER 22

Good Advice

"Advice is not meant to provoke confrontations with relatives. Mature physicians exert their authority subtly, kindly, gently and unconsciously."

—THE ART AND SCIENCE OF BEDSIDE DIAGNOSIS

Alecia is the first to buy: a black, knee-length leather jacket with dark fur on the collar.

"But that's *real* leather," Di says, appalled.

"It's *used* leather," Alecia says. "The animal died for the person before me."

The three of us are in Camden Town rummaging through the racks of clothes, coats, and jewelry in the outdoor market—used goods, mixed with not-so-used.

It's funny how natural it feels to be here after I resisted Alecia's invitations to go shopping for so long. Only it wasn't Alecia but an e-mail from my mother's friend Jexy that finally made me agree to come today. She wrote to say she'd be in London in a few weeks and wanted to take Ben and me to lunch. An imminent date with a fashion designer made me open my closet and see that my wardrobe could use some work.

So far, I've stuck with one conservative purchase—a lavender cashmere sweater—and one frivolous: a shiny, pale blue, "bad ass" (according to Alecia) leather jacket. The day I have the guts to wear it will be a day I can shout, "I don't know!" with confidence. Or, more optimistically, maybe it'll be the day I finally know something.

"How long do you think we can leave Ben alone with the baby?" I ask Di, wondering if we'll still be able to stop for pizza. It occurs to me belatedly that I've come all the way from Winchester without any sandwich Baggies of food. I even forgot my doctor's bag. *Is this progress?*

"He'll be fine. Mom's there to help," Di says.

She's actually right. For the last week Roxanne has been vigorous enough to direct Ben in the care of her grandson. The cancer, while not in remission, has at least stalled enough to give us this sliver of time. It's better than waiting.

"So, what are you guys going to give up?" I ask.

"What do you mean?" Alecia asks.

"My mother always said that nothing new should come into your life or your closet until you decide to throw out something old," I say. "It's called the Closet Rule."

"My mother says the same thing. She calls it the Closet Commandment, only she never abides by it," Di says. "The only reason Mom says it is so I won't leak into her closet space."

"I have a silk scarf I could get rid of," Alecia says, sounding doubtful. "Holly?"

"I already got rid of Ed," I say.

"Maybe someone should tell him," Di says.

It's true. Every Saturday that I don't have to be in the A&E, I try to go to London and sit at Roxanne's bedside. Except that whenever I arrive at the flat on Lorraine Avenue, Ed is already there, playing with Max or fixing Roxanne some tea. It's bad enough that I have to see him in Winchester at work and in the kitchen and—half-naked—leaving the shower. Now my London haven is ruined, too. Over and over, I get to be reminded that this sexy man didn't really want me.

"I think he's secretly in love with my mother," Di says.

"I think he's in love with Max," Alecia says.

"I think he's in love with you, Di," I say.

"Me?" she says, and then laughs. "Well, that's never gonna happen."

"Because he and I—"

She sighs so gustily that her bangs take flight. "For so many reasons."

WE END UP wandering into a dress shop called Lena's, owned by a woman who begins scowling the moment Alecia walks through her jangling door.

"Hey, guys! Look!" Alecia points to the racks. "It's a Going-Out-of-Business sale!"

"No, it *isn't*," comes the frosty reply from behind the counter. "It's simply a *sale*."

"SHE *DESIGNED* THESE DRESSES," Di tells Alecia, outside my dressing room. "She's *Lena*. You shouldn't use the word 'sackcloth' in front of her."

"I'm the customer. It's not my problem she's standing in a room full of dresses she can't unload. She should thank me for being here instead of trying to make me leave because of my lemonade. This store's about to go under, and she wants to get on my case over clear liquids."

I unlatch the door to my dressing room and come out in a red dress. "Is this cherry?"

They must hear the skepticism in my voice. "Brick," Di says, shaking her head.

"Burgundy," says Alecia. "Wine."

"Garnet," Di adds.

"I'd be afraid it was cherry," I say, shutting myself back into the stall to take it off. My mother is—was—the only redhead I've known who could pull off wearing cherry.

"Holly, you have to tell Mom that she's not strong enough to take a vacation," Di says.

"I do?" I ask, struggling with the zipper. "A vacation to where?"

"The Isle of Skye. Off the coast of Scotland," Di says. "Ed told her that she has to go there to get her spirit back."

"He told her *what*?" I ask, reaching for the next dress to try on.

"Did we know that Clifford was Scottish?" Alecia asks.

"She's not strong enough," Di says.

"What if she thinks she is?" I ask.

"You have to tell her she isn't!"

"She didn't like the last one," Alecia says. Apparently, Lena is back, so I open my door to hand off the vetoed dress, just in time to see a woman coming out of an adjacent stall. Her dyed hair clashes horribly with her cherry-red Nancy Reagan suit. My grandmother would scold me for staring, but then, she'd have to scold the woman for suddenly pointing at Di.

"Ah, hello! Diana, is it? Gloria Newton-Bly!" The large lady in red says. "From next door!"

"Oh . . . right," Di says, looking a little confused. Or maybe, like me, she's just startled by the exuberance of this stranger.

"I saw your mother just after the holidays. She looked so *different*."

"You could say that," Di says.

"I heard she was sick. How is she—apart from the cancer?" Gloria Newton-Bly asks. If she wants an opinion, I will say that the cherry red suit looks fabulous, just so she'll buy it.

"She's terrific . . . apart from the cancer," Di says slowly.

"Right, then," Gloria Newton-Bly says, nervously touching her orange coif. "Do say hello from all of us."

Watching the woman gather up her purse to leave, I realize she's wearing her own unfortunate suit.

"What a bitch," Alecia says, after she's gone.

"I am so sick and tired of everyone saying hello. It's, like, you think that's what Mom needs? Your *greeting*?" Di says.

"Who says hello to her?" Alecia asks.

"Everyone who knows she's sick. Neighborhood people. The mailman. The butcher. The dry cleaner. The Indian takeaway guy. They all say to tell her hi—or *hello*," Di adds with an exaggerated English accent as she rolls her eyes.

"I didn't know Roxanne had so many friends," Alecia says.

"She doesn't!" Di says.

"I think it's a convention," I say. "To sort of pretend everything's normal, while at the same time they're letting you know that they're thinking about Roxanne."

"Everything's *not* normal!" Di says, her voice breaking. "Everything is a mess! And what's so unacceptable about admitting that you truly care?"

"Hello?" the store owner calls, coming back into the dressing room area. "Everything all right?" Her eyebrows go up when she notices that Di is red-faced and that she's wiping tears from her eyes. "Can I get you anything?"

"A couple of minutes?" Alecia replies, and then, after Lena is gone, Alecia adds, "A better selection?"

"Di," I say, reaching out to touch her arm, a gesture that only seems to make her cry harder.

"I don't want her to die," she says, nearly choking. "There's nothing I can do, and it sucks."

"I know," I say. "I'm sorry." I think of Roxanne telling me that I won't always ache over my own mother and how, slowly, that's becoming true. But it's too soon for Di to even imagine, just as I wouldn't have been able to.

"At least you have a good relationship with your mother. At least she's not a wack job," Alecia says. When she opens her mouth to say more, I stare her into silence. *This is not about you.*

"Mom and Max are all I've got," Di says, weeping. "My father's dead."

"What about me, ya bitch?" Alecia says, making Di chuckle and cry at the same time.

"You live in America," she says.

"I live with you! Besides, you're not English. You can come back to the States whenever you want."

"I lost my passport when we moved from the Netherlands!" Di says. "I have no other proof of identity. They'll never let me come back."

"As long as you have a credit card, you can apply for a new passport, right, Holly?"

I shrug and nod. She's going to need more than a credit card, but that's probably not the point right now.

"She's my best friend, and I hate to see her suffering," Di says, blowing her nose, and for the first time, I am glad that my mother never had the chance to suffer long, even if it meant that we never got to say good-bye.

All of a sudden, Di seems to notice me. She wipes her face and says that she likes the latest dress I've tried on.

"Oh . . ." I look down at myself. "Really? I don't know." It's a little black shift dress. It's exactly the thing that I don't have an occasion for, which I tell them.

"You can dress it up or dress it down. You can wear it to my wedding," Alecia says. I assume she's talking about marrying my brother again, considering she's wearing the emerald ring. "Get what you want," she adds magnanimously. "I'm not having bridesmaids."

"When will this be?" I ask.

"I don't know," Alecia says. "But that is a dress that will never go out of style."

"Yeah, Holly," Di says with a sniff. "What's the problem? You look stunning."

"Maybe I don't want to look *too* good," I say.

"Oh, I know, I hate that," Alecia says. "Sometimes I wake up in the morning and think, 'Don't look too good. Please, God, just don't let me look too good.'"

I think of shopping with Mama. *Just get it,* she'd say. "Can we put it on hold?" I ask.

"Don't put it on hold. You'll never come back," Alecia says.

"Well, we can't take it *now,*" I say. "We still have to go out for pizza. It could get crumpled. Or tomato sauce could spill on it."

"We'll pay for it now," Alecia says, and then turns to the store owner. "Do you have a size large sandwich Baggie we could put this in?"

"HOLLY, YOU'RE HERE!" Roxanne says with a smile, when we finally get back from shopping. It must be a good day, because she's actually standing up, holding on to her IV pole in the middle of the living room as if she's a shepherd with a staff for sheep. Somewhere in the future, I feel myself already missing her greetings—the way she converts the simple fact of my presence into a promise of something good.

"I'm here," I say, feeling cheerful until Ed appears from the hallway bathroom.

"Hey, woman," he says, scooping Max up off the floor to flip him upside down. As Ed swings Max back and forth, back and forth, I look away, unable to watch his little neck snapping to and fro like that. If only Max would stop encouraging Ed with his hysterical laughter.

I glance over at Ben, who's reclining in a leather chair pretending to read. I know immediately he's pretending, because his forehead is wrinkling the way it used to when my parents would fight while we watched TV. Only I'm not sure what's bothering my brother today, unless he's anticipating a conflict between Ed and me. But Ben doesn't have to worry. I'm not about to tell Ed to stop showing up. How can I, when Roxanne seems to like him so much?

"Well, I spoke to your mother today, Alecia," Roxanne says.

At the kitchen island, Alecia stops unpacking her parcels from Camden Town. "You spoke to my mother?"

"She told me that she'd just spent the last month in a psychiatric ward. She said she tried to kill herself."

"Yeah, I know," Alecia says, nodding slowly. She cocks her head to the side. "How'd she find me?"

"Oh, I called her," Roxanne says. "But she said to tell you 'hi.' "

"Ha!" Alecia says, a declaration. She looks at Di, who shakes her head. "Why were you calling my mother, anyway?" Alecia adds.

"I wanted to invite her on our family vacation," Roxanne says. "We're going to the Isle of Skye over the Easter bank holiday."

"Mom, are you *crazy*?" Di erupts. "What happens if you go into septic shock again? What the hell are we supposed to do then? You've still got that bag on you! Holly, tell her! What if she needs another blood transfusion?"

"Look, Ed says that if I want to get well, I should be making a journey to retrieve my power animal," Roxanne says.

"Retrieve your *what?*" Di asks.

"My pow-er an-i-mal," Roxanne enunciates. "It's the only way to get my strength back. And Skye is the place I picked to do it."

Ed reaches down once again for Max, who, hands overhead, sits on the floor making doglike begging noises. Straightening up with the baby, Ed seems to notice that we're all staring at him. "I read it in the *Way of the Shaman,*" he says with a shrug. "Sometimes, if you're too sick to visualize your power animal, you gotta go get it back."

"So your *shaman* wants you to go, but what does your doctor say?" Di asks.

"Hey, I was just passing on some theories about illness," Ed says.

"I'll get jacked up with a couple of units of blood right before we go," Roxanne says. "I've got a good vibe about the place. Baedeker's says it's got otters and seals, and two hundred species of birds, including golden eagles. Stop worrying. I can sense that nobody's gonna die that weekend."

"Say that, Mom, and you're pretty much guaranteeing one of us will," Di mutters.

"I was an internationally ranked psychic before this shit happened to me!" Roxanne shouts, making me smile. I can't help myself. It's nice to see her looking so vigorous for a change.

"Yeah, well, how psychic are you now, when you're going to make us travel hundreds of miles to bring Clifford home?"

"How many times do I have to explain this?" Roxanne asks. "Clifford is my spirit guide. He is *not* my power animal." She takes a few steps forward, still clutching the IV pole. "Now, I'm not a very demanding person. I ask very little of people. Di? Have I ever asked anything of you?"

"You asked me to leave the States and never see my father again."

"Oh, besides that!" Roxanne says. "Now I just want a few

things. I want to take this trip to Scotland. I want to see this place the Vikings named Isle of the Clouds. I want to see its hills and valleys, its caves and waterfalls. And I don't want to go alone."

Nobody speaks.

"I think we should go," I say. "We need to get out of here before we kill each other or . . ." *Before someone dies.* "I mean, it's the island of the *sky*! We might not get another chance to see it."

Ed turns to look at me gratefully. Even Di lifts her head.

"And I want Alecia to forgive her mother," Roxanne goes on.

"Take it up with her," Alecia says. "She's the selfish one."

"You can choose to forgive her. It'll only help *you*."

Alecia shakes her head. "Never."

"Alecia, do you want to live the rest of your life bitter and unhappy?" Roxanne asks. "Because that's a choice, too."

She's right, it occurs to me. If I can pick a state of mind, why do I hold on to my grief and anger?

"Why did she leave me?" Alecia finally asks, in a voice too laden with agony to even reach full volume. I stare at my future sister-in-law and feel like I'm watching myself. Could I finally let her go—let go of the Mama I thought she was and the Mama she turned out to be?

"Look, Alecia, I don't know. I can't say I understand Maddie. But I want you to forgive your mother. It's why you're here, isn't it?"

Just hearing Roxanne say it aloud lets me know the truth: that's exactly why I came to England. To forgive my mother. I just didn't know it when I left.

"I don't know why I'm here," Alecia replies, only without her usual fight. She runs her hand through her spiky hair and admits, "I really don't."

"Maddie loves you," Roxanne says.

"She doesn't know me," Alecia says, staring at the floor.

"She doesn't know anyone. No one truly exists for Maddie except Maddie herself," Roxanne replies.

"And you're telling me that's acceptable?" Alecia looks up, angry again.

"Honey…" Roxanne says, moving to touch her shoulder. "You exist to *me*. And you exist to Ben. To every one of us in this room. Okay?"

Alecia nods, and when she finally looks up again, I can see her eyes are glassy with tears about to spill over. But instead of collapsing back into her own seat, she goes to join my brother on the arm of his recliner.

"I also want Ben to bless the baby," Roxanne suddenly says, her eyes now fixated on my twin.

"Roxanne, no. I can't," Ben says, his arm encircling Alecia's back. Given his quick response, it occurs to me that this probably isn't the first time he's heard her request. My brother points to Ed. "Have the shaman do it."

"Oh, no, no," Ed says. "Seriously. I just read this cool book—"

"Why don't we just take Max to a real holy man to be baptized?" I suggest.

"Because I don't know who is a real holy man. I look around me and see a lot of holy men and women, or I see none at all," Roxanne says. "Most of the time I look around and see a world of people who are only parallel playing, occasionally waving hi from their sandboxes."

Padding toward my brother on her swollen feet, Roxanne stops and sits down right on the coffee table so she can face him.

"Ben, do you think I care if you dropped out of your ministry program? You think I give a shit about making this official? Play the 'Circle of Life' and hold the baby up to the sunlight! I don't care. Whatever you want. Just invoke something with reverence in front of that baby."

"I don't feel comfortable. I'm not a minister, and I don't want to be. I'm trying to live quietly," Ben says.

"Oh, Ben," Roxanne says. "You're hiding whenever you tell me that. You call quiet living a testimony? At best, when you die people will say you were 'nice.' At worst, they'll say they never suspected such a quiet man was capable of killing all those people. But no one will ever invoke the idea of God when they remember you."

Ben shakes his head. "I just don't get what you want from me."

"I told you what I want. I want a blessing."

"But what would I *say*? That sometimes I believe in Jesus and sometimes I don't? That sometimes when he makes the most sense I am most positive that I'm having a—a *seizure*—and I'm okay with that?"

"Guess what, Benjamin. The blessing is not about you," Roxanne says, moving with her IV pole toward the kitchen.

"Well, if it's not *about* me, then why does it *require* me?"

She doesn't answer, just keeps walking past the island and down the bedroom hallway, letting Ben's words hang there like a still life on the wall waiting to be considered.

CHAPTER 23

Letting Go

> For there will be...
> ...the letting go
> For love is what death would always intend if it
> had the choice...
>
> — "GAUDEAMUS IGITUR," JOHN STONE, MD

ook at you! You're beautiful!" Jexy says, as soon as she opens the door to her flat in Earls Court. But she's the beautiful one, slim and tall, with a head of brown waves that's been tamed down from her "big hair" that my mother saw when they met in the '80's. In her long wool skirt and boots and green sweater, she could exist in two time periods at once: the 1940's and now. Only the neck on her sweater is so oversized that she's baring a little shoulder—probably one of her own designs. I'm almost surprised she's not wearing a pair of her world-famous jeans.

"You look different. Are you in love?" Jexy asks immediately after we've finished hugging.

I can't help laughing. My mother's best friend has always been this direct, though it's been over a year since we saw each other last—or nearly two now, since we're nearing the second anniversary of Mama's death. "Actually, no," I say. "I'm not even seeing anyone."

I have taken care with my outfit, though, dressing up for this occasion in the black shift dress from Camden Town and

Alecia's long leather jacket. When eating with a fashion designer, it's hard not to pay attention to what you're wearing.

"Where's Ben?" Jexy asks, leading the way into the living room from the front hall.

I tell her that he's working at Starbucks today, but that he wants to see her while she's here. "So, they put you up here?" I add, looking around at the French provincial furniture and the ornate rug that could've been stolen from Versailles.

"Who, the filmmakers?" Jexy asks. She's dressing the cast of the latest Harry Potter movie. When they aren't in their robes, the young wizards will be outfitted in Jexy Jeans and the rest of her line of clothes. "Oh, no. This place belongs to my friend's friend. He told us to use it, while he's in Italy."

"Us? So, someone else is living here, too?" I ask, a question that seems to make Jexy look just a little giddy. In fact, she seems to be twinkling all over.

"My friend came with me," she says, but her brown eyes dare me to ask more.

"Are *you* in love?" I ask, which makes her burst out laughing.

"Oh, you're wonderful, Holly. It's just like seeing Sylvia again."

I laugh, too, and tell her she didn't answer the question.

"It's an old flame," Jexy says, blushing. "From, like, a million years ago."

"Thor?" I ask, remembering that Jexy and Thor were married for a time.

"Oh, God, no. Me and a transplant surgeon? Never again."

"Babe? I'm going," a woman says, emerging from the hallway, wearing a backpack over her shoulder. Her frizzy, orangish ponytail reminds me of hay. I can't help noticing her jeans couldn't possibly have been custom-made by Jexy: the crotch sits too low.

"Wait, I want you to meet my best friend's daughter," Jexy says, standing up and holding out her hand, the perfect hostess. "This is Holly," she says as I form my face into a smile.

This is Jexy's friend? *This* is Jexy's new lover? I am crushed. If Jexy ends up with a woman, she's not supposed to be in a slouchy flannel shirt. She should dress in Armani and know how to accessorize.

Only, the woman apparently hasn't discovered the technique of a Courtesy Smile; instead she looks perturbed as she repeats, "Your best friend's daughter. So, who was that? Sylvia?"

I'm surprised, not used to Mama's name being spoken so intimately by someone I've never met.

"Oh, wait, I forgot," Jexy says with a laugh, covering her mouth. "You knew her."

"Yeah, I knew her," the woman says, staring at me so intently now, I feel naked. "You look a lot like her," she adds.

"Did you go to school with my mom, too?" I ask.

"Me? A doctor? No way. I was visiting my brother at the time." She hoists the backpack farther onto her shoulder and comes toward me, holding out her hand. "I'm Jude, by the way."

"Oh, geez, I'm sorry," Jexy says. "I'm so bad with introduc—"

"Who's your brother?" I ask, appreciating the firmness of her handshake. At least it feels sincere.

"Simon Berg."

"Simon Berg?" I repeat, startled. *So, this is Jude. The one who didn't want to see her brother happy.*

"Yeah, Simon Berg," Jude says, looking amused. "You heard about him?"

"I guess he and my mom shared a body," I say, which makes Jude start to laugh, while Jexy looks at the floor.

"They sure did," Jude says.

"I mean, they shared a cadaver. In anatomy lab," I say. *Why does it feel like she's laughing at me?* "What's he doing now?" I hastily add.

"He lives in New Jersey with his wife and daughter."

"But right now he's on vacation," Jexy says.

"Well, yeah," Jude says with a shrug. "Sasha's doing a year abroad at the London School of Economics. So he's visiting."

"Visiting...here?" I realize slowly. "He's in London, too?"

"My niece is 'having a hard time adjusting,' so Mommy and Daddy are here to bail her out again. She's such a spoiled child," Jude adds.

"Well, why don't you set her straight?" Jexy says, sounding just a bit playful.

"Not today. Today I'm off to the archives. The British Museum calls." I watch as Jude leans in and kisses Jexy. "Give my brother my love," she says with a smile. At least the smile makes her seem softer. Even her hair seems less brittle. Still, I can't help wondering why, if they're an item, Jexy doesn't hold a fashion intervention. Maybe opposites really do attract.

"Is that okay?" Jexy asks, once Jude is gone.

"Is what okay?" I ask.

"If Simon joins us for lunch?"

"Today? Now?" I say, nearly panicked. *I never expected to—I have to prepare for—it wasn't supposed to happen—he didn't show up at the funeral! That's when we should've met.* "Does he want to meet me?" I ask.

"Well, I'm sure that he'd love to," Jexy says.

In other words, no. In other words, he has no idea that I'm going to be there.

I tell her that I just have to use the bathroom before we go, even though I don't even need to pee. Jexy has never been one for playing games, yet why do I feel like I am in one? Probably because it's suddenly a mission: I must comb my hair and reapply my lipstick. For Mama's sake, I have to look good for Simon.

JEXY DOESN'T DO the Underground. Instead, she pays for a taxi to take us over to Carlos Place, which deposits us just outside the Connaught. It's ironic when I realize that Simon is staying here and remember my last unfortunate meeting associated with this hotel: Matthew's mother. At least this time I'm dressed for the lobby.

As Jexy leads us to the concierge desk, I can't help thinking wistfully back to the drunken night when I climbed the mahogany staircase to Matthew's hotel room, lay on his bed, and tasted his champagne. If only I hadn't been so selfish, so determined to be with someone so obviously wrong for me.

Suddenly, a well-dressed woman is bustling toward us with outstretched arms dangling gold jewelry. Simon's wife must be in her early fifties, yet her hair hasn't aged a bit: honey blond without a visible gray root. Mama would say she's aged well.

She hugs and kisses Jexy, who again introduces me as "my best friend's daughter." I can't help being pleased. It makes Mama sound so alive.

"So, you're having lunch with Simon, I hear. The three of you, then?" Lisette asks. If she knows anything about the history between Simon and Sylvia, her face doesn't show it.

"Apparently," I say.

Lisette tells us that she and her daughter, Sasha, are going shopping at Harrods for the day to brighten her spirits. "Such a tough time for her, trying to fit in. Her boyfriend broke up with her. She's not sure what she wants to do with her life. And the whole point of the London School of Economics was to help with that. Now she's thinking she should be a poet like her aunt Judith. Tell Jude she must stop trying to help. Oh, here he is!"

And here he is. Simon Berg. The man my mother loved. Walking toward us in the lobby of the Connaught. He's wearing a stone-colored suit with a burgundy tie and a wry smile. He's dark and dapper, thin in all the places that my father is chubby— in the face and gut—and olive-skinned where Dad is sunburnt. Yet I'm surprised to discover how slight Simon's shoulders are. I imagined him larger, stronger.

"Hey, Jex," he says, leaning in to kiss her. "You look great, as usual."

Straightening up, he glances in my direction and looks away before his eyes shoot back.

"Simon, this is Sylvia's daughter," Jexy says, pulling me forward.

"Sylvia Bellinger's daughter," I add, just in case he's forgotten, as I shake his hand. "Holly."

Simon looks stunned; in fact, he doesn't say a word as he shakes my hand for several seconds. "Hello, Holly," he finally manages. The way he's staring at me makes me understand why Mama fell in love. His eyes are so intense that I can feel the insight in his gaze—insight and kindness.

"I better consult with the concierge on how to find all the

major department stores," Lisette says. "Sasha and I are hopeless with directions."

"How is your mother?" Simon asks, once Lisette has moved off toward the front desk.

I glance at Jexy, who's looking at the chandelier or the staircase, at anything but us. Suddenly, I get it. That's why she wanted to bring me here today. Jexy never told Simon that the last time she saw my mother, she was picking out clothes for Mama's casket.

"Um, she's . . . dead," I say.

"She's dead?" Simon repeats, his brown eyes widening in horror.

I nod my head, unable to stop staring at him, scrutinizing his expression. He looks genuinely upset. "She was in a car accident. Two years ago," I say.

"Two years ago?" he says again before turning to Jexy. "How long have you known?"

"I didn't know how to tell you," she says.

"You just say it. You just tell me the truth. Christ, no wonder you didn't become a doctor."

Suddenly, Lisette is back, babbling about Harrods and the upcoming shopping adventure. "Honey, are you all right?" she asks, when Simon doesn't even smile in reply. His face looks different now: the confidence he wore moments ago replaced by tension. I can't decide if this is the look of sadness, regret, or simply fear. Maybe it's all three.

"I'm fine," he says, giving his wife a squeeze. "Go spend lots of money."

"Now I know you're not all right," Lisette says with a giggle. She's the only one of our circle who laughs.

"You're mad," Jexy says to Simon later, once we're seated in the restaurant.

I pick up my leather-bound menu to hide behind it. This is a conversation they should be having alone. *I've done the hard part; I broke the bad news. Can I go now?*

"Well, what'd you expect? I feel broadsided," Simon says.

"We were all broadsided," Jexy says.

Technically speaking, I was the only one who got broadsided, I can hear Mama saying in my mind, as my eyes keep scanning the menu for something reasonably priced. *Twenty pounds for a plate of warm asparagus? Do we get to keep the plate?*

"What about a glass of wine. Holly?" Simon asks, folding up his menu to hand to a tuxedo-clad waiter who has appeared at our table.

"Sure," I say.

Jexy orders a mimosa, while Simon and I ask for glasses of Chardonnay.

"Did you think I couldn't handle it?" Simon asks once the waiter is gone.

"I was afraid you'd show up at the funeral," Jexy says, only it's practically a mumble. "The others agreed."

"Afraid I would—what *others*? Who was there? Has everybody known about this?"

Jexy shrugs. "Just Thor. Ernie. Ubiquitous Vic."

"And not me," Simon finishes.

"It wouldn't have been fair to Holly's father," Jexy says.

Simon shakes his head and looks away, saying only, "That was a long time ago."

"Don't stay mad. I haven't seen you in years," Jexy says, almost pleading.

"And now you're doing my little sister. I don't know what to think," Simon says.

Thankfully, nobody has to think, because the waiter is back with our wine, which I gulp a little too quickly.

"So, Holly, your mom went into ophthalmology, didn't she?" Simon asks after we've ordered. I hope to hell I don't get stuck with the bill, because besides the warm asparagus, I ordered a salmon salad that costs thirty quid. I spent less on my cashmere sweater.

"Ophthalmology, right," I say with a nod, wondering how he knew, wondering when they last spoke. "What about you?"

"ENT," he says. Just like Matthew, it occurs to me. Ear, nose, and throat specialists: nicer than your average surgeons.

"Holly's a doctor," Jexy says.

"Great," Simon says, but he doesn't sound enthusiastic and doesn't ask me what kind. That's okay: I don't really want to talk about medicine either, when we have something much more important in common.

Lunch passes by with only small talk, but the food itself is profound. The warm asparagus, lightly dusted with salt and butter and some secret ingredient, is the best I've ever tasted in my life. In fact, I'm so engrossed in my meal that I'm startled to be directly addressed by Simon, though I am the only one left at the table, since Jexy just left abruptly to go answer a cell phone call in the lobby.

"So, how old are you now, Holly?" he asks. "Twenty-seven, twenty-eight?"

"Thirty-one," I say. It feels like a thud in my chest.

He tells me his own daughter is just twenty-two, that I don't look much older than she does. Then he asks if I'm married or have children.

"No," I say, putting down my fork with a small sigh.

"Well, that's good," Simon says. "I think your mother would've said that it's best not to rush into your life and make irrevocable decisions." He starts to say more but hesitates. "Oh, you knew her much better than I did. I shouldn't be talking about Sylvia like that."

"No, I mean, you knew her—" I start, but the waiter is back before I can finish my thought.

"What do you say, Holly?" Simon asks, as he hands off his empty lunch plate. "Dessert?"

"Sure," I say, like a little kid. Not only am I completely stuffed, but a slice of carrot cake is probably going to cost him the equivalent of fifty bucks. Still, I don't want the lunch to end yet.

"Is your guest finished?" the waiter asks, motioning toward Jexy's half-eaten lunch.

"We think. Go ahead and take it," Simon says, offering

up her plate. Once the table has been cleared, he looks at the door of the restaurant and wonders aloud, "Where did Jexy go, anyway?"

"You were in love with my mother?" I blurt out before I realize that I'm about to say it. All I know is: I have to ask him everything now, before the meal is over. This is it.

If I've caught him by surprise, he doesn't show it. Instead, Simon turns his gaze back to me and says so tenderly that my heart could break, "Very much so."

There is a pause while I try to swallow.

"She was funny and brilliant and honest and . . . silly. So silly." Simon chuckles to himself. "Oh, Vee."

"Did you ever want to marry her?" I ask. "If she hadn't been already married?"

"If she hadn't been married, it wouldn't have been an issue. The fact is, she was, and I still wanted to marry her. And she wanted to marry me, but she didn't want to risk losing you children."

"You didn't want children," I say.

"Oh, no! I wanted children. Eventually. I wanted your mother. I would've been willing to..." Simon seems to struggle with the words, "*deal with* the entire package of two children, but your mother wouldn't hear of it. She was convinced that the... *adulterer*"—he cringes—"never gets custody of the children."

I must look shocked because he hastily adds, "I'm sorry. I just assumed you knew everything."

"I do," I say, even though I didn't. "I mean, I knew that you and she..." I trail off. "But I never knew she seriously considered...I never knew you were almost my stepfather."

"What did Sylvia tell you about me?" Simon asks, holding up his coffee cup without drinking from it. His brown eyes look shiny and nearly afraid. *I know that look,* it occurs to me. *He's waiting for bad news.*

"She didn't tell me anything. I found your letter," I say. I tell him that it was dated July 1983, that he wrote it after my mother had said that they couldn't be together ever again.

"I remember," Simon says, letting go of my gaze and placing the cup back in its saucer.

"So, what happened when you got back to the island for second term?" I ask, already knowing the answer.

"Well, it was the rainy season," Simon says with a distracted smile, as if that explains why a married woman would sleep with her ex-lover all over again. As he describes how lush and green Grenada was then—how, on a sunny day, the sky would suddenly break open, and before you could ask, "Is that rain?" you would be drenched—I think of Simon calling the island "a conspiracy of wonder designed to bring us together." Maybe, for him, the rain explains it all.

"It just seemed like we couldn't be together without *being* together," Simon says. "And down there, we were never apart. I know that your mother felt incredibly guilty," he adds.

"Why didn't she just divorce my dad?" I ask.

"She didn't want to lose you children. At least, that's what she always told me. And I suspect that she probably still loved your father, too. I'm sure she did," he adds, in a quiet voice.

"Did she ever say..." I say, hesitating. "Did my mother tell you things were bad with my father before she left for Grenada?"

Simon shakes his head. "Your mother was very driven to become a doctor. She was also driven to get away from her own mother. As for your dad, I don't think their relationship really soured until she left home."

"When she met you," I say.

Simon shrugs as he stirs more sugar into his coffee, though he still hasn't tasted it yet. "She had always felt ignored by him. It wasn't until she was gone that he suddenly wanted her back. But your mom wanted to finish what she went there to do. Your dad was pretty oblivious to my part of the equation."

"Until he came down to the island," I say.

"Oh, right," Simon says, sounding grim. "That was ugly. Mostly because she wasn't even there." He tells me that the whole group of them (except for Vic, who insisted he had to keep studying) had flown to St. Vincent's for the weekend to hike the volcano. My father had never told my mother he was coming, and Sylvia had never told him she wouldn't be there, so Dad had flown three thousand miles to discover his wife was missing.

I think of the picture of Mama and her friends on the crater's edge and how happy my mother looked standing in the wind, four thousand feet in the air. Meanwhile, my father was sitting alone in his empty hotel room waiting for her to return to the island—or waiting for his flight home, whichever came first.

Simon tells me that when they got back to Grenada, Ubiquitous Vic—bursting with the excitement of a scandal—was waiting to give them the news. Sylvia was holding Simon's hand while Vic said that someone was waiting for her and then pointed out to the beach. My father was standing by a gnarled tree in the sand. Simon didn't know who the stranger was until he turned from the horizon, and Sylvia gasped and dropped Simon's hand. Then he knew. Everyone else seemed to know, too. Thor said, "Oh, shit," and Jexy said, "Oh, my God," and they all watched Sylvia jump over the ledge that separated the food area from the beach and then trip across the sand toward him.

"And then they got into it," Simon says. "Everyone watched. Even the stray dogs."

My mother said she was sorry for not being there. My father said he was sorry, too. My mother started to explain that a whole big group of them had gone hiking on another island, but my father didn't want to hear about it. He wanted to know who the guy was—the one she was seeing. And Simon heard her say, "There isn't anyone else," and that's when Simon couldn't bear to listen anymore and walked away. By then, everyone in the food court was staring at him, too. Even the stray dogs.

"How did my father know she was having an affair? Did Vic say something?"

Simon shakes his head. "It was your grandmother."

"My . . . are you sure?" I ask.

"She's the one who told him to go down and win her back. She apparently told him if he didn't go down, then he might lose her forever. But I'm not sure that's the case."

I think of my grandmother telling me that Mama might have had a crush, but that she never would've acted on it. Meanwhile, she knew the truth all along. Eve was like me, hiding painful secrets in her fireproof heart.

"How do you think my grandmother knew?" I wonder aloud.

"According to Sylvia, your grandmother knew *everything,*" Simon says, as he finally tastes his coffee. Only he must've oversweetened it; he winces before setting the cup back down.

Luckily, the waiter is back to top off our drinks from a fresh silver pot.

"So what was the invasion all about, anyway?" I ask, taking a sip of my own hot coffee. For just a moment, it's easier to talk about the country than the relationships that took place there.

Simon tells me that the prime minister of Grenada had been overthrown by a military coup. First they held him hostage, and then, to avoid a countercoup, they murdered him. "It was a very weird time," he says. "You would've thought our school might've issued some sort of opinion on the matter of political unrest, but no, they left it up to people like Ubiquitous Vic, who went around like the town crier, urging everyone to book our flights home, while there were still flights out. He said the airstrip was being converted into a communist launch pad." The way Simon talks, looking behind me, it seems as though he's watching the memory unfold somewhere over my left shoulder.

"God, I'll never forget showing up at the physical diagnosis lab and Professor Barnsworth was still there, telling us to examine ourselves," he goes on. "It was like he was telling us to keep peering into our belly buttons, while the whole world went to hell around us. And then, of course, we were stuck there. The teachers were gone, classes were canceled, and we couldn't get out. There were tanks in the streets and the new Marxist government had ordered a curfew." Simon adds that in his mind, he always remembers it as though he and my mother were the last ones left, but he knows that wasn't true, because when the Marines landed, a lot of students needed to be rescued.

"How did you make it out of there?" I ask.

"Daddy," Simon says, and I know that he is not talking about his father or my father but instead their landlord on the island, a 250-pound black guy who'd christened himself "Daddy" after the birth of his second son. Before that, Daddy's name was Trouble. My mother had told me the story of how she arrived on the island for second term with instructions that any bus driver would know where her landlord lived. Outside the airport Sylvia approached a man leaning against a van pumping reggae tunes.

"I'm looking for Trouble," she said.

"No," the man said. "You lookin' for Daddy."

"He arranged for us to escape by fishing boat to St. Vincent," Simon says now. "Then we had to catch a puddle jumper to get to San Juan." He adds that the plane was a four-seater whose left propeller didn't work, until the pilot got out and spun it with his own hands. The pilot told them not to worry, that propellers were a lot like lawn mowers: once they got going, they would keep going. Simon said he tried hard not to think about his old mower that always died in the middle of the lawn.

By some miracle, they made it to the airport in San Juan, Puerto Rico; the last time Simon saw my mother was as they rushed through the mayhem, running for Customs and Immigration as if it were the chute at the end of a marathon. "The place always reminds me of pictures I've seen of Ellis Island—just with a bit more energy," Simon says. "Somehow, in that mess, we got separated. I never saw her again. That was it."

"Did you call her, back in the States?"

"I waited for a while. She'd asked me not to call or contact her, but I couldn't bear it after a while. Finally I did call, and your grandmother answered. Needless to say, she was very cold. She said she would let Sylvia know that I called, but I was pretty sure she wouldn't. I called one more time, and one of you kids answered. I'm pretty sure it was your brother. Just hearing his voice made me feel like some horrible interloper, and after that, I stopped calling."

"And then you decided to marry your fiancée after all?" I ask.

"Not quite," Simon says. "She was a dancer who was already in a committed relationship with her anorexia, so we broke up."

"So, when did you and Lisette get back together?" I ask.

Simon blinks. "We didn't."

"Isn't she your wife?"

He shakes his head. "I married Gabrielle. The woman you met in the lobby."

It occurs to me that she never did introduce herself. I just assumed both Mama and Simon had returned to their respective lives.

Jexy comes back, blustering around the table like a gust of wind. "Guys, I'm sorry. I have to go. There's a big mix-up with the costumes. The wrong shipment came, and we're shooting on Monday!" She grabs her purse off the floor. "Will you guys be all right?"

Simon smiles at her and tells her we're doing just fine.

AFTER HE'S WATCHED me eat my carrot cake, and after I've watched him pay the bill, Simon and I walk back into the lobby. He's told me that he's flying back to the States the day after tomorrow, and I find myself wishing our meeting didn't have to end.

"Listen, if you ever need anything," Simon starts, and then shakes his head. "No, of course you don't need anything. You're a grown woman."

"Well, you never know," I say, aware that we'll never see each other again—aware that if I ever need anything, there are lots of other people I would bother first.

"I'm glad to have met you, Holly," Simon says, shaking my hand and holding on to it a moment longer than necessary. He seems to hesitate before asking, "Tell me, did she ever wear the ring?"

"What ring?"

"It was an emerald set in arms of platinum. Little diamonds on either side..."

"How do you know about that ring?" I ask.

"I gave it to her. On St. Vincent, when we took the trip to the volcano. We spent the night in this little hotel...." He trails off, looking wistful. "I proposed, and she refused, as I knew she would. But I told her to keep the ring." Simon shrugs. "The emerald reminded me of her eyes."

Mama always pretended that she'd bought that ring. *It's a present to myself for finishing medical school,* she said. It's too sad to imagine. My father sits alone in his hotel room, while his wife is somewhere else being proposed to. *Poor Dad. Poor Simon.*

"She wore the ring," I say. "My brother has it now. Well, his fiancée has it."

Simon considers this for a second, then nods with a smile. "Good. As long as it wasn't lost."

"It wasn't lost," I say.

"Do you happen to have a picture of her? I mean, from sometime in the last twenty years?"

"Well, yeah, but none of them are on me," I say.

Simon nods again, looking almost stoic this time, reminding me, strangely, of Matthew for a second. It's either the jawline or just the expression of resolutely accepting something he wishes were different. "It's probably better that way," Simon says, the corners of his mouth turning up.

"But wait," I say, suddenly remembering my purse. I reach inside and pull out the letter, Simon's letter, and give it back to him. "This is yours."

Simon looks at the envelope, nods, and puts it in the breast pocket of his suit jacket. Then he grabs my hand to give it one last squeeze. "You take care of yourself, Holly."

"You, too," I say, swallowing so hard that it makes my neck hurt.

OUTSIDE THE HOTEL, the cold air of March hits me in the face and makes me shiver in my leather coat. Despite the bright sunlight, it must be twenty degrees in the wind, and just to warm up, I run all the way to Hyde Park and then keep going down the winding bike paths once I get there. It doesn't matter that my stomach is so full it's hard to move or that my black flats aren't made for running. It just feels good to move forward.

Finally, out of breath, I choose a bench partly shrouded by trees, sit down, and start to cry. It's a good thing that, unlike my mother and father, who were watched by everyone—even the stray dogs—I really am alone, just me and the trees bending in the wind. As tears stream down my face and snot runs into my silk scarf, I hug myself and cry for so many people: for my mother, who died too soon, for Simon and Will, who loved her. But most of all, I'm weeping for me, because I miss her terribly. Because Mama should've been having lunch at the Connaught today, catching up with her old flame and reassuring herself that everything turned out just right.

CHAPTER 24

Pressure

"Start out with the conviction that absolute truth is hard to reach in matters relating to our fellow creatures, healthy or deceased, that slips in observation are inevitable even with the best trained faculties, that errors in judgement must occur in the practice of an art which consists largely of balancing probabilities;—start, I say, with this attitude in mind, and mistakes will be acknowledged and regretted; but instead of a slow process of self-deception, with ever increasing inability to recognize the truth, you will draw from your errors the very lessons which may enable you to avoid their repetition."

— "Aequanimitas," Sir William Osler

t is April again, nearly two years to the week since Mama died, when I kill someone for the very first time. I am in the A&E, chatting with Mr. Danvers about Mr. Despopolous, my demented and alcoholic "frequent flier," when the first "stat!" page is announced overhead: a female voice summoning Dr. Jacobs, the radiologist, to the CT scanner.

"Why on earth would you ever need a radiologist 'stat'?" Danvers asks with a chuckle, looking at the ceiling. "Jacobs chose radiology specifically to avoid the emergency page."

I shrug and finish describing the rash that was on Mr. Despopolous' lower extremities, slightly raised patches that you could feel with your hands. "A palpable purpura," I say. "Plus, he's having abdominal pain and bloody stools. I was thinking he might have HSP."

"Henoch-Schonlein purpura?" Danvers repeats, looking doubtful. "Dr. Campbell, what age group is most commonly affected?"

"Children, but there've been a few adult cases here and there," I say.

"Dr. Campbell, have you not heard the saying 'If you hear hoofbeats, don't automatically look for zebras'?" Danvers smiles. "Mr. Despopolous has cirrhosis and routinely comes in with spontaneous bacterial peritonitis. He also bleeds from his esophogeal varices quite frequently."

"Well, yes. It could be either of those things. But that doesn't explain the purpura."

Mr. Danvers considers this for a moment before booming, "Come. Show me this elusive rash."

"Oh, well, I can't. He's in the CT scanner right now. But I'll let you know what I find out when all the labs and tests are back," I say, moving to put my initials next to another patient's name on the Great Wall of Problems. But after picking up the marking pen, I hesitate and turn back. "If it's not zebras, what are the hoofbeats, anyway? Wild buffalo?"

"Horses," Danvers says.

That's when the Code Blue is called.

It's obvious Mr. Despopolous is dead from the moment I run into the CT scanner. Surrounded by nurses, I can see that his chest and neck are blue, while the heart monitor hooked up to him isn't even registering a wave—instead, there's just the flat line of asystole.

"It happened almost immediately," Sister Gemma says as soon as she sees me. "We gave him the IV contrast for the CAT scan, he turned blue and started writhing around, like a fish on the sand. He kept gasping, clutching his neck. By the time Dr. Jacobs arrived, the patient's heart had stopped."

"He wasn't allergic to IV contrast," I say, which only makes the radiologist scowl at me as he performs CPR with his white comb-over flopping to the wrong side of his head. "I mean, that we knew of," I add. "It's not listed on his chart, is it?"

"Marian, kindly give the patient a dose of epinephrine and one of atropine," Danvers says from behind me. He sounds calm, as if he's ordering a poppy seed muffin and a cup of tea, which is probably a good thing, considering I'm nearly woozy with panic as I flip through the chart, trying to find any known allergies.

"Hold compressions, please," Danvers says, so that Jacobs will stop CPR. We all turn and stare at the monitor, to see if my patient has responded to the drugs. Unfortunately, the flat line appears unchanged, while Mr. Despopolous looks a little stiffer, a little bluer. It's hard to believe this is the same energetic man who tries to sell me a TV every chance he gets, despite the fact that he lives in a box under a bridge. "Have we got a pulse?" Danvers asks.

"No pulse," Jacobs says.

"No known allergies!" I say, finding it listed in the chart.

"He's dead," Danvers says, ripping off his gloves. "Time: 3:53 P.M."

"WELL, DR. CAMPBELL, every doctor feels like Lady Macbeth at some time or another," Danvers says later, in the cafeteria, where we're having cups of tea: Earl Grey for him, chamomile for me, because I need some comfort. Though shots of whiskey would probably feel better right about now. "Inevitably you kill at least one person along the way."

"Every doctor *kills*?" I repeat.

"At least once. It's difficult to pay attention to all the leaves and branches winking at you, while in fact the whole forest is coming down."

"But all I did was order a test," I say, and then shut my eyes, waiting for Danvers to lecture me on my physical diagnosis skills, how I should've put them to better use rather than ordering yet another test.

But he surprises me by saying, "You did nothing wrong."

I open my eyes. "I mean, he had an acute abdomen. I had to find out what was causing it."

"You did nothing wrong," Danvers says again, slowly and emphatically.

"But if only I'd ordered an *unenhanced* CT scan, he'd still be alive."

"Yes, well, everything is clear when we're wearing our retrospectroscopes," Danvers says, holding up his teacup as if in salute.

But I feel too guilty to smile. "Have you ever accidentally killed anyone?" I ask.

Danvers puts his cup back down. In the pause that follows, I decide that he's probably not trying to come up with a story. He's just debating whether or not to tell it to me. "I sent a young man home after he took a fainting spell at choir practice. He was sixteen years old. I assured him he was simply overheated. Less than a week later, he was running and collapsed. Died on the spot, at the track. Hypertrophic cardiomyopathy. I felt terrible." Danvers shakes his head at the memory and then stops to look at me again. "It is a risk of the profession, my dear. It is a risk that you own every single time you make a decision."

"I'll never get used to that," I say.

"You have no other choice."

BACK AT PARCHMENT HOUSE, I sit in the kitchen waiting for my pasta to boil, even though I'm not even hungry. Staring at the blank ceiling, my head is filled with one recurring thought.

I killed a man today.

It doesn't really matter if his quality of life was miserable, if he had nothing to live for, if he would've died anyway. *I'm the one who wrote the order.*

If only I could get the picture out of my head of Mr. Despopolous, laid out in the eerie fluorescent light of the CT scan room. I try to tell myself that he looks peaceful, but I'm lying. His face is frozen in an expression of terror, as if he just realized who he is, what he's been living like, and that *this is it*!

"Hey, woman," Ed says, sauntering through the swinging kitchen door. At least he's fully dressed for a change, in a gray T-shirt and jeans. He puts a hand on my shoulder and leaves it there longer than necessary. "Heard about what happened today. Man, that's rough."

"Yeah, well," I say, getting up from the table and heading for the stove to check my noodles. I don't want to trust his touch, no matter how innocent. "Especially rough for Mr. Despopolous," I add, fishing out a floppy pasta noodle with a wooden spoon. *Definitely done,* I decide.

"Hey," Ed says, putting his hands on my waist from behind. He leans over so that his chin is resting on my shoulder. "I miss you."

I stand perfectly still, not moving, not breathing, until my pasta starts to foam up and spill over. When I ask him to step out of the way, Ed straightens up and drops his arms, then watches me pour out the steaming water and pasta into a colander in the sink.

"You okay?" he asks. "You seem kind of miffed lately."

"You're everywhere I go," I say. "And we broke up."

"Yeah, about that . . ." Ed stops and chuckles, but I'm not sure what the joke is. As soon as he realizes that I'm not going to smile, he finishes his thought. "I'm afraid I never gave us a chance, you know? I mean, you seemed to want to be serious, and hell, I wasn't there yet, but . . . now I don't know." He leans against the counter, pushes some of his hair out of his eyes, and gives me one of his dazzling smiles. "Max is great, you know. It would be so cool to have kids."

My eyebrows go up. "Are you asking me to have a child with you?"

"No, no . . . I don't know," Ed says, emitting a small, tortured groan. "I'm just saying that I never thought I'd get married again. Didn't really see the point. But now I do. It's about family. I like your brother," Ed adds. "He and I have had some great conversations about religion and stuff."

"I'd tell you to date him, but he's already taken," I say, taking out some Tupperware to pack up my pasta, because my appetite is definitely gone by now. Only, none of the lids seems to fit the dish that I've pulled out. When Ed reaches over and hands me the right plastic hat, he watches my face as if he just handed me a ring.

"Thank you," I say, sealing the dish shut.

Instead of asking me why I'm putting my dinner in the fridge, Ed comes toward me and reaches out to touch my cheek. "I want to know you, Holly. We don't really know each other, do we?"

"Not...really," I say slowly, thinking of Simon Berg telling my mother that he wanted to forget everything he'd ever learned and learn her instead. Ed must notice the sag of my shoulders, because he pulls me toward him and wraps his arms around me.

"Oh, yeah," Ed says, hugging me closer and even swaying a little bit. "This is what I'm talking about. This feels great."

It does feel great—touch, warmth, arms—but wrong, too. It would be too easy to sleep with him again.

"What about Di?" I ask. It's enough to make Ed straighten up and open his eyes.

"What about Di?" he asks.

"How do you feel about her? You seem enthralled by her son."

"Love Max. Never really...put the two together."

"Mother and son."

"Yeah," Ed says, perplexed.

"Do you love me?" I ask.

"I just told you—"

"You say you want to know me. But do you love me?"

"Why, do you love me?" Ed asks.

That's when I realize, no. I don't. I never did, and I never will.

I hug Ed one last time and tell him that I'm going back to my room and to bed, alone.

* * *

IT'S EITHER MY HEART, beating inside my throat, or the sensation of lying naked in the dark that startles me awake. Who stripped me and left me here to rot in my own bed? The terrorists who are holding me hostage? Do I dare open my eyes? *No, no, too dangerous—not when they're probably hulking nearby.*

Testing my surroundings, I make only the slightest movement with my big toe. *A blanket. They left me a blanket.* Then the elbow: I move it a fraction until it touches T-shirt. *My pajama T-shirt?*

Trying to calm my wild heart, I suck in a breath and then recklessly open my eyes. Surprisingly, I find myself fully dressed in scrub pants and a T-shirt. I am still in England, and I am safe in my bed, so why can't I breathe?

I get up and open my window just to get some air. It's a cool night that makes me shiver, and a light moves across the sky, but not a shooting star, only an airplane. I sit there for a few minutes, panting, until a scratching sound from in my closet makes me freeze in the middle of a breath. *Someone's in the closet.* That must be the reason I woke up feeling like this.

Relax. It's probably just a mouse, I tell myself. Nevertheless, as soon as I can overcome my temporary paralysis, I bolt for the hallway. Outside my room, it's empty except for the sound of the fluorescent lights, a buzz that'll probably keep going long after a nuclear holocaust.

In desperation, I knock on Ed's door, escalating from timid taps into petrified pounding, until a voice in the hall makes me scream with surprise.

"Have you gone mad?" Marian says, standing there in a white flannel nightgown, her hands on her hips.

"I'm looking for Ed," I say, turning to push on his door handle. *Locked. Damn it.*

"You've gone off the rails. It's almost one o'clock in the morning," she says, her voice sharping on "morn" as floppy curls rattle about her head. It occurs to me that before now I've never seen Marian's hair out of its tight bun.

"Sorry to disturb your precious quiet hours," I say, "but there's someone in my closet."

"Someone in your...?" Marian stares at me. "What exactly do you mean?"

"I heard a noise in my closet!" I say loudly.

"Have you been drinking?" she asks.

I lean on Ed's door, almost bang on it with my skull just out of weariness. "Just go away. Please. Just go. Away."

When Marian turns around, I think for a second that she's actually listening to me. But instead, she opens the door to my bedroom and marches inside, apparently mistaking it for her own.

"Wait a second. Marian. What are you—" I say, moving after her.

She stands at the foot of my closet door and then fearlessly throws it open, making me flinch. Except for Big Bertha, it's completely empty. Not Mr. Despopolous, not even one article of clothing is hanging inside—probably because my entire wardrobe is already on the floor.

"There is no one in your closet," Marian says, turning to face me. "No one at all. All right, then?"

"Okay," I mumble, looking at the brown carpet.

"Will you sleep now?"

I nod even though I know I can't sleep, even if Mr. Despopolous isn't in there. He's in my head. And besides, my room is as stuffy as a sealed coffin.

Once Marian is safely gone, I change into jeans, my sneakers, and a sweatshirt, walk briskly for the stairs and then down into the front hall, where the windows are filled with the blackness of night and unseen eyes. After grabbing the phone and dialing, I curl up in a corner of the room, under the row of hanging mailboxes, trying to make myself invisible.

With each ring, my panic grows: that he won't be home, that he's vanished to the same unknown place that has Ed or even Mama. The thought is enough to get me panting again.

At last, he picks up. "Hullo?"

"Matthew? Oh, thank God," I say with a sigh.

"Holly?" He sounds confused. I can just imagine him feeling around in the darkness for his glasses by the bed. "What seems to be the trouble?"

"I'm dying," I say.

"How . . . are you . . . dying?" His voice sounds disoriented.

"I can't breathe. I just woke up this way. I can't get any air in, and I'm not even an asthmatic. I was thinking maybe it's a spontaneous pneumothorax. Or a pulmonary embolism. Or an aneurysm—who would know until it was too late? The first sign is sudden cardiac death."

I hear him shifting around, rearranging things, or himself. "Holly . . ." he starts.

"Maybe I should go across the street to the hospital," I say. "But I hate hospitals. They're houses of death! God, I can't breathe."

"But you're talking quite normally. There's nothing ragged in your breath sounds."

It's odd, but Matthew is right. I do sound fine.

"That's strange," I say. "Except when we hang up, I won't be able to breathe again."

A pause ensues, a pause I've read about where I'm supposed to wait for the patient to come to her own conclusion. My head feels like it's about to explode, but not from pain.

"Oh, God—I must be—I'm having anxiety attack?" I realize. My face scrunches with tears, just as my heart seems to scrunch and tear, and I cry with a well of force from inside that almost makes me vomit. "Please don't hang up," I whisper.

This is what I fear the most: unwrapping the panic I have neatly packaged inside me. My heart is a knot, instead of a pump, while the rest of my body clenches. Dizzily, my eyes swim in the pools of their sockets. Meanwhile, Matthew stays on the line, waiting patiently like a computer support technician who, called up to troubleshoot, sits around on long distance while the computer boots up.

"I don't want to die like this," I whisper. *I don't want her to die.*

"Why are you preoccupied by such gruesome things?" he asks.

Death is slippery, not gruesome, I want to protest. *It's the clink of glasses, the smell of good food and laughter from the other room, when all you can do is lie there.*

"I killed someone today," I say. "I ordered a CAT scan, and it turned out he was allergic to the IV contrast. He coded right there in the scanner, and we couldn't bring him back."

"It happens," Matthew says, only he doesn't sound cold or even matter-of-fact, just reassuring.

"I know, but . . . I can't do this anymore."

"Do . . . what—anymore?"

"This putting my hands into other people's lives—it's a recipe for badness."

"Holly, badness happens. You're the one trying to help."

"How do you keep going every day?" I ask.

"I remember I'm not alone," Matthew says.

"You mean . . . there's God?"

"I *mean* there is always someone I can wake up who knows more than I do," Matthew says. "A patient's not doing well, and I'm confused about what to do? I turn on all the lights, get anybody and everybody on the phone. I wake them up. I wake them *all* up! You have to when a life is at stake."

Isn't that what I'm doing right now? Only the idea of a life at stake reminds me of Mama after the car accident, when nobody could save her from the pulmonary embolism, and it makes me cry. I can't say anything for a few minutes.

"Holly?"

"Do you hate me, Matthew?" I ask.

"I could never hate you, Holly," he says, with the same tenderness that reminds me of Simon talking about my mother.

"You never answered my e-mails. Or my thank-you card," I say.

"I didn't think there was anything left to say."

"Last time we saw each other—"

"I was an inappropriate ass," he finishes.

"You weren't. You didn't say anything that wasn't true."

"Holly, I have to tell you . . . it's . . ." Matthew hesitates. "It's after eight o'clock here in the States and I'm rather late for a dinner with a friend. . . ."

"You should've shut me up!" I say, embarrassed to realize I interrupted his social life instead of his sleep.

"Not when you were dying," Matthew says. "Listen. Are you absolutely alone? Is there anyone closer than I am? Anyone in the U.K., perhaps?"

"Oh, Matthew, I'm fine," I say, wiping my eyes.

"You know I would come straightaway if I could," he says. "But I can't."

"Will I ever see you again?" I ask.

Matthew tells me that he'll be in England over the Easter bank holiday, that perhaps we can arrange something then. It's not until we hang up that I remember I'm not going to be in England that weekend. That's when we're going to the Isle of Skye. It'll be the last time that we'll be together, before Roxanne disappears forever.

Suddenly, it starts getting hard to catch my breath again. I stay huddled under the mailboxes and stare at my skin, deceptively concealing all sorts of decay. My heart pounds, my aberrant cells divide, and my hemoglobin suffers from poor oxygenation. *Just breathe, breathe, breathe,* I tell myself. But the only way to calm down is to start moving, so I pick myself up to go for a walk.

Outside, the sky is clear and bright with a full moon, and the cool wind feels refreshing after the stuffy, sick-building air of Parchment House. I amble past the other dorms, past the hospital, and then cross the street, heading into the cemetery where I first traipsed through with my suitcase nearly a year ago. There are the same headstones lying on the ground, untouched since the bombs that brought them down more than half a century ago.

Suddenly, I'm so tired that it's hard to stand, and even the cold grass looks more inviting than my bed. Lying down on my back, I stare at the sky and listen to the night. There's not a single sound in the graveyard from wind or thunder or even a car driving by. Nothingness. *Is this what death feels like?*

The thought is enough to make me weep into my hands with sobs that grow audible and with shakes that rearrange my organs, until, after a while, the same stillness that has enveloped the cemetery and the night envelopes me. I open my eyes. There is nothing to see, but everything to see. The stars seem closer now, friendly witnesses to the passage of time. I am alone in the dark, and I am okay. Finally, I really am okay.

CHAPTER 25

Heart Sounds

> "If we apply the ear, with or without the stethoscope, to the cardiac region of a person in health, we perceive most distinctly a series of sounds of a very marked and peculiar kind.... The first is...a graver and more subdued tone...the second is brief, smart and clear, like...the cracking of a whip...."
>
> —THE LIBRARY OF HEALTH, 1927

This is Scotland. Anything can happen," the man singsongs as he holds up the keys to our rental van. It's the weekend of Easter, and we've just flown to Edinburgh.

"We're still not paying thirty pounds extra for daily car insurance," Roxanne says dryly.

Thankfully, we ordered a van with two rows of seats, considering there are now eight of us, ever since I disembarked from the airplane and found myself locking eyes with a man in Buddy Holly glasses. Only, in his jeans, hiking boots, and fleece jacket, this guy looked too athletic and outdoorsy to be Matthew. *How funny,* I thought, not for the first time, *the way you can go to a foreign country, and people make you look twice, make you think you already know them—*

The man in the black specs grinned, making me stop short. *I know those teeth.*

"Matthew?" I asked, baffled.

"I was wondering if you were going to say hello," he said, looking sheepish and even a bit sly.

I moved to grab him in a hug but accidentally slugged him with my camera case and doctor's bag instead. "What are you doing here?" I asked, trying to untangle myself from the straps.

"You invited me," he said.

"This is just like that time we ran into each other at the Whispering Wall!"

"Not really, no," Matthew said. "That was a coincidence. This time, you told me your flight number. I arrived just before you."

I reminded him that *twice* he said that he couldn't come, that he had plans with his mother and sister for the holiday. Matthew said he changed his mind, that he would have two weeks to see them, since he was taking all of his vacation for the year. Besides, he said, he'd never been to Skye.

"I'm so glad you're here!" I said, this time managing to complete the hug.

Matthew squeezed back, holding on for a few seconds, until something over my shoulder caught his eye. "Bugger!" he exclaimed, his face screwing up with disgust.

I looked back and spotted Ed making his way down the chute from the plane.

"Oh, that's just—he's just—Ed's here for Roxanne," I said hastily. "Not me. He hangs out a lot."

Matthew closed his eyes for a few seconds longer than a blink. "I read your e-mail several times," he said in a low voice. "I am most certain you never mentioned he would be coming."

"He's her shaman," I said, turning away from Ed, who was in the middle of making exaggerated smiles at Max in Di's arms. "Or something like that. Believe me, I didn't invite him. I invited you."

Matthew nodded slowly, as if weighing whether to leave or stay, and in fact, he might've booked the next flight back to London if Ed hadn't suddenly stopped walking. "Hey, it's the ex-boyfriend!" he said.

I watched Matthew's jaw tighten. "If it isn't the ex-elementary-school-mate," he replied.

Thankfully, Ben appeared then and slung an arm over

Matthew's shoulder. "Hey, buddy, ready for Skye?" he asked, as if Matthew had been expected the whole time.

"Ready," he said, without even a flicker of hesitation.

"Awesome!" Ben said, and then added to me, as if I could forget, "This guy saved my life!"

And so Matthew is here for our journey to the Isle of Skye. Despite warnings that without the Roadside Assistance option, we would run out of gas or run out of air in our tires, the only thing we run out of on the drive are adjectives. Every twist in the road across the Highlands reveals a more astounding sight—mountains both snowcapped and green, water dancing with light, while over the lochs live little islands of Scotch pines that look like floating tribes of wise, fairy elders. The weather is a miracle of clarity; clouds are dissolving by the minute. We pass through Glencoe, by the Glenfinnan viaduct, then continue down the road toward Fort William. *Scotland, the soul of a good emerald.*

After lunch at Fort William, we follow the changing scenery through forests of slender trees laced with ivy, then along looping roads of white sandy shoreline out to Mallaig. A collective silence falls over the van. It seems useless, trying to come up with new exclamations of amazement. The appropriate response is maybe a thank-you, the secret kind, just on the inside of my lips.

We arrive at a small fishing village after four o'clock, just in time to make the last ferry over to Armadale on Skye. Standing underneath a sign that reads, "Pisces Fishing and Rigging," we each examine the tickets that we were lucky enough to snare.

"The last ferry. Thank goodness. That could've been a disaster if we'd missed it," Di says with a sigh.

"There's always tomorrow," Roxanne says.

"Yeah, but we wanted to arrive today. We just had to arrive today," Di says.

"Let's not get so fatalistic," Roxanne says.

As if on cue, a man runs by suited up in rubber boots and rubber pants. "You think there's a fire?" I ask, inhaling for smoke.

"Now, it's simply a hunch," Matthew says, wrapping an arm around the shoulder of my blue leather jacket, "but I believe he may be a fisherman."

"That guy's oars kind of give it away," Alecia adds, pointing to another fellow in the distance carrying two long wooden oars.

"So those aren't shotguns," I say.

"Didn't I tell you a long time ago that you need new glasses?" Roxanne asks, patting my arm.

FINALLY, the *Lord of the Isles* pulls into the Mallaig Harbour to take us across the Sound of Sleat. After crewmen on the ferryboat direct the van on board, we pile out and split up. Di needs to find a spot to breast-feed the baby, and Ben and Ed seem to need to feed themselves. Alecia, on a quest to find a bathroom, barges ahead of a small, white-haired woman whose equally frail husband is struggling to fold up her walker at the foot of the steps.

"Look at them. Aren't they dear?" Roxanne says in a low voice, as she and I watch the older woman and man, holding on to each other and tottering up the steps one at a time. If they know they are holding up a line of people behind, they don't seem to care. His few remaining scraps of hair are practically blowing away in the wind, while her cotton skirt is lifting up, à la Marilyn Monroe. He says something that makes her laugh and say fondly, "Oh, Farwell." *I want what they have,* I think.

"Hey, kiddo, let's go over to the rail," Roxanne says. She looks beautiful all dressed up—or rather, just dressed at all—in baggy linen pants and a wool sweater colored the periwinkle of her eyes. Putting my arm on her back, I can't help noticing the way her shoulder blades stick out like two wings already folded there. Very soon Roxanne will be nowhere—or at least, like Mama, permanently unreachable to touch, hear, smell. The thought gives me a lump in my throat.

"Oh. You've got the crease down your forehead," Roxanne says. "You're stressed out."

"No...well, a little," I say, looking at both of our hands

gripping the rail, mine young and white and healthy, Roxanne's purple and bruised from IV sticks. "Are you?"

"Stressed out?" She turns to look at me again. "About dying?"

"Well, yeah," I say with a gulp.

"I'm afraid of suffering...but I'm not suffering at the moment. And I don't want to leave anyone behind, but...we're all here right now. Dying itself doesn't exactly...I mean, does a baby get stressed out about being born?"

I puzzle over that for a moment but can't make sense of what she means. That Death, the unfathomable entity, arrives like a baby? That leaving your body behind can be something exhilarating?

A loudspeaker interrupts my thoughts to announce that otters have been spotted in the Sound of Sleat. Passengers are invited to observe the spectacle of sea life over the side of the ship.

"But aren't you nervous?" I ask.

"Nervous?" Roxanne repeats, her eyes shining. "Nervous is an adjective I gave up a long time ago."

"Are you worried..." I trail off. "What *are* you feeling?"

"Kinda thankful. Nearly hopeful. The wind," Roxanne says.

I smile and wrap my arm around her thin shoulders.

"You know what I've decided?" I ask.

Roxanne muses for a moment. "Actually, I don't."

"Well, my dad called me again the other day. He's talking about marrying this woman he met on the Internet. He wants me to come home and help him pack up the house and probably give my blessing. But I might extend my contract for another year and stay right where I am."

"Holly!" Roxanne breaks away from my arm, annoyed. "You'd be crazy to stay. Go start your life. Go watch your father get married."

"Yeah, but—"

"No buts! I don't need you here."

"It's not about your needs, Roxanne, it's about mine," I say. "Time spent with you is always a gift to me."

"I don't need you here. I don't need you waiting. And you can't get closure on your mama's death by watching me die. I just don't think it works that way."

"I'm afraid I'm scheduled to leave England before I've really appreciated being here."

"Oh, Holly," Roxanne leans her head on my shoulder. "You've got the month of May, honey. Soak it all in. Then beat it, kid." She shakes her head. "What's Matthew doing here?"

I turn around to look up and behind us. He's talking to Ed. *Why the hell is he talking to Ed?* They both wave, which unsettles my stomach.

I say, "He's visiting his mother for the next two weeks, and I convinced him to come along."

"He's visiting you," Roxanne says. "He loves you."

"Oh, I don't know about that."

"Holly, let me tell you something. The most daring thing your mother could do with her life was to take herself down to that island. The most daring thing you can do with your life is to take yourself off of yours. Now, do you love him?"

I look above me, first at Matthew coming down the stairs from the top deck and then at Ed, who's watching the horizon, searching for his balloons.

"I love you, and you're leaving," I say, my voice rising in pitch to stave off the cry behind it.

"You love him, too, don't you? So give him the chance he deserves. And remember: you are not your mother. You can choose."

Trying to swallow without crying, I nod and stare at the sea foam spilling up from the back of the ship.

Roxanne grabs my arm and says with sudden urgency, "Holly, visit New York. Go to Broadway for me. See a really good show and pay extra for good seats."

"Okay," I say.

"Oh, promise me you'll be glad you're allowed to go home." Roxanne says, squeezing my hand before she starts walking away.

"I will. I am," I say.

And suddenly, instead of Roxanne, Matthew is standing next to me.

"Are you crying?" he asks, touching my shoulder.

"No. Well, sort of," I admit, wiping my eyes.

"I suppose you're wondering what I'm doing here."

"No. Of course not," I say, staring at the water. "I mean, I invited you."

"Holly, do look at me."

I turn and look at Matthew's face, his earnest green eyes. *He is so kind,* I think. *Brilliant without being pompous. Funny without being arrogant. Passionate without being shy. Matthew Hollembee is an entirely rare bird.*

"I love you," he says with a gulp, his Adam's apple bobbing up and down like some other fruit, maybe a clementine. "I truly believe that you and I are supposed to be together. I can't say why. It's just . . . we were meant to be."

"Matthew . . ." I say, hesitating, even though I want to believe him.

"Please, do let me finish," Matthew says, pulling his hands out of his coat pockets.

I look down at his palm, thinking he's going to reach out for my own, but instead he's fumbling to open a box. Blinking away the wind in my eyes, I realize I'm staring at the most beautiful emerald that I've ever seen, a small but dazzling stone that's only in need of a setting. *My very own emerald.*

"Hey, Holly!" Alecia calls, coming toward us from the far side. She's pointing starboard, the side of the *Lord of the Isles* where people are gathering to see the otters. "Oh, shit!" she says, when she sees Matthew and the ring box.

I turn away from her.

"I bought this for you before you'd gone. Now it doesn't seem fit for anyone else. I wanted to make this into a necklace, but then I was afraid you'd imagine a choker," Matthew says, miming strangulation. "And I thought of a ring, but that seemed awfully premature. A bracelet seemed all wrong . . ." He trails off.

"Holly!" Ben yells from above.

"I love you, Holly Campbell, and I wish you'd come home," Matthew says.

A scream from behind me makes me turn my head and look up just in time to see the white-haired lady—the elderly Marilyn Monroe—toppling down the ferry stairs. A collective gasp resounds from the myriad otter-searching ferry riders as her knees—then her head—then her knees—then her head—hits each iron step.

As shocking as the fall is, I'm ashamed to admit that it still doesn't compare to Matthew's emerald.

CHAPTER 26

Statistically Significant

> "In a good treatment trial, the blind lead the blind."
>
> —OXFORD HANDBOOK OF CLINICAL MEDICINE

hear the question first, shouted by a starboard passenger. "Is there a doctor on board?"

Oh, shit.

"I'm a volunteer!" someone volunteers.

"Let's go," Matthew says, shepherding me in the direction of the stairs.

I shake off temporary paralysis and wave, yelling out, "Over here!"

"Holly's a doctor, let her through," Alecia says as Matthew and I try to approach the throng of concerned passengers surrounding the lady crumpled at the foot of the stairs. "Doctor's here, let her through." Then, like a bank robber approached by a security guard trying to be a hero, Alecia yells, "Everybody back the fuck up!"

It's amazing. The sea parts, and everybody backs the fuck up.

"Ma'am?" I crouch down beside her, thinking of my ABCs: airway, breathing, circulation. The woman breathes raggedly and rapidly as blood drips down the side of her head.

"It's Helen," her husband—Farwell, she called him—says in a British accent. "Her name is Helen." He adds that she's seventy-five, and that, apart from arthritis, she's never been sick in her life.

"Helen, can you hear me?" I ask, trying to look into her mouth without tilting her neck, to assess her airway.

"Don't move her neck!" Ed says. "It could paralyze her!"

"She just fell down a flight of stairs," Matthew says. "She may have taken care of that herself."

"She's movin' her own neck," someone says, pointing at Helen. I glance up and see it's one of the crew, in a neon green vest. "Ye see thar? She's no paralyzed," the man adds.

"You're not a doctor," Alecia says.

"Don't I know it," the crewman heartily agrees.

Helen groans, grabbing at the left side of her chest.

"Can someone get me my doctor's bag?" I ask, looking around until I meet Ed's brown eyes.

"Got it," he says.

"Helen, do you know where you are? Do you know who you are?" I ask.

She moans again as her nostrils flair and her sternum heaves. Matthew opens her blouse and lays his head down on her bony chest to listen like an Indian straining for the sound of a stampede.

"Absent breath sounds on the right," he says before starting to percuss on her rapidly rising and falling chest. Her scalene, intercostal, and subcostal muscles are retracting, all the accessory muscles of respiration at work. "Resonant on the right, compared to her left."

"Pneumothorax?" I ask, and watch Matthew nod.

"I need a sixteen-gauge needle," Matthew yells to the crowd. "Can somebody—please!—get the doctor's bag?"

"Trachea's not deviated," I say. "Her neck veins aren't distended."

"That's a late sign. Where's the bag?" Matthew asks.

"It's coming up from the car," Di says, just as my black bag drops to the deck. I look up to see Ed standing there.

"Is she having a heart attack?" he asks.

"Tension pneumothorax," Matthew replies without even looking up.

With shaking fingers, I count down Helen's ribs to the second intercostal space, mid-clavicular line, the place where the needle should go, if we can find it in time.

"Good Lord, Holly, what've you got in here?" Matthew says, rooting through my bag. "A central-line kit? Sterile gloves? Have you been ripping off the National Health Service?"

I ignore Matthew, recount the ribs.

"Ye all right there?" the boatman calls.

"I'm fine," I reply, before realizing he means Helen, who is blinking her eyes, gasping for breath, and trying to sit up. The crowd draws in their own sharp sighs and makes protests. General consensus: Helen should remain flat.

"Take it easy, Helen. This might hurt," I say.

"Aha!" Matthew says, holding up the sixteen-gauge needle connected to the three-way stopcock that he's managed to rifle out of my bag. "Do you want . . . ?" he asks, the ultimate gentleman. *Do you want this procedure or shall I?*

"You're the surgeon," I say. "Go for it."

Matthew goes for it, with precision and skill. He is, frankly, amazing to watch. Some girls might appreciate generic tall, dark, and handsome men, but give me crooked teeth and Buddy Holly glasses and deft hands that can expertly stick a needle into someone's chest. I watch with admiration as Matthew pulls back on the syringe, twists the stopcock, and expels the trapped air in Helen's chest so that her collapsed lung will reexpand.

"Check for breath sounds," Matthew orders, and I quickly use the stethoscope to listen for symmetrical sounds.

Emergency blasts sound from the smokestacks of the *Lord of the Isles:* seven toots followed by one long blast. This seems to confuse the audience of otter lovers: *Is the boat sinking, too?*

"He's no safe," the crewman comments, words that make me bristle and say, "He's a surgeon!" until I notice he's speaking into a walkie-talkie and not about Matthew's resuscitation efforts.

"I'm tellin' ye, she's no safe.... I dunno, but she's pretty puir. Ye best come directlay. Acht, he'll tell ye."

The boat hand says, "Paramedics," as he gives the radio to Matthew, who starts shouting into it, "I have a seventy-five-year-old woman who fell down a flight of stairs. She'll need a chest tube. A chest X-ray before and after placement, and a head CT. She may need to be airlifted to Glasgow." He hands the radio back to the crew member and then looks at me.

"I love you, Matthew," I say.

His eyes open just a little wider. "Now?"

"I love you to pieces... and parts... and to the smallest possible atom... to smaller than an atom. If there is such a thing as being smaller than an atom."

"Leptons and muons," Matthew says evenly. "Smaller than an atom."

"I love you to leptons and muons and the space in between." I start laughing then, because we're on a boat to the Isle of Skye, because for the rest of our lives, we'll remember Helen and Farwell, and because—finally!—my tears feel good. It's a massive relief, the kind I imagine Ben felt when God called him back.

"Well, it's about bloody time," Matthew says with a smile.

Farwell stoops down next to his wife, takes her hand, and squeezes it. "Helen? Darling?" he asks. Suddenly, I am certain that she'll be fine. Before she got sick, Roxanne was an internationally ranked psychic, and if she said no one would die this weekend, then no one will.

In the parking lot of the port of Armadale, an emergency vehicle swerves, sirens blaring. I'm suddenly struck by how blurry it all looks from the back of the ship. The letters on the side of the ambulance—no matter how hard I blink—stay hazy and indistinct, spelling something like "Doober... Mackissen...?" Even the sign on a store, equally nonsensical, reads, "Can't Shop!" It isn't until the boat drifts closer that I can see the words are actually "Craft Shop."

Roxanne is right. I should've gotten new glasses a long time ago.

CHAPTER 27

The Blessing of Maximilian

> "Like toddlers we should always have the
> question 'Why' on our lips... not that we are al-
> ways searching for the ultimate cause of phe-
> nomena... it is so we can choose the simplest
> level for intervention."
>
> —Oxford Handbook of Clinical Medicine

On the brick patio of the backyard, cast-iron chairs are arranged in a circle around the big, comfy recliner that looks like a throne. The table, wearing its green-and-yellow-checked tablecloth, is set out on the grass and laden with food: fruit salad, lobster bisque, grilled barbecue chicken, sourdough bread, sliced tomatoes, and a towering chocolate cake.

Ed helps a swaying and rocking Roxanne settle into the recliner while we all stand around and watch as if the *QE2* is being docked.

Her bilirubin is rising every day like a thermometer. Roxanne's doctor told her she'll be confused when it goes as high as twenty and that she'll slip into a painless coma somewhere after that. Right now we're at thirteen.

"Well, do we have to play musical chairs to get you all to sit down?" Roxanne asks, beckoning to Di, who's holding naked baby Max in her arms.

"Ben should stand," Alecia says, pulling out a chair for herself with a rumble and squeak of iron on brick. "Don't you think the preacher should stand?"

"I am *not* a preacher," he says, wringing his hands in agitation.

We just had a fight in the kitchen, after I found him filling up a wooden bowl with bottled water and realized what was going on.

"You're using Evian?" I asked.

"What do you want me to use?" Ben snapped. "Mountain Dew?"

"Is anyone here offended that I've asked Ben to preside over Max's baptism?" Roxanne asks now. "If so, go wait in the kitchen until we eat."

Everyone generally agrees that no one is offended, but Ben seems to be waiting to hear it from me. "The water's fine, Ben," I say. "And stand up."

"Aren't we waiting for one more?" Ed asks just as the back door opens and Matthew appears, holding a covered dish and looking hesitant.

"You're in the right place!" I say, jumping up to rescue him. In fact, I'm so intent on finding a spot for his casserole that it's not until I've rearranged the table that I finally stop to look at him. He looks different standing there in the breeze. I can see him so clearly now.

"*Holly.* You look so studious," Matthew says, pointing to my new frames, before kissing me on the lips right there, in front of everyone.

"Matthew? You look so *good*," I say, dropping my voice to a whisper. "Where are your glasses?"

He waves his eyebrows at me. "Contacts," he says.

"Contacts?" I repeat. My eyebrows are possibly furrowing right through to my brain. "What about your Buddy Holly glasses?"

"They were getting awfully faddish."

"Are you kidding? Contact lenses are a fad! *Lenses* directly in your *eye*?" I say. "Besides, you have to wash and clean them every night. It's like having a pet!"

"Why, don't you like them?" Matthew asks, brushing away his hair so I can fully appreciate the gleaming green of his eyes.

He looks downright dashing. I tell him we seem to be having a role-reversing *Grease* moment, now that I'm the studious Sandy in glasses and he, cool in contacts. Matthew laughs and asks if I really thought he was ever as cool as John Travolta.

"Can we get started?" Roxanne asks, only she's smiling at us as we go to take our seats.

Ben glances around, rising uncertainly. "Okay. Well. I didn't plan on doing this alone, which is why I asked you all to bring something to read," he says, gesturing to the potluck collection of books and papers on the table.

After explaining how John the Baptist, through water, prepared the way for Jesus' coming, Ben opens a cloth-bound book, *Great Dialogues of Plato,* and begins to read the "words of a wise woman":

> "In the first place he is always poor, and anything but tender and fair, as the many imagine him; and he is rough and squalid, and has no shoes, nor a house to dwell in; on the bare earth exposed he lies under the open heaven, in the streets, or at the doors of houses, taking his rest; and like his mother he is always in distress... he is bold, enterprising, strong... keen in the pursuit of wisdom, fertile in resources; a philosopher at all times, terrible as an enchanter, sorcerer, sophist. He is by nature neither mortal or immortal, but alive and flourishing at one moment when he is in plenty, and dead at another moment, and again alive by reason of his father's nature. But that which is always flowing in is always flowing out, and so he is never in want and never in wealth...."

Ben looks up from his book. "The Wise Woman wasn't talking about Jesus, actually. As recorded by Plato, Diotima was instructing Socrates on how to recognize Love. She went on to explain Love as the medium between mortals and immortals, the interpreter between the gods and man, 'the mediator who spans the chasm which divides them, and therefore in him all is bound together.'

"What really went on two thousand years ago? I don't know. But Love has woven this umbilical cord between me and the sky. I can't reason him out; Jesus will remain an enigma, just like my existence, just like Max. I look at Max and who knows what he sees, understands, who he'll be? Max is untranslatable, but I love him overwhelmingly. Whatever way we want to name Love, we want it to live and thrive in Max. That's why we're here today."

Alecia gazes at my brother with electricity that makes me turn away in embarrassment for having intercepted it.

Love and sex, I think, my gaze falling on Matthew. *The mediator that spans the chasm that divides them.*

Diotima reaches for *Anne of Green Gables* on the table. "My quote is short," she says, opening to an earmarked page. " 'Kindred spirits are not so scarce as I used to think. It's splendid to find out there are so many of them in the world.' "

Ed goes next, balancing his guitar on one knee as he fishes in his pocket until he comes up with a crumpled piece of paper. "This is from a poem by Sylvia Plath," he says. " 'You're

> Clownlike, happiest on your hands,
> Feet to the stars, and moon-skulled,...
> Vague as fog and looked for like mail...
> Right like a well-done sum.
> A clean slate, with your own face on.' "

"Sylvia Plath. She stuck her head in an oven and gassed herself to death, didn't she?" Roxanne remembers. "Or was it an overdose? I used to know this. Must be the bilirubin."

Ed shrugs in his unconcerned way. "Anyway, it was Max."

With sheepish reverence, Matthew goes next, delivering "a bit of poetry by Mary Oliver": " 'When it's over, I want to say ... I was the bridegroom, taking the world into my arms.' " When he sits back down, I tell him that I thought he'd pick someone British.

Matthew is followed by Alecia, who stands up and begins reading from Emerson's "Self-Reliance" with such fervor that I have the feeling she's trying out for a play. Hopefully Gloria Newton-Blys won't call the police for a noise violation.

> " 'Trust thyself: every heart vibrates to that iron string. Accept the place the divine Providence has found for you; the society of your contemporaries, the connexion of events. Great men have always done so and confided themselves childlike to the genius of their age, betraying their perception that the Eternal was stirring at their heart, working through their hands, predominating in all their being.' "

"Maybe he will grow up to be a dictator," Roxanne says.

Alecia ignores her but continues the reading—projecting her voice as if it needs to reach the back of a theatre—and passionately waving her fist.

> " 'Misunderstood! It is a right fool's word. Is it so bad then to be misunderstood? Pythagoras was misunderstood, and Socrates, and Jesus, and Luther, and Copernicus, and Galileo, and Newton, and every pure and wise spirit that ever took flesh. To be great is to be misunderstood.' "

Roxanne makes a face. "I'm sorry, it's just...I don't want Max to suffer *that* much. I'd settle for him to be good and understood."

Ed gives a silent whistle and says, "Tough crowd."

"Why don't you lay off?" Alecia snaps. She flips around in the book and then decides, "Bah, I'm done."

There's a small silence. I wonder if I should have her hand me "Self-Reliance," so I can pick another passage.

"Are you sure you're finished?" Roxanne asks uncertainly. "I mean, I don't want to speak if you're not."

"It's your turn, Roxanne," Alecia mutters. "Go for it."

Roxanne glances around at each of us, as if looking for the approval in our eyes, and then starts with my brother. "First of all, Ben, that was beautiful. ReCalled, or not, you have made me very happy today. All of you, just by speaking... you, too, Alecia," she adds, reaching out to press her fingertips into Alecia's hand. "You have a lovely stage presence, and I mean that."

Alecia shakes her head, annoyed, and then involuntarily snickers.

"My passage is from a poem by Rita Dove," Roxanne says, before she begins to quote from memory.

> " 'I hear wings, and spiders
> quickening in the forgotten shrines,
> unwinding
> each knot of grief,
> each snagged insistence.' "

She swallows and peers around. "My prayer for Max is that he'll never need to hear the wings and spiders to wake him up."

After that, Ben says a few words about water versus the fire and the spirit, and then we stick naked Max, who chortles and screams, into the little tub. Ben reaches into the spring water and makes a wet sign of the cross on Max's forehead, which makes him wave his arms and squeal.

"Now we're supposed to make a pact. Our pact will be that, to whatever extent we can, we will uphold love and amazement and faith, and preserve that in Max."

Then we sing, or at least they do—songs of Creedence Clearwater Revival; and Crosby, Stills, and Nash; and Cat Stevens. But I can only grasp the chair arms tightly and try to contain my agony. How can they sing when nothing will ever be the same again? I'm leaving this place. Roxanne is leaving this place. Max will never be a baby again. Even if we come back, we can never return to the same moment.

The song "Tuesday's Dead" is over, but everyone wants more.

"Oh Very Young," Di suggests, which seems like a cruel request. How can I even look at Roxanne and be expected to sing,

"And though you want them to last forever, you know they never will...."

My brother is staring at me as if trying to figure out what's going through my mind. "Holly, you never spoke earlier," Ben suddenly realizes aloud.

"How did Holly get off without a quote?" Alecia asks.

"Oh, Holly, you have to speak!" Di says.

"I didn't really prepare anything..." I say.

"Here, Holly Bear." Ben pulls wet, happy joy-boy out of his tub and hands him to me. "He oughta help inspire you."

"It doesn't have to be published, Holly," Ed offers.

Max kicks his legs happily in my arms. *Say something. Anything.* Seven expectant faces—Ben, Alecia, Ed, Di, Roxanne, Matthew, and even Baby Wonder—wait. I wait, too, for all of my dreams and all of my losses to stop rushing at me together. When I open my mouth to speak, it accidentally caves into a sob. "I'm so glad we met," I blurt out. "I mean—all of you—it's just been—this year has been—I can't even tell you—ow, Max, ow. Let go of my earring."

Luckily Matthew rescues me with a hug, and I keep laughing and crying, thinking how lucky I am to have been saved from myself.

CHAPTER 28
Fossil Sisters

> "The ward sister is usually right. Respect her opinion."
>
> —Oxford Handbook of Clinical Medicine

One thing I'll always regret is Gabe," Roxanne says later.

We're in the bathroom. I'm leaning on the sink waiting for her to finish peeing. "Falling in love with him?"

"Stealing our daughter," she replies, accepting the wad of toilet paper I offer. Roxanne pauses to look at the crush of tissue and observes, "I am just no fun anymore."

"I think you're fun," I say, reaching over to flush for her.

Roxanne grasps my shoulder as I hoist her to her feet. "I'm so sorry you're ending your trip this way," she says as we shuffle our way back toward the bed.

I'm so sorry you're ending your trip this way, I think, maneuvering her and the IV pole.

Helping her back into bed, I'm reminded of my mother in a moment I haven't thought of in years. It is the summer of 1983, and Mama has just come home from a semester away. I'm nine years old, standing in her bedroom and proclaiming that she's the Best Mother in the World. For some reason, Mama looks worried. She wants to know if I'd still love her if she had no arms and no legs.

"Why would you even ask that?" I ask, horrified.

"Because you're so proud of me," she says.

"Of course I'm proud of you. You're going to help people!" I say, mimicking my grandmother.

"But what if I couldn't do anything useful?" Mama asks. "What if I had no arms and no legs?"

"I'd still love you," I say.

I still love you, I think now, packing pillows under Roxanne's swollen feet. Somehow, when she manages to give me a smile, she's still more beautiful than a blue-eyed Cher. *I still love you, Mama,* I add in my head. *No matter what.*

"Oh, you're sweet, Holly," Roxanne says, before letting her eyes fall closed.

"Sweet, like the Devil?"

Roxanne smiles again. "Sweet like a gentle, true spirit. Sweet like the original intent of the word."

I pull the white blanket up over her shoulders and then climb into bed next to her, lying on top of the comforter, but close enough to soak her up.

"Sometimes I look around me, and I still can't believe this is happening to me," Roxanne says softly. "The house looks pretty. Di brings me orchids. You bring me hardbacks. It doesn't seem real. But then I'm too weak to lift your hardback, and Ed has to rip out the pages, and I vomit after three ounces of soup and a little bit of fruit salad . . . and I know it must be real."

She glances at me with only her eyes and says, "I wonder if Gabe died hating me."

The ceiling fan creaks and shudders above us. Trying to assess the likelihood of an imminent fall, I watch its tilting revolutions before wondering, "Well, what do you think?"

"I guess . . . we both had plenty to be sorry for." Roxanne's voice is thoughtful. "He fell in love with another woman. I was tremendously hurt and took Di, the only way to hurt him back. It can't win me any points with God or anything, certainly not if I'd do it all over again. . . . But what if the only way to fix my bad karma would've been to ask Gabe to forgive me and now he's dead and I can't."

"Why don't you just forgive yourself?" I ask.

"Myself." Finally, she studies me dead-on.

"Yeah. Why not?"

"I just told you! I'd keep reliving my regrets over and over and over...."

"Roxanne, even if you didn't relive the *same* regrets, you'd have *new* regrets to take the place of the old ones. Why is it so noble to say you'd do things differently? Just admit that you'd react exactly the same all over again. Face the blame and then forgive yourself for being you. Maybe that's the best way to fix your karma."

Roxanne sounds like a little girl when she asks hopefully, "You think that'll heal me?"

I tap my head, just like she did a few months earlier. "Up here," I say. "Then maybe once you could forgive yourself, you could go on to forgive Gabe for what he did to you."

"Oh, I already have forgiven him. And I am sorry he suffered. If that's anything." Roxanne frowns. "I suppose the person I should be sorriest for is Di. I took her away from her father, and now she'll never be able to find him. I hope she doesn't hate me after I'm dead."

"Roxanne. Di has never held a grudge. I'm sure she's *already* forgiven you."

"I hope you're right."

We lay side by side, inhaling and exhaling the silence of wings and spiders. Tree leaves lap against the window screen; scales of guitar notes breeze in from outside; and overhead, the fan keeps turning in its circle.

"No, you may not," Roxanne says.

"No, I may not what?" I ask, leaning up on my elbow.

"Stay right here forever."

I smile at her internationally ranked wisdom and stroke her cheek and kiss her forehead. "Oh, how I love you."

"Oh, how I love *you*," she replies, letting her eyes shut, and I watch her breathing for a while. It amazes me that the room can seem so full when so on the verge of emptiness.

"Don't let Di keep all my clothes after I'm gone," she says, under closed lids. "I want her to purge the closets. You tell her; she'll listen to you."

"Okay," I say, thinking of how I'll encourage Di to cut small pieces of each fabric from each one of Roxanne's dresses—

"And for God's sake, no commemorative quilt either."

"Okay," I agree, meek this time.

I WAIT until she's fallen asleep before slipping out of her bedroom. Outside the flat, the sun is shining like a novelty—an entire spring day without rain. On the front stoop, I find Alecia and Di, who stop talking as soon as the door opens.

"All right, what's going on here?" I ask, sitting down on Diotima's free side.

"I was just feeling sorry for myself," Di says, wiping her teary eyes.

"Oh, Di," I say, squeezing her shoulder.

"I'll be okay. Of course I will," Di says, blowing her nose with conviction. "It's not like I won't see Mom again."

"True, but . . . it'll be hard until you do," I say.

"Oh, she'll visit," Di says. "I mean, my grandma Hazel just appeared the other night."

"Your grandmother?" Alecia turns her head and stares, amazed. "What'd she say?"

"Well, nothing. Or if she did, I couldn't hear her. But she was smiling. They all were."

"They?" Alecia repeats, perturbed. "She's made friends?"

"She was with Grandpa Nelson and my father," Di replies.

"Uncle Gabe?" Alecia looks startled. "What was he doing?"

Di shrugs. "Hanging out."

"So . . . they looked happy?" Alecia asks.

"They were smiling. Although . . ." Di hesitates. "Grandpa Nelson was wearing this silly white suit that made him look like Colonel Sanders."

Alecia shakes her head with pity, as if Di confessed that Grandpa Nelson was gnashing his teeth.

"But my grandmother was breathtaking in crimson silk. Or it looked like silk, anyway. It flowed so nicely."

"I never imagined wearing clothes in the afterlife," I say, hugging my knees. "I thought when you die, you'd go back to becoming part of God. Like your spirit merges with something larger, and you become just another particle of light."

"That's what *I* used to think, too, until I was about nine years old." Di isn't putting me down. Nine was the age she first spotted her grandma Hazel.

"I don't know—maybe you *are* a particle of light," she adds. "Maybe you're everywhere, in any form. But if you wanted to communicate with someone here, someone like me, you'd have to take on a recognizable shape, wouldn't you say?"

I smile slowly and tell Di that from now on I will strive to be the pregnant soul that she is.

"God, Holly, don't leave," Di says, leaning into me with her head on my shoulder. "I can't handle you and Mom going at the same time."

"I'll come back. I promise," I say. "But I need to go home for a little while. I have to clean out some boxes and help my father move. And Roxanne has you guys."

"I'm really happy for you and Matthew," Alecia says with a smile.

"Yeah, he's such a good egg," Di agrees. "Hey, shouldn't we make a vow since we're leaving each other? The Fossil sisters always did." Until this moment, I forgot that Di had been planning on naming her baby Petrova if it had been a girl. It also occurs to me that I never did see Cromwell Road, and somehow it just doesn't matter anymore.

"That's right!" I remember. "They made a vow to get the Fossils in history books, since it was their name and no one else's. And it was Petrova who they decided would get them there—since she flew planes and all."

"So . . . what . . . we say a vow that Di will launch herself into history books like Petrova was supposed to?" Alecia jokes.

"Oh, no. Not me," Di says seriously. "I just want to be a good mother. It'll be you, Holly. You care about causes."

"No I don't. I avoid causes. Causes are too overwhelming. I care about people," I say, simultaneously remembering how overwhelming people are. "You're the one who picks up gum wrappers and bottles in the park."

"Well, there's always me," Alecia says.

"But I never touch the really gooey trash," Di says.

"Hello? There's me," Alecia says. "I'm going to become a lawyer ... or a life coach."

"Um, yeah, sure," I say, which makes Di start laughing.

"Okay. Okay. A vow," Alecia says. "That Di will be a good mother. That I will maybe ... be a *Something*. Or a really content Nothing. And that Holly makes it into a history book ..." she pauses, making a sly face, "as the oldest virgin who ever lived."

"Not anymore!" I say, but Alecia and Di are laughing too loudly to hear, and I can't help but join in.

Down the sidewalk, the fat postman with bulbous earlobes looks up to see the source of the ruckus and then stares at where we're sitting with our arms around one another's shoulders, as if the sight of three sirens on a doorstep has frozen him and his handful of mail.

"Oh, gross," Alecia says.

"Did you know that if you kill a postman you could be hanged, because he carries the royal mail?" I ask.

"Why *is* that lascivious man staring at us?" Di wonders.

"He's hoping we're lesbians," I say.

Alecia gives me a shove over Di's shoulder, and once again we erupt.

Epilogue

> "Remember that however busy the 'on-take,'
> your period of duty will end."
>
> —OXFORD HANDBOOK OF CLINICAL MEDICINE

Three weeks after the baptism, Roxanne died. She took her last breath with Di holding her hand, and as her doctor predicted, she didn't seem to be in any pain. By then my contract with the Royal County Hampshire Hospital had ended, and I moved out of Parchment House to spend my last days abroad in the flat on Lorraine Avenue with everyone else. Roxanne told me to go home, but I knew I'd regret it if I left before she did.

"Well, Dr. Campbell, was it worth it?" Mr. Danvers asked in the A&E when I went to hand him the code pager for the very last time.

For a moment, I was puzzled by what he could mean—was it worth leaving my life behind, learning what I'd learned, or becoming a doctor in the first place? Then I decided it didn't matter, because I could answer the same thing to all three.

"Yes," I said, reaching out to shake his hand. "And thanks for everything. It's been quite a year."

"Indeed," he replied, carefully observing me. "Did you accomplish all you intended to?"

I thought about dragging my mother's suitcase through the cemetery one year ago and told him yes again.

When I held out the code pager, Danvers looked wry and asked if, now that I was handing off the "bleep," would I be going to the airport straightaway? I explained that my friend was dying, and I wanted to stay to say good-bye.

"And medicine?" he asked, and even without him saying so, I knew Danvers was asking if I would be saying good-bye to that, too.

So I told him that once I got back to the States, I was planning on applying for a couple of family practice positions—outpatient only. I waited for him to be disappointed, but Danvers surprised me with an encouraging smile.

"I daresay I was afraid we'd lose you entirely, my dear. And I kept thinking, 'What a pity,' " he said.

IT WASN'T until three days after Roxanne passed away that I finally flew back to Maryland with the idea of helping my father move. But it turned out my grandmother needed me first.

"I used to say that hell is a nursing home, but I was wrong," Eve says now. "Packing for the nursing home is hell."

It is the beginning of July, and Matthew and I are at her house, helping her pack things up. At eighty-five, Eve has decided that maybe a six-bedroom Victorian on seven acres is getting too big for her to manage, especially if my father is really going to move out of Columbia and go to Annapolis for his "Internet bride."

"Grandmother, it's not a nursing home," I say. "It's a retirement community. You'll have your own apartment and kitchen."

"But I'll be surrounded by old fogies," she says. "I refuse to believe that I'm one of them. Aging is a very strange thing, Holly. One day you'll understand."

"If I'm lucky," I say.

"Holly," Matthew calls, coming down the stairs. "Perhaps we should make this our last load, if we're meeting your father at the boat by three."

"Not yet!" Grandmother says, practically shrieking. "I'm missing one important box! Her father can wait—after all, he's notoriously late, isn't he, Holly?"

I nod reluctantly, while Matthew looks at me and winks. We both know that Grandmother is stalling. We were supposed to be out of here hours ago.

"Go make yourselves some tea while I look for that box," Grandmother says. "English people like tea. Am I right, Matthew?"

"We certainly do," Matthew replies, smiling at me as we make our way into the kitchen to wait. He moves to put the kettle on the stove, while I sink into a seat at the table. A sigh escapes before I realize I'm letting one go.

"Are you all right there?" Matthew asks. He knows that Ben called this morning to say that he and Alecia, Di, and Max just arrived in Edinburgh and were on their way back to Skye.

"I'm okay," I say, thinking of them scattering Roxanne's ashes over the Sound of Sleat like she wanted. My father asked me if they'd be coming home afterward, and I told him I didn't know. Ben is talking about writing a screenplay, and he'd prefer to stay abroad to do it. Alecia, on the other hand, has started toying with the idea of returning to TV news again and wants to go back to New York or even Pittsburgh. She's ready to face the cameras, she says, but not her mother. "If she wants to talk, let her come find me," she told me on my last night there, as we cleaned out Roxanne's closet, which was when we discovered Di's missing U.S. passport. (Despite her relief, Di has no interest in returning to the States right now. "Max and I need time to be on our own," she said.)

And Ed, I think with a sigh. Ed is not on his way to Skye right now, because Ed is on a plane to Iowa. His ex-fiancée, Nicky, called the day after Roxanne's death just to let him know that his son, Noah, was nearly six months old. "I can't believe it! I have a son!" Ed said, smiling broadly despite Nicky's request for child support. "Maybe he'll turn out like Max!"

I'm happy for Ed but almost happier for Noah, a boy who will get to experience Ed's truest affections.

"Aha!" Grandmother says with a girlish, gleeful laugh from the other room. "I knew I'd find it."

Emerging from the living room, she plunks down a shoebox in front of me and says, "Go ahead. Look. You should recognize some of what's there."

Slowly, I lift the lid. It's not my third-grade diorama, but the box is filled with bits of my own handwriting. It must contain every card and letter that I gave to my mother from the time I could write. In fact, there are scribbles from my first doctors' appointments, badly drawn stick figures, and even spelling tests.

"How'd you end up with this?" I ask, looking up at my grandmother, whose hair-sprayed bouffant is blonder than usual. Maybe she wants to look even younger for the retirement village.

"Oh, sometime after the funeral. Your father couldn't handle having Sylvia's things around him. He told me he was going to be giving everything to Goodwill, and I said that wouldn't be necessary. I said I would come sort through her closet and take to my house whatever shouldn't be thrown away."

"That explains all the sweaters and shoes," Matthew says.

"Well, I wasn't about to let him give away perfectly nice outfits!" she says. "Anyway, I found this shoebox, and I must've taken it with me. Look, there are the letters your mother left behind when she went to the island," Grandmother adds.

I unfold one of them.

Dear Holly,

Remember to listen to Grandmother. Remember to take your bath today. Remember that no one has ever loved you like I love you, and you're not alone.

"The mail on Grenada was so unreliable," Eve tells Matthew, "so Sylvia wrote all these letters in advance and made me give them to Ben and Holly, once a week. They loved mail day, didn't you, Holly?"

"Yeah, until Ben figured out there was no address on the

envelope, just our first names and the date," I say, reaching for the next scrap of writing with Mama's chicken print on it.

October 13, 1984—

Dear Simon,

I was afraid you might call, even though I told you not to call, and then when you never did, I was disappointed.

It's not one of our Grenada letters. It's even better.

The teakettle starts to shrill, and while Matthew moves to shut off the stove, and my grandmother rushes to find some teacups, I quickly separate these pages from the rest of the box and put them in my pocket.

IT'S NOT FOR ANOTHER HALF AN HOUR, after we've had our cups of Earl Grey and exhausted my grandmother's current favorite topics—Ben not living up to his potential; my father's plans to "shack up" with his girlfriend before the wedding—that we manage to convince her that we really should be going to meet Dad at the boat.

"Good-bye, Holly. And keep this man around—he's an excellent packer," Eve calls, waving from her front porch. "Oh, and Matthew, I hope that next time you can do better than an emerald *bracelet*," she adds pointedly as we duck into the car.

WE MEET MY FATHER at the dock on the Magathy River. If he's even noticed that we're late, he seems too happy to care. Dad grins and waves from the bough of a twenty-seven-foot sailboat—not Noah's Ark, which is still broken down in our driveway at home, but the boat that belongs to his woman, the one who's taking him away to a house on the Chesapeake Bay.

"Hey, kids!" Dad calls with glee. "Come on aboard!"

Behind the tiller stands Carly, a slim lady with permed hair and overly tanned skin, probably from years outside on the boat. She looks about ten years younger than my dad, although, at the moment, my dad looks about ten years younger than my dad.

As we motor out to sea, Carly and Dad put Matthew to work. He follows their instructions, tugging on lines and cranking devices. Meanwhile, no one seems to mind when I slip up to the front of the boat, where the only sound is of the wind and the waves lapping against the stern. I think of my brother and friends on their way to toss Roxanne's ashes off the boat in Scotland and imagine that's what I'm doing today as I unfold the pages in my pocket and begin to read.

October 13, 1984—

Dear Simon,

I was afraid you might call, even though I told you not to call, and then when you never did, I was disappointed. But it's for the best, really, because if you had called, then I would've been tempted to talk to you, and we couldn't talk for the same reasons that we can't see each other now . . . so why am I writing this letter?

It's been nearly one year since we saw each other last: Oct. 23, two days before the Marines landed. I was so grateful to have made it home again that for the first few weeks that I got back, I didn't miss you like I thought I would. I'm not saying that to be hurtful. It's just that at the end of my "tour of duty," it was the closest I've ever been to going crazy. First there was the ordeal of Will showing up after the volcano. (Oh, the show we gave people that day! All the screaming on the beach, and the security guard asking if I was "okay, sista?") Then midterms were rapidly approaching and I couldn't concentrate, couldn't be around anyone anymore. If you recall, I started studying in the storage closet outside the lecture hall. It had a million boxes stacked up to the ceiling, one desk, and the microscope that I'd swiped from the path lab. (Oddly, when I showed up one morning, there was a sign on official school letterhead that said "No Studying in the Closet," which seemed strange—that one could be forbidden to study anyplace on campus. But now I wonder if it might've been a joke...maybe Ernest made the sign, or Thor.) Anyway, I was so shaken up by Will's visit and the possible dissolution of my marriage that I couldn't study without thinking I had contracted whatever horrible thing I was reading about. Parisitology was the worst—I kept envisioning Barnsworth's slide show with me in place of that poor boy who had worms pouring out of his ass—the dreaded ascaris lumbricoides! Then came the afternoon that I stopped scratching and studying long enough to come out of the closet to buy a bottle of Coke, and everyone was talking about Prime Minister Bishop being overthrown by a coup. I guess we should've listened to Vic and got the hell out when we could, but at that point, I just couldn't deal with the immediacy of going home before Christmas. It was like going into premature labor. I knew what my due date was, and I was sticking to it. Of course, the Marxists didn't care about my marital problems, or that I was in love with you, or that once I left the island, I would probably never be a doctor. They murdered Bishop anyway.

I remember packing my suitcase for home, when the tanks were outside, and I hated myself for being so stubborn and so in love, for getting myself in this predicament in the first place. All I wanted was to make it home alive and to hold my children again. I promised God that if He got me home, I would be a faithful wife, and a good mother, that I'd forget about medicine if I got to see them again—all those bargains you make when you're terrified. But I meant it.

And I'm still grateful—grateful to God, grateful to Daddy. I should probably write him a thank-you letter for arranging the fishing boat. It was the strangest feeling *leaving the island behind, wasn't it? I'll never forget look-ing back at the shore as we sailed away at dusk, just amazed at how desolate the landscape looked, when it had been so full of life for me, at least for a little while.*

The last time I saw you, we were in San Juan Airport. Somehow I knew this was it—I even said it aloud and squeezed your hand for one second before letting you go into the madness. "I'll meet you on the other side!" you said in a rush, moving the opposite way, toward Customs and Immigration, with your cart of suitcases, as I went, lost, looking for Big Bertha. I assume you meant to show up at my gate to say good-bye, but that didn't happen. I never got to hug you or kiss you again. There was no time to even grieve until I was on the shuttle bus to my next flight and saw a suitcase lying open near the runway. All of its contents were spilled everywhere for strangers to see. Panty hose were strewn like guts, and papers flew away in the wind. Just the sight of such open wounds made me tear up, but then we pulled up in front of my plane, and I had to let it go. Let you go.

And now I'm back, and it's good. The children are thrilled that I'm home—and I'm thrilled, too. There is nothing in the world like a ten-year-old in your arms! How could I have ever forgotten? They are fifth-graders now, who amaze me every day. Only seven months left of elementary school. They say that children are resilient and get over illnesses that would kill an adult—maybe it's the same for emotions. I can only hope.

I talked to Ernest recently. He told me that you and Thor and Vic ended up in New Jersey, along with every-one else. So it turns out St. George's University was good for something after all, considering they managed to place everyone in U.S. schools. Except Jexy, that is. You must've heard that she's leaving medicine to go to school for fash-ion design, still looking for the ultimate day job. And me, I ended up at University of Maryland School of Medicine. It's been my mother's dream for me all along: I'll graduate from a "real" medical school. U of M will never be my alma mater, though. I don't even really fit in with all these "real" medical students. I'm just the transfer who came from a more interesting place. They are the Poor Saps and I am Secretly Lucky.

By now you must be married. If I remember correctly, Lisette had the reception planned for the Waldorf-Astoria this past summer. I couldn't bring myself to ask Ern about it. As much as I want you to be happy, it's too painful to think of you with someone else. But I do hope your wedding was beautiful, Simon. God, I am crying just thinking of it.

Will and I are struggling. Struggling to be more than just roommates who happen to be in charge of a couple of kids. Struggling to get over my relationship with you, which I finally ended up confessing. He already knew, and besides, I didn't see how we could ever grow closer in a marriage based on a lie. I don't know if he'll ever trust me again—in some ways, I think he wished he didn't know the truth.

It's become an unspoken rule in the house: we never talk about Grenada. Everyone feels better pretending it never happened. But sometimes I do miss being able to share the memory of the place. It's funny, inhabiting another world. You stay long enough, and you start to feel like it's all you know: the moonrise over Prickly Bay, all low and holy, the Southern Cross, the crazy cloud formations hanging over the water. You almost forget how loud the crickets are.

But back home it's autumn, and there is nothing like autumn in the Northeast: the crispness, the geese, the pine trees. I'm almost forgetting my walks to school at dusk— the moon, and the stillness, and the bats whipping over my head so peaceful and aimless, like thoughts. And you, dear Simon. I am almost forgetting you, too. But I don't want to forget.

The thing about Grenada was how simplified my life

became for a little while, and how quickly it went. I was utterly and blissfully and completely happy with you, and I was guilty about it every day. Time slipped by, and yet I felt every minute, because I knew it would end before I was ready. I wanted to hold on to the stars that I can't see at home, and those crazy cloud formations, and the bats that could've been doves.

And you. I wanted to hold on to you forever.

I would say that San Juan was the last time we'll ever see each other, but I know better than to speak in finalities. Things revert. Nothing is permanent. As you once told me, the Southern Cross will find itself in the northern latitudes once again. At any one time you are one thing, and give it a moment, you are something else. It's a blessing, really.

Even if Will can't ever forgive me, I have forgiven myself for everything I did: leaving, forgetting, cheating. What choice do I have? Otherwise, I am just a sitting duck, waiting for my eternal punishment. Which doesn't mean that I'm not sorry. I am so sorry for everyone I hurt, including my children, my husband, even you, my love. But the fact is, I am not perfect. I was never perfect, and that's okay. I am not expected to be. Jesus may have been perfect, but he was merciful, too.

Sometimes I remember that night we spent on the dock during the meteor shower. You were telling me about the pole star, how the earth is wobbling on its axis, and its center keeps changing as the planet moves through its circle. It's like my relationship with God. I oscillate toward and away from Him—one minute singing His praises, and the next minute I can't form a prayer on my lips. But all the while I'm circling Him, even when I can't feel the pull, wobbling toward Jesus, away and back, away and back. And maybe that's the only way to know Him. To know myself better. To accept the contradictions in myself, my imperfections, and to know that I am still loved.

Remember when we dove the Bianca Sea, the way we looked for the shipwreck, searching through the blue, blue water, and suddenly it was there, so gargantuan that we couldn't believe it could've snuck up on us? Heaven must be like that. You aren't sure where the clarity ends and the vision of God begins, but it turns out He was there all along, looming and massive, right in front of your face, until you wake up saying, "Oh, Spirit, when did I End and when did You Begin?"

The letter stops without a signature. Overhead, the sail starts to rattle and flap, along with the pages in my hand, and I hold on to them tighter, remembering Mama, remembering Roxanne, until, finally ready, I let them go. When Matthew calls out from behind the tiller, I think for a second he's pointing at my papers tossing and turning on a wild ride of air currents over the water. But he's just telling me to keep my head down. It's time for the next tack.

Acknowledgments

There are so many people whose support I am deeply grateful for.

My professors at University of Delaware: Anne Hatfield, for reading a seventeen-year-old's story and asking so seriously after class, "What else have you written?" John Jebb, for the best course ever in American Literature. Bernie Kaplan, who led our fiction workshops with humor, honesty, and encouragement.

Thanks to one of my earliest readers, my sister, Katherine Brown, who always gives me good advice and a comb, who loves to "talk writing." Thanks to the Squirrel Hill Writer's Group, especially Pat Schuetz, Many Ly, Madalon Amenta, and Scott Smith, whose critiques were invaluable to this story. I am forever grateful to Cindy McKay for her writer's instincts, her fabulous ideas, and her friendship. Thanks to everyone at Aspen Summer Words—especially Caryn McVoy and Doris Iarovici, for reading this tome and offering suggestions. Thanks to Laurie Horowitz, for telling me not to give up on this rewrite or the one after that, and to Hilma Wolitzer, for a memorable workshop at the Key West Literary Seminar—thanks for keeping my mother and me laughing all week long. Thanks to my agent, Jodie Rhodes, for finding my novel a home, and to my editor, Caitlin Alexander, for her enthusiasm and guidance.

Thanks to Shannon Perrine, for being a wonderful friend and a reporter who is nothing like Alecia—here's to getting "written up" for singing too loudly. Thanks to Elizabeth Finan, for the Holland bicycling tour, for going in circles and never solving anything. Thanks to Ernie Lau, for knowing my courtesy laughs, and for letting me sing the blues using his name; Jay Lieberman, for making the pilgrimage to the Isle of Skye, where nobody booed once; and Dave Leopold, for being the guru of B7. Thanks to Ryan Labovitch, for gin and tonics on the balcony and lots of promises that the best was yet to come; Adam Yopp, for forcing me to climb on that lion in Trafalgar Square; and Danielle Aufiero, who misses airplanes—except those bound for Amsterdam—for getting me through surgery and the USMLE.

Thanks to Dr. Richard Williams at Harbor Hospital, a mentor in the art of paying attention; and Dr. Rand Allingham at Duke

University, who told me go home before I could say I needed to leave. Thanks to Dr. Catriona Purl, who answered a stranger's letter (mine) concerning emergency logistics surrounding the Isle of Skye.

Thanks to the author Michael Shermer, who wrote a fascinating article for *Scientific American,* called "Miracle on Probability Street," that explained the Law of Large Numbers and why coincidences are always happening to me.

Thanks to my parents, my grandparents and my siblings, including my brother Chris Leffler, for his clinical pearls, and my little brother, Brad Lincoln, for getting my jokes.

Thank you so much to my husband, Tim, whose unflagging support and love mean everything to me.

About the Author

Maggie Leffler is a physician who lives in Pittsburgh with her husband and son. This is her first novel.